AS
GOOD
AS IT
GETS

Other books by Judith Greber

MENDOCINO
THE SILENT PARTNER

AS GOOD AS IT GETS

JUDITH GREBER

CROWN PUBLISHERS, INC.
New York

Grateful acknowledgment is given for permission to reprint the following:
"Little Boxes," words and music by Malvina Reynolds. Copyright © 1962, renewed 1990, Schroder Music Corporation, all rights reserved.
"This Be The Verse," from *High Windows* by Philip Larkin. Copyright © 1974 by Philip Larkin. Reprinted by permission of Farrar, Straus & Giroux, Inc.
"The Gestalt Prayer." Copyright © The Estate of Fredrick Perls. Reprinted with the permission of *The Gestalt Journal*, publisher of *Gestalt Therapy* Verbatim.

Published by Crown Publishers, Inc.,
201 East 50 Street,
New York, New York 10022.

CROWN is a trademark of Crown Publishers, Inc.

Manufactured in the United States of America

Library of Congress Cataloging-in-Publication Data

Greber, Judith.
    As good as it gets / by Judith Greber. — 1st ed.
    I. Title.
  PS3557.R356A9   1992
  813'.54—dc20   91-36424
                                                    CIP

ISBN 0-517-58731-9

1   3   5   7   9   10   8   6   4   2

First Edition

For my husband Robert
and our sons,
Matthew and Jonathan

Three cheers for the home team

Acknowledgments

Grateful acknowledgment to the following for their invaluable expertise and generosity: Gloria Feldt, Executive Director, Planned Parenthood of Central and Northern Arizona; Bonnie Rose Hough, Executive Director, Family Law Center, Marin County; Joan Kelly, Executive Director, Northern California Mediation Center; Ruth W. Rosen, Deputy County Counsel, Marin; plus a trio of Writers/Critiquers/Friends par excellence—Jean Brody, Susan Dunlap, and Marilyn Wallace; and an exceptional duo—Jean V. Naggar and Betty Prashker, whose titles, to me, are the same as this book's.

Contents

Contents

AS GOOD AS IT GETS

Going to the Chapel

1960–1961

And so
the Prince and the Princess
were married
and
lived happily ever after . . .

1

I T LOOKED like a munchkin's Frisbee and it was stuck to the bathroom wall.

Hallie sat naked and defeated on the edge of the tub. *Modern Bride* hadn't even hinted that a wedding night could be this frustrating. Certainly not before it involved the groom.

Perhaps she was anatomically incorrect, because each time she grasped the greasy rim, spread her legs and pushed, the diaphragm collided with her—her *private parts*, for God's sake! When had they become public, pathetic, and in need of prosthetics?

Three times the rubber disc had whizzed free, obeying a law of physics—something else she didn't understand—in a woeful trajectory from her groin to first the sink, then a framed print of Paris at night, and finally the blue and white wallpaper above the toilet.

She could scream. Stay on the tub rim forever. Enter marriage au naturel and be impregnated. Or try again. She pulled the diaphragm off the wall. A hair, not hers, was stuck to the spermicide. For the fourth time in fifteen minutes, she soaped the rubber circle.

Bet Ted thought she had the wedding-night jitters, like some silly movie bride, locked in the bathroom for fear of . . . IT.

Which was ridiculous. Wasn't it?

Twenty years of whispers, speculation, and everything-but had now ended with "I do," which should have been "I will" or "I can." Permission finally granted.

But she'd never been afraid. Except after reading *Love Without Fear*, which made sex appear technically difficult, potentially crippling, and definitely grim. "Both partners should, in coitus, concentrate their full attention on one thing: the attainment of simultaneous orgasm," sounded like a dreaded school assignment that was easy to flunk.

She wasn't scared, but still, it wasn't easy to retool your thinking. Her whole life, nice girls didn't. Boys wanted only one thing and girls didn't want anything. They had a "precious gift" to preserve.

Now it was time to give the precious gift—in its precious gift wrap. The diaphragm lay in her palm like half a rubber scale of justice, reversing the old rules.

No more pretending The Act never entered your mind, let alone your other parts. Instant amnesia about messages received from mothers, teachers, advice books, religion, songs, movies, and even boys who talked about other girls. About cheap and fast. About how they wouldn't respect you.

She had learned so well how to hide a racing pulse, disguise desire and pleasure because they'd get the right idea, called The Wrong Idea.

What if she was permanently set on automatic shutoff?

She wished the hurdle of this night was behind them. If they hadn't been at schools hundreds of miles apart, if she didn't live at home, if Ted's roommate hadn't broken his leg and been unable to leave the studio apartment—if, if, if—they'd be past it and she'd know how the hell to get this thing inside herself.

2

She took a deep breath, picked up the tube, and reread the instructions, which once again didn't address the problem of gripping a greasy rubber ring. Instead, they promised to kill male sperm. Female sperm were obviously to be spared. How could she entrust her fertility to a company that stupid about the facts of life?

She folded the slick diaphragm like a rubber taco and bent over. It zipped out of her hand, did a back flip, and landed on the fuzzy white bathroom rug.

The hell with it. Let the male sperm live, too. Let them do what nature so obviously wanted done. Nobody would be surprised.

"Everybody will think you're pregnant." Her mother's gray eyes had scanned her, as if she could see through to Hallie's womb.

"I'm not."

"Did I ask? I trust you. But I don't understand why you can't wait till you graduate."

"A whole *year* while he's *there* and I'm here! *Mom!*"

"But marriage is *forever!* For the rest of your life!"

Hallie glared.

"You're in love, and he's different than anybody else on earth, am I right?"

"He *is!*"

"Romance. Hearts entwined. Off into the sunset, but it isn't like that! And you're supposed to be so smart."

"You don't understand."

Her mother set her lips. "I understand love, thank you. And I understand marriage. However, I also understand the difference."

"We'll be fine. A tiny wedding, no fuss. Ted has a good job offer, and—"

"You're throwing away your scholarship!"

"Penn's here. Ted's there. I'll finish school in Boston. It'll work out. Trust me."

"You're a child! Marriage isn't like in songs. It's long and complicated and not only about the two of you and what you want. It's about everything that happens to you and to the world, too. It's about luck." She gesticulated wildly, annoying Hallie.

"There's the people, the marriage itself, and the world, all sharing space and being tested, all the time."

The same irrelevant babble. Soon she'd start in about the Depression, the War.

"It's nice the way they sing that the two of you become one, but it's a lie. There's always two of you. You don't change diapers as one or cook dinners as one or—"

"Oh, Mom, really!" Why was she so negative?

Her mother changed tacks. "Then why in March? Why spring vacation? You can't even live together until June."

Her unbearable practicality threatened to ruin it. It was so romantic, so impetuously wonderful. "Will you marry me?" Ted had asked, voice thick with longing.

They'd known each other barely six months, and more by letters and phone calls than in person.

Ridiculous to consider marriage so soon. Bizarre. Dangerous, even. But yes, she said. Yes. She would marry him.

"Tonight."

She worried that he'd been joking. Then worried that he hadn't.

"We'll find a judge in a picket-fence house. Just like in the movies."

But she still had a chapter and a half left of *Bleak House* before tomorrow's exam in the Nineteenth-Century Novel.

"Then when?"

They'd ticked off days and weeks and the half-joke became fact, and they wound up with spring vacation and it was written indelibly on her brain that she must marry Teddy Bennett and do so six weeks later, in March.

And she had. Now the new Mrs. Bennett again washed her rug-fuzzy diaphragm and put cream around the edge, this time leaving two empty spots for her thumb and middle finger to grasp. Hoping sperm weren't wily enough to find the breach in her armaments, she bent the wire rim over and squatted.

Voilà. She poked an experimental finger inside and touched victory. Test completed, full speed ahead.

She lifted a demure, lace-trimmed and gossamer-soft negligee from its hanger. Bizarre for her practical mother to have given her this, to have insisted on this part of wedding tradition. Sylvia

4

Saxe was unadorned salt-and-pepper hair above utilitarian garments. A woman in love with good causes, not material objects. But despite her denials, a bit of a romantic, too, it appeared.

Hallie settled the gown over her body, pulled the peignoir around her, and slipped into high-heeled blue satin slippers.

She saw her frothy self in the mirror. Translucent fabric, easy access. The Virgin Prepared for Deflowering.

Ready. Set. Go.

Ted Bennett looked over the night city, wondering if the point of the fuss was to make the most instinctive and basic human activity terrifying.

Since the day he met her, he had wanted to be with Hallie Saxe. He loved the way she looked, the brown-blond curls that so annoyed her, the almost supernatural pale blue eyes, the curves of her body. He loved the way she was, bright and funny and more alive than anyone he'd ever known. She didn't look or act like anybody else. Uniquely herself. Uniquely desirable.

Miraculously, she wanted to be with him, too. They wanted to be together. A simple enough idea.

Why, then, did the marriage machine butt in, take over, and turn a private desire into a public event in which they were bit players with less than full votes? Guest lists and invitation squabbles and food choices and going-away outfits and now this interminable stay in the bathroom while Hallie mutated into The Bride, performing God knows what ceremonial act.

He lit another cigarette.

He wanted to make love, not orchestrate a goddamn capitalized, ornamented, formalized Wedding Night. He was half afraid the photographer would barge in to document this, too. Or that at dawn, his mother-in-law would seize the bloody sheet and hang it outside for the villagers, proving her daughter's virtue and her son-in-law's virility.

Maybe marriage was so terrifying that this hoopla was meant to distract and confuse you until the doors clanged shut.

In any case, he was now a married man.

Impossible. His timid *father*, forever apologizing for his existence, was a married man.

You have a wife, Ted.

No. His *father* had a wife.

Mr. and Mrs. Bennett.

His *parents*.

Who was that in the bathroom and how had all this happened?

The door clicked open and he turned and saw her. His wife. His bride. She looked as horrified as he felt.

Who Is That Man?

Ted. You remember. Your groom?

But who was Ted? A complete stranger she had vowed to stay with until one of them died. Chained to the creature in the silk robe forever.

"Mrs. Bennett, I presume?"

Oh, my God!

"I thought you'd found a back door out of this place."

"Movie-star handsome," her father had said after meeting his future son-in-law. It wasn't clear if he felt such striking looks were an asset or a liability, but he was accurate.

Ted was gasp-out-loud gorgeous. Too good-looking for a husband. Trouble.

Besides, she had always imagined a desperate and romantic life of poverty and extremes with a tortured genius in a garret, not forever with an electronics engineer in an apartment near Boston.

I have sold out. Condemned myself to the wrong life.

"Champagne?" the wrong man asked.

"Yes!" She quickly downed a glass.

"Are you frightened?" he asked.

"Of course not! Not that way—I mean not of . . ." Her voice dribbled off as she privately admitted yes, she was, of *something*, and maybe it didn't matter what she called it.

He studied her carefully, then put his champagne on the night table and stood up. "I'm afraid I have something horrible to tell you."

She felt a nervous smile twist her face.

"I'm serious!" He stepped back. "I can't keep it secret any longer."

Fragile smile gone, she sat, hands in her lacy lap. What was that person going to tell her that she should have known all along, except "Marry in haste, repent . . . repent . . ."?

He stood tall, handsome, and clean-featured. How awful could his secret be? She had explored him, knew he was in working order.

But a girl in her Sociology class had married last Christmas and separated seven days later, saying only that it had been a nightmare. There could obviously be major postmarital shocks.

"It isn't really my fault." Ted slowly untied the belt of his robe.

She poured more champagne, spilling some.

He slithered the robe from his shoulders, like a stripper, and revealed caution-yellow pajamas with burgundy dragons on each breast and tiny green Chinamen, linked one to the other by pigtails, marching around the borders. Even the cuffs had their parades of men. "Frogs, they call these things," he said mournfully, pointing to ornate, twisted fasteners that looped over lumps of silk where buttons might have been.

She burst out laughing. "Teddy, your clothing is usually so . . . how—"

"Yesterday my mother asked me what pajamas I'd gotten, and I admitted I never wore them." He sat down next to her. "She was horrified. Said my . . . the sight of my . . ." He divided the last of the champagne between their glasses.

"The sight of your what?"

"My 'member,' was her precise locution. Said it would terrify a nice girl. As my father's had terrified her, she graciously added. So she bought me a trousseau."

And before Hallie could stop laughing and remember to be afraid of the unknown man beside her or of the endless future they had promised to endure, Ted wasn't separate and he wasn't in his wretched pajamas and she, unterrified, was free of her costume as well and they were familiar skin, scent, and longing. And unfamiliar luxury, rich with time.

And if the earth didn't move the way Hemingway promised, if her automatic shutoff valves hadn't yet retired, if it wasn't quite what she'd imagined, it was still a beginning, and sufficiently magic to make familiar boundaries dissolve, to be reassembled as a part of a mystery, to be an interlocking piece in an intricate, endless puzzle.

To be for keeps. To be married.

—————— 2 ——————

"Hi, Mrs. Miller," Hallie said.

"She's upstairs, kiddo." As on most evenings, Megan's mother, Kat, sat at her oilcloth-covered dining-room table, directly below a paint-by-number "Last Supper," a cigarette in one hand, a glass in the other. The TV in the adjoining living room blared.

"I had my last final today, and I'm leaving tomorrow." Hallie's parents were driving her to Boston, which felt depressingly childish, like being carpooled. It was the cheapest way to transport clothing, books, photo albums, desk lamp, her complete set of aluminum pots, and the wedding gifts that hadn't yet made their way north—a rotisserie, a percolator, nested white casseroles with small blue flowers, monogrammed flotsam and jetsam. Nonetheless, even via unglamorous transit, it was still true that after two months of a part-time, weekend marriage that was like a sexy, semi-illicit game, she was about to begin the real thing.

"Who's that funny guy in *Some Came Running*?" Kat asked.

"I don't know." Hallie was drowned out by the Miller boys, physically debating who would choose the next TV show.

Kat was good at ignoring things. "Rolls his eyes," she said. "Makes faces. Twitchy. Come on, kiddo, you're so smart."

Hallie shrugged. Upstairs, a radio whined about an itsy bitsy, teenie weenie, yellow polka-dot bikini.

"A food name. Or a taste. Sugar? No. Bitter?" This was spoken by Kat's red-faced gentleman caller, Sweets.

Ten years earlier Kat's husband Charlie had walked out on his family, but Kat was still optimistic about his imminent return. Sometimes she thought he'd been kidnapped, sometimes she was sure he had amnesia, but never did she consider that he'd left her. Meantime, Sweets, a man with gold front teeth and an endless supply of Scotch, had drifted in right after her husband evaporated, almost as if he and Charlie Miller had planned the exchange.

"Sour . . . lemon! Jack Lemmon!" Kat beamed. "Thanks, Hallie."

"But I—"

The boys became bored with wrestling. "You look pretty, Hallie," the shorter one said. Michael, the youngest Miller, was everybody's pet human being, even at a gangly fourteen.

"Thanks." Hallie blew him a kiss. "Looking good yourself."

He ducked his head and punched his brother.

"Jack Lemmon," Kat said. "Loved him in *Some Came Running*."

"I think you mean *Some Like It Hot*." Megan's family amused Hallie, who came from serious stock, parents who served guilt about starving foreigners along with dinner. Megan, however, had no time for her mother's nonchalant approach to life. The two girls had filled countless adolescent afternoons detailing how their marriages and families would be nothing like the second-rate systems that had spawned them.

"I'll get Megan now, if that's okay. I'm leaving early in the morning, and . . ." Good-bye, good-bye, to everything familiar. Tomorrow really began the happily ever afters.

"No problem, kiddo. Girls will be girls."

Kiddos would be kiddos, and upstairs, Megan would be Megan, straightening a mess of tubes, brushes, and bottles.

Megan's roommate and younger sister Bonnie had brick-colored smears under her cheekbones, a white line down the middle of her nose, and multitoned eyeshadow under heavily penciled brows. "I was teaching Megan how to sculpt her face," she told Hallie when she entered the room.

Megan herself had peacock eyelids, scarlet lips, and thick black eyebrows. "Sorry," she said. "Give me a minute to unsculpt." She was petite and slender, which Hallie, who always felt too tall and soft, envied, and she had dramatic black hair and tortoise-shell eyes that Hallie also coveted. "And turn that radio down, Bonnie!" Megan said as she left. Elvis dropped a decibel.

Hallie, wondering why a love song would use the words *mean*, *cruel*, and *fool*, picked up a book lying facedown on Megan's bed. *The Navy Wife*. She should have known.

The tidy half of the dresser featured a framed photograph of Megan's fiancé, Daniel Farr, in his Naval Academy uniform. Strong-jawed, he looked ready to defend his country single-handedly.

When Hallie thought of Ted, she thought of laughter and looseness. Of a smile, a wonderful ease about the way he breathed.

Daniel Farr had none of that, but his solid strength attracted Megan because he was nothing like the flighty, unreliable Millers. They said women married their fathers, but Megan was trying hard not to.

Rules depressed Hallie, but Megan craved them. She'd described the Academy's rigid precision with admiration. One tear in your regulation undershirt and you had to throw it away. Perfection or nothing. She searched for the rules of life, clipping articles that enumerated "Twelve Ways to Make Him Happy" and "The Five Most Common Newlywed Mistakes." Daniel was the logical prince to methodically hack through the Miller thicket and rescue Megan. He, too, was escaping chaos. Both his parents had died years back, and finding no guidance in foster homes, he'd designed and engineered himself. It was a match made in heaven, so who was Hallie to question it?

Hallie looked at Megan's book, open to a section detailing the fundamentals of calling cards. First of all, she read, they were to be engraved with one's full married name.

The name business upset Hallie. She loved being married. Often whispered the exotic, erotic word *husband* for the taste of it. Nonetheless, her fully married self, "Mrs. Theodore Henry Bennett," showed no trace or residue of Hallie Elizabeth Saxe.

She'd read Shakespeare. "He that filches from me my good name . . . makes me poor indeed." But Iago was a man. A woman was supposed to be honored by having her name filched.

She concentrated on Megan's book. "Junior officers call upon their seniors . . . except that seniors call on the bride of a junior officer attached to their command. . . . A woman leaves as many cards as there are adult women in the household, but never more than three, so if . . ."

Megan was backpedaling into a Henry James novel. How complicated, how different a world from Hallie's, where, starting tomorrow, she and Ted would play life by ear. Just the two of them.

She sat on the bed and waited, not for Megan and the farewell dinner, but for tomorrow, when real life began.

—————— 3 ——————

"Damn!" Her hand was burned and the black and white linoleum splattered with string beans, mushroom soup, onion rings, and a fractured white casserole dish.

Gingerly, Hallie lifted a sponge. Her finger throbbed. The air was yellow with humidity and every sweaty inch of her was uncomfortable. Thank God Ted's mother was out of the apartment, unable to comment on further evidence of Hallie's domestic inadequacy.

Married five months and barely a relaxed hour together. When she'd moved to Boston, she was immediately neck-deep in summer school and the even more overwhelming curriculum of marriage, everything new and strange, from the joy of meeting his body in the middle of the night to keeping a mental inventory of bread and toilet paper to figuring out how to have the meat and vegetables finish cooking at the same time.

And now, finally, a few August days between finals and fall classes to enjoy her life and husband. Instead, she had visiting in-laws. When Ted's parents invited themselves, Hallie decided to be optimistic. Perhaps entertaining them in her home would stamp her officially married, less a girl playing house.

A fine theory, but, in fact, their visit was nearly unendurable. Simon Bennett was cheerfully addled, obsessed with the mathematics of travel—how long it took to get somewhere and what alternate routes might mean in terms of time saved. Miriam Bennett confused conversation with a catalog of the insults and indignities she had suffered from birth.

For five days now, while Ted toiled at Summit Electronics to bring Americans bigger color-TV screens, his bride played tour guide and hostess.

For five nights, after Miriam was sated with criticizing Hallie's poor maintenance of her linens, copper, furniture, windows, time, and husband, the elder Bennetts retired on the living-room sofa bed and Ted and Hallie fell into each other's arms, but not onto their creaky bed. They made awkward, silent, sometimes painful love away from the tissue-thin walls and the noisy mattress—on the bare bedroom floor, in the bathtub. Hallie had acquired a

11

bruise on her coccyx, a chip on her shoulder, and now a burn on her hand and green-bean casserole on her floor.

Ted suddenly materialized, propped against the wall, holding his banjo. "There you are," he said. "I've been looking for you."

Despite her woes, she flushed as she did every time he said that, as she had the night they'd met, when those were the first words he said to her.

He strummed and sang, parodying an Elvis lament: "It's not forever, it's just too long. They'll leave, my darlin', they'll—hey, are you okay?" He put his banjo on the floor.

She showed him her burn.

He retrieved the butter dish and gently slathered her finger, his face filled with love and concern way beyond the severity of the situation. "Husbands can be useful," he said.

Husbands. My husband. The words still part of a game of let's pretend and not quite hers, like her first pair of wobbly, slippery-bottomed high heels.

Their buttery hands together, he moved closer until their thighs pressed. He kissed her mouth, her eyelids, the side of her throat while he unbuttoned her blouse. Then he lowered his head and kissed the flesh above her bra.

Her sore coccyx pressed against the lip of the sink, but except for the burned and pulsing finger, she felt wonderful, sliding toward a dizzy inability to know where she ended and he—they—began.

She reached for where he swelled and pressed against pin-stripes, reached for flesh meant for nakedness, not tailoring. With both hands, she touched. He moaned. She undid his belt, eased apart the metal clasp at his waist, touched the zipper—and laughed. "Oh, no! Butter. All over your fly."

"Damage done." His voice was husky. "They're gone. No point stopping."

So she didn't, and he didn't, easing her Bermudas down while his trousers slid to the floor and she took his weight in her hands, massaging butter onto him as she pulled him even closer, adjusting herself for him.

And then, behind the kitchen wall, the front door opened with a deep groan.

Frantically, like clowns in a silent comedy, they grabbed, buttoned, zipped, coughed, sputtered, and smoothed.

When Miriam Bennett walked into the kitchen, her rumpled son, shirt hanging loose, was washing a dish. "You should change clothes after work, Theodore," she said. "Especially if *you* do the housework." She gave her daughter-in-law a withering glance. "You're flushed, Hallie, and no wonder. Heat in this apartment could kill you without adding the oven to it!" She snapped off the dial and extracted four potatoes. "We'll finish them on the barbecue with the roast."

"Have some wine," Ted said, his back still to the women.

"Do you two always drink?"

"Not always," Hallie said, lighting a cigarette. "Not after we pass out."

"The little woman has an offbeat sense of humor." Ted shot Hallie a warning glance.

A sudden gust ruffled the apartment, freshening the heat-heavy furniture and occupants. It was immediately followed by a blaze of light and noise, and then the welcome splash of rain.

They watched the downpour ricochet off the barbecue on the fire-escape landing.

Hallie stubbed out her cigarette. "I'll put the roast in the oven," she said, "and finish the potatoes."

Another crack of lightning and roar of thunder, then silence. The kitchen clock didn't tock.

"The stove's electric," Hallie murmured. "I'm sorry. I'm sure the power will be back on soon and we can—"

"Potato, anyone?" Ted helped his mother into her seat. "With sour cream and chives. And I'll get the butter."

The stick of butter had been gouged by their fingers. Miriam raised an eyebrow but said nothing. Around them, the rain made shadow rivulets on the walls.

"This potato isn't done," Miriam said.

"Mmm," Hallie agreed. At least dining together meant she didn't need any form of address. "Mother" was already taken. "Mrs. Bennett" sounded stiff, "Miriam" rude, and "Mother Bennett" like imitation Jane Austen. When they were away from the table, she spoke only after she caught the woman's eye. She wondered how such dilemmas were resolved.

"Potato edges aren't bad." Simon's voice was mild, as always.

Miriam eyed Hallie's pocketbook, hanging over the edge of her chair, a red, white, and blue KENNEDY FOR PRESIDENT button on its strap. For obscure reasons of her own, Miriam didn't approve of her daughter-in-law's political involvement.

Now she inhaled slowly, as if breathing were a challenge. "How do you manage to work on his campaign? I certainly don't have time on my hands after my house is properly cleaned and my dinner cooked."

Bitch. *All I wanted was Ted.* She hadn't married these sticks, but they blew into her landscape along with him like debris in a windstorm.

"But maybe Theodore's easier," Miriam said. "Unlike his father, who needs everything just so." Miriam had two husbands. One, the mild teacher, the other, a mythical Simon-monster who tyrannized her. "You know how *he* is," she'd say in defense of whatever she wanted to do.

Simon, oblivious, whistled "The Battle Hymn of the Republic."

How had they produced Ted? By some miracle, their every good recessive gene had triumphed. Ted was a mutation, and having his child could be dangerous. Hallie might give birth to her in-laws.

"But if you must push doorbells, then why race through school, too?" Miriam asked. "Summer school, extra classes. Why the rush? It isn't as if you'll starve to death if you don't work. It isn't as if my son doesn't make a good living." The woman had an ancient quarrel with life. Simon was to have been an architect, but his Depression marriage had necessitated a safe career as a high-school teacher and she had never forgiven either him or fate.

"I *want* to work." Hallie hoped Simon understood her coded message that he was all right and blameless. "If I finish my degree by next June, I can get a real appointment. If I graduate midterm, I'd have to be a substitute."

"And no creature is lower or more mistreated than a sub." Simon's chuckle was melancholy.

It had grown dark and Ted lit the candles. "I heard a riddle today," he said, not at all subtly changing topics. "A man's with his son when there's an accident and the boy's hurt. He's rushed to the hospital, but the surgeon says, 'I can't operate on this boy—he's my son!' How's that possible?"

"The boy was adopted," Hallie said. "The doctor's his natural father."

"He's the grand—no . . . I give up," Simon said.

"I know! The father who rushed him in is also the doctor. The same man," Miriam said, "too flustered to—"

"All wrong," Ted answered. "The surgeon is the boy's *mother*! Nobody got it at work, either."

"I hate trick questions." Miriam's voice had barbed edges. "And I don't know what drives girls today. In my day, we enjoyed being homemakers." She leaned into the table. "Hallie, will you stop working when you and Theodore . . . well, when the time comes, will you stay home for your children?"

"Of course she will," Ted said.

Don't answer for me! But before she dared say it out loud, as if censored from above, the room glowed with fluorescent intensity and another bolt surrealistically illuminated pale faces above white plates, inedible potatoes, and crumpled foil. The rain intensified, as if someone had suddenly turned a faucet.

Hallie's stomach growled. "I'm sorry," she said.

"About the weather?" Simon looked amused.

"About that, too."

"Cheer up," he whispered in the dark. Rain pounded the roof, but the thunder and lightning had stopped. "They're leaving soon."

"It's not altogether about them. It's about being married."

"Isn't that good anymore?" His voice was black-velvet ribbon lacing the night.

"My parents say they're happy, but they quarrel all the time. Yours never fight, but they're angry and sad."

"None of that is news."

"Everybody's parents seem bored or annoyed. Maybe decay's inevitable. Maybe your parents were once like us."

"Impossible."

"Cinderella and Charming probably wound up bickering. Even Lucy and Desi split."

"We're different. Even if there's no precedent, we'll make it good and make it last."

"It's still scary."

He sat up. "Not if you know the antidote, which is to maintain an infantile mindset and stay away from grown-ups. So let's get out of here."

"Now? Where? It's pouring!"

"Right. They'll never follow us."

"It's midnight."

"It's immature." The bed squeaked as he got up. She watched his naked body, pale in the night room, move to the closet, pull out his Burberry and button it. "The kind of married people we will never be would screech that we could get *sick* out there. They'd insist our life has to be just as boring as theirs. They wouldn't understand that we are something new and different."

"You're right. I wasn't thinking. I must have been contaminated." She, too, went in search of her raincoat.

"Saved in the nick of time."

4

"Are you sure this is where she said she'd be?"

It was the third time Ted had asked. Hallie didn't bother to answer. Megan had said the statue of the Indian, Tecumseh, which is where they were, along with hundreds of other people. It offered a fine vantage point for noon-meal formation, the watching of which seemed a popular prerequisite to spending time with midshipmen.

"She's so short," Ted said. "She could be two feet away and we'd never find her."

Oh, but she'll find you. You're so findable, Hallie thought. A woman with a Jackie Kennedy pillbox hat openly eyed Ted. Women always did. It was a chill spring day with a damp wind coming off the river, but Ted radiated his own glow, as if there were a heat lamp inside his skull.

"Hey!"

Hallie saw a waving white glove, then black bangs and a red headband, and then Megan Miller, not in her customary art-student leotards and turtleneck, but a pleated tartan skirt, white blouse, and low heels.

"Sorry." It was Megan's habitual greeting, as if it were a given that she was guilty of some offense. "I tried to leave the drag house—"

"The what?" Ted asked.

Megan shrugged. "They call us their drags here, although nobody will say why. And drag houses are old sea captains' mansions used as our weekend dorms. Anyway, this landlady made me stop and hear a warning that if anybody turned off her living-room lamps, she had a spotlight triggered to zap on."

"So use another room," Ted said.

"It's obvious you don't know this place." Megan pursed her mouth. "For example, you are at this moment holding hands and therefore committing the major offense of public display of affection."

They disengaged like guilty children and Megan laughed. "Forbidden for me, not you."

"Really," Hallie said, "isn't your personal life off limits?"

"Definitely. So far off it doesn't exist. Rules are the price of admission. For example, if you stayed over, you guys could go to Jewish church tomorrow."

"Tomorrow's Sunday, and it isn't church for us, Meggie."

"The Academy doesn't care. Forget that the Jewish Sabbath has been Saturday for a few thousand years. Here, religion is church and church means Sunday. Period. Rules are rules. Oh, but look!" She stood on tiptoes and pointed. The show had begun.

Three thousand blue uniforms and white hats, three thousand low male voices answering roll call. Man, Essence Of.

Megan looked proud, as if she'd invented the whole sex.

Ted snapped a picture. Hallie stared. Incredible to do this wheeling and heel-clicking because they were about to have lunch. Hallie began to appreciate Academy pomp and looked forward to Megan's crossed-swords wedding in two months.

Ted, camera dangling from his shoulder, looked bored and handsome. Megan had once tried to draw his portrait but failed. "I'm not good enough," she'd said. "He's mostly color." Hallie

understood. His features were pleasing, but he was special because of his palette: tawny skin, streaky amber and flaxen hair,
dark honey eyes.

Still, striking or not, Teddy Bennett was only one man. Right
now her attention was riveted by thousands of oval faces, white
hats. She felt the plural force of the troops and mentally lay flat,
conquered like a weakly defended country.

Daniel, Megan's fiancé, led them to a steamy sandwich shop
crowded with midshipmen and drags. Hallie was relieved. She'd
been afraid restaurants in Annapolis would be as formal as the
rule book, as quaint as the cobbled streets, and the Bennetts'
budget couldn't handle elegant dining. Even this anniversary trip
stretched their funds.

When the waitress arrived, Ted as usual ordered for both of
them, while Hallie, also as usual, wondered why women were
supposed to whisper their preference to their men, as if it were
a dirty secret that they wanted something.

"A fellow I work with went to the Academy for three years,"
Ted said, once the order was in. "Finished at B.U., though."

"When we graduate," Daniel said, "we owe the Navy four
years, but industry recruits mids before then, pays them to quit,
finish their degrees outside, and work in the private sector instead.
They want our combination of engineering and management
training."

Daniel had a flat and final voice, as if his words were not open
to interpretation or comment. Hallie smoked and considered him,
remembering the huge male noise, the single organism of the men
in formation.

"Daniel thinks quitting that way is unethical." Megan was visibly proud of her man's code of honor.

"The most interesting job I can think of now is"—Hallie waited
until their sandwiches were set in front of them and the waitress
left—"the Peace Corps." Her BLT had arrived falling apart and
she pushed tomato and bacon between the slices of toast. "If I
weren't married, I'd join."

"It's ridiculously idealistic," Daniel said with his customary
finality.

"I don't mean to be rude," Hallie said, "but you're biased. War's your best route to becoming an admiral, but we have to think in new directions, find alternatives. We're the new generation President Kennedy passed the torch to. We can change things. Look at Cuba. What good did storming in, dying, and being captured do? People have to—"

"Forgive my wife," Ted said. "Her parents thought standing on a soapbox improved digestion."

He'd said "my wife" as a low-grade insult, an easy laugh, like a shabby comedian. His Wife. His. She couldn't believe how foreign and unrelated to her he suddenly seemed.

"When human nature changes, I'll change my mind," Daniel said.

"The Peace Corps is the best idea in years!" Hallie hated sounding aggressive and unfeminine, but she hated being silenced and treated like a disobedient child even more.

"The cherry blossoms were beautiful," Ted said.

"I'll bet you took lots of photos." Megan's voice was thin and bright, like tinsel.

"The real issue is the space race," Daniel said.

"Just because the Russians sent Yury somebody up there," Hallie muttered.

"*They* sent him. We didn't. That's the point."

"No it isn't!"

"Honestly, Hal," Ted said.

She pretended not to have heard him. "The point is if people worked together, like through the Peace Corps, not everything would be a contest." Hallie glanced at Megan the way you might at a passerby while you fought off attackers, hoping for help, but Megan sat primly. A model good girl.

Hallie's face burned. She always intended to mind herself, behave properly, and make Ted proud. She had no idea why she so often failed.

Hallie looked at their reflections in the mirror above the ladies' room sink. "Am I disgustingly fat?" Mutt and Jeff, people joked in high school. Hallie was almost a head taller, and always on a diet, and Megan was not only short, but thin. But when they'd first met, in fifth grade, they were the same size and they laughed at the same jokes and the same boys.

That was the year Charlie Miller took a walk and Kat went to work and Megan, age ten, was suddenly in charge of a household. Most afternoons, Hallie accompanied her home, and together they coped with three younger Millers, everybody's homework, and meatloaf.

Then Megan moved and they didn't see each other for three years, until eighth grade. They were no longer the same height, and Megan had become quieter and more self-conscious, but the bond of history and affection held. And then Hallie's younger brother, Eric, ran after a ball and into a speeding car and Hallie's parents barely spoke to their surviving daughters or each other for a year during which it felt as if the entire Saxe family had been lost.

Megan understood how it was to be bereaved and without moorings, to be estranged from everyone at home and at school, from life and normality. She also knew how to survive it.

The two girls' bond was double-forged and solid at the core, but perhaps incomprehensible on the surface.

"I blew up so much on the Pill," Hallie said, "I switched back to the diaphragm, but I kept the weight. Ted was sure the Pill was a hoax anyway, a plot to get people pregnant."

"Don't you want a baby?"

"Not yet." Hallie applied fresh lipstick. "I've only been married a year. Besides, practice teaching makes me realize I don't want to do that forever. I will, long enough to pay back the loans, but . . . promise not to laugh? I've been thinking about law school."

"Are there women lawyers? Besides in Katharine Hepburn movies? And what would you do when you had kids?"

"Stay home, of course." Everybody knew it was vital to be there for your children.

"Then how could you?"

Hallie blotted her lips and tried to suppress a too-familiar tremor of doubt. "I don't know yet."

"What does Ted think?"

"I haven't told him. I don't want him making fun."

"Would he?"

"Not on purpose." She smoothed her hair and sighed as it sprang back into curls. "But I'm not always sure he understands I'm the same kind of real he is."

Megan applied clear red lipstick that matched her headband.

"You should use the Pill," Hallie said.

Megan laughed. "You don't get it yet, do you? This place is more effective than any pill. Tonight, for example, we can go to the movies or the dance. If it's the movies, we might get time alone in the drag house—with the lights on—but then Daniel would have to be back in his room earlier than if we'd gone to the dance. But at the dance, you have to stay until the very end, then you have a half hour in the drag house along with everybody except lower classmen, who have less time."

"You mean you'll all be in that living room—"

"Sober, with the lights on and a time limit. Add that to the basic terror of knocking somebody up because you can't be a married midshipman, and who needs the Pill? Besides, I'll be married in two months and I want a baby. I want dozens. Sometimes I get such a craving, I take care of Grady's baby."

Megan was oddly fascinated by her cousin Grady, a musician who'd been unlucky enough to impregnate a former classmate of theirs, a spoiled girl named Christina whose only talent was dressing well, and who, much to Hallie's annoyance, had dated Ted Bennett during a summer he worked in Philadelphia. Hallie cut short Megan's baby rhapsody. "What about your plans to design clothing?"

Megan shrugged. "There's nothing more important than making a home, starting a family. Not that your ambitions aren't fine," she added.

"And vice versa." Hallie snapped shut her purse.

And then they returned to their men, and to chitchat about Hallie's teaching, Ted's work on an improved, enlarged TV monitor, and Megan and Daniel's pending wedding. Yury Gagarin, the Bay of Pigs, the Peace Corps, and other potential irritants, like Hallie's and Megan's futures, were not mentioned again.

When they left the luncheonette, Hallie walked beside her husband on a daffodil-lined path. She was still full of the memory of how he had squelched her, made her feel as if her outspoken

21

opinions, her separateness, was somehow subversive and unsuitable. They were a couple, two as one, but that one wasn't necessarily her. Mrs. Theodore Henry Bennett's institution was beginning to seem almost as regimented as Daniel's.

Why had nobody hinted at how tricky—sometimes impossible—it was to be married, a couple, and still be yourself? How many people were in The Bennetts, and who were they?

Tug of War

1961–1964

Love is an ideal thing, marriage a real thing; a confusion of the real with the ideal never goes unpunished.
Goethe

———— 1 ————

"HONEY, I'm—" Ted Bennett stopped himself. Sounded like a TV husband, and what ruffled apron and wooden spoon dripping cake batter did he expect to find?

He flicked on the entry light and shrugged off his coat. The empty apartment felt alien and rejecting.

He stamped snow off his feet. Not even Thanksgiving yet. It was going to be a hard winter. He brushed his muffler and hung it and the coat on the edge of the closet door to dry. Then he flipped through the mail. A flyer advertising a twenty-nine-cent special on chicken and swordfish. Telephone and car-payment bills. A postcard showing thatched huts on a lush beach, greetings from his college roommate, the still-single James Harris. It said only, "Eat your hearts out, Boston marrieds." A letter for them

23

from his mother and another for Hallie from "Mrs. Daniel Farr," postmarked Baimbridge, Maryland, where Daniel was training in nuclear-powered subs.

He wondered what women found to tell each other incessantly, what Megan found to say about Daniel, who was pretty much a stick. Hallie thought it was because he was military, but that was her typical knee-jerk reflex. The man was unlikable. It had nothing to do with his profession.

Ted turned on lights in all three rooms, making the apartment less forbidding, but it was still ugly with all its hand-me-downs and leftovers. Wobbly, blistered tables and upholstery the color of dirt. They'd painted the walls with tints labeled "lemon" and "buttercup" and hung posters of Van Gogh sunflowers, hoping to duplicate sunshine. Instead, the yellow and brown rooms looked like cold scrambled eggs.

He carried a Coke from the small refrigerator to the living room and put the bottle and a pack of Pall Malls on top of a pile of unread *Newsweeks* and *National Geographics*.

As usual, his mother's letter contained coupons, this time for ketchup, Pepsodent, and paper towels. Hallie interpreted them as criticism, but they were simply part of Miriam Bennett's frugality, a bit of which wouldn't hurt the new Mrs. Bennett, who tended to give up on inanimate objects and throw them away. "How do you know how to fix everything?" she'd asked, so dazzled that he felt like Superman instead of somebody who'd merely planed and painted a door.

". . . and when the repairman said the price, I nearly fainted," he read. "So we won't have a fallout shelter, and I pray we won't need one and thank God we don't need to ask our child for support, but when your father retires, I don't know how it'll be, and . . ."

How did she whine in a Palmer-method script? And by what dark magic did her voice, in person or on paper, grate her real and incessant message across his brainstem—"Don't be a failure like your father! Don't!"

There might be dust under their bed and laundry accumulating, but to her credit, Hallie didn't sit idle, complaining. She was helping them get a foothold, and doing it with good grace, considering how her job disappointed her.

"It's not teaching," she said. "It's custodial care. Prison, and I'm the warden."

A few months earlier, out with a lawyer friend and his wife, Hallie had remarked, speaking softly and rapidly as if embarrassed, that she was thinking about becoming a lawyer. "Bad idea," the fellow said. "Women are too emotional for the courtroom. They'd cry if they got a run in their stockings." Hallie looked on the verge of tears right then, even without a run in her hose. The guy was probably right. She hadn't mentioned it since.

Ted put his soda back on the crinkly circle it had made on the magazine and tossed his mother's letter onto the table next to Mrs. Daniel Farr's envelope. He thought about that lunch in Annapolis half a year ago, his watershed.

The fused blur of uniforms and faces at noon-meal formation had bored him. They were zeros, not individuals, a circuit engineered to make something else work.

But then at lunch, when he heard that the faceless pegs had the inside track with business, he felt as if he'd missed the shot that began a race.

He didn't tell Hallie because he didn't want a tirade about how life was not a competition. Life *was* a competition, and one that Ted Bennett did not intend to lose.

He needed to be as desirable as the Daniels. He needed that edge, the management training Daniel had mentioned. If he waited, he'd be trapped the way his father had been, obligations piling up into a barricade blocking all other possibilities.

Besides, his career was for both of them, and for their kids.

If Hallie put up with a few more lean years, stayed with a job that wasn't ideal, she could spend the rest of her life doing whatever it was women did, and in comfort.

He pulled graduate-school applications out of his briefcase, sat back on the sofa, feet on the unread magazines, and, greatly relieved, filled in blanks.

"Gonna flunk me, Miz Bennett?"

The words fell into the long shadows of the empty afternoon classroom while Hallie tried to find an answer. Leola was in twelfth grade and Leola was illiterate. Hallie was the first teacher to mention it.

"I don't understand," the girl's mother said.

"Nor I." Mostly, Hallie didn't understand what being a teacher had to do with teaching.

She'd entered this profession because Shakespeare and Edith Wharton and Charles Dickens and Amy Lowell were her personal friends and she wanted to spread the word and the delight. But so far this one week, she'd broken up two fights: one male, involving racial slurs; one female, involving razors hidden in hairdos. So far this week, she'd held hands with a hardworking senior girl whose pregnancy canceled out nursing school. So far this week, two drunk and singing juniors had visited her eight A.M. sophomore English class, and when she ushered them out, their good natures curdled and they threatened her life at the hands of their gang.

Yesterday, Willie Field, a bright but disruptive sophomore, had stormed out of school after she confiscated his hunting knife. Around midnight, according to today's paper, Willie Field killed his father for beating up his mother once too often. Hallie wanted to beg forgiveness for not having cared about him as much as about classroom order. And for still not knowing how she could have behaved any differently in the chaos of her overcrowded, disjointed days.

Leola's mother was round faced, the color of a fawn. "Made it to last year of high school." Her voice was soft and pained.

Hallie passed over a spelling paper covered with gibberish, although she was unsure whether the mother herself could read.

"No other teacher said." Yesterday, Leola Johnson had a wiry, almost offensive swagger. Now she looked feeble, victimized.

Hallie had been sanctioned by the state to make massive decisions about Leola's fate, but she felt cloddish and dull-witted in the face of the girl's problems. Did it make sense to flunk her, keep her from graduating? Would her future be changed with *Dick and Jane* under her belt? And where would she be sent to learn reading? A humiliating first-grade class? She'd quit school instead.

Leola picked at a cuticle. Her mother regarded the spelling paper with a morose, defeated expression.

Older teachers joked about students who didn't try and about

Hallie, who tried too hard. "Can't change the world," they said. Frustration was as visible as dust motes in the old school's air.

Hallie looked at the clock. She couldn't be late for her graduate class, giving Dr. Adams cause to humiliate her again.

"Curlylocks," he'd called her in the middle of the last seminar. She blushed, even at the memory. "Hey, Curlylocks, you have brains!" he'd said after she made an observation.

She'd taken the class in order to work toward her permanent teaching certificate. She was getting an A. And he humiliated her. "Curlylocks," like some character in a nursery tale, reducing her to an amusement for his "real," male students.

She hadn't told Teddy, knowing he'd either say Adams meant no harm—which was possible, but didn't make it better—or he'd say, "Women are so emotional!" as if feelings were a defect.

Made her feel like . . . like Leola probably felt.

"What'll my girl do?" Leola's mother blurted out.

Hallie was exhausted. This evening, after class, she had one hundred and twenty other spelling papers to grade, a paper on *Billy Budd* to begin for Dr. Adams, who didn't believe that any woman, including Curlylocks, should be in graduate school, and a ditto master to type for a "Theme and Meaning in Literature" unit.

And dinner. Damn. And laundry.

But none of that mattered to waiting, anguished Leola. "Would you come be tutored by me after school?" Hallie asked. Still more of her time fragmented, and for what, to what end, but she had no other solution. "Nobody will know but us. No grade, but if you do it, you'll pass English."

Leola's mother sighed with relief and looked at her daughter, who blinked hard as she contemplated the gray vista beyond the classroom windows. Then Leola nodded.

"Thank you, Miz Bennett," her mother said. "Leola's a good girl. You giving her a chance."

But not much of one, Hallie knew. And much too late. They walked to the door, and Hallie flicked off the lights, checking that the desks were clear and the window shades properly aligned. Those were the only things the principal was passionate about.

If I were a lawyer, she thought, I'd have Leola sue the whole damned system. If I were a lawyer, I could defend the Willie Fieldses from their fathers.

"See you tomorrow?" Leola whispered, and Hallie nodded.

It wasn't too late to apply for next year. Their student loans would be almost paid back by June. They could manage on Ted's salary for three years. Their nest egg would have to wait, but it would be worth it.

She would tell Ted tonight.

"It's for our future." He forked a French fry and dipped it in ketchup.

"You're a scientist, not a businessman. An engineer. I thought you loved tinkering, inventing, working out technical problems."

"It's about freedom. When the time's right, and the opportunity, I want to be able to do anything." He took her hand.

Feeling selfish, she nonetheless translated his freedom into what it meant to her, not them.

"What are two years out of our whole life?" he said. "I know you're not crazy about teaching, but—"

Not crazy! She woke up every day mourning something.

"—we could swing your graduate courses, too, so—"

"I don't want to go on with that."

He didn't ask why or what she meant. "I'm not surprised. What's the use of a doctorate in English? How many women professors are there?"

Comprehending a husband involved much more than she'd suspected, and she had no idea why they called this emotional seesaw "settling down." He was so innocently selfish. "I want to go to law school." She controlled an urge to apologize.

He swallowed audibly. "I thought you changed your . . . we can't afford to both go to school."

She heard every electrical wire in the wall hum in the silence. "Guess it makes more sense for you to go," she said.

"No. I'll go later. I can wait."

Sweet, sweet man. Wonderful, incredible man. To say this even though—she didn't want to admit it, but still—anybody else would point out that Ted was the man, the breadwinner. Ted was the one with a career. Anyone else would ask when Hallie planned to use her expensive legal education. After all, she wanted children, knew that it was best to have them while you were young, understood that raising them would be her career. Those were the real facts of life.

Her mother always said that marriage was a matter of making compromises. Hallie took a deep breath. "It makes more sense for you to go, Ted. I can teach two more years. That's not so long."

He had a smile you'd do anything to produce. "You're the best, Hal," he said, beaming. "The absolute best."

So. Sharing a life was no different than sharing anything else— you both couldn't have it at the same time.

"And then, year after next, when I'm finished, we could start thinking about a family. Our family," he said. The idea trickled warmly through her system. But why did it sound so terribly like a bribe, or a payoff? Her husband, her one and only love, wouldn't manipulate her, would he?

She concentrated on the pleasure of being the source of the joy on her beloved's face. That was something, too.

Still, she wished they could have tugged more, debated longer about whose turn for what it should be. She wished he hadn't accepted her capitulation so readily. So happily. So smugly.

2

The spaghetti was boiling, the meat sauce simmering, and Hallie, spreading garlic and butter over slices of French bread, felt pretty good about herself and life. For once, she had everything synchronized. The apartment was reasonably tidy. She was almost caught up with her teaching paperwork. They hadn't gone over the budget this week. Their life was in order.

And then she gagged.

Ten feet away, in the brown and yellow living room, Ted and a classmate from Harvard took a study break and talked about the President's sending troops to Birmingham, Alabama. "Like their Governor Wallace isn't part of the same country," she heard, "refusing school integration, defying—"

Tomato, onion, and garlic essence congealed at the back of her throat and made her gorge rise. She put down the bread, took a deep breath, and walked through the living room. The men ignored her. They each held a beer, and she could feel it slosh in its glass. She doubled her speed toward the bathroom.

Inside, she leaned against the door and breathed deeply. Teachers should get hazardous pay for working in classrooms, for being petri dishes for every new virus.

She'd left the spaghetti boiling. It would become inedible, thick and mushy as slugs. At the thought, she rushed to the toilet and bent over, but the nausea subsided. Good thing. She couldn't be sick. She hadn't left a decent emergency lesson plan.

She splashed water on her face. There were dark circles under her eyes. If she didn't have dinner still to serve, she'd crawl into bed right now, at eight P.M. She'd been dragging for a while, nearly dozing off while the kids did oral book reports yesterday, blinking hard to stay awake during her department staff meeting.

She was exhausted with supporting the two of them and taking care of the apartment and their meals. No wonder she caught every bug.

She opened the medicine chest in search of a stomach-soother, but found only aspirin, a bottle of congealed nail polish, an empty tin of Band-Aids, mouthwash, athlete's foot powder, a bottle of antiperspirant, and a pain prescription that had expired when Ted began business school, eight months ago.

Perhaps under the sink. She had to be tidier, keep things in order and inventoried. She bent to check the plastic shoebox where they tossed medicinal odds and ends and became so dizzy she clutched the sink rim above her, for support.

And while she squatted, facing the open cabinet's chaotic innards, she saw among the toilet-bowl cleansers and fingernail brushes an open box of tampons, empty but for one. She'd meant to buy more before she had an awkward emergency, but had forgotten.

When? How long ago? She put her hand to her throat, where her pulse suddenly thumped and raced. Ridiculous. They took precautions. Ted had over a year of school left. They lived in a tiny apartment with no room for the two of them, let alone a . . . It was masochistic foolishness to even entertain the idea that she, their sole support, could be . . .

She looked down at her belly and the V of her legs in their slacks as if they were foreign matter, unrelated to her brain and coolly capable of treachery.

She wanted to scream for help. Or cry in panic. Instead, she went out and rescued and served the spaghetti. Ted and his friend were grateful. They didn't notice that she ate nothing. She was already full, with questions.

3

"Chocolate mousse for dessert?" Ted said. "After lasagna, wine— why do I feel like I'm in an old 'I Love Lucy' and you're about to say, 'Ooooh, Ricky, I have something to tell you'?"

But on TV, she thought, I'd knit booties and he'd hug me. He'd be happy, no matter what. He wouldn't say "How could you have let this happen?" In the movies they were always happy about it, except when they were so unhappy they killed the mother-to-be.

"Did you wreck the car? Gamble the food money? Did you and Ethel sign on as belly dancers in a—"

In the movies, she never had to say it. The guy saw the booties. "Is it? Are you?" he'd gasp, burbling with joy.

"I'm pregnant."

She'd forgotten to knit booties. Maybe that was why Ted forgot to burble. Instead, his face turned as yellow as the painted pegboard. Stunned. The possibility of reproduction had never crossed his mind or loins. He coughed, swallowed hard, gulped wine, and stared at Hallie as if she were a mutant form of life.

"You're—we're—we're having . . . having a . . . a baby?"

"In seven months."

"How did this . . . I mean I know how, but . . . *how?*"

No, no. He was supposed to be incoherent with *delight*. But in the movies, the bundle of joy didn't ruin their life, break the trust, betray their future. "I think, maybe, on our anniversary." Since the doctor's call had confirmed her fear, she'd spent the day counting backward.

"Why? Didn't you . . ."

Surely, he didn't mean to interrogate her, act as if she'd committed a crime. "I think, in the middle of the night—that second time—you're supposed to add more stuff, or maybe it wobbled. The doctor said nothing's foolproof." And here's the fool to prove it.

"A baby. My God."

A kiss? A handshake? It was theirs, plural. But hers was the body that contained the intruder, hers was the body that was changing their life.

He sat like a lump. She should have mailed him the news. "It's due in mid-November." She meant her voice to be matter-of-fact, reassuring, but it quavered and broke.

"Hallie?" He stood up.

"I thought," she wailed, "when we'd have a baby it'd be this wonderful, perfect thing—but *later*, *much*, when we're ready, which I'm not, even if you didn't have a whole year left to finish your degree!"

"Shhhh!" He held her close, stroking her hair. "It'll be fine. I hope it has your eyes."

"My—" She pulled back. "What are we going to *do*?"

"Stop crying, for starters."

"How can you be calm?"

"I'm not. My heart is racing and I can't catch my breath. Does that satisfy you? Should I faint, which I also feel like I could do? I think that's your part."

"All I've been thinking about is how angry you'd—"

"What's the point? I assume I had a part in this, Hal."

"That you'd think I did it on purpose."

"So I'd have to marry you?"

"I wouldn't blame you, either."

"Shouldn't you sit down?" He led her to the mud-brown sofa and sat down beside her. "Everything will work out."

"How? How will you finish school?" She started crying again. "What about your degree? How will we live?"

It was going to be bad. Scary. There was the poverty, the

absence of room for a baby, for a place and the quiet for Ted to study. She'd become like her mother-in-law, fearfully frugal and angry all the time. "I was thinking I could make some money typing dissertations," she said. "And tutoring, after the—after it—but I'm scared! Aren't you?"

"Honestly?" His expression became serious and inward. "It's terrifying. Permanent. Forever. Like . . ." He shrugged. "Like real life." He put his arm around her protectively.

Babes in the woods, she thought. "One of my eleventh-graders knew I was pregnant because my neck was thick," she said.

"It is not." He lifted her hair and inspected, kissing beneath her left ear, and then her right, and then the back of her neck, and then the hollow of her throat. "I love you. We'll figure out how to do it. Remember me? I fix things. Besides, a baby's not smart. It can't even talk. We can *fool* it if we don't know what to do." His hands, under her sweater, ran up her sides, and then he stopped. "Is it okay?"

"For once, no chance of getting into trouble. We're already in it."

"Ah, Hal. Loss is trouble, death is trouble. Not life. Not us. This baby's made out of love. That's not trouble."

"Forgive me," she said.

"For what?"

She hadn't trusted him the way he deserved. But now she did, and it felt like relaxing muscles that had been for too long tensed in her soul. Now she knew they were, as promised, for keeps. "I love you more than I ever did."

He moved her gently until she was on her back, kneeled above her, painting designs with his fingers on her belly, mystical writings that tied her into the earth's history. She arched to meet him, feeling like creation. Oh, yes. This was how this had happened. Only when he touched her was the map of her body discovered. His hands made her beautiful, like a cartoon magician, glitter spilling from his fingertips. Everything was wonderful.

But once, while they rocked in unison, she opened her eyes and found Ted staring at her, and his expression reflected the terror she still felt.

Both of them immediately closed their eyes.

33

—————— 4 ——————

Trying to update premarital friendships was like trying to do a jigsaw puzzle with poorly cut pieces. Not that Megan wasn't still her friend, but they were both half-couples now, and their sets meshed as poorly as a jammed zipper.

It seemed easier, somehow, when the men were the presynchronized halves. Women—wives—searched more intently for common ground, making sure the social event stayed sociable.

Hallie had looked forward to this visit. She had Boston friends now, and she knew she'd make more in playgrounds and parks after the baby was born. But they'd be new, and the need for history was the strongest craving of Hallie's pregnancy.

First, she'd blamed their discomfort on the two years between visits—if you could even count Megan and Daniel's wedding a visit. Then she blamed the heat. Then herself. She was enormous and her feet were swollen and maybe she was cranky.

However, inspired by the new "French Chef" TV show, Hallie had expanded her repertoire beyond the broiler, and tonight she'd pulled all the stops. After two weeks of chili and spaghetti to loosen the budget for whipping cream, Madeira, arborio rice, artichokes, almonds, and decent wine, she'd produced *suprême de volaille à blanc* and *gâteau à l'orange et aux amandes*. It was delicious and appreciated, but it didn't help. She gave up on finding a cause of the ongoing tension.

"How about we walk Griselda while you wash up? We'll bring back ice cream," Ted said.

She was grateful for and surprised by his tenacious hosting.

"Not that the cake wasn't terrific," Ted added. "This is for later. It's so hot."

Their puppy, Griselda, all feet and hair, tangled her leash two times before the men left the apartment.

"Isn't it odd that a man's best friend is a dog?" Hallie asked when she and Megan were back in the muggy kitchen. "Women say their husbands are their best friends. Or, if not, then a *friend* is a best friend." The kitchen was a mess, spatters of cream, splots of butter, and sprigs of parsley on the counter plus a sink full of dirty pans. The presence of super-tidy Megan made her doubly aware of her incurable sloppiness.

"Sorry," Megan began, "but—"

"For what? Why are you always sorry?"

"Sorry," Megan said automatically. Then she slapped her hand over her mouth. "Only meant to say Ted's best friend has an awful name."

"Chloe Wister named her."

"Class of 'fifty-seven's Most Likely to be Peculiar. Still, naming a poor puppy Griselda." Megan dried a wineglass and tried, unsuccessfully, to reach its cabinet shelf. "Hal," she said, "I'm sor— I mean I'm *short*."

"Much better." Hallie deposited the glass where it belonged.

"Nice that Chloe visited. She's always fun." Megan sounded oddly wistful.

"Invite her yourself. She's not yet a star on Broadway. She's unattached and poor, so she's keen on being a houseguest."

Megan carefully dried another wineglass. "Daniel doesn't like company. He's . . . kind of private. We don't see other people much. We used to go to the Officers' Club, but not anymore."

Hallie poked at the pot with her scouring pad. "Why not?"

"People danced with me. You know how jealous men are."

Hallie could almost see Megan's life shrinking.

"Oh, who can figure men out?" Megan laughed weakly. "Tell me instead why Chloe named the dog Griselda."

Hallie gave up on the dirty pot and filled it with soapy water. "It's from an old story—thirteen hundred something, and I can't tell it the way our actress friend did, but, in brief, a nobleman married a country girl named Griselda, who promised to please and obey him. She had a baby girl and zap, he whisked it away. Had it killed. She produced a son and he did it again. And Griselda said, 'If it makes you happy to kill my kids, go ahead. I promised to please and obey you, so I will.' A dozen years later, the nobleman dumped Griselda for a new, young wife. But first, since Griselda knew how to run his castle, he asked her to make arrangements for his wedding. Cater it, get the place prettied up. And then leave with nothing but the dress on her back. And did our Griselda say anything?"

She turned off the taps. "Griselda didn't make a peep. She all but scrubbed the floor with her hair, sprucing things up for her replacement, because she wanted her man to be happy. And then her husband said 'Guess what? The last twelve years were a *test*. I wanted to teach you how to be a wife. This cute gal isn't my intended, she's our daughter, and the fellow with her is our son! Ha-ha! I didn't murder them, after all! You're a good wife, Patient Griselda.' "

"And what did she do?" Megan pushed a stray lock of hair off her forehead.

"*Nothing*. That's supposed to be the happy ending. He gets a doormat, and she gets him. Isn't it sick? But Chloe thought, and I agree, that Griselda's personality was perfect for a dog."

Megan didn't comment. They took iced tea into the living room. Megan curled her legs under her and looked for a place to put her glass on the cluttered end table.

Hallie removed a stack of paper. "I'm in the middle of a horrible typing job. A pharmacology dissertation translated into German. I have to do it letter by letter, and proofread it that way. I cry every time I work on it." She rested the stack on the tops of shelved books and tossed a blue paperback on top of it. "*The Feminine Mystique*. Another gift from Chloe. I haven't opened it yet, what with the typing and tutoring and housebreaking the dog and reading about natural childbirth." She couldn't stop babbling, compensating for Megan's muteness. "Ted's mother thinks it's disgusting that I want natural childbirth. My mother thinks it's dumb. And my doctor says it's fine for dogs, horses, and monkeys. Screw them." She smoothed her white smock over her black maternity Bermuda shorts. "I look like Humpty Dumpty. I wish we'd had more time alone, and more money. It's hard to fit somebody else into our lives, into a one-bedroom, third-floor apartment. I keep thinking of Anne Frank and those awful people who moved into the attic with her."

"You're talking about your own baby!"

"Doesn't some law of physics say you can't create matter?" Hallie drained her iced tea and poured more.

"Who cares? Girls don't understand physics." Megan sounded a little more like herself.

Hallie rested her head. Her curls, tight with the August heat, were pulled up high, and they fanned over the sofa back. "Nonetheless, you're smart to wait." She was weary and would have liked to lie back, clear her mind of everything except gentle reminders to her baby to grow all its fingernails and vital parts.

Megan's voice was nearly too faint to hear over the whirr of the fan. "We're not waiting. Not voluntarily. I don't seem able . . ."

Hallie sat up as straight as she could. "Stupid of me to assume. Have you been to a doctor?"

Megan nodded. "They can't find a reason. I bet if I had messed around when I was so afraid of getting pregnant, I would have, but now . . ."

"You will," Hallie said. "Of course you will."

"It feels like everybody in the entire world is except me. You, and my sister Bonnie—out of high school fourteen months, married ten, and due two weeks from now. And my cousin Grady's having a second baby. They made a deal. If Chris got a full-time housekeeper, she'd have another baby."

"She hasn't changed."

"But to be in charge that way, to decide to have a baby, to pick the month, to have it work out. Spring comes and coats come off and every woman has a belly." She looked tinier than ever and sad beyond measure.

"You always hear about people who took forever," Hallie said. "Maybe you should go on a vacation, relax—"

"Try to relax when you have to monitor your body, your temperature, your sex life every day! It's two years now and there are no vacations, no getting away from it. You're either waiting for your period and hoping, praying, you won't get it, or in despair, or hoping again that this month, this chance—when nights are circled and it doesn't matter how you feel—or if your husband is away on a ship on the night, the chance for that month." She shrugged, as if defeated. "Tonight had a circle around it."

"Then it still does. We will not come near the living room." Hallie glanced at her watch. "The news is on. Mind if I watch? I saw a part of King's speech, and it was incredible." She yawned. "Let me get the linens, in case I keel over." She hauled herself off the sofa, turned on the TV. An earnest young man moved his eyebrows up and down for emphasis as he described President Kennedy's meeting with the demonstrators.

His voice trailed her down the short hallway. ". . . crowd estimated at two hundred thousand heard representatives of the NAACP, the Student Nonviolent Coordinating Committee, baseball star Jackie Robinson, singers Peter, Paul, and Mary, Joan Baez . . ." She returned with bright floral sheets balanced on the shelf of her belly and dumped them onto the sofa.

Megan smiled. "Everything in this place is so yellow, it must be bright while you sleep." Then they watched the screen, because there was what looked like all mankind, and Dr. King's voice rocking them into his ideas. "I have a dream that one day this nation will rise up and live out the true meaning of its creed . . ."

"Gives me the shivers." Hallie winked at her old friend. "What a historic day to start a baby."

The door opened, the ice-cream hunters returned, and the room felt packed with people and livestock.

". . . the sons of former slaves and the sons of former slave owners will—"

"Christ," Daniel said. "Aren't you sick of that? If it isn't a sit-in, it's a speech."

Hallie wished she could like him more. She looked at Megan, who watched her husband with concern. Thy annoyances will be my annoyances.

". . . free at last, free at last—"

"As if they were the only ones who ever had it hard," Daniel said. "I had it just as bad. Only difference is some of us get on with it without whining. We make things better for ourselves."

"—great God Almighty, free at last," Dr. King said.

Daniel snorted.

Nobody else said anything.

Hallie tiptoed out of bed, moving silently in the dark. Shouldn't drink iced tea or anything before bed when her bladder was baby-squashed to the size of a thimble.

She yawned and quietly turned the bathroom doorknob, opening the door slowly, avoiding its chronic creak. She put one bare foot out and, instead of tile, touched fur that yiped.

"Griselda! What—how did you get closed in the—"

"She's with me." Megan huddled in the dark in the empty bathtub. "I'm sorry. You need the toilet. No problem."

Hallie closed the door behind her. Only a pale yellow night light thinned the darkness. "Why, Megan?"

"I couldn't sleep. I didn't know where to go, except here. She followed me and scratched on the door, and I was sure she'd wake somebody up, so I invited her in."

"I don't mean to pry, but did you have a fight?"

Megan shook her head. "We—I—" She made a sound halfway between a giggle and a sob. Griselda tried to offer comfort, but her nails scratched down the tub side, and she sat heavily, confused enough to lick the floor tiles. "She," Megan said, pointing at the puppy. "She—"

Hallie walked to the far side of the tub and sat down on the toilet. Only a vague silhouette showed through the shower curtain, as if Megan were a hospital patient in isolation.

"She—" from behind the curtain. "We—I—"

Hallie flushed, closed the lid, pulled back the shower curtain, and sat down again. "No more pronouns. What's going on?"

Megan was pale and insubstantial in the thick shadows. "Daniel wasn't much interested. He's weird about this baby-making. Thinks I only want his sperm."

" 'Not tonight, dear, I have a headache'?"

"All those jokes about wives, right?" Megan shook her head and whispered even more softly. "He doesn't like it if I'm unfeminine, if I'm . . . cheap or too forward, you know? But I persisted. He was asleep, but I only needed to wake up part of him." Her hands fluttered in the dusky light, minimizing her requests. Only that small portion, please.

"I about had that part convinced," she said, "and then the sofa bed squeaked so loudly—"

"Oh, God, I forgot to warn you. But nobody was listening. Nobody cared. I hope that didn't ruin your . . ."

Megan looked down at her hands. "We wound up on the floor, so that seemed okay." She laughed and shook her head. "The rest of Daniel finally got involved, you know? And then Griselda—"

Hearing her name, the puppy lurched to her feet, slipping on the tiles, wagging her entire rear, panting and straining, trying to claw through the tub to Megan.

"It was slapstick," Megan said, nevertheless sounding morose. "Daniel levitated—leaped straight up into the air, shouting. I can't believe you slept through it! I thought he'd gone insane. His pajama bottoms were around his ankles, and he tripped and fell splat, and Griselda danced around him, licking whatever parts she could get to, which is what she'd been doing while we were otherwise engaged. She looked like a hairball with a tongue, jumping and panting and slobbering. Like a monster movie crossed with Loony Tunes. Canine interruptus."

Hallie thought of the charts Megan had mentioned, the X on the night, the two years of wanting a baby. This was serious business. This was the beginning of life itself, or might have been. Nonetheless, giggles softly shook her as she tried to swallow the laughter. "I could wring your hairy neck, Griselda."

The dog smiled.

"Look at us," Hallie said. An egg with curly hair, sitting on an ill-fitting toilet seat, and a pair of baby-doll pajamas huddling in an empty bathtub.

And deep inside, flutters and kicks. The baby holding its sides in a watery, silent guffaw at the foolishness of the people outside the belly button who called themselves adults.

—————— 5 ——————

"You're doing great! Don't push yet, give your baby time to— That's it, great—"

Hallie couldn't always hear the words, only the roar of the cheering section urging her on, saluting her run for the goalposts. Except the football was inside her, pulling her to a high center, like a tent, and she was inside it, too, sweating with the hardest, most solitary work of her life, and there was no backing off, no changing her mind, no passing the ball to another player.

A nurse wiped her face. "Scream if you need to, honey." But Hallie couldn't let go of even that small amount of energy. She had to concentrate on the heaving ball at the center of the world.

She no longer remembered why that was so or what exactly she was doing, only that it was vitally important. Sometimes it was to please the doctor. Sometimes it was for Ted, who held her hand and made her feel both less and more alone. But most of the time, it was an elemental struggle for mastery, endurance, survival, between Hallie and the ball, the pain itself. Almost never did her mind unclench enough to remember that she was helping a baby—her baby—be born.

"Now! Push now—*push*, Hallie. Good—okay, hold it, pant—wait, let's give it a—okay, now—*now* a giant push, the biggest push, the best push—"

From her eyeballs down, she pushed with everything inside, everything she knew, everything she hoped for and imagined. And suddenly, the ball elongated and sculpted itself into head, shoulders, belly, and rump, smoothly sliding through her, stroking and imprinting itself on her soft tissue. With a stunned shudder of ecstasy, she felt her child rush from her womb to the world.

Nobody had ever described or even suggested that sensuous thrill, but before she could think about it, she heard a cry.

"Not all out and carrying on," the nurse said. "You've got a real pisser there."

Hallie saw the still-connected glistening creature, all feisty mouth and long limbs and skin turning red and real and beautiful. Perfect.

Her wiring went into overload and she cried and laughed, clenching Ted's hand, kissing it, mouth open, bawling like a great overgrown echo of the child cupped in the doctor's hands.

"A beautiful daughter," the doctor said.

Oh. Beautiful. Daughter. Puny, inadequate words. Ted's eyes brimmed over. They shook their heads, smiled, cried. Awe, not words for miracles.

The cord was cut, the baby swaddled and given to Hallie. Her daughter, tiny hand curled around Hallie's index finger, stared at her gravely, as if estimating her destiny, her vulnerability in this world of strangers. She was no longer "the baby." No longer Hallie's. She was Erica Bennett, a small, separate, and unknown human being with pale blue eyes.

41

"I will take care of you forever," Hallie whispered. She wanted to once again encompass her child, to carry and shield her in absolute safety. "I'm your mother. And this is your daddy and, oh you, oh you—I love you so much!"

Erica bawled nonstop. Hallie offered her entire arsenal of comforts: breast, diaper, pats, pacing, and soft songs. Nothing worked. God, she thought. Please. I have no idea how to be a mother.

And it was a life sentence. Permanent, irrevocable responsibility.

Erica caterwauled, her misery untouched by the impostor mother. "Ted," Hallie whispered, almost as distraught as the baby was. "Ted," she said more loudly. Her husband. Helpmate.

Ted awoke, groggily took the baby, and swayed in place. Erica was not consoled. Ted handed the howling baby back. *"You're* the mother," he said. "Do something!" He got back in bed and pulled the pillow over his head, and then both Hallie and Erica bawled.

But it was no better when the troops arrived, loaded with gifts, food, cameras, and a need to help, hover, instruct, control, disagree with one another, and drive her crazy. "Ask not what you can do for your in-laws," Simon Bennett said. "Ask what we can do for you." Sweet man, but what they could do was leave.

And leave her frightened and stranded again. She had never known such ambivalence. Now she sat in bed—they all agreed she should rest and she was grateful. She could not imagine how that tiny child produced this much exhaustion.

The grandparents were at it again in the living room. "Postpartum depression, is what I think. *Hormones.*" Her mother-in-law's voice shot through the wall like shrapnel. They were wrong. She was suffering Miriam And Simon And Sylvia And Ivan Depression. There would be elation post their partum.

If only the grandmothers didn't monitor every fumbled, stumbling action with the baby, hands out, as if Hallie would surely drop Erica. Didn't contradict each other's child-rearing theories. Didn't repeatedly point out that a puppy and an infant in a third-floor walkup was insane. Didn't blind the baby with flashbulb photos, treat Hallie like dairy stock with warnings of dried-up milk. Didn't treat Griselda, Ted, and all of Hallie's friends like walking germ banks.

"You don't know how it is," Hallie told Ted every night. "You're in class and then you hide in the library."

"*Hide?* I have to study. And what's so awful, really?"

He seemed miniaturized and remote, as if stuck on the wrong end of a binocular. "Your father constantly regurgitates the news," she said. " 'Isn't that interesting?' he says. 'Old Ike rededicated Gettysburg.' Then my father starts in about Eisenhower, pro and con. And then my mother disagrees with whatever my father says and your mother says they're waking the baby and that nobody has any consideration for anybody."

"It's not forever."

"They wanted to see the baby and they have—more than I have."

"They're trying to help."

"I feel invaded. *I hate it!*" The tears began before she noticed, and then she couldn't stop them. "I want it to be us. *We're* the family." Ted left to study at the library.

Hallie looked at her baby, sleeping in a cradle her father-in-law had made months ago. He was a truly nice man. They were all good people. Hallie was an ingrate. She took a deep, calming breath and concentrated on Erica, curled in her long nightgown like a sack with a baby-head and ten pink fingers.

The living-room symposia on Hallie's Mental Health had run out of steam. The new topic was the imported white knit snowsuit from James Harris. His taste in women and baby gifts was impractical, frivolous, and gorgeous. John-John Kennedy could wear that snowsuit when formally presented to visiting heads of state. But as soon as Sylvia and Miriam agreed that Hallie should exchange it, Hallie determined to keep it. Erica Bennett deserved the best.

Snowsuits triggered the memory of that long-ago winter day, blue as spring but edged with snow clouds along the curbs, and of her brother, Eric, almost ten, in a maroon parka, running into the street after a pimple ball and colliding with an Oldsmobile. Hallie shuddered, unwilling to admit how helpless parents were. Hostages to fortune, like somebody said long ago. Even the President, because his poor baby Patrick lived only a day and a half. What a cold world where you couldn't save what you most loved, you could only remember, name something new for it, and begin again.

There was heavy rustling outside her room, whispers. The door creaked. Hallie's fists clenched.

"Surprise!" It was her sister, Vicky, bundled in a vintage raccoon coat. She looked out of the Twenties, or the woods. "I'm on antiquity leave—maternity leave for aunts. Where is my niece?"

Hallie gestured toward the cradle and her sister tiptoed over and scrutinized Erica. "She's scrunched," Vicky said. "Can't see much except her nose, but word is, she's a knockout." Vicky turned back to the bed. "Named her for Eric."

Hallie nodded.

"I was thinking about him the other day, right when you went into labor. Isn't that weird? I didn't know you were in labor, and I almost never think about Eric."

"And I was thinking and talking about you," Hallie said. "About how it must have felt for Mom to deliver you on V.E. Day."

"I assume victory in Europe felt good, or why saddle me with Victoria?" She pulled off her coat and suddenly looked shy. They were both out of context: the baby sister, a college freshman, and Hallie, a mother. "So. How is it?"

Who could describe that wordless moment of birth, or the deep peace while nursing Erica, when much more than milk traveled between them? Sometimes, a deep, long thrill, a pull and press at the same time, ran through her body from her groin to her nipple and she wondered at it, just as she still pondered the memory of her daughter's slide through the birth canal. Why didn't anyone talk about the sensuality of it? Or was sex that didn't include men too dangerous to be acknowledged? "Indescribable," Hallie said.

"Listen, they said you were de—" Vicky stopped herself. "You don't seem sad," she said.

"About what?" Stupid postpartum garbage.

Vicky looked at the cradle. "I don't know. About having a baby, I guess. Being ordinary now."

Ordinary! How could Vicky use that word for a miracle? "That baby is precisely what I've wanted my whole life," Hallie told her. "Having a child is part of being a woman. Of being in love. You're in favor of love, aren't you?"

Vicky dropped her coat on the floor and sat on the edge of the bed. "Actually, there's a music major with a red mustache. Just between us, I signed out yesterday. Spent last night with him."

Hallie glanced at the cradle. "Are you careful?"

"Thank God for the Pill."

"You'd better. All we could use was our imagination." Oh, the substitutions, yearnings, worries, anatomical hair-splittings that were codified as their morality. Weird.

Erica awoke with a startled cry.

"Good lungs," Vicky said.

Hallie's milk let down at the precise moment Sylvia materialized at the door. "I'll freshen precious up." The changing table was in the corner of the living room now designated as Erica's.

"Gotta see her unscrunch," Vicky said. "Isn't this fun?"

And suddenly it seemed as if it might be. Might as well be. What the hell. They'd go back to their own lives and return hers to her. And then she'd become a mother by doing it. On-the-job training, like her marriage. Like her life.

She smoothed her robe and walked into the living room. Her mother-in-law hammered in the kitchen, either tenderizing or repairing something. Her father-in-law listened to the barely audible radio, hissy-whistling "God Bless America." In the corner, her mother diapered Erica, cooing along with Vicky. Ivan Saxe sat in the rocker by the frosted window reading the *Globe* and muttering about Mrs. Hicks and the Boston school system.

Miriam Bennett wiped her hands on a kitchen towel tucked into her skirt. "Sauerbraten for dinner. Want a sample?"

"Not yet, thanks," Hallie said. In a moment, her mother would suggest in a high, strained tone that nursing mothers shouldn't eat sauerbraten, and her father, expert on everything, would disagree. She reminded herself that these were temporary disruptions.

There was a snug hibernation ahead, maternity leave from the world. She'd be okay. Her mother was more expert only because she'd stumbled through it herself. Now it was Hallie and Erica's turn. She had a vision of intense peace and intimacy and joy.

Simon Bennett stopped whistling. "Strange. They've interrupted the broadcast. A special bulletin from Dallas. The man sounds—"

Without questioning why, Hallie went to the changing table and lifted her daughter, holding her close, lips against Erica's downy head.

Ivan Saxe put down the paper. "What's that, Si?"

Hallie inhaled the powdery, vulnerable silk of her baby.

Thin winter light strained through the small windows, making the room look like a faded photograph. Simon Bennett blinked behind his glasses. "The President." He spoke with soft incredulity. And then he broke with habit and didn't repeat the news. Instead, groping blindly for the knob, he turned up the volume so they could hear for themselves.

6

It was well past midnight and bitter cold. Three stories below, the chains of a car clanked a lonely greeting to a new year. The country still mourned and staggered in shock, and blessings had to be recounted. Hallie listened to her husband sleep, measuring her good fortune by the rhythm of beloved breath in the dark.

Ted turned, his hand brushing her, pausing, waking up on its own and stroking her nightgown. She smiled at the hand that instinctively paused to love a part of her.

Then the rest of the man moved closer, his eyes still closed. Her smile became uncertain. She was so tired. And vaguely worried that her insides were still unstable, no matter that they had withstood and even enjoyed the resumption of sex. But when it was over, it was more over than it had ever been and she sank into the true sensual goal of her days—sleep. Desire required energy. After a day of her breasts in Erica's mouth, sex seemed another loan-out of body organs. Shameful, but there it was.

She loved Ted and wanted him. Only not urgently. Not now.

Soon, maybe. When Erica slept through the night, when Hallie wasn't so overmuch, exclusively, a mother.

Snow swirled at the window and Ted's warm hand tracked her stomach, igniting buried networks of nerves. Fingers circled and teased, backtracking across her midriff, over the silky material, to the underside of her breasts. She let herself sink and float deeper into darkness. Oh, she thought with surprise. Now I remember.

It would be all right again between them, here in this warm bed on a freezing night in a brittle new sliver of an uncertain year. She leaned toward the pale blur in the dark. He cupped her breast, then skimmed across it, his palm deliberately, slowly, brushing the nipple so that pleasure ran from the center of his hand into and through her.

He smiled before his eyes opened and murmured a private, wordless greeting. Her lips moved to his, to that smile, to the man.

Then, wetness on her chest, the gown sticking. His hand, surprised, lifting from a dribbled slick of milk.

And Erica, from her cradle, shattering the night with a reminder that the breast on the bed belonged to her.

Ha! Teddy said in mirthless exhalation. So!

Her kiss mutated into Sorry-I-wish-but-what's-to-be-done. Hallie, all motherhood and inevitability again, went to make a different kind of love. This was the real eternal triangle, and even though someday things would be all right, they would never be the same.

Little Boxes

1964–1967

Before going to war, say a prayer; before going to sea, say two prayers. Before marrying, say three prayers.
Proverb

―――――― 1 ――――――

A LOVELY house," Sylvia Saxe said.
Ivan Saxe frowned. "Plumbing's on its last legs."
"We'll fix it. Ted's handy. We couldn't afford good plumbing."

"Penny-wise and pound foolish," he muttered.

"Oh, Dad, just once." Hallie shifted Erica on her hip.

"I believe in telling the truth," he said. "Now we'll take a walk. Take a look at the neighorhood."

And find something else to bicker about.

"A house in the suburbs," Vicky said after they left. "One-point-five children." She lifted her guitar, strummed a few chords, and sang:

Little boxes on the hillside
Little boxes made of ticky tacky,
Little boxes on the hillside
Little boxes all the same—

Back from Mississippi, a veteran of Freedom Summer, Vicky was heavily into tolerance—except for the middle class.

"Stop." Hallie angled churning arms and legs into the high chair. Griselda stationed herself for dropped food.

And the people in the houses
All went to the university,
Where they were put in boxes
And they came out all the same.

And Hallie had been so proud to have her family visit before Vicky went back to Antioch. So proud of her house ringed with green grass.

Since Ted had completed his M.B.A. and gone back to Summit, she no longer typed dissertations or tutored. Humble as it was, the house meant they had made it to the far shore and now, despite the loans they still had to repay, all was well. But Vicky made it ordinary, even sordid.

And there's doctors and lawyers,
And business executives,
And they're all made out of ticky tacky
And they all look just the same.

"Cut it out!"

"I didn't write it." Vicky's sandy hair frizzed so that she looked as though she'd been electrocuted. "I wouldn't live it, either. Occupation: housewife. That's you."

Housewife, the new dirty word, thanks to Betty Friedan. A housewife did not experience "full participation in the world as an individual." The words had reverberated through Hallie's system since she'd read them. Even now as she put steamed carrots and hamburger granules on Erica's plastic dish, as she felt the queasy beginnings of her second child. Her mother said *The Femi-nine Mystique* was twaddle. "The Feminine Mistake," she called it. Still, Friedan's words played like a jingle through Hallie's brain, cryptic, annoying.

"Mama," Erica said. "Mmmmmm, Mama." At nine months, she trilled and gurgled nonstop, experimenting with sounds.

Hallie smiled and looked to Vicky for acknowledgment of the child's progress, but Vicky was above her picayune nickel-dime history.

Her father reentered the house. His plaid Bermuda shorts looked droopy. "I forgot my hat." He retrieved a squashed white cap from the top of the refrigerator. "Think about it, Vick," he said. "Listen to me. You'll get in trouble signing petitions and lists."

The debate that would not die. They had been at it when they arrived, had probably argued Vicky's political involvement the entire seven-hour drive up from Philadelphia, and they were not about to stop.

"My father, the so-called revolutionary," Vicky said. "I can't believe you're talking this way."

"I didn't believe it either when my friends lost their jobs to McCarthy because they'd signed lists years earlier." Ivan slammed the sailor cap on his bald skull. "Maybe I know a little more than you do." And he left.

"Fascist," Vicky hissed.

"He's scared for you. How do you think he felt when kids like you were killed in Mississippi?"

"Who'll change things if we don't? Or should we simply watch the country go to hell? You'd think he'd notice. Even our own City of Brotherly Love had its riot."

Erica gasped, choking. Hallie pulled her out of the high chair, pulse racing as she patted her back.

She'd capped the light outlets, removed poisons from low cabinets, put locks on kitchen cabinets, gated stairways, checked that crib slats met safety regulations. She'd bathed her infant in shallow tubs with diaper linings for anti-skid safety, protected her from the sun, the cold, the rain, from inactivity and overstimulation. She'd tested every bottle and bath on her inner wrist. But she couldn't eat her daughter's food for her.

"Stop. She's fine." Vicky put her guitar on the floor and lit a cigarette. "Your overprotectiveness will make her crazy. Didn't you ever take a psych course?"

And indeed, Erica smiled, tiny tooth pickets gleaming. Hallie put her back in the high chair and sipped coffee although lately it gave her indigestion. She was trying to stop smoking until after the baby was born. "I didn't think you'd been on campus enough to know there were courses," she said.

"There's more to learn than intellectual bullshit. Civil rights mattered to you, too, before your brain turned to baby food. You've forgotten those kids you taught."

Hallie felt her summer tan drain away. "No," she whispered. "I remember. One of my kids wrote me last month from Vietnam."

"Where?"

"Where that Gulf is. Tonkin? Where the ships were bombed last week, remember?"

Erica carefully dropped a carrot slice from the high chair, bending to watch it land.

Hallie cleared her throat. "In high school, Donald refused to join a gang. He got into fights because of it, so he quit school and joined the Army." To participate fully in the world as an individual.

"And?"

Hallie was dislocated for a minute, then she remembered. "I called his aunt to make sure I had the right address, so I could write him back. She told me he was dead. An accident, but all the same, he died because he wouldn't join a gang. I know there's no safe place for kids like him. I'm not an ogre."

Vicky looked at her hands. "Sorry."

Hallie was bone tired. Not an ogre, but not a participant, either. A bystander, like the people in New York who watched that girl get murdered.

"The problem is Dad can't handle honesty," Vicky said.

"You seemed much more interested in Mississippi's men than its politics. No father wants to hear his daughter's sex life." Would Erica someday torture Ted with true confessions?

"Just because I'm not hypocritically selling myself for a wedding band like your generation did!"

Hallie was too tired for this again. Too tired to fully participate in the world as an individual. "My generation? We're sisters. Five years apart. The same generation."

Vicky lit another cigarette. "I'm talking reality, not genealogical charts. My generation considers women equals. People. And people have sexual feelings."

The waistband of Hallie's shorts was too tight and her blouse gaped and pulled across her chest, but she didn't feel ready for maternity clothing again. She felt like a slob.

"He hates that Ronny's Negro." Vicky looked sulky.

"Are you capable of saying the word 'Ronny' without mentioning his race? You could be Klan, you're so obsessed. Look, folks, I'm a liberal because I slept with *A NEGRO!* They're upset you're sleeping with a *guy.*"

"Do they think I consult *The Facts of Life and Love for Teenagers?* That I won't kiss good night before the third date and never let them touch below the waist? I've been with guys since—"

"They didn't know. And if they did, they didn't have to discuss it or give their seal of approval. It's not nice."

"*Nice?* Who are you? Doris Day?"

Dinosaurs must have felt this way on the eve of extinction. Why, with the terrible finality of Kennedy's death, hadn't Hallie realized that when something ended, something else began? That gunshot had wounded everybody her age. That torch they'd been handed flickered and stopped lighting anything clearly, so they'd dropped it and their baby brothers and sisters rushed to become the new torchbearers, the next generation.

"Your life's so damn safe!" Vicky said. "Everything by the book—the degree, the husband, the kids—" Vicky stood so abruptly, her chair toppled and Erica, startled, dropped her cup and howled.

Hallie lifted her daughter, but she couldn't make her voice or actions soothing. "My life isn't a fill-in-the-blanks! I'm not following directions!" Oh, but she hoped it was true that she wasn't an automaton. That she was shaping her own life.

The baby, face and hair streaked with mashed carrots, screamed. Hallie clutched her in apology, holding her like a shield. "Last month there was a demonstration about the schools. I wanted to go, but it was raining and Erica had a cold and I couldn't get a sitter."

"Don't get so—"

"Should I sacrifice my kid like some Old Testament weirdo? Would you think more of me? Is that what you want? Is that—"

"I didn't say . . ."

Hallie turned away and rinsed the baby's face and sponged the high chair. Griselda waited. Dogs were the last optimists.

"The truth is," Vicky said softly, "white girls became bad politics and Ronny dumped me." Her nose reddened. "I didn't even want to think about him again, but I couldn't stop blabbing."

Of course. It wasn't political theory at all. It was men. They were sisters and the same generation in some ways, still.

"I wanted to stay. He said there wasn't any place for me. Now I don't know what to do."

"Join the crowd."

2

The triumphant urge to roar down Route 128 was difficult to control. The Beatles were singing "A Hard Day's Night" and Ted joined them at the top of his lungs.

He was going to make it happen.

A year ago, only days after he returned to Summit, and too soon, politically, Ted had suggested that the company consider a new direction: medical applications for their video monitors. His project manager had pretty much dared him to prove it, hoping, Ted was convinced, he'd screw up.

He hadn't. He'd done his homework, interviewing surgeons, medical school administrators, medical equipment companies—anybody whose work might be enhanced by a state-of-the-art color monitor, so many that even in his dreams he mumbled about cost versus benefits. And once he confirmed that there was a hungry market, he found the way to beat the competition in the shape of a small company already producing exactly what was needed.

Today the monitor company had made it clear that they'd love to be acquired. They agreed that they had everything to gain with Summit's power and market force working for them, but it wasn't going to be as easy to convince McPherson, the V.P. of Business Development and the stereotype of stinginess.

Ted had to seduce the man with cold facts and hope that the process didn't take so long that somebody else grabbed TeleVue first.

The music stopped for the news. If he worked fast, there was time to draft a rough memo before the squash game. Good thing he wasn't rushing home as usual, because he'd be late and Hallie would be angry. Sometimes, especially since Andy's birth, she acted as if the children and house were also his responsibility, his job a flimsy excuse for shirking his duty. He imagined her waiting by the front door all day, holding both kids, tapping her foot until he got back where he belonged.

He mentally began the memo, searching for words that stressed urgency without making McPherson feel pushed, planning strategy to get the rest of the team solidly behind him so that they bulldozed the man.

The news rolled on. The Chinese premier had badmouthed the U.S. What else was expected from people who'd said they were happy when Kennedy was shot?

"Seventeen thousand people responded to the news that President Johnson committed U.S. ground forces to combat by staging an antiwar rally today in New York—"

War? The man—as candidate—had said he wouldn't send American boys to do what Asian boys should do for themselves. End quote. Ted drove more slowly, while the newscaster, in the same noncommittal voice, noted that the Supreme Court had banned curbs on birth control, which would no longer be limited to married people. Good. But his mind was stuck on the word *war*. Hitler had shown what happened when you let a tyrant take an inch, and you didn't want to be a coward, or unpatriotic, but all the same, another Korea? Still and all, the government must know what it's doing, he decided.

"The Supreme Court today voided the conviction of Billy Sol Estes because his trial was televised against his wishes," the announcer said.

What a scam! The guy swindled twenty million bucks. Some people did whatever they pleased.

He stopped for a light next to a gray stone school and smiled at kids playing basketball. Somewhere, their mothers called their names into empty backyards, told them to get ready for dinner, do their homework, but they were mother-deaf, drunk with approaching summer.

A block farther, lost in memories of school yards and spring, Ted saw a glint, gasped, and jerked to a brake-squealing stop. Then he gripped the wheel and sat shaking as a boy on a blue and silver bike recklessly, wildly, caromed past his fender and through the intersection.

His breath back, Ted rolled down his window and poked his head out, ready to shout at the oblivious kid. But the words froze and his hand dropped because he recognized the boy. Remembered when he himself wore that skin.

At the other side of the intersection, the boy jumped the curb and sped onward, up a gentle incline, so weightless he'd be airborne in another block.

I remember, Ted thought. I remember the feel of June, the blood rushing because soon school would be out for the forever of summer, when absolutely anything could happen but nothing had to. And meantime, you rode so fast freedom ruffled the roots of your hair, then you coasted, then you flew.

In the gray expanse of his Johnstown neighborhood, there'd been a single oasis, a grassy hill of sycamores. In spring, when the trees were hazed with green buds but were still a web you could see through, Teddy Bennett took his bike to the top of his mountain, surveyed the expanse of city below him, then raced down, wheels barely touching earth, bike snaking grand slaloms around tree trunks, flying through the blue air of spring.

He hadn't known then that he would never again be that free. Then, he'd thought he was having a taste of the future.

No way he'd break the boy's bliss. Life would take care of that in due time.

Honks behind him made him realize he was blocking the intersection. He lurched forward, turning left until he remembered that was the boy's route, not his. He redirected his car toward the office and drove on.

"Good game," Jack Demetrius said again, after they showered. He was that kind of man, enthusiastic about everything. "We have to have you join the club, get a standing court date."

"Great," Ted said, even though he probably shouldn't. But

why the guilt? A man was entitled to relax. He wondered with whom he was arguing the point. "You know," he said as they walked toward the dining room, "there was a kid on a bike today—" But Lenny Peters and Vic O'Neill spotted them, and after greetings and game comparisons, the four men went in to eat. Ted checked. Six-thirty. Plenty of time before Hallie expected him. No problem.

The three other men were older and comfortably established in the Summit hierarchy. They called Ted the Young Turk, and sometimes treated him like a mascot, but they were allies, and he valued them.

He had a beer before dinner and sat with the relaxed satisfaction of having worked his body as hard as he'd worked his mind. There was gossip about an expansion of Summit, other gossip about being bought out.

"There's always talk," Jack said. "The day I joined the company, ten years ago, I was warned some giant was buying us." He finished his Bloody Mary and ordered another.

Ted swapped soft information about the monitor for news of impending promotions, personnel changes, and suspected liaisons. Men's gossip, Hallie called it, annoying him.

Over prime rib and lobster with drawn butter, they talked about sports they'd played and watched. About best games and individual records. About Cassius Clay becoming Muhammad Ali and what it meant.

As coffee was poured and the dessert cart wheeled over, Ted glanced at his watch and winced. Already an hour late.

Before he began his apple pie, he thought about finding a phone, but Jack turned to him. "Didn't you say something earlier about a kid on a bike?"

"I nearly hit a boy zooming through an intersection," Ted told him. "He was fourteen, fifteen. And I couldn't get angry because he looked so damned happy and I remembered that springtime high, that freedom." He stopped. They'd think him a sentimental fool.

But the great thing was, whether or not they actually remembered, or had felt, as adults, that piercing bolt of nostalgia, all three men said they had and reminisced about the times before you had to do much of anything except be. Together, they wished for one more chance at a summer. The real kind.

By after-dinner drinks, all of them not only remembered how it was to be young, but sounded like fourteen year olds.

"—and she said, Christ, she said come back in ten years! So humiliating. Like you'd talk to a toddler. Humoring me." Lenny was laughing so hard he was wiping his eyes. "The thing is—I actually did see her ten years later. And she still wouldn't give me the time of day!" He pulled out a handkerchief, blew his nose, then laughed again. "Oh, the fantasies of youth."

And they were off again, on what they had thought the world and business would be like. What they still hoped for. Ted felt comforted in ways he hadn't known he needed. Somebody eventually yawned, and all four of them made their way to the parking lot. He didn't want to be the only one to break formation and find a phone. Besides, what would he say? She knew he was late. And she was undoubtedly asleep, so why wake her?

She could look like Medusa, snakes coming from her head, pale eyes chilly as metal shields. Medusa in a ratty bathrobe and knee socks, sitting at the kitchen table.

"I thought you'd be asleep," he said.

"I was scared to death! I thought you were dead!" She looked weepy and furious.

"I'm perfectly fine, as you can see. You shouldn't have worried." He bent to kiss her temple.

She stiffened and brushed him off. "Where *were* you? Eight o'clock you said and it's nearly midnight! I was going to call the police in exactly four minutes. I imagined you crushed, bleeding, alone on the highway—"

"We got to talking. I didn't notice the—"

"Erica got cranky waiting up for a good-night kiss, and—"

He thought about his friends, who understood.

"Is it asking too much to take five minutes from your fun?"

He'd wanted her to know about the boy and the bike, but now he saw what a stupid idea it was to tell anything like that to Medusa.

"If I'd known you were all right, I could have gone to bed. I'm exhausted with Andy getting up every— *One lousy phone call!*" She stood, nostrils flaring, hair in wild tendrils. "You have absolutely no consideration for—"

"Why don't you install a time clock at the front door?" He picked up his briefcase. "Or buy me a leash?"

"So arrogant! Not even sorry for—"

"You're right! I'm not sorry! I could have called and I didn't want to! I didn't want to *have* to! I had a great time, and the way you're acting makes it crystal clear why it felt so good, just once, not to sign in and out!"

She looked stunned, then hurt, then enraged. "Don't—what are you—don't try and make *me* the villain!"

The joy of the evening was as far gone as if it had never been, trashed by the woman in the stained robe. "Nobody's the villain," he said. "We're both tired, and I have a memo to get out by morning, so forget it."

"*Forget it?*" Her voice was painfully shrill. "One lousy phone call, that's all!" Her voice drilled through his skull, eradicating springtime, now and forever.

"*Stop acting like my fucking mother and leave me alone!*"

She stood, mouth agape like something in a bad old movie, and he went up to the attic, taking the stairs two at a time.

He sat in his makeshift office under the eaves, one window opened to the noise of crickets, the unfinished memo on the desk, and below him, the muffled sounds of Hallie soothing the baby back to sleep.

Why couldn't she understand? You hoped, your own wife . . .

He switched on the radio above the desk and heard a Cole Porter love tune, witty and wry. He lowered the volume.

"Last year," he wrote, "TeleVue monitors were given six-month trials in three medical schools. The attached study demonstrates conclusively that—"

He should apologize before she went to sleep. Never go to bed angry—wasn't that what she said?

But she said too much. Let her follow her own rule. Come up and say she was sorry.

He was surprised when another serenely untroubled announcer

summarized the news. One A.M. and nothing much had changed except that the odds for rain were now sixty percent. Otherwise, China still hated us, we were still maybe starting a war, and Billy Sol Estes was still free.

And somewhere the kid on the bike was asleep, oblivious to everything except dreams of the wind and his own heart pumping.

In the attic, Ted Bennett wrote his memo, wishing with all his heart that his wife had understood, mourning his conviction that she never would.

3

His name was Byron, but he wasn't poetic. Barely verbal and not Hallie's idea of romantic, despite flowing locks, a lavish handlebar mustache, and a profile worth a swoon. He sat on her brand-new navy and cream sofa with the animation of one of its throw pillows.

He was undeniably exotic in tie-dyed shirt and threadbare jeans stuffed in Robin Hood boots, as was Vicky, in a short skirt and long ironed hair. They'd arrived looking like royal refugees, he in an ancient velvet-trimmed topcoat and she in her moth-eaten fur.

Ted had lit a fire, and the room was a warm ark against the ice age visible through the swagged drapes. Across the street, Christmas lights punctuated a snowy roofline.

Within the walls of this house, everything central to Hallie thrived. But her contentment shriveled under the impassive gaze of visitors who valued none of it. She was Mrs. Organization Man in her color-coordinated living room on a street that looked like a winning Monopoly property with its identical peaked-roof houses. She had the ticky-tack life Vicky had mocked.

Hallie considered Vicky's . . . what did you call him these days? *Boyfriend* was archaic, left over from Mickey Rooney movies and her own teens. *Lover.*

The times certainly had a-changed. Hallie imagined presenting a rag-tag bedmate in the era of I Like Ike and Peter Pan collars. She cleared her throat. "You're at Antioch, too, Byron?" It was not her voice that emerged, high and strained. Julia Child's, perhaps, enthusing over *pot-au-feu*. She lit a cigarette for stability. She absolutely had to stop smoking. Ted had six months ago and was obnoxiously moralistic about it. He frowned at her now.

"I'm more or less there," Byron said.

"He's not enrolled," Vicky said. "We met in front of the White House last April. Fifteen thousand of us and LBJ leaves to make it clear he doesn't give a shit. I was so pissed, I clobbered Byron with my picket. Accidentally."

"I'm not into formal education." Byron hollowed the words and filled them to overflowing with scorn.

"He was at Berkeley." Vicky sounded like a proud parent. "Arrested in the Free Speech Sit-in."

"My!" Hallie said. Should she tell them about the dark ages of 1961, four entire years ago, one college generation back, when *in loco parentis* meant school rules were as tight as your mother's, and your mother's were tourniquets? Who would have dreamed that all of it could be abandoned, broken, ignored, this easily?

Byron held his cup between his palms and studied its contents. "Screw authority, you know?"

Hallie was in a foreign country with benign but inferior interpreters, so eager for definition that she crackled and squeaked. "So then, you're visiting Vicky?"

"More or less," Byron said.

More or less *what*? She looked at Ted, who, after checking that neither visitor would see, crossed his eyes.

"Coffee or tea?" Hallie chirruped. "Sandwiches? You guys must be starved." Oh, God. Possessed by Donna Reed now.

"I'm more or less macrobiotic," Byron said.

"Byron's off to friends in Maine."

And then to Canada. The War. A year and a half ago, Vietnam had been so remote that when her former student wrote her from there, she'd had to look the place up on the map. Now it was too familiar, a chronic infection. Every night on the news, like stock footage, ferns and fronds and small men with bony faces over there, teach-ins and pickets and shouting students over here.

"Draft boards are a bummer, huh?" Byron mumbled.

Ted wore the glaze of one not truly present. He dismissed

Hallie's antiwar sentiments as uninformed and overemotional, and did a good imitation of General Patton for one who'd done his service in peacetime, through summer camp and the reserves. Their disagreements about the war rubbed a small but permanent sore spot between them. Hallie disliked being reminded of how different she was from her husband.

"Brainwashed since kindergarten," Byron said. "Air-raid drills. Feared the bomb and the Reds more than God. Scared a war would start, and I'd be stuck with Miss O'Neill in the school boiler room forever, you know?"

Hallie envisioned a beautiful little boy, blond hair slicked, ruddy cheeks clean, peanut butter sandwich in a bag with his name on it. Portrait of a future fugitive.

"My dad says every man needs his own war," he added.

Hallie didn't ask what his mom said. So clichéd—Confederate and Union mamas weeping while dads said they were proud, or rode off with their sons. Dads didn't sing "I Didn't Raise My Boy to Be a Soldier." Dads didn't raise boys. They raised draft counts.

Coldly, Hallie stared at Ted across the great divide.

"If Byron's leaving for Maine, how will you get back to school?" Hallie asked Vicky.

"More!" Erica pounded her cup on the high chair.

Vicky lifted the milk carton.

"No! Mommy do it! *My* mommy!"

"Two year olds." Hallie poured milk. In a second high chair, nine-month-old Andy Bennett slapped palms into his applesauce. Puree splatted on a Polaroid on the windowsill. Megan's long-awaited baby, Stephen. There was applesauce all over the image of his black hair. Just like his mother's, only hers would never have food on it, even in effigy.

"I'm not going back to school," Vicky said.

"But . . . finals?"

Vicky shrugged.

"You're already short credits, aren't you?"

More shrugs.

"Are you going to Maine with Byron?"

"I'm pregnant." The word, whispered with face averted from Erica's wide gaze and expanding vocabulary, nonetheless sounded like a howl. Vicky's face was so bleak that Hallie felt like an intruder and looked away.

There were shouts and groans from the playroom, where the men watched football.

"I can't go through with it! I'd rather die. I'm sorry to dump this on— Don't hate me, Hal, I didn't know who else—"

"Shh, don't be silly." But her hand missed the mark and more of Andy's applesauce dribbled. "What can I do?"

"Don't you know somebody who could—you know."

"I know obstetricians, not—and in *Boston*? They have problems selling contraceptives here!"

"Then Teddy? Could he ask around?"

She imagined him in a gangster's fedora, pulling coworkers aside. "I think we'd better take care of this ourselves."

"How?"

"What about not doing anything? Stay here until—"

"*Have it?*" Vicky looked naked, stripped of her bravado and self-declared independence. "I can't! I'd kill myself first—I would! I could never tell them! Dad would *die*. No. Even if I went away and lied—it'd be nearly a year. Where would they think I—how could I? Where would I—oh, God, *please!*"

Hallie wondered, with a degree of despair that surprised her, how there could ever be new women if there were always such old, old stories.

Vicky sagged forward, her face buried in her hands.

"Vicky cry," Erica said. Andy's bottom lip quivered.

Hallie reached over and patted her sister's hair.

"Mommy makes nice," Erica said with approval.

"I thought with the Pill . . ." Hallie whispered once her children were involved with their food again.

"So did I. I don't know how this happened, I swear. Go on, say it. Say I'm a—I deserve this after the way I—"

"You deserve what you wanted. To find things out. I'm a little jealous, but I'm on your side. That's why you're here." She took a deep breath. "I hope this isn't too middle-class, but why doesn't Byron marry you?" She sounded angry, and she didn't think she meant to. "Maybe it'd help his draft status," she added, to soften her words.

"It isn't his."

"Jesus, Vick!"

"Lay off! Byron's my friend. I think maybe he digs men, but even if he didn't, I can't have a baby. I can't!" She looked around the kitchen, as if solutions were up with the spices, or down with the dog dish. "I've asked everybody," she whispered. "The only ones I heard about are in Puerto Rico, except for one in New York."

"New York? Is he safe?"

"Somebody's friend used him. And lived." Her voice was flat.

"Then we'll find him." She'd do what was needed. Pray that he was clean, antiseptic, kind. Her heart raced. Mrs. Organization Man wasn't used to being a criminal.

"He costs a thousand dollars."

Hallie's mouth flapped, wanting to object, to demand fairness, to point out that legitimate doctors in real hospitals supervised nine-month pregnancies and safe deliveries for less. But you couldn't protest crimes while committing one.

"I have a hundred and seventy-five. Plus Byron said he'd give me fifty, but that's all he has."

Noble Byron the fugitive. Another criminal. Something was horribly wrong with the world.

Hallie busied herself with a damp sponge and the apple-sauced high chair. A thousand dollars. She had thirty in her wallet and an emergency twenty-five upstairs. *They* had a thousand dollars. Both their names on a savings account. But it was one thing to discuss a much-needed sofa, one thing to agree the fee for Ted's racquet club was worth it, another altogether to negotiate her sister's abortion. She realized that she didn't really have a cent, except by Ted's gracious permission.

In the end, Vicky would get her money. But Hallie wished negotiations weren't required. Wished she had her own funds so that what was a woman's problem and woman's work could also be a woman's decision. Period. She mentally filed this new knowledge.

"I'll pay you back," Vicky said. "I swear."

"Who's the father? Can't he help?"

"He said I tricked him and he cut out. We'd been together six months. I thought it was for real, forever."

Gone. That's what was for real. As real as sperm.

So much for women's right to be people, to be sexual. Hallie should have known Vicky's ideas were too good to work.

"I drank gin and puked. I ran up and down the stairs. I moved furniture, even the refrigerator. I took pills."

What was left? Back alleys. True-confession magazines and cautionary tales.

"Puke!" Erica grinned. "Ginnenpuke! All gone!"

Vicky held her midriff and leaned forward.

Infection. Death. Butchers. Hallie helped Erica out of her high chair and washed her hands and face. "Go to Daddy, love. Maybe he'll play the banjo and sing."

Hallie squeezed Vicky's hand. "Don't worry," she said. "Everything will be all right." The lie sliced her like a scalpel.

She was afraid she'd run out of gas, and it wasn't a neighborhood to be stranded in, so she turned off the ignition. If Vicky didn't walk out soon, Hallie was going in no matter what. What could he do?

Anything he wanted to. She and Vicky were outlaws.

She shivered through dusk and a light snow flurry. Please, she prayed. Don't let her die.

The brick building loomed, high and wine dark. Really. If Vicky didn't show up immediately, Hallie would call the police, even if it meant going to jail herself.

But Vicky did appear, huddled and bleary in her raccoon coat. Hallie rushed to help her and glimpsed a retreating man and woman.

"It hurt." That was the way she'd sounded when she was little, running to her big sister after somebody picked on her. "I had to wait for him to show up. That's not his real office." She sat gingerly. "He made me feel like trash." Hallie hugged her, then let go and started the motor again. "He said that if tramps like me kept our pants on and—but the whole time, he was—Hallie, he was feeling me up. It makes me sick. He said he was examining me, but it wasn't right and I felt—against me—he was hard. So disgusting. Humiliating." She put her head into her mittened hands, slumping in the seat. Her back heaved with her sobs.

Hallie pulled the car up into a bus zone. At the curb, snow dusted the sidewalk grass. "It's no more than a bad dream now," she said. "Let's get you in back, so you can sleep. It's over."

She was wrong, fooled by the necessity to concentrate on the long and difficult drive home, by Vicky's silence, and mostly by the need to believe her own reassurances.

But when Ted came out of the house to help them, he saw the dark stain on the backseat. "She's hemorrhaging," he said. "And she's burning up. Infected." It wasn't over at all.

Hallie burst into tears, because Ted offered to take Vicky to the hospital, to face questions and perhaps the police, and because she had that, had him, and Vicky had only desertion and fear and blood and infection. "I'll go," she said, kissing and holding him.

And even when the starched woman at admissions withheld treatment until Hallie provided the police with the name of the abortionist—surely a false name and address two hundred miles away in another state—and even, days later, when Vicky's infection was halted and she no longer bled, and she came back to Hallie's, and even weeks after that, when pink-skinned and energetic again, she packed and left, almost herself again, though not quite as confident, with not quite the joy and power or newness— even then, each of them knew that the pregnancy was over, but what had been done to her in that back alley wasn't, and never would be.

4

Even out in the parking lot, they heard the greasy sobs of "Love Is a Many Splendored Thing." "Reunions should be outlawed," Ted said.

"That song reminds me of my junior prom," Hallie said. "Dancing with my ass in the air to avoid contact with my date's erection."

"And here you are, pregnant once again because you stopped contorting that way."

"Will Kaplan. God, was he embarrassed. His eyes rolled up, so I could only see the whites, like he was convulsing."

"Girls are so smug."

They walked across the gravel. "If only Twiggy weren't in style. Or if I were as mini as the dresses." Or if I did anything, she thought, anything but breed.

"You're beautiful. Why are you so nervous?"

Husband comfort didn't count. She had spent her life battling her body's determination to enlarge. Her legs had never been thin enough for mid-thigh hems; her waist, which she'd been fond of, had disappeared; her formerly reasonable, likable breasts had ballooned at the moment of conception so that they tugged at the narrow-chested cut of the dress; and her hair, despite flat beer as setting lotion and enormous rollers, curled unfashionably. The one night in ten years it was imperative to look great, nature and couture conspired against her.

Through French windows she saw people speaking with exaggerated motions, overemphasized glee, trying to look as if they were having fun.

"Stop peering in like Orphan Annie," Ted said.

"I wish I—" She stopped herself.

"I hate when you stop mid-sentence that way."

She'd wished she were different, not the same as every other female classmate. She had meant to be unique. If she'd become a lawyer, maybe.

How come? she suddenly wondered. How come he got what he wanted? How come I didn't? How come it works that way? But what she said was, "Reunions feel like dental checkups."

"Why worry? You've got everything a girl could want—great kids, great house, and a great husband, if I say so myself. The American Dream fulfilled."

"1957–1967" stretched on a silver banner across the entry to the ballroom. As they walked under it, "True Love" began. The band seemed determined to remind them how soppy their music had been.

The Fifties' pleated skirts and crinolines were long gone. Some

women, like Hallie, wore Carnaby Street minis. A few were outrageous in vinyl dresses, plastic boots, fishnet stockings, Twiggy
lashes on their lower lids, and hair long enough to sit on; another
group looked like overaged flower children in poison greens and
pinks, beads and fringes, and a small sprinkling of diehard conserv-
atives resembled their own mothers in cocktail dresses that
brushed their calves. Adventurous men wore English nipped-
waist suits, the trousers belled. Some expressed themselves
through luxurious hair, but not one was hippie-long, and although
there were sideburns and a few daring mustaches, there were no
beards.

"Look there." She elbowed Ted. "Will. But he's not rolling his
eyes."

"He will if you tell him your image of him. Why do we fixate
that way? Like Arnie Stein, who picked his nose in third grade.
He's a gastroenterologist now, but to me, he'll always be the nose-
picker."

"He still does it in his car."

"How would you know?"

"All men do. They think they're invisible there." The awkward, funny-pathetic problems of adolescence were history, replaced by the awkward, funny-pathetic problems of adulthood.
One good reason to enjoy the moment, whenever. She smiled
and, for the first time, looked forward to the evening.

He hated reunions. His, hers, anybody's. Strutting your stuff for
people you never liked and hadn't sought out since graduation.
To make a point. To make up for.

High school was forever.

Enough of this togetherness crap. "Anybody for a drink?" He
interrupted a toothy woman enthusing about her five children.

"No thanks," Hallie said. "I'm queasy for a change."

Megan shook her head.

Ted excused himself and tried to figure out what was going
wrong with Megan Farr's looks. There was something pinched
about her now, something not quite believable, like an old woman
wearing a young mask.

He passed Daniel, sitting in full military regalia, like a taunt.

He held a glass of dark liquid that matched his eyes. Maybe he was what was wrong with Megan. Anywhere except here at a reunion of the silent generation, Daniel's uniform would have provoked demonstrations. Hallie was probably controlling the urge to picket Daniel right now.

She was weird lately. Irritable, easily annoyed. This pregnancy was affecting her differently than the other two.

He ordered a martini on the rocks and wondered if he would ever tell this child how it came into being. How out of the noisy blur of a weekend, there was sudden silence. Erica was at a birthday party two doors down, Andrew was napping, Hallie and he were reading the Sunday papers. It began to snow, an unexpected, unseasonable spring flurry, cloaking the already quiet hour in absolute, otherworldly stillness, except for the crackle of the fire, the muted tocks of the mantelpiece clock, their own breath, and the sense of the baby heavily asleep upstairs.

The white whirling against early budding trees outside pressed on the silence inside and insulated them from anything they knew and any place they'd been. It was the very beginning again, full of mystery, surprise, and need, only better, because they were no longer timid and unskilled, because now they knew so much more about love, pleasure, and each other.

Luxurious midday love in front of the fire, their flesh and the flames the only color in the dancing white universe. Later, still naked, with smudges of newsprint on Hallie's back, they opened a bottle of wine they'd been saving for "someday." "Someday" had arrived.

One of the best somedays of his life. They had toasted each other, intoxicated before a single sip by what they had, and what they were and would be.

That day's baby was a gift, wanted, if not planned, even if Hallie was distressed because she'd been wearing some metal gizmo to prevent it.

The band charged into "Rock Around the Clock," and giggling couples filled the floor. Holding his martini, he glumly maneuvered through alumni clusters.

". . . an encounter group, he calls it. Strangers tell each other their garbage, but he swears it's made all the—"

"—getting so that when the temperature's high, I'm scared. Philly could go up, poof! The whole city, not just their neighborhoods."

The darker-skinned members of the Class of '57 had congregated on the other side of the room. Ted wondered if they, too, were discussing the summer riots.

". . . doing drug counseling. With the LSD business and all this tuning out."

"Tuning *in*, Hank. He says tune *in*, turn *on*, and drop *out*." The voice of a smug student of contemporary sloganeering.

Ted scouted for a hiding place.

"Theodore Bennett! My goodness!"

The hairs on his arm rose. He felt as if he were coming down with the flu. Her.

Long ago, he'd obsessively speculated on how it would be if he ever saw her again. Now he wasn't sure how it was except for remembered humiliation and, for one shocked moment, such an acute memory of desire it felt like actual longing.

She held a plate of food. "Christina Young," he said, his brain playing on too slow a speed. "What a surprise to see you here."

A decade ago, he'd planned for such an occasion, determined to spout witty epigrams. And she would be tongue-tied and matronly. Dusty, pathetic, gaping at his elegantly tailored back as he raced off to a glittering party.

But look, he hadn't become Noel Coward, and Chris wasn't dusty. In fact, the red-gold hair, the glittering green eyes, and the lanky body had not visibly suffered for wear.

"This is my reunion," she said.

"I didn't know." The words brought a flush, a reflex memory of the burning sickness that followed those words years ago.

He could still hear the nasal voice of the girl on phone duty at the dorm. "Chris isn't here," she'd said.

He'd asked when she'd return.

"You don't understand. Chris is gone. Married."

"What are you talking about?" They'd spoken last week, discussed plans for Easter vacation. "Who are you talking about?"

"Christina Young is who and married is what. As in wedding? Husband and wife? With this ring?"

"I—I didn't know." It was impossible. The very first thing he'd done this new year was make love to Chris in her own bedroom. They'd talked every week. Several times each week. How could she be married? "There's some mistake," he said. "Would you check her room? This is a long-distance call."

"We aren't allowed to tie up the phone." She'd hung up.

Chris had never called or explained. He'd heard she'd had a baby seven months after her elopement. That didn't reduce his pain.

Now she moved closer, with the same cockiness, the same amused assumption that she was irresistible as she'd had ten years ago. She touched his lapel. He was glad his suit was the very best wool, ashamed that he cared.

"Please." She spoke so softly he had to lean close to hear over the music and the din. "Say you don't hate me."

"I could use some air," Hallie said. "Keep me company?" The perfumes of too many bodies had intensified her queasiness.

Megan's boyish body was in a mini-dress the color of poppies, a fringed white shawl with a floral pattern over her shoulders. Her black hair hung straight. Next to her, Hallie felt as massive as the Statue of Liberty. "I'm jealous," she said. "You look so absolutely right. I never have and I never will."

Hallie scanned the crowd like a lighthouse beacon, comparing herself, always unfavorably, with the sexy, flat-bellied unpregnant. "Look! There's Mark Robinson. He's still cute, Meggie. Ask him to dance for old time's sake."

Megan laughed mirthlessly. "You think we're having trouble in Asia? You want to start World War Three here? I told you how jealous Daniel is."

"Is everything all right?"

Megan looked pensive. "Michael," she said. Her brother was being sent to Vietnam. "My being scared for Michael annoys Daniel, like that means I don't care about him as much, or enough." She shivered as her shawl slipped off her shoulders, revealing a splash of fading black and blue marks.

"What happened?"

Megan pulled the shawl back on. "Nothing. Sometimes Daniel forgets how strong he is."

"Men," Hallie said. They passed Sissy Foley, whose smile was like a rictus. Hallie nodded a cool greeting, but inwardly felt a rerun of junior-high humiliation.

In ninth grade, Sissy had convinced the entire cast of *The Man Who Came to Dinner*—except Hallie—to buy gold tragedy-comedy pins. "Eighteen carat," Sissy said. "Why settle for a cheap imitation?" Hallie lacked the courage to cast the only veto.

Her father did it for her, not surprisingly outraged by what he labeled "materialistic wastefulness." She begged, she pleaded. She could not bear being the Only One, the Outsider. Her father refused to either loan or advance her the money. She couldn't babysit fast or often enough, so she tried to cancel her order. Instead, Sissy devised a public and mortifying plan. The entire cast would post her bail, and she would repay them in installments. It took her nearly a year.

She'd disliked the pin and Sissy all along and had gotten furious with her parents in the interim, but by the end of the business most of all, she loathed her own self.

She hoped she was a stronger person now, but Sissy still made her anxious. Nobody ever grew all the way up.

Outside, silhouetted under black cutouts of trees, faces blurred into the night, Megan suddenly spoke. "Is it the way you thought? Life, marriage, anything?"

"I'm not sure I did any thinking at all. Then or now." She put her palm on her belly. She certainly hadn't thought about or wanted a third child. Ted, however, was delighted. They were still and forever the blue-ribbon all-American family, and if she felt that something else waited for breath inside her, something obliterated by the baby, she was a malcontent.

"Hallie?" Megan's voice sounded chilled, uninsulated against the night. "Does it ever seem too hard?"

Ever? *Did it ever seem easy?* should be the question. "Sure."

"We were unrealistic, weren't we, though." Megan's relief was audible. "Everybody said you had to work at it, only I didn't think that meant *work*-work. I thought it'd be like in 'Can This Marriage Be Saved?', you know?"

Hallie nodded. She was as compulsive about the feature as Andy was about his security blanket and for the same reason. Both guaranteed comfort. The marriage could always be saved.

Given a stitch here and a tinker there, happily ever after was pretty much guaranteed.

"The problems there always seem easy, straightforward. . . ." The white portion of her shawl and her hands, gesturing, glimmered in the dark.

Hallie waited.

"I try, but I don't understand his moods. It's probably what we said. We had unrealistic expectations."

Hallie felt off balance, as if she were standing on the slippery edge of a stream and had to be careful.

Megan was a few paces away, a blur of white shawl spots and thin legs. Her wistful voice floated on the dark. "Sometimes I miss the before-marriage sex, frustrating and weird as it was. Do you ever?"

"Sometimes." There was much to be said for the force and power of pure yearning. That was one aspect of sex her sister's generation would miss, after all.

"The way they touched us then," Megan said. "As if we were real. Precious. But once they're husbands, they touch like the witch squeezed Hansel—to see if we're edible yet." She laughed at her own bitter joke.

Hallie felt cornered. She wanted to believe, just as Megan did, that they spoke the same language with the same referent points. Friends understood each other, except it was now obvious that their words didn't describe the same things. Still, admitting that their men and marriages were not alike felt like a terrible betrayal, further isolating Megan. She searched for words both kind and true, and ended up saying nothing. Then she realized she was no braver than when she'd bought Sissy Foley's gold pin. "Actually, Meggie," she began, "I'm not sure I feel the same way about—"

"Megan? What are you doing out here?" And Daniel, face rigid as his posture, suddenly loomed over his wife like a vice-principal dealing with a delinquent.

"Oh, Daniel." Megan sounded almost amused by his foolishness. He took her elbow and led her back into the reunion. Hallie followed.

*   *   *

Chloe Wister was center-stage, her favorite place. She was the only unmarried female who'd come out of hiding and attended. "Yes," she'd say with a laugh. "I'm an old maid! I played too hard to get, just like Mama warned." Another laugh. "Always a bridesmaid, never a bride! Maybe I need Listerine?"

But she could say such things, because everybody knew she'd always been determined to stay single. Eccentric Chloe. Still, they were surprised to discover she'd been serious.

". . . her mother had a breakdown after Walt died," Chloe was saying. "Lily's taking care of her."

"Walt *died?*" Hallie remembered Lily's brother, all muscles and energy on the junior-varsity basketball team. "Of what?"

"The war."

"The school should put up a plaque," somebody said.

"A big one the way things are going," Hallie added.

"Hallie Saxe has become a peacenik!" Declared by a bespectacled woman who'd long ago danced a clumsy but sincere Dying Swan in assembly.

"Remember Joel? He played the flute and worked at the veterinarian's. He enlisted, can you imagine?"

A chorus added names. "Esther Toll's brother was drafted." "Remember my little cousin? Joanie's boyfriend? Carol Davis's brother's in Amsterdam, to avoid it."

"Her other brother's on drugs."

"All those kids are, don't you think?"

"Oh, God, and hippies?" The Dying Swan again, wrinkling her nose. "Did you hear what their governor called them?"

"Hippies aren't a state. They don't have a governor," Hallie said.

"The *actor*, the governor of California. He said they dressed like Tarzan, had hair like Jane, and smelled like Cheetah. Isn't that a scream?"

The actor actually was Vicky's governor now. She'd never gone back to college, and for the past two years, she'd crisscrossed the U.S. Shortly after her wanderings began, a package had arrived with a card saying, "I can't repay you yet, but nobody believes in money anymore, just in helping each other the way you did. This is the way I do. Enjoy!" No signature. Marijuana, their link with the noisy sequel to their silent generation. Hallie loved the giddy, sexy high, worried about getting fat with the munchies, shared it with friends behind drawn shades, and joked that it was good to still have a dirty secret.

The dope was the first of Vicky's counter-culture CARE packages. A Grateful Dead album, postmarked Santa Cruz. A peace symbol necklace and a Jefferson Airplane album from Taos. A "God's Eye" of crossed sticks and colored thread from Mendocino. And recently, from San Francisco, a Day-Glo poster with a swirl of melting letters reading, "Wherever you go, there you are."

She searched for Vicky's face when the news showed Be-Ins, Peace Marches, or the Summer of Love, all of which seemed as exotic as *National Geographic* reports.

My generation got hand-me-downs, Hallie thought. And then, as soon as we were outfitted, they told the next group to choose whatever they wanted, or to invent it. We were cheated.

Hallie found the barefoot life romantic. Ted considered the flower children's antitechnology stance barbaric and dangerous except, of course, for the sex part, the "If it feels good, do it" ethic. He didn't say much about that, but he seemed as envious as she felt, as a lot of people their age seemed lately.

Out there, sex bubbled like stew on a back burner. The unconnectedness of it appealed. It was a political necessity, a moral imperative to make love, not war.

Of course she loved Ted and was happy with him. Of course! But what was her measure? How could she be sure?

"Hallie Saxe? It's Craig. Craig Forman."

The name was dimly familiar, the face, a tall, good-looking stranger's.

"Honors English. Stage crew?"

"Craig? Oh, my goodness—*Craig*!" Craig Forman had been emaciated, practically mute, and definitely short. All I.Q. and acne. This man, this non-Craig, spoke in a melodious voice. His hair was Edwardian, as was his suit. The bumps were gone.

"Dance?" he asked as "Stranger in Paradise" began.

Within a few bars, before anybody was a stranger no more, she'd recited her married name, her husband's name, her children's names, and her town's name. Then she was out of material and into panic.

Gracefully leading her around the dance floor, Craig explained that he had spent a few years in Europe after college, finding out, with a minimum of agony, that he most likely would never compose the Great American Symphony. He'd been married, briefly, to a French actress. No children. Now he wrote background music for TV shows and love songs for himself. "Sad love songs," he said, "because there isn't one of us who isn't hurting inside from somebody."

She felt lithe and delicate in his arms.

He smiled down at her and spoke softly. "I want—need—to tell you that I came to this reunion because of you."

"Me?"

"You're my sad love song. I spent high school staring at you, as I'm sure you knew. Fantasizing about you, writing sickening poems about your beauty, your incredible eyes—alpine lakes, windows to the cosmos, that sort of thing unfortunately—your cleverness, your perfection. But when I'd try to speak to you, my tongue wedged against the top of my mouth. It makes me sick to remember."

She was in danger of swooning like some antebellum flower, overwhelmed by the saccharine music, Hollywood, French actresses, European sojourns, his aftershave, and mostly, his words. "I'm . . ." Flattered? Honored? No. She'd embarrass them both because she had—absolutely must have—misinterpreted him. "I'm not sure I understand what you're saying." She sounded prim, Miss Grundy, instead of recherché.

"I'll make myself absolutely clear. I needed to know if the attraction I felt then still held. It has. It's still there for me, Hallie. Don't laugh."

"It wouldn't occur to me to laugh." She'd forgotten how being looked at that way could melt the spine.

"I get to Boston now and then," he said.

"Well, call next time! Come for dinner!" She detested herself. That wasn't it, not it at all.

The music faded. They stayed on the dance floor. "Are you happy?" Craig asked.

"Of course!"

"The question's too important for 'Of course.' "

Her hands were freezing. She clasped them behind her in an inverted, secret position of prayer. She looked around and saw Ted talking to a thin redhead, but watching Hallie, instead. He motioned for her to join him. "I'm happy," she told Craig. "If you mean all the time, constantly, as in ever after, then no. But that isn't the same as being unhappy."

"And you're still a good girl. A lot has changed since the Fifties—but not for you."

"I still think being married is more than a statistic for the census taker, if that's what you mean."

He pulled out his card and handed it to her. "Call me if your definitions change. Ever. This offer has no expiration date." He kissed her, a moment too lingering for pure friendship's sake, with his hand tilting her chin toward him. A second too much eye contact before he broke away. "It was worth the trip, Hallie Saxe," he said.

"Bennett," she told his retreating back. "Bennett," she repeated, this time for herself.

She left the dance floor and went to Ted. He lifted an eyebrow, silently questioning.

She pretended not to understand. She was unwilling to toss Craig into the communal pot of her marriage.

The redhead flicked a disinterested glance at her. Christina. Of course. Ted had once dated her.

"I assume you two knew each other in school," Ted said.

"Not really." Christina's tone made it clear she'd lost no sleep over not knowing Hallie.

"I'm Grady Houston, Chris's husband." A stocky, rumpled man walked toward them. He held a plate of food, as did Christina, and Hallie was sure he'd been waiting for her for a long while.

Megan's cousin Grady. He wasn't what Hallie had imagined, but he looked kind, which is more than she could say for his wife. "You people want to join us?" he asked.

Christina kept her gaze on Ted.

"Don't let us keep you," Hallie said.

Christina leaned into Ted. She put her hand on his chest, covering his tie, as if claiming possession of his heart. "It was so good to see you again," she murmured. "I've thought of you so often. Call me when you're in Philadelphia." And without another word, she walked off.

Grady and Hallie, extras in the drama, glanced at each other. By the time Grady excused himself, his eyes were opaque.

"What was that about?" Ted asked.

"That's what I'd like to know."

"Who was he?"

"*He?*"

"The guy kissing you on the dance floor."

She took a deep breath. "A former classmate. I told him I was married. Like you could have told Christina."

"She knows."

"Not so you'd notice!"

"Come on, Hal. What did I do?"

"Nothing. But you could have. You could have laughed at her. You could have said, 'How incredibly rude you're being to my wife and your husband.' "

Ted looked shocked. Then a slow grin began. "You're jealous."

Hallie glared.

"I don't intend to accept her invitation," he added.

Say you don't want to. Say you're not even tempted.

"While we're at it, I have problems with long, lingering kisses from other men on the dance floor."

Say you weren't tempted. Say you didn't keep Craig's card. Say you aren't a self-righteous prig.

"Peace?" Ted made the two-fingered sign.

"Peace." They joined hands and moved toward the buffet. But en route, she caught him studying her, as if he had suddenly realized, as had she, how dangerous they both could be, how capable of wounding each other, as long as they both shall love.

Laundry and Lilacs

1968–1970

> Marriage is the only adventure open to the cowardly.
> *Voltaire*

---— 1 ---—

THE HOUSE was at its late-afternoon worst, littered with coloring books, crayons, miniature trucks, and more socks than there were small feet to have shed them. Half-eaten apples and floppy banana skins lay on the coffee table. Erica and Andy jumped on the dismantled sofa's pillows. The baby loudly sucked a pacifier, and Griselda sniffed, inspected, and shed over the wreckage.

Hallie sat at the dining-room table trying to ignore everything but two hundred Mothers for Peace flyers she'd promised to address.

Andy turned on the TV. "Turn it off," Hallie said. They were running newsclips of the Chicago convention. Too dangerous for little eyes to see what was impossible for her, an adult, to comprehend: how, at the very symbol of the democratic process, American policemen could club American kids, brazenly, in front of television cameras.

The TV was silent again, but not the children. "Don't push me!" Erica shouted.

Maybe mothers should strike for mental peace instead. Or was that another futile campaign? It took courage or stupidity not to lose hope. How many petitions had she signed, how many congressmen had she written, and for how long had she packed diapers, pushed carriages, pulled toddlers, and taken to the streets without any change, except for the worse?

"My turn!"

Martin Luther King. Bobby Kennedy. Vietnam. Even Andy Warhol, not worth the effort, shot by a woman who thought men were scum. The world had tilted off its axis and everybody was angry about something.

"Tell him to stop hogging."

"Share, Andy."

"I'm hungry."

Instead of deciding whether civilization was grinding to a close, she'd decide what the kids would eat for dinner. Once, she'd worried about missing the great issues of her times. Now she knew she would.

"It's mine!"

"I'm hungry!"

When Sarah was born, in February, the nurse was delighted. "More boys are born in wartime. We have eight babies in the nursery and Sarah's the only girl," she said.

Nature didn't quibble about semantics. She reseeded the earth with males, future fodder, whether or not the war was officially declared as such. The harsh practicality made Hallie cry. They called it postpartum blues.

Thud. Maniacal laughter.

"Mommmmmmmmy!"

She marked her place with a finger. "Stop it, you two."

"Didn't *do* anything!"

"Did so! He did so, Mommy! You saw, didn't you? Mommy saw and you're gonna get it."

"Did not, did not!"

Hallie addressed the next flyer.

Sarah came unplugged and screeched. Hallie gave up.

"Okay, you guys. Dinner." Her next-door neighbor Jeanette,

a nonstop proselytizer for human perfection, had given her Adelle Davis's *Let's Cook It Right* and made her promise to stop poisoning her babies with additives, synthetics, or prepackaged fodder. But who'd know? There'd be no witnesses except three very small children, one of whom couldn't speak. Ted was working late. Again. He'd become frenzied, a prizefighter sparring with his future. Director of Marketing now for G.T.U., the mega-company that had absorbed Summit. Further and further from his real work, she thought, more distracted and harried, stopping by home for fresh shirts, food, and sex.

"How 'bout hot dogs?" The kids cheered. She boiled water and slit plastic, averting her eyes from the list of ingredients. For herself, she put a tea bag in a mug her sister had sent from California and read again the calligraphy on its side:

> *I do my thing, and you do your thing.*
> *I am not in this world to live up to your expectations*
> *And you are not in this world to live up to mine.*
> *You are you and I am I, and if by chance we find each*
> *   other, it's beautiful.*
> *If not, it can't be helped.*

"Right on," she muttered, doing her thing, which happened to be helping Erica and Andy onto their booster seats, mixing Sarah's rice cereal, taking the chill off a half-full jar of pureed apricots, pouring milk for the older two, and avoiding Griselda, who was everywhere food might fall. And wondering. If she had seen a crystal ball showing scenes from real life, such as this very evening, would she as eagerly have tumbled into Ted Bennett's arms eight years ago?

Why did descriptions of love sound accidental? Falling. Head over heels. Tumbling.

Tumbling Hallie. Tumbleweed. Floating debris. Nothing, really, but enough nothing could smother you.

Shopping for food, preparing food, cleaning up after food, being food for the baby. Her entire existence was tied into the food chain, all the way through dirty diapers and toilet training.

Repairmen.

Laundry.

Terrible twos. Terrible threes. Pretty rotten fours.

Car seats. Snowsuits. Pediatrician. Vet. Chicken pox. Teething. Earaches.

No time to push the tumbling weeds aside and see civilization—friends, books, the world. Oh, and husbands.

"Anchored to life by laundry and lilacs, daily bread and fried eggs." God bless Sylvia Plath for soothing sentiments, but look how she lost her anchor, stuck her head in the oven and killed herself. Maybe not the best source of domestic inspiration.

"Mommy! You cut my hot dog! You're not supposed to cut my hot dog like that!"

Hallie took a deep breath. "Listen, Erica. We're in the Sixties. I'll do my thing and you'll do yours. I am not in this world to live up to your expectations."

"What?" Erica's eyes were wide. Her mouth hung open.

"You are you and I am I."

"You cut my hot dog like a baby's!" Erica pushed her plate away and put her head in her hands, the portrait of despair.

"Whoops." At three, "whoops" was Andy's favorite word. He smashed and crushed and smeared and split, having a rip-roaring good time, and then he said "Whoops" with such heartfelt regret, it was impossible to be truly angry. She sponged up his milk. "Please, honey. Watch what you're doing."

Oh yes, oh yes. Meaningless mothertalk. Doing her thing.

Sarah looked like a baby bird, mouth wide open. Hallie filled the beak with liquefied apricots.

Truth was, if she had seen a vision of today in that crystal ball, she wouldn't have undone her life or avoided it. She would simply be less surprised.

They were all bathed, at their absolute sweetest, even if Sarah was whimpering. Hallie had felt the beginning of a tooth when she was nursing. Too soon. Time that moved in slow motion in late afternoon now pushed ahead at breakneck speed.

"Read, Mommy." Erica handed Hallie a library book. She had Teddy's silky fair looks and endless energy.

"The Velveteen Rabbit," Hallie said. The baby sobbed. "Why

don't we sit on my bed so you can see the pictures and I can hold Sarah," she suggested.

They cuddled together, pillows stacked behind them, freshly washed and shining—except for Hallie in a misshapen Mexican embroidered shirt over jeans with stains at child-hand's height. Even Sarah settled into anxious but silent pacifier sucking, and Griselda lay beside the bed protecting them like Nana in *Peter Pan*.

" 'There was once a velveteen rabbit, and in the beginning he was really splendid.' " Erica and Andy sighed in contentment. She read the story of the stuffed Rabbit and the Boy who loved him. "And the Skin Horse said, 'When a child loves you for a long, long time, not just to play with, but *really* loves you, then you become Real.' "

That's what this is about, Hallie thought. I'm becoming Real. She kissed each of her perfect children and Sarah forgot her distress and smiled so hard the pacifier needed to be replaced.

There is nothing else I require. I am blessed.

In their safe harbor of light, they read how, when the Boy recovered from his illness, his toys, including the Velveteen Rabbit, had to be burned. But before the gardener got to the job, the nursery magic Fairy made him a real rabbit who could run and jump and whirl.

"I love that story!" Erica said. "Read it again. It's the best story in the whole entire world!"

"I hate it!" Andy grabbed the book and hurled it. Griselda yiped and lumbered to her feet.

"Andy! You've hurt—"

"Read it again, Mommy!" Erica scrambled to retrieve it.

Andy hurled himself across Hallie, tackled his sister and socked her, creating seismic waves that shocked the baby, who set off her personal Klaxon. Griselda barked.

"Stop it, all of you!" Hallie scrambled to her knees, balancing the baby.

"I hate that story!" Andy's nose was red. "It's *mean*." He started to cry.

"Read it again, Mommy." Undaunted, Erica clutched the book to her chest. "You're a crybaby, Andy, like Sarah. Crybaby, crybaby!"

"I don't believe this. I honestly, truly don't—"

"He could have *died*! He could have burned up!"

"But he didn't," Hallie said.

"The gardener was too busy—but if he *wasn't* too busy, the rabbit would have burned up before that fairy got there! *I hate that story!*" Tears streamed down his face, he gasped between phrases, his nose ran, and his hands were tight fists.

"Crybaby, crybaby!"

"Don't, Erica." She put Sarah, who screamed in protest, on the bedspread and held Andy close. What was she to tell him? That the lack of logic, justice, or guarantees in the universe troubled her profoundly, too?

"He could have *died*," Andy whimpered. "What if the gardener didn't have to dig potatoes and gather green peas? What if the fairy hadn't come that night?"

"But, darling, they did."

Sarah screamed sharply in ear-piercing yelps. Hallie freed one arm from Andy and tried to scoop up her baby.

"*But what if!*" He had just realized that happenstance and good fortune weren't enough. It took a lot longer to realize that enough or not, they were all you got.

"You're never ever going to read my favorite book in the whole world to me again, are you? You spoiled everything, stinky Andy!" Erica smacked him and then she, too, sobbed.

The dog pushed her nose at Erica, at Andy, at Sarah, at the bed, and finally at Hallie, urging her to do something. Anything. But Hallie had no idea what.

"Hi," Ted said two hours later.

She tilted her head up above the laundry basket to receive his perfunctory kiss. The children were finally asleep. Hallie had promised Erica private *Velveteen Rabbit* readings. She'd sat with Andy until he drifted off. She'd rocked Sarah into fitful dreams. Then she'd gone to the basement to retrieve the clean laundry. She had hoped to shower before Teddy came home, but trucks and crayons still littered the rug, and unaddressed flyers, the table.

He followed her into the kitchen. She nearly tripped on a half-chewed dog toy. "Don't go to any trouble," he said. If only once he meant it.

"You'd think McPherson would trust my group by now," he said.

His job had become air and weeds, too, and it was burying him. He hadn't noticed, however.

"I'm *thirty*." Ted's new refrain. She had given him a surprise party. Thirty friends. Dinner. She did all the cooking during the children's naps, hiding food, orchestrating a wonderful party, a perfect night.

It hadn't made Ted one iota happier about his age. Thirty was his mental turnstile into management, but several months after the fact, he was still in a twenty-nine-year-old's job.

"It's all politics. I'll never get a break," Ted said.

She turned the chicken breast to broil the other side. Tension or tumbleweed knotted at the top of her spine.

". . . unless McPherson . . ."

She stifled a yawn. She had felt more true concern for the endangered Velveteen Rabbit. She filled his plate with chicken, rice, and green beans, poured herself coffee, checked the "You do your thing" mug, searching for the small print that exempted wives and mothers, and sat down. She'd already eaten leftover, wrongly cut hot dog and the extra portion of chocolate pudding, vowing to touch nothing else all night. But she picked her way through a roll, and then a second one.

The war would never end, the children would never all be happy at the same time, the laundry would never be folded, and she would never lose her pregnancy weight. She was flabby and fat and greasy-haired and lonely.

Sooner or later, Ted would finish using her as a decompression chamber and it would be her turn, time to move beyond "It'll be all right," "Ummm," and "Tsk, tsk." Sooner or later. Mostly, later. Often, too late.

Usually, by the time he asked about her day, she was beyond speech, so exhausted that her love of the man had to be carefully sifted through a mesh of fatigue.

Rabbits and marriages could be saved or lost by happenstance and the Good Fairy didn't always arrive in time.

Teddy flicked through the day's mail while he ate and complained. She lit a cigarette to keep from gnawing a third dinner roll. Shouldn't eat, but shouldn't smoke, either. Must stop, but not tonight. Shame settled on her like ash.

She was fading fast. The kids' dishes were still in the sink along with cups and plates from the afternoon. She saw herself, a sleepy, fat slattern with a filthy house and clothing stained with baby burps and sticky hugs.

"Hey!" He turned his magazine around. "She reminds me of you. You'd look great in an outfit like that."

Hallie blinked and focused on an advertisement for brandy. A lean, long-boned woman with cornsilk hair reclined in front of a fireplace. She wore black satin lounging pajamas and a diamond necklace. In the background, an elegantly tailored man, who looked a lot like Ted, cradled his snifter and smiled adoringly.

No animal cookies were ground into the brandy drinker's carpet. No dog hairs like tweed on her lounging pajamas.

"For those nights," the ad read, "when you celebrate yourself."

"What do you think?" Teddy said. "For your birthday? The pajamas, not the necklace, alas."

"Haven't you noticed—" She waved her hands at the chaotic family room, the dog's water slopped on the kitchen tile, the sofa pillows still on the living-room floor, the unfolded laundry, the flyers, the war inside the TV, silent though it now was, her stained, bedraggled self. "That lady," she said. "She really—she reminds you of me?"

He nodded. "Except your hair is curly. And your body's curvier. Sexier."

"You're . . . you're not making fun of me, are you?"

"Why would I?" He reached across the table for her hand. "It's good to be home. Good to see you, be with you."

She looked at her husband, who probably didn't really resemble the man in the ad either, and then at the life and confusion around them. She looked at their life. "It's good to have you home, too," she said. "Everything's good. As good as it gets."

─────────── 2 ───────────

"You look no worse for taking the plunge," Ted said.

James Harris settled into the booth. "A married man. Where did I go wrong? And you with three kids, for Christ's sake!"

The bar was noisy with Friday-night mating calls. Ted recognized several G.T.U. men delaying family reentry. How disgustingly domesticated he was, going home after work like a mechanical toy, and even when he didn't, he didn't detour into pickup bars. Hallie and the kids were visiting her father, who was recovering from a prostate operation. Otherwise, Ted would have brought James home.

"What can I do for you?" Orange hair, bosom, fishnet stockings, and a voice that said any request was permissible.

"I'm fine." Ted pointed to his vodka tonic.

"I'm pretty fine myself," James said, "but I could use a Bloody Mary, nonetheless."

She flashed a truly wicked smile and left.

"Okay," James said. "You show me yours, and I'll show you mine." He studied the snapshot Ted handed him.

"Sarah's . . ." Ted counted it out. "Six months. She was my birthday present. My *thirtieth* birthday present." Both men groaned. "Andy's three and a half and Erica's almost five."

"Cute," James said. "And Hallie still looks great."

"The complete Bennett dynasty. No more to follow. Your turn to go forth and multiply."

"Don't hold your breath." He gave Ted a folded magazine page. "Veronica," he said. "The little missus." Even in the dim light of the table's electric candle, she was a certifiable knockout, a sultry brunette, hair streaming down bare shoulders, pale flesh discreetly covered by lace-trimmed sheets. She held a flacon of perfume to her cleavage. Ted shook his head in wonder.

They established where and how both of them now lived. They described trips and vacations—or, more accurately, Ted, who hadn't had a real vacation since the summer after tenth grade, listened as James jetted from Monaco, through Manhattan, and onto a place in California where he and Veronica bared souls and bodies in naked encounter groups.

They sighed over the assassinations, the hijackings, the Soviet tanks crushing Prague, America's stale war, about which Ted had become much more ambivalent than James, who was still a hawk. They paid homage to Billie Jean King's Wimbledon victory and wished they could get on the courts more themselves. They ordered another round and compared notes on classmates and then they settled into shop talk. James was a consultant, based in New York. "My own firm," he said. "My own migraines. My own ulcer." But he laughed as he said it. "And you're still a company man."

"But not always happy about it. I'm excited about videotapes, new applications, but G.T.U.'s so damned enormous it moves like a . . . like a . . ." Slowly Ted realized that James's interest was focused elsewhere, and as if on cue, elsewhere materialized.

She held a frosted glass and looked barely out of her teens. A top-heavy brunette, with thickly lashed vacant eyes, wearing one of those psychedelic prints that looked like stained glass on acid. "I have a bet with my friend." She gestured vaguely behind her. "You're from Digital, right?"

"Should I lie so that you win the bet?" James asked.

"You look just like this guy in Operations. Honestly! I wasn't— this isn't some kind of . . . you know."

"My name's James. And this is Ted."

"Pleased. I'm Sabrina, like that Audrey Hepburn movie?"

"Lovely," James said.

"My friend Lara—"

"Like that Dr. Zhivago movie," Ted said.

Sabrina beamed. They were in cultural synch. "Like me and Lara and a couple of other people, we have the back room, it's private, for a T.G.I.F. party tonight? Open bar. So, like you're invited, even if you aren't Mike McConnell from Operations." She giggled and backed up a step. "James and Ted. See? I remember. So consider yourself—yourselfs—invited, and come on back."

"She forgot to ask our signs," Ted said.

"Do we have dinner reservations to cancel?"

"You're going to her party?"

"So her I.Q.'s smaller than her boobs. We don't have to talk, and it's only for one night."

"But . . ."

"Oh, no—it isn't aesthetics—it's morals! Why? Who gets hurt? Veronica's doing a Christmas layout in Anchorage and Hallie's with her folks. On what cosmic scale does it matter if we eat steak and talk electronics or drink vodka and have a friendly screw? Where have you been? Heard of the sexual revolution?"

Ted didn't know what to say.

"A quote: 'Life can little else supply but a few good fucks and then we die.' John Wilks, 1763." James grinned.

"You made that up."

James shook his head. "It was always thus, man."

Ted turned his glass and looked into it. "In fourth grade, there was this kid called Stinky. The kind your mother made you be nice to, but every time you wanted to have fun, Stinky whined. 'It's stupid,' he'd say. 'It's dangerous.' 'We promised we wouldn't.' Stinky was a cowardly, unimaginative asshole. I hated him. And now I feel like him."

"So tell me I promised I wouldn't do it."

"Don't forget stupid and dangerous."

"You've been married eight years? Straight through and beyond the itch and you haven't?"

Ted shook his head.

"Never? Girls were always after you. And that was in the dark ages. Nowadays—how can you resist?"

"I flay myself. Plus, there's Hallie's threat that she'd come after me with pinking shears."

"You're a romantic," James said. "You still believe that one woman is different from the next."

"I'm *married*," Ted said softly. "I'm *happy*."

"One has nothing to do with the other. I would never get involved with something that could affect my marriage."

Ted looked at all the men at the bar, wedding bands flashing as they flirted. "No hard feelings if I pack it in?"

"Ciao."

He didn't say fool, jerk, coward, but Ted heard it all the same.

They finished their drinks and James walked Ted to the exit. "Hey!" James shouted after Ted was on the crowded late-day sidewalk. "When did they stop calling you Stinky?"

———————— **3** ————————

Sarah's screams shredded the dark.

"WHAAAAEEEEeeee . . ." A pause for a furious, fragmented intake of breath felt all the way down the hall as Hallie's muscles woke from sleep and immediately knotted.

The night before, they'd gone to see *Funny Girl* with Jeanette and Bill, and stayed out too late because Hallie's mother was visiting and babysitting, so there was no rush.

"WHAULLLLLLLL!"

Teddy lay inert, turned away, but his hand tapped her, like you'd flick a fly.

Sarah screamed. Outrage. Despair. Starving to death in the bosom of her family, her wail insisted.

The bosom of her family pulled on a robe against the early-autumn chill.

Sarah yowled, alerting the neighbors, the next county, the children's rights people.

Infants should sleep near their mothers. Cut the commute. But Ted couldn't handle the noise. Wouldn't be able to concentrate at work.

The hall nightlight outlined Hallie's bare ankles as she shuffled along. Seven months postpartum and she still walked the morning mile like somebody with a fresh episiotomy. Her stomach sagged, her cow breasts flopped. She was used up and old at twenty-eight.

She passed Griselda, sleeping on the landing with her head over the top tread of the stairs. "Thank me for spaying you," Hallie told her. "You get to sleep in."

Time to wean Sarah. Get a little freedom. Make *him* wake up and feed her.

Oh, but. Sarah was the last. Goes so fast. Look, now, Erica with a Bozo the Clown lunch box, starting kindergarten this very day. The yellow bus would vacuum her into the system from which there was no escape.

She'd wean Sarah in a while, but for now it was worth the morning sirens to see her gummy, gaspy smile. Momma, food, God, existed. Felt good to make somebody that happy.

The nursery was forbidding in the dark, its paintbox colors mute. Hallie wondered, not for the first time, how Sarah viewed her world. Terrifying to be enclosed in hard-edged slats, a duck mobile and stuffed bear your only charms against a cavernous void. No wonder babies screamed so desperately.

"Not my idea to have you down the hall." Hallie kissed the baby-chick head. "Shout at your father, not me."

"Mommy, look! I dressed myself. Look at me!"

"Erica? Why are you up?" The child looked grotesque.

"School, remember?"

Hallie lifted Sarah from the changing table and turned on the baby lamp—wooden lambs frolicking on a painted base.

"Don't I look pretty?"

"Stunning." Like a blow to the head was stunning. Erica wore an outgrown red plaid wool skirt that barely skimmed her crotch, an orange T-shirt with Tweety-Bird and a spinach stain on its front, one red knee sock, one purple knee sock, and her dress Mary Janes.

Griselda shuffled in, her entire rear end wagging.

"Not yet!" Hallie snapped. The dog crumpled down with its head on its paws, eyes mutely accusing her.

Erica pirouetted. "Ha-ha, Sarah," she said. "I'm going to kinna-gard and you can't, 'cause you're a baby."

Sarah revved up for the give-me-milk blues. Hallie sat down in the rocker. The baby sucked, sighed happily, and went into a trance. "Shhh," Hallie whispered. "We don't want to wake up Grandma. Or Andy." Not until we get you out of that costume, that's for sure. "Didn't we put that skirt away for Sarah?" she asked her older daughter.

"It's mine."

"But you've gotten so tall!"

"My favorite skirt in the whole world."

"But short and too hot for today, honey, so—"

"MY. FAVORITE. SKIRT. IN. THE. WHOLE. WORLD!"

"Shhhhh . . . then about those socks . . ."

"Aren't they pretty? My favorite colors."

"Except we usually wear the same col—" Her daughter backed up, as if Hallie were physically attacking.

What am I doing? "I will not raise cookie-cutter conformists." Hallie Bennett, last night. After the six o'clock news, before *Funny Girl*. Never, Wonder Mother said, would she fight about hair or clothes or politics, stifling creativity and individuality. Their bodies and ideas belonged to *them*.

"She's having a Kahlil Gibran fit." Teddy had tried to soothe Sylvia Saxe, insulted by Hallie's inference that she had not been as enlightened as her daughter now was. "You know, 'Our children are not our children,' et cetera."

"That's what's sick about this country," Hallie had pontificated. "Beating up kids because their hair's long, because they don't dress like their parents."

Comes the dawn, her first test case and all she could think was that the teachers and other mothers would see that her kid's underwear was longer than her skirt, her socks didn't match, and her shirt was stained, and ask what kind of mother?

"Too much noise." Another country heard from. Andy in his sleepers, thumb in mouth, hand clutching his security blanket, the "bom-bom" that Hallie was sure he would someday drag down the aisle and pack in his briefcase.

Griselda scrambled to her feet, nails scratching the hardwood floor, tail thumping.

"Not *yet*," Hallie said. The dog looked to the children for assistance, then sank back into martyrdom.

"I go to real school now," Erica said, "not baby nursery like you. Hurry up, Mommy. I'll be late."

Late. No. Impossible. Hallie craned to see the clock on top of Sarah's yellow and white dresser. "It's five-thirty!" she wailed. "Five-thirty in the morning."

"I can't tell time," Erica said.

"It's dark out."

"I'm hungry," Andy said.

"There are three hours before the bus!"

"Oh, no! One, two, three! Hurry, Mommy!"

"You don't understand. That's long."

"Whhhaaa!" Sarah's mouth had slipped, sprung. Hallie shoved her nipple back in.

"Mommy, come on, the bus!"

And he sleeps! Pushes me out of bed and sleeps. Big, busy man. Resting up for the real world. Ha!

"Is this a private party?" Her mother stood in the doorway, clutching her robe.

Griselda, savvy at last, waved her tail half-heartedly.

"Look at me! Look at me, Grandma!"

I could pretend I'm blind, wear dark glasses and a white cane when I go to school conferences, Hallie thought. Nobody blames a blind woman for her child's fashion offenses. Except there were twelve years of schooling ahead. More. Add in Andy and Sarah . . .

"You're not wearing that to *kindergarten*, are you?"

Go to it, Mom. Lay your narrow-minded, conformist, bourgeois, crippling dictates on her. *Please.*

"Mommy said I'm stunning."

"I'M HUNGRY!" Andy took his thumb out of his mouth, the better to bellow.

"Shhhh—Daddy's asleep." She put the baby on her shoulder and patted her back.

"Well," Sylvia said, "your teacher will certainly know you're not a cookie-cutter conformist."

Touché.

"I'M HUNGRY!" Andy needed an exorcist.

Sarah belched, long, satisfying. Wet. Christ, she'd forgotten to—

"Shouldn't you have a diaper on your shoulder, dear?"

"How come Sarah always eats first?" Andy looked jealous and a little dangerous.

"When you were a baby, you—"

"I want real school, too," Andy said. "I'm not a baby now."

"Are so," Erica said. "Are so, are so, are—"

"I'm not going to nursery school again! Not ever!"

"—so, are so, are—"

"How about I make breakfast?" Sylvia chirruped. "Since everybody's up."

"Not quite everybody." She sounded like a witch, her voice a cackle, her words a curse. But it didn't matter. The "not quite everybody" couldn't hear a thing. He was blissfully asleep.

*   *   *

"You look tired," her mother said.

She laughed, re-threaded her needle, and sewed a name tag onto the waistband of Erica's corduroys.

"Feel like you forgot to read the job description before you signed up?" Sylvia turned on the mixer. Her grandmothering always involved cookies.

Hallie suddenly thought of the times, rare but infuriating, when Ted did his disappearing act, not coming home on time and not calling. She resented him anew, not only for his lack of consideration, but also for his having the ability to assert his freedom, the luxury of sporadic irresponsibility she lacked. "Sometimes," she murmured, "I wonder what else there is."

"You talking about sex? The stuff in the magazines about how many orgasms you're entitled to?"

"Mother!"

"I'm trying to be modern, au courant. I never even heard the word growing up. Then I found out you were supposed to try for one and now I hear you're supposed to have a dozen. Give me a break."

"Sex is the last thing on my mind."

"So you mean work. If you wanted to be a career woman, you shouldn't have married and had three children. Too late now, but frankly, nothing's as important or rewarding as raising good children. You made the right choice."

The same soothing facts of life as always. Still, Hallie felt a fuzzy, futile anger. She fiddled with the name-tag roll. Five thousand repetitions of Erica Bennett. Enough for school, summer camps, college, and trousseau. "Why does kindergarten require name tags? Do the kids undress every day?" She clipped a thread, then put down her sewing and lit a cigarette. Absolutely positively must stop.

Sylvia sprinkled chocolate chips into the bowl. "How's Megan's new baby?"

"Michael? Coming along fine. She brought him home last week. Wish I could visit." Megan had been living in San Diego for several years now, even after Daniel resigned from the Navy.

Her second son, Michael, had been dangerously premature.

Born too soon, in grief, the day of his namesake and uncle's funeral.

"Such a shame about her brother."

Hallie nodded. Such a shame about all of them. Such a waste. Michael Miller, the adorable little boy she'd helped babysit after school all those years ago, was now Hallie's face of war. And so was his mother, Kat, who had believed that bad things could simply be ignored. Hallie would never forget her mutely staring at her son's coffin, holding the flag they gave her.

Her mother scraped the spoon against the bowl, but Hallie knew what she was thinking about. Her own lost son was always in Sylvia's mind, tracking invisibly the unlived portion of his life. Now he was over there, as Michael had been, or fighting the war at home.

The umbilical cord was never completely severed. The part made of hope, the part connected to the future, to a life that continued beyond yours, was forever. Hallie knew she was able to change diapers, kiss hurts, and stitch name tags only because she refused to fully acknowledge that children could be suddenly and forever dead.

The timer went off and Sylvia stood up. "Enjoy what you have while you have it," she said. "We bitch until it's too late, and then we realize how precious every second was."

"You sound like Emily in *Our Town*." Hallie stubbed out her cigarette and picked up another name tag.

"All the same, try not to waste it." She removed two trays of cookies. "We were poor. It wasn't picturesque washing diapers by hand and hanging them in the wind. Or turning shirt collars and wearing ill-fitting shoes. And then, God help us, it got worse. War. That's what I would have said was my life back then."

She transferred the cookies to a wire rack, coating the air with butter and chocolate. "But what I remember now is the life and the laughing and the kissing and the touching. Babies' bellies. The backs of their necks. Feeling useful and used."

The second batch of dough dropped onto the sheets. Sylvia sighed heavily. "Now my life's too big, a fat lady's dress on a skeleton."

"Mother!"

The grandmother part of Sylvia worked methodically, the cookie sheets put in the oven, timer set, but she, the large-boned, competent woman, receded. "Forgive me. Forget it. I'm not saying it right. Besides, it's my problem, not yours."

"What? Is it Vicky?" The problem almost always was.

"No. After all that worry about Mississippi and San Francisco, bigots and drugs, she's finally safe and happy."

Vicky was living in a farmhouse in Sonoma. The Summer of Love had ruined everything, she said. Kids hitching in from Kansas to get hip. Tourist buses. Bad drugs. Time to leave San Francisco.

"She's baking and selling her bread," Sylvia said. "Her, um, friend's trimming trees for a landscape company." Sylvia tried to be broad-minded about Vicky's unsanctified partners, but she stumbled all the same. "They live on peanut butter and brown rice and vegetables they raise. Surplus food from the government. They make their clothing. Everything we were so proud to overcome after the Depression, she chooses. I don't get it. I wish she'd finish college."

"I'm not sure why." Hallie concentrated on her stitching. Maybe the teacher would notice what tidy work she did with name tags and forgive her daughter's ensemble. "I spent more time preparing for a profession than working at it."

"It makes you a better mother," Sylvia said. "If only I could have gone to college!" There'd been a partial scholarship, but her parents had forbidden it, fearing the corruptions of the wide world. So Sylvia left home by marrying Ivan Saxe at age eighteen. Now she stood up and walked across the room like an old woman to turn off the timer and take out her cookies. "Everything's over," she said, sending a chill through the fragrant kitchen.

"I'm not," Hallie said softly. "Your grandchildren aren't. Vicky isn't. And Dad's not."

"Oh, Hallie, what do you know?" Her mother grabbed a napkin and blew her nose.

"What?"

Furiously, Sylvia Saxe shoved the napkin in her apron pocket and spooned cookie dough onto the sheets, pushing it off the teaspoon, staring intently at her hands. She reset the oven timer and put the empty mixing bowl under the faucet.

"Talk to me." Hallie stuck her needle into a pincushion.

Her mother left the sink and the bowl and sat down again. "Mo Henry died last week," she said. "Like that. Massive coronary. He retired five months ago. The golden years, they call it."

Hallie reached over and took her hand. "I'm sorry."

"You think the coast is finally clear, the hard work done, the children on their own."

Her mother looked like a dark mirror reflecting her own future. The same light eyes, the same resolute chin, long, narrow nose. The same cells and marrow, but Sylvia's all stained with sorrow.

"They should call them the leftover years."

"Mother!"

"Your father . . ."

"But the operation was a success, wasn't it?"

Sylvia seemed absorbed erasing a coffee drip from the side of her mug. "His prostate's fine." She stared at her thumb. The timer clicked. "You know what? I forgot to put that batch in the oven," but she stayed where she was. "Since the operation, certain . . . marital acts, you know, are impossible. But that's not the problem. The problem is he moved into Vicky's old bedroom."

"Why?"

"He says . . ." She cleared her throat. "He says that since he can't 'be a man' with me—those are his words, not mine—there's no point sleeping together. He's ashamed of something he shouldn't be, but he won't talk about it. He was never exactly demonstrative. The only time he really touched me was when we were going to . . . well, let's say I knew what a kiss before dinner meant. So now we don't ever touch. We're Tupperware containers of flesh, refrigerated, waiting to be thrown away."

"Have you told him?"

"I said it, you know, doesn't matter. He got angry, said that meant it never mattered. I even talked to his doctor, a young man who told me about growing old gracefully, and protecting the male ego. He didn't see anything wrong with how your father wants to live because, of course, we're old. I was a dirty old lady to think about sharing my bed."

She scratched her thumbnail on the side of the cup. "He says he can't be a man, but he *is*, if only he understood. Why are they so concerned with that one thing? That one part of themselves? None of us know how much time is left, and I don't want to waste it. I want to be near him in the dark. He's my *husband*." She put her head in her hands. "I'm so lonely."

Hallie walked over and stroked her mother's hair. "Making nice," Erica would have called it. If only nice were something she could make.

The buzzer sounded, but both women stayed in place. There was nothing in the oven anyway.

4

"Ten years. Incredible." He clicked his wineglass against hers. "Happy anniversary."

Hallie filled with a fierce burst of love and longing. Ted was still, always, the one. Her single-minded vision of love was considered narrow and ridiculously old-fashioned by the new social scientists, but that didn't make it less true. My husband, she murmured. The words thrummed, light and quick as hummingbird wings below her heart. My husband, my husband.

Golden, shining man. But that wasn't half the attraction. He was *right*. Fun. Clever and wise. Good.

He was her history now, too. A third of her life had included him. Her eyes welled. He shimmered across from her, a mirage.

"I'm only sorry you have a cold," he said.

Her fever gave her a surrealistic, hallucinatory buzz. She pulled out a tissue and blew her nose.

"And Cape Cod in March doesn't seem the place for a cure," he added.

"I thought it'd be wildly romantic. Windswept dunes. Catherine and Heathcliff in New England."

They sat with a pizza carton between them on one of the low-ceilinged, musty room's twin beds. The center of their chenille bedspread was transparent, as if countless bodies had been slammed down and ground out on the spot. Every other place she'd called had been shuttered for the winter.

"Being alone with you is romantic enough," he said.

Good thing, because the dunes were legally off-limits and with wet, icy winds whipping the coast, even Heathcliff wouldn't have followed Catherine out there. All the nearby good restaurants were shuttered until spring. Alone was all that was left.

"You know," he said, "your eyes are even more dramatic when they're bloodshot."

He put his pizza slice back in the box and took her hands. "I love being married to you, Hallie Saxe."

If she cried, her nose would run even more.

"Guys talk about their wives and their problems," Ted said, "taking it for granted that every woman's like the one they're stuck with. I never say how it is with us. It would be rude to flaunt my good fortune."

He floated in and out of focus, blurred and glowing gold. His eyes, when she could see them, were the color of burned sugar.

"When James was in this summer," he said, "we went to a bar."

No. They were more like dark caramel.

"There were these girls having a party. . . ."

Or maybe . . . "What?"

"Nothing. It's irrelevant. I love you."

"Lub you, too." She had to disengage and grab tissue.

He held her free hand in both of his. Held it for real. The way that said no life could be long enough for all the touching they had to do.

"Know what?" she whispered much later. "When we were first married and the bed was wet after making love, I thought I was defective, like a dribble glass. I was sure normal women didn't leak, and I kept hoping you wouldn't notice."

"I figured it was my incredible masculinity," he said. "You know, too much for any woman to contain."

"Nice how our ignorance meshes." She pulled him close.

"Everything does," he murmured, and then she heard his breath slip off into sleep.

She lay warm and fever-dizzy, still softly echoing with pleasure, and pondered the euphoria that gave the lie to postcoital miseries, the mildewed room, the miserable weather, and her head cold.

It was more than sex and was not induced by brandy, wine, champagne, or antihistamines. It was finding themselves, like misplaced objects.

They were on vacation from ten years of complications, the clutter of their roles back home. Their luggage didn't include three children, laundry, milk spills, car pools, mortgage payments, shopping lists, tantrums, repairmen, or the war. Like an image in a darkroom sink, their true selves, the chemistry, congruencies, and contrasts that were too often blurred, rose sharply and clarified.

She could see it now, the original blueprint of the marriage.

"There you are," she whispered to his sleeping form. "I've been looking for you."

Now she remembered who she was and who he was. Now she remembered why she so wanted to be Ted Bennett's wife. The only thing she couldn't remember was why there were times when she forgot.

Encounters

1971–1972

Marriage is a repressive bourgeois institution for the
enslavement and exploitation of women.

1

CHLOE WISTER was in Boston with a show in tryout,
but today she was spending "Sunday in the country,"
as she put it. Patronizingly, Hallie thought.

The swing set's paint flaked after a long winter, but
the day was rich with the wet green of early spring and Griselda
had not yet stomped the pale lemon crocuses and white snow-
drops blooming near the fence.

The backyard view always unsettled Hallie with its identical
grids of windows, dormers, and doors, suggesting that one house,
one family, was like the next. Examples of the "mindless conform-
ity" her generation supposedly espoused. Only the colors varied,
and not much at that. Hallie's was Colonial Gray. Jeanette's—hers
alone now that husband Bill had "found himself" and followed his
guru to a tantric commune—was Colonial Green. "Bum," Sylvia

Saxe labeled Bill, failing to understand that in the new age, commitment was only to your own self-growth. Bill called Jeanette a "diminisher" for trying to prevent his escape from the psychological bondage of his family, for squelching his fun.

Two doors down, Andy Bennett celebrated another six-year-old's birthday behind a Colonial Blue. Hallie could hear his basso exclamations all the way here, above the squeak of the swing.

"When's lunch? We're hungry." Erica had Debby, a silent, braid-chewing friend, in tow.

"In a minute."

"More swing!" Sarah screamed.

"She is sooo spoiled," Erica said.

Chloe's hair was long, straight, and russet, as were her nails. She wore a white vest with cap sleeves over a blouse the color of peach ice cream. Her hip huggers had barely anything to hug. Hallie felt like tugging her forelock and bowing.

"Where is your husband?" Chloe demanded.

"Working," Hallie said. "In the attic, in his study. Why'd you ask? You saw him when he came home from tennis."

"What do you call what you're doing?"

"Pushing a swing."

"Christ, Hal, it's *work*! You're working, too!"

"Okay, it's my job, and you don't understand marriage."

"I know it's about power, and I know you can't admit that. Yet. I'm single because I understand marriage, all too well."

She always had a man, however, usually a married one because they were grateful for so little, she said.

"When is it your turn to play games and catch up?" Chloe demanded, hands on hips. "Or are you an indentured servant?"

"Gotten militant, haven't you? Going to call him a male chauvinist pig?"

"More!" Sarah shouted. "More, Mommy!"

"One more push, then lunch," Hallie said.

"Don't cook. Starve a rat today." Chloe arranged her hair on her peach and vanilla shoulders.

"Around here, nobody talks that way." The new, vocal women were marching and battling too far away to be heard or noticed.

Chloe put her manicured hand on Hallie's shoulder. "I'm in a

CR group. Consciousness raising, and it's wonderful. I never knew women before. I thought men were smarter, more interesting. I bought their propaganda."

Hallie thought of all the parties she'd gone to where she wound up talking to the men. Men were more involved, their interests more significant than women's. Wasn't that so?

"Remember in elementary school when Africa was called the dark continent?" Chloe asked. "The map was basically blank? Now we're the dark continent and it's time to study ourselves."

Hallie helped Sarah off the swing.

"I know you have a good marriage. But after talking with women, and reading stuff, I know Ted has an even better one, because he has you. He gets to be a star in the world of gizmos—"

She shouldn't have bragged about his promotion.

"—while you smooth the way for him."

"I'm doing what I chose to do," Hallie said softly. "It gives me pleasure."

Chloe shook her head. "You're doing what you've been brainwashed to do." She tucked a strand of hair behind her ear.

Sarah had hopped onto a dandelion and now squatted, trying to repair the broken stem. Griselda shuffled over, watched the child, then snapped her jaws at a fly. Hallie felt as if Chloe's imperial stance threw the joyful tableau into shadow. "Your friends in New York don't have a whole lot in common with a woman like me, who's married—happily, with kids—trying to make it work. Your friends care about taking off bras. I did that, you know? And then, all I thought about was my tits. Were my nipples popping from the cold, or the blouse fabric, or from the way men stared? I made a whole lot of men—and myself—uncomfortable before I finally wondered what the hell naked boobs had to do with anything real. And when did hairy armpits or legs take on philosophical importance? And now there's one lunatic saying underpants are oppressive and another insisting pregnancy is barbaric and we need artificial wombs. Don't blame me for not rushing to your barricades."

"You were one of the smartest people in school." Chloe shrugged. "Well, never no mind. Didn't mean to pester."

Hallie's annoyance melted away. "This doesn't mean I'm not interested."

Chloe raised an eyebrow. "How about I tell you a story? A group of us put on a reading, a fund-raiser, Women on Women—WOW for short. I was assigned Chaucer."

"The Wife of Bath?"

"How did you know?"

"She's Chaucer's lusty lady. Five husbands. Who else?"

"That's the prologue. I did her tale. Remember that?"

Hallie shook her head. "You are my legend bearer. First Patient Griselda . . ." Chloe cocked her head and managed to make the attitude one of silent accusation. "I'm not a Griselda!" Hallie snapped. The dog licked her hand.

"Did I say anything?"

"Sorry. Lunchtime, Sarah." The child looked up, the dandelion head in her fist.

"Story time." Chloe spoke to Hallie and an unseen grandstand as they crossed the small backyard. "A rapist is given a year to save himself from his death sentence if he can find out what women really want. For twelve months minus a day, this fellow gets the standard answers—love, money, diamonds are a girl's best friend. He knows he's dead meat until"—she opened the kitchen door and ushered them in, pausing for dramatic effect—"at the very last moment, he meets a crone who *knows* what women want and who will tell him—if he'll marry her."

Sarah gaped. Chloe galvanized even three year olds.

" 'Wommen desiren have souereynetee,' the crone says, which translates, clear and simple, into women want sovereignty, control over their lives. Jackpot. The queen agrees that's the answer."

Erica and silent Debby paused from pouring milk to watch her.

"So he keeps his life and his promise and marries the crone, although making it with a hag is a bummer, and he says so. And she says okay. You can have me as I am, old and ugly and faithful, or you can have me young and gorgeous and take your chances on my fidelity." Chloe grinned. "Which do you think he chose?"

"The young one?" Erica asked.

"On behalf of all us over-thirties, I hope he chose the faithful crone," Hallie said.

"Listen up, because this is the great part. That knight, that former despoiler of women, had learned his lesson." Chloe's voice deepened. "He let *her* choose. He gave his wife what women want—sovereignty." She laughed out loud.

The four of them were spellbound—Sarah wide-eyed on her booster chair, Erica, milk carton still in hand, Debby, the tip of her right braid in her mouth, and Hallie, holding the refrigerator open. "Which did she choose?" Erica whispered.

Chloe bent forward and spoke as if only to her. "Because he had given her sovereignty, had asked what would make *her* happy, she chose both. She became young and beautiful and faithful and did only those things that made him happy. And so they lived forever in perfect joy." Her voice rose to declamatory level again. " 'Jhesu Crist us sende Housebond meeke, younge, fressh a-bedde . . . and eek I pray Jhesu shorte hir lyves That wol nat be governed by hir wyves. . . .' "

"What's that mean?" Erica asked.

"A good man was hard to find then, too," Chloe said.

"What does *that* mean?"

"Trust me, you'll understand soon enough."

"Grown-ups," Erica muttered.

"I like the 'fresh a-bedde' requirement." Hallie smiled and whipped egg whites for a cheese soufflé.

"How come Chaucer knew what women wanted in 1400 and five hundred years later Freud acted like it was the riddle of the universe? And even today, otherwise well-educated, intelligent women haven't gotten the message?"

"Don't start. Don't spoil a perfectly wonderful story."

"Don't be afraid to think. Don't be afraid to change. The personal is political," Chloe said.

"And strident. And tedious."

But two weeks later, while Sarah napped and the other children were in school, Hallie crept up to the storage part of the attic. In among the outgrown toys and cartons of old school notes she found the hefty anthology. She blew off its dust, took it into Teddy's study where there was light and space and a comfortable leather chair, and she sat with The Wife of Bath, whispering about sovereignty, feeling excited, furtive, and guilty of multiple trespasses.

—————— 2 ——————

"It's high time we spoke frankly." Hallie wore a man-tailored blouse rolled up at the sleeves and looked vaguely rumpled.

Frankly? Teddy braced himself. As compared to what? Did they usually speak dishonestly? And why "we" and "high time"? He'd been frank forever. He sat at the center island of the kitchen, watching her make sandwiches. Another of her petitions lay on the work island. He tilted his head to see what it was now. Recycling. Her eco-freak side this time. She wanted the good people of Waltham to stop wasting their trash. Good luck. Typical of her.

"We have to talk." She opened a can of tuna. Oil splashed onto the corner of the petition. "Honestly."

He had brought the Sunday paper into the kitchen as a convivial, husbandly act. Drink coffee, chat about the news, keep her company so she wouldn't feel alone or ignored. Now his muscles tightened as he understood that he, the well-meaning innocent, had walked into a trap. "Do you mean it's honestly time to talk," he asked, "or that it's time to talk honestly? And why? Have we spent the last eleven years not talking? Or lying to one another?"

"You are barely aware of the children."

This was the fourth straight day of rain that had drowned the roses and left the swing set in the middle of what they'd named Lake Bennett. The family was condemned to close proximity indoors, a weekend of squabbling over funnies and cartoons, of cereal dropped into sofa creases, raisins dumped on the rug, and cranky complaints from his offspring wherever he settled. "I am aware of the children. Sometimes painfully so."

Hallie chopped celery. "But perhaps not aware that *the* children are *your* children."

"What the hell does that mean?"

"Don't get defensive!" A tendril of hair stuck to her forehead, and she flicked it back, then tucked the curls on the side behind her ear.

He recognized that gesture. It was Chloe's. Hallie borrowed shtick and rhetoric from the actress agitator. An insane blowup about *The Canterbury Tales*, for God's sake! And since then, mutters and dark hooded glances. He'd assumed she was getting her period, but a woman couldn't be premenstrual for four months.

"For example, this is Sunday on my calendar, too," Hallie said. Chop, chop.

"And probably on most other people's calendars." He despised her new ponderous, meaningless pronouncements. Don't cook. Starve a rat today. A woman without a man is like a fish without a bicycle. "I know you're trying to be honest and frank, but could you also be comprehensible?"

The knife slammed down. "I have tried since spring, but you won't listen! I'm tired of being their only parent!"

"That is the most unfair, ridiculous—"

"The primary parent, the responsible, bottom-line parent. You drop in for a fun trip to the zoo, a bedtime story, but not if it interferes with your tennis, or your work—"

"What's that tone for? You think I don't really work?"

"—or an important game. Then they're one hundred percent mine."

"A handful of games in eleven years—some men watch all the time, some men—"

"Making me hire a sitter last Saturday while I went to your coworker's fiancée's bridal shower!"

"I had to work. I couldn't babysit!"

"Is it babysitting when I do it?"

"Let's not fight about semantics."

"We're not fighting." She picked up the knife and resumed mincing celery. "We're having a discussion."

As argumentative as her father. It must be genetic, inevitable.

"We are discussing your lack of sensitivity."

If he got any more sensitive, he'd bleed through his pores. "I try to help you," he said patiently.

"That's exactly it! You see?"

What he saw was the girl he had promised to cherish forever going berserk. How the hell could that movie's slogan be "Love means never saying you're sorry"? Lately, love meant always saying he was sorry. For existing. For doing his job. For being male. For being who he'd always been.

"You aren't *helping* me." She waved the knife and he had a

moment of dread. "This isn't noblesse oblige! You're being their parent! I don't have to be grateful for every crumb. I'm not *helping* you every time I bathe them or read them a story, so why when you do it is it a favor?"

Because it *was*. She had her job, he had his. Weren't sixty hours a week sweating blood for G.T.U. *enough*? If she'd deal with McPherson and the old guard and make sure the managers he supervised were on top of their projects, if she'd maneuver through the stupidity and inertia and red tape and politics and come up with ideas that could get him into line management—he'd thank the hell out of her!

This was Chloe's fault. And Hallie's new pals who'd sucked her into a women's group. Maybe he should monitor her friends, watch out for bad influences the way they tried to do for the kids.

Really, what the hell was a women's group besides a fancy title for bitching about men? About him. Real groups had a purpose, not a sex. His mother's groups raised money. Hallie's raised her consciousness, like a dredging operation. He imagined sweaty women heaving something gelatinous out of the muck.

"Look, Hal, I know it's hard on you now, but it evens out in the end."

"I cannot imagine what you mean." She methodically mashed tuna chunks and celery with mayonnaise. Her consciousness was so elevated she didn't deign to look down at him.

"Here's the deal," he said. "I work my whole life. I never get off the treadmill except for short breaks. A game on TV, squash, tennis, a vacation. But it's different for women. You work very hard now, but once the kids go to school, you never work again. You watch soaps or paint or play canasta or tennis, whatever you want, all day long. A permanent, lifetime vacation."

"That is not the deal, Theodore Bennett!" Her voice was harsh and foreign. "Maybe your mother's, but not mine!"

"What exactly do you want?" he asked quietly.

"Sovereignty."

That word again. "What does that translate into?" He'd asked the same thing before. She never knew.

She glared and put the bread in the toaster oven.

He believed women should get equal pay. But what did that

have to do with his home becoming a war zone? And why was he—the man who paid for the place and kept it going, the man who literally supported every one of them, the man who broke his balls for them—suddenly the enemy? "You've changed," he said mournfully.

"Thank God for that!" The darkly lashed pale blue eyes that had for so long fascinated him were frightening. She looked like an enraged prophet, a furious oracle. "Wake up," she snapped. "The Fifties are history."

The summer storm raged around the house. Ted lifted his coffee and silently toasted the good old days when women were mysterious, unfrank, and low of consciousness.

3

Theodore Bennett sat on a concrete bench shivering, the sports section in his hand, his right thigh holding down the rest of Sunday's *Globe*. He thought wistfully of his attic study where the space heater toasted the March air and a man could comfortably read his paper.

He felt like a retiree or a bum on a park bench, a frozen sacrifice to women's liberation.

He loved Sunday afternoons in his study. Loved the angles of the ceiling, the blurred family sounds seeping through the floorboards. He could think up there, and he needed to. He had a lot on his mind.

Instead, he'd been sent into exile. The personal was indeed political, as she now insisted, and he was Napoleon on Elba. And God, but he'd never quote from *Adam's Rib* again and tell her she was cute when she was causey. She wasn't.

She didn't care about him anymore. Looked put upon when he spoke, as if he were trespassing. He'd tried to explain his restlessness, his frustrating struggle to be recognized and tapped for senior management. And she just about held up a silver cross and said it had to be her turn someday, which was patently insane because the only turn he'd ever had was a permanent one at supporting all of them.

Hallie had started treating her family as if it were a principality, dividing up duties and drawing boundaries. But like Hitler, you gave her an inch and she demanded the world. Appeasement did not work. And in the background, instead of "Deutchland Uber Alles," that stupid "I Am Woman" song.

The fact was, Ted was the only man at the playground. Normal women eyed him from across the swing sets while their husbands stayed home watching the game. He realized he was holding an old yellow diaper bag with a bunny rabbit on it. And the women, having taken every detail in while pretending to check on their children, turned their backs and whispered. Just like the seventh-grade schoolyard when giggling girls cupped their hands and leaned into one another's ears.

"Mind if I join you?"

She was traveling solo. A pocket-sized woman. Spinners, the guys called them—God forbid Hallie should ever hear. "Not at all." He smiled. He knew, had always known, his smile was potent.

There were shrill cries from the sandbox. A long-faced woman dislodged herself from the back fence and mediated.

His bench companion put a pink gingham diaper bag between them. He pushed his bunny bag behind his feet. Now she'd say, "What's a nice guy like you doing in a place like this?"

"I'll go crazy," she said, "if I have to only hear little kids." When she smiled, her nose crinkled.

All right, so Hallie, not this woman, would have said the other thing. He glanced at this very different person's hands, a feature he always noticed and cared about. Hers were delicate and tapering. And ringless.

Her smile was wry. You've checked me out, it said. I'm cute, agreeable and unmarried, right? Your move.

His hand was on his leg, wedding band completely visible. Interesting. There were absolutely no rules anymore. Last week a woman at the racquet club had said wedding bands made men's hands sexier. She'd stroked his fingers, one by one, while she said it.

It used to be only wild kids like Vicky and her friends. Hippies. The very young, or the James Harris types. But now the sexual smorgasbord was open for business to anyone. Even the good girls of his youth had shed their pointed bras and impenetrable girdles and become soft, touchable, nipple-happy sex-starved predators like their younger sisters. Quasimodo wouldn't go needy. God bless the Sexual Revolution—but why had it waited so long?

He had friends racing backward through the generation gap, except you were who you were, and their screams when they got caught in a time warp were old-fashioned and fatal. There was a betting pool as to when Wally Cryor, who never went home until he'd made it with a pre-commute pickup, would have his heart attack.

A better bet was when Cryor would have his divorce. Within the last month, two couples they knew had filed. One because of his shenanigans, one because of hers.

Too much was at risk. They couldn't predict the fallout from an affair, whoever had it. One of the few things Hallie and he still agreed on.

Old farts, that's what they were. Last ones into the pool. No. Last ones still dry on the sidelines, watching the water sports.

"Brrrr! Chilly! I was fooled by the sunshine!" She pushed her hands into her pockets and smiled up at him. "I didn't bring a hat, but it'd ruin my hair anyway." She had one of those puffy hairdos and a pink headband, and below it, sable, admiring eyes. He looked away before eye contact registered as too long and meaningful or even long enough and potentially something.

"Which is yours?" she asked.

"The boy on the balance beam and the little girl with the yellow snowsuit and the two ponytails."

"Your boy's handsome. Looks just like you."

My, oh, my.

"How old are they?" Asked as if it were the most interesting information in the world and she'd die for it.

She was a nice break from all the angry women. "Sarah's four and a half, and Andy's seven. I have another daughter, nine. She had a better offer today." Babble, babble, like a nervous kid.

"Three! I can't imagine. I'm exhausted with just Stacy—the one in the pink snowsuit?"

"Of course. She looks like you."

The woman beamed. "Maybe a little, but your son, well! He's your walking image!"

"Not really." Not at all. Andy was Hallie translated into a masculine language. However, there seemed no reason to mention the co-designer of the beautiful boy.

Hallie. He felt a twinge to which he applied a direct compress of anger. What did she expect? She'd pushed him onto female turf, unarmed except for a bunny bag and the Sunday paper.

The woman bathed him in her glance. Nothing like Hallie's hostile, speculative examination. She looked at him the way women used to look at men.

She took a decorating magazine out of her pink gingham bag but didn't open it. Instead she stared, rather dreamily, ahead.

"Watch me, Daddy, watch me!"

He nodded and clapped as Sarah showed him how she could hang by one arm from the top of the climbing dome.

"Cute," the woman said.

He looked over at her, ready to say something about Sarah, but the woman was looking directly at him and he was no longer sure which Bennett she found appealing. Or maybe he was.

"Mind if I ask a personal question?" she said.

The temperature escalated along with untried possibilities. "I can't answer," he said, "until I hear the question."

"You must be a lawyer!" Her laugh was high and feminine. She was dainty even unto tinkling vocal cords.

He forced down a crazy urge to tell her that every single year of high school, he had been voted Best-Looking Boy. His senior year he was also Most Likely to Succeed. "Actually," he said, "I'm an engineer."

"Like on trains?"

So she wasn't wildly bright. He knew from experience that a too-smart female was exhausting. "An engineer who designs electrical systems," he told her. "The inside of your TV, for example. Although my son would be more impressed if I did work on the railroad." He was immediately sorry about that last bit, about using Andy that way. "Actually, I don't design anymore. I do what's called 'strategic planning.' Looking ahead for the corporation, seeing what we should get into."

"Management," she murmured.

"Yes." Modestly. As he should. To be a middle manager was to be nothing. The restlessness that had become an all-season allergy buzzed through him. He needed to move up or out of G.T.U. Whatever, wherever that meant, whether or not Hallie understood.

"I'm impressed," she said.

"Ah . . ." He cleared his throat. Hallie said it was rude not asking women about their work, never showing interest in their world. "Do you have a—what is it you do?" It sounded stupid. Why was he following his wife's guidelines to seduce a stranger?

"I think being a mother is the most important job in the world, no matter what those women's libbers say." She emitted another trilling tinkle. I'm a pink and cuddly, old-fashioned *girl*, it burbled.

"What was the personal question, then?" he prompted.

She sighed and faced forward. She probably felt awkward. They were all new at this, but they'd get past it. "Well," she said, "I thought since you have a little girl, you could tell me how you trained her."

"Trained her? Sarah?"

She nodded.

"To do what?" She was too young to juggle, or lift weights, and what, frankly, did Sarah have to do with anything?

"Stop joking! To go potty, of course."

He bit his bottom lip.

"I read every article, try every new theory, but Stacy refuses. And if she isn't trained soon, she can't go to Montessori."

She could not actually be discussing this with Theodore Bennett, best looking, most likely to!

"My husband says I'm too easy on her." She pouted. "I asked him to do Parent Effectiveness Training with me, but he says she's my job, not his."

Husband? Where was the wedding band? What was her game, sashaying up ringless, asking leading questions?

"How strict was your wife about it?"

"I—I really don't know, but in general, she's not a very strict . . ." So spoken by Theodore the Eunuch Wet Nurse.

"She is trained, isn't she?"

"My wife?"

"Your daughter!"

"Oh. Her. Ah . . ."

"I mean I see you have a diaper bag there, but surely—"

"I have pretzels in it. Want one?" He tried to picture Paul Henreid passing Bette Davis a pretzel log instead of a lit cigarette. He tried to imagine Bette Davis asking about toilet training.

The woman shook her head. "When was it?"

"What?"

"That she stopped using diapers. Sarah. At night."

"I'm sorry." Was that the kind of date a truly liberated father knew? He didn't think even Hallie could say precisely when it happened.

"Well, did she have problems with them? At what age did she start with number one? Um, pee-pee, uh—"

"I have to grow," he said. "I mean go."

"Really?"

"I have to buy things."

"Food shopping? Where do you—"

"Not food. A car." It shimmered just ahead. A two-seater, incompatible with families. "And a sailboat."

"Wow," she said.

He offered her the newspaper, but she shook her head and watched him, mouth half open. A dangerous boat, it'd have to be. A racer. "And a stereo," he added, lifting the bunny bag. "Lots of stuff. Anything I want." He waved farewell and went in search of his children and every undomesticated object that would make sure nobody ever again mistook him for the kind of person who knew about toilet training.

He needed liberation, too.

4

"What did you think of your insides?" Suzanne, who last week had gifted each woman with a speculum and explained how to use it, smiled. "How was it to finally see them?"

The CR group was gathered in Hallie's family room, filling the air with cigarette smoke. Hallie lit up, as always with a twinge of guilt, but not enough to stop.

"Not how I expected." Hallie was embarrassed, though the whole point was getting over this stupid shame. God knew men weren't unfamiliar with their reproductive organs. She forced herself on. "I expected to be, oh, murky. The kind of place you'd keep secret. My privates, my mother called them. Or 'down there,' as if it were the void on those ancient maps where it said, 'Beyond this point lie monsters.' But it was pink and healthy and *right* looking. I wish I'd known all along."

"I thought it'd be like my basement," Joan Elkins said. "Plumbing and heaters. Only a desperate choice for visitors."

"I imagined warty and gray, like an octopus." Harriet passed pretzels. Competitive cooking—"entertaining"—was forbidden.

"An octopus looks like a scrotum." Virginia was a reference librarian with a passion for precision. She spoke in clear sentences and needlepointed, her hands and mouth operating simultaneously and independently. "A homely, pulsating scrotum. Very unlike a vagina."

"I bought the speculums because self-examination seemed outrageous, so what the hell," Suzanne said. "Tony's such a pig about these meetings, I wanted to make him angry. I didn't know it mattered until afterwards. I thought nature made it impossible to see ourselves for our own protection. It was a revelation. Plus, it convinced Tony that we are subversive."

Ted had also been weird about the speculum, unable or unwilling to understand its point. "What's next?" he'd asked. "Proctoscopes?"

"I am so tired," Diane said, "of being made fun of. Of being told I'm foolish. I love being here where nobody does that."

Yes.

"Where we can be honest, for once, for the first time."

Yes.

Heady stuff, to find out who you were and what you wanted. Put the speculum to your entire self without knowing what you might find and what else the discovery might lead to.

Frightening, too. Old ties frayed when weighted with new consciousness.

Wendy Scanlon had walked out on her husband last week,

tired, she said, of his inability to accept her as a full human being. Another member had taken her daughter and departed for an all-woman ranch out west. After five attempts at contracts detailing household duties, Liz had separated from her husband because he wouldn't share the shit work. Suzanne and Tony battled and reconciled, always on the brink of a final explosion.

"Marriage is a repressive, bourgeois institution" popped from the lips of women who'd spent their childhoods preparing for the "big day," who'd gone to college for their "MRS's," who'd made sure they were engaged by their junior year, who had always answered "What do you want to be when you grow up?" with "A wife and mother."

These were the times that tried women's souls.

One of the things Hallie had begun to see was that marriage wasn't something that happened to you, but something you did. And not once and forever after, but over and over. Until, maybe, you didn't anymore. Maybe.

The whole business was infinitely more complex than she'd suspected. Sometimes Ted and even love seemed peripheral. She weighed him on her new scales. Imperfect, yes. But still, and she kept this unfashionable, politically suspect opinion to herself, he seemed the best of breed, and life was better with him than without.

So on she groped, unwilling to join the separatists who treated the flawed institution the way Nixon treated Vietnam, blowing it to smithereens in order to save it.

"I'm angry," Joan said, "for the years I felt bad about how I was made, even if I didn't know I felt bad about it."

"How could you not know?" Divorced Steffie was a correspondent from the front lines of the sexual frontier. "A guy's going down on you, but first he disinfects you, then puts on nose plugs. It's a clue."

Soft chuckles from around the room. Hallie's eyes skimmed over the copy of *Ms.* on the coffee table where she always left it, hoping Ted would want to know what women wanted. Instead, he acted as if it were radioactive waste.

They moved on to the official topic of the night, early memories of being trained to be girls.

Hallie listened to Rachel's account of being called a tomboy, to

Joan's story of being warned against taking math in college because boys wouldn't like her, and then she recounted the memory that the week's topic had prompted.

"When I was little," she said, "I read every fairy-tale book in the library. Obsessively. But when I daydreamed, I inverted them and I rescued a prince from the tower where a witch kept him prisoner. I once wrote my version out in class, and the teacher told me I had it all wrong." So she'd kept her dreams to herself, guilty, tingle-inducing secrets. What would Freud make of her first sexual fantasies?

The newly regained memory of the lost little girl heroine hurt. She wanted her back. She needed her.

5

Hallie muttered to herself as she inched into a parking space near Kat Miller's apartment. It made no sense to seek Megan out, almost force herself on the woman, and then to be hostile. Still, Megan had been odd—cool—for a while now, writing rarely, and even then sounding remote and evasive. And when they talked— always because Hallie called—conversations were brittle and quick.

Friendships eroded, especially when an entire continent was wedged between two people. Still, Hallie couldn't shake the feeling that something specific and injurious had happened, but at the same time she couldn't figure out what it could have been. Even this contact was accidental.

Hallie was in Philadelphia because her father had suffered what Sylvia called "a bad scare." A heart attack—minor. Now he was on the mend and Sylvia was sure the sight of his grandchildren would help him. Hallie doubted that. Ivan Saxe was not particularly appreciative of small creatures made of emotion and mess. It was for her mother, who undoubtedly needed some hugging silliness, that Hallie had driven to Philadelphia. She had also convinced herself that her father's illness would give him cause to stop being a belligerent semi-stranger and really talk on a personal level about life, work, family, anything.

She'd been right about her mother and wrong about her father. Yesterday, while Grandma and the children baked and decorated eccentric cupcakes, Hallie tried to find out about her father's youth, but instead heard what Nixon's reelection meant for the war and then about terrorism and the past summer's Arab massacre of Israeli Olympians. Depressed, she excused herself and, on impulse, called Kat Miller to see how she was and to get news of Megan.

Except Megan herself answered. "Sorry," she sputtered. She hadn't let Hallie know she was in from California because she'd only come in for her mother's birthday, and Boston was so far from Philadelphia she hadn't wanted to make Hallie travel or feel guilty about not doing so. The rational, even considerate excuse didn't end Hallie's unease.

The only possible time to see Megan had been this afternoon, and even then, Hallie would be a third wheel at a preexisting lunch date with Megan's sister. Hallie picked up a bouquet from the front seat and locked the car.

Trash cans lined the curb, waiting for pickup. All but three had been overturned. A long-legged dog eyed Hallie, then returned to his garbage buffet.

She automatically smoothed her hair, although there was no reason left to worry about whether it was "in place." It had been cut and freed to be its curly, untamable self. Reminding herself that she was liberated from the hair follicles down, Hallie Saxe Bennett stood straight and pushed Kat Miller's doorbell.

"Happy Birthday," she said as she entered the apartment. "These are for you."

"Thanks, kiddo, but I'd as soon people stopped making a fuss. Fifty's real old."

"Nonsense!" Her insincerity was audible. Fifty was ancient.

"Hi." Megan tidied the sofa bed.

Kat frowned. "Your hair looks like that Angela Davis!"

"My revolutionary new look." Kat wasn't impressed. But she was a hairdresser of the old school, still teasing and shellacking. Naturals like Hallie's were a threat. And maybe Ms. Hallie Bennett herself threatened "Mrs. Daniel Farr" as well.

Megan brought a vase for the flowers. Her right arm was in a sling.

"What happened?" Hallie asked.

"Such a klutz. I tripped on the one step in our house and broke something in my wrist."

Maybe she couldn't wear her real clothing with the sling. Maybe that's why Megan looked so unnaturally drab. In her dark skirt and long-sleeved white blouse, she looked like a nun in modern street clothes.

Kat was more colorful with her platinum bouffant and pink work smock. She pushed at her lower back. "Moved here because I'm alone now, you know. It's cozier."

Also affordable, Hallie suspected. How many still sought Kat's clips, perms, and hair spray? The apartment was dreary, with one narrow front window and furniture worn to a noncolor.

Kat fumbled in her smock pocket for a tissue and wiped at her eyes. "Lost both my boys." After Michael's death, Megan's other brother had left the States rather than protest the war any longer. Kat, the former Pollyanna of mothers, seemed devastated, as if the living parts of her had quit.

"A husband's an iffy thing," Kat said. "You miss him when he's gone, but you can't pretend to be surprised. But a child's for keeps. A child is *you*, is everything, and God help me, that war took both my sons. Can only reach Larry through friends. Best not to know his address. The F.B.I. . . ."

"When the war ends . . ." Hallie couldn't bring herself to finish. This war was forever.

Kat waved the unbearable subject away. "I have a seventy-two-year-old woman wants to look like Liz Taylor by three this afternoon." Slowly, as if weights were tied to each appendage, she found her car keys, put on her coat, and left.

"Where are the boys?" Hallie asked.

"Daniel took them to a movie." Megan fiddled with a button on her blouse. "He's here, too. Had some time, so . . ."

Daniel had resigned from the Navy, ready to be seized by the business world, as predicted over a decade ago in Annapolis. But it appeared that he was speedily grabbed and just as quickly let go. He'd had three positions in four years.

"I'm sorry there was no more time," Megan said. "I had promised Bonnie, and last night was a full house with Grady and Chris and their kids. I didn't think you'd want to spend time with her, anyway." She pulled one of her mother's ancient coats over her shoulders and her good arm, grappling with the baggy garment.

"I don't own a winter coat anymore." Hallie hovered nearby, arms out to help, but Megan shook her head.

They walked down a flight and out onto the monochromatic street, where bare-limbed trees erupted from cement and brushed stone walls. The only color was on cereal boxes spilling out of the trash cans and the skin of a rotting jack-o'-lantern.

"Excuse the mess," Hallie said. The backseat was littered with picture books, a car seat, ear muffs, a Viewmaster and plastic 3-D disks, a rumpled copy of *Jack and Jill*, and a half-empty bag of pretzels. She knew Megan's car would never look like that. "How was dinner last night?" she asked, to prove that she was socialized, even when it came to Christina.

"Remember how she always knew the latest fad?"

"You know I wasn't part of that crowd." The Cashmere Cuties, somebody had called them.

"Well, anyway, these days it's workshops that, quote, 'unmask' you. Encounter groups. Actualization seminars. She couldn't believe that I, who live in California, had never been to one. Anyway, now that she's more in touch with her feelings, to quote her again, she has realized that she needs space and—oh, hell, in plain English, she and Grady date other people. My mother nearly had heart failure and Bonnie turned mauve."

"Open marriage," Hallie said. "I read the book. I thought it was like those old key party stories, or the wife-swapping that everybody was sure everybody else did." She pulled at one of her large hoop earrings. "Messing around is a dangerous fad. Sooner or later, a new person has to appear when your husband is at his worst, and then what? I'm too—"

"How do you know when your husband's reached his worst?"

"Is that a riddle?"

Megan bit at her lip. "Forget it."

"Megan," Hallie said softly, "I've been worried. We're so out of touch, and you seem—"

"I get busy, with what I don't know, and . . . What were you going to say? I interrupted you with that dumb question."

"Only that I'm too insecure. I know we're not supposed to be jealous anymore, that we have to understand we don't own anybody and we shouldn't feel possessive, but I haven't evolved that far yet."

"This corner, turn right." They were in the new, northern end of the city, where rows of small brick houses with struggling foundation plantings were centered on thin oblongs of grass.

"Last time I saw Bonnie, she was a kid playing with makeup, and look—a house, her own kids."

Bonnie's door was trimmed with a wreath of tiny shellacked corncobs and squash. The interior of the house was as precisely accessorized, with six tiny, perfectly square rooms furnished in Early American eagles and duck decoys and oval rag rugs. Every surface gleamed, and the living room smelled of wax, lemons, and the tang of yellow chrysanthemums on the coffee table. And Bonnie matched, not a hair out of place and a yellow-and-white-checkered apron over her A-line skirt. Her pride was obvious and unashamed.

The dining-room table was set with flowered place mats and napkins, and a wicker cornucopia overflowing with artificial fruit. Bonnie retrieved three plates from the kitchen, each with a mound of turkey salad in half a winter squash shell, sitting on a lettuce leaf beside a garnish of carrot sticks. "*Better Homes and Garden*'s 'Autumn luncheon for friends,' " she said.

"This is fun," Megan said. "I wish I lived closer. It gets lonely out there." She poked at her food with little interest, a trait Hallie had long envied.

"Friends? But you always had tons of them," Bonnie and Hallie said more or less in unison.

Megan directed her comment to her sister. "Daniel isn't . . . His house is kind of his private escape from the world, his . . ."

"Castle." Bonnie looked proud of herself.

"Maybe you should get a job," Hallie said. "Meet people."

"The boys are too little."

She didn't mean to say anything, because as long as she kept it a secret, as long as she was the only one waiting, she was less vulnerable. But she suddenly felt a need to hear it said, to test it against other ears. "I'm going to. At least I hope so. I'm not telling Ted until I'm accepted, but I've taken my law aps and—"

"Law," Megan said. "Still?"

"When Sarah starts school in a year, so will I. I hope. I'll apply everywhere I can commute to, and then I'll hold my breath."

"No offense," Bonnie said, "but little Sarah needs Mommy there after school."

Hallie ran a fingertip over the pebbly surface of the water goblet and kept her mind cool by pretending she was in court, facing a jury. "It's been eleven years since I first thought about going to law school. Eleven years while I was too busy for that or to fight for civil rights or against the war—I mean really be engaged and out there. Eleven years could stretch into forever while I was too busy helping my kids with their lives to live my own. Haven't you felt that way?"

"No," Bonnie said. "Absolutely not."

"I almost went to school. Almost took a pattern-making course." Megan smiled disparagingly. "Does that count?"

"But you didn't?"

"It was at night."

Bonnie rubbed the base of a brass candlestick with her napkin. The silence persisted.

"So?" Hallie finally asked.

"You used to make fun of your mother for saying 'so?' that way."

"Don't change the topic. Why didn't you take the course?" Hallie heard her grand-inquisitor tone. Not everybody had to do what she was doing, she reminded herself. But all the same, Megan was so talented. And so visibly unhappy.

"Daniel wanted me to stay with him," Megan explained.

"Of course," Bonnie said. "Why else would he come home? There's plenty other women to keep him company if you won't."

"How about what you want, Megan?" Did these women live under rocks? "How about what you want, Bonnie?"

"I want whatever Tommy wants."

Hallie took a deep breath. "All the time?" she asked, as patiently as she could.

"I make myself want what he wants." Bonnie put her hand up as Hallie sputtered. "Is it better to aggravate him? To fight and be angry? Who wins that way?" She crossed her hands on her apron and sat back.

"Giving in isn't winning!"

121

Bonnie unclasped her hands and looked at her nails, which were polished a pale pink. "I used to fight with Tommy day and night." She spoke slowly, carefully. "And then Ivy Lee Schmidt moved here from Georgia and told me about Completely Female and my life changed. Now I get flowers instead of hell. Think you can convince me that's losing?"

"What exactly did Ivy Lee tell you?" Megan watched as if Bonnie was likely to reveal ultimate truth.

"My problem was that I thought of myself all the time."

"I cannot believe that in 1972 women could still talk like—" But Hallie was shushed by her hostess, who leaned forward, one finger raised.

"Lots of women follow this program. Lots of *contented* women, which you cannot say for the libbers, can you?"

"At least women who are trying to figure out their—"

Smiling, Bonnie interrupted her. "The Good Book says, 'Wives, submit to your husbands' leadership the same way you submit to the Lord.' Ephesians, 5:22. It's the natural order of things."

"That's the most pathetic, paternalistic—"

"God made it up, not me." Bonnie's voice was lyrical and soothing, her presence so tidy and carefully styled, Hallie wanted to throw turkey salad at her.

"Ivy Lee's program should be called Griselda, like my dog! What if the wife needs something that her husband doesn't think of himself? Or worse, doesn't want himself?"

Megan watched Hallie, then Bonnie, as if thinking were a spectator sport.

"If you're sweet and pleasing and patient," Bonnie said, "you'd be surprised. I get lots more than flowers. When I used to aggravate him, make demands, nag about his jobs and his drinking— I got nothing but grief."

Megan made a choking sound, or a sob.

"You okay?" Hallie asked.

She nodded and sipped water. "Something went down wrong," she said, but she still looked troubled.

"Now," Bonnie continued, "I keep Tommy's house as perfect as I can, and I pamper him. When he comes home, I'm dressed

in my best and his favorite food's ready. I start dinner after breakfast so there's no way I won't be ready for him, and I wouldn't
dream of leaving him here alone at night, or of going to work and
pretending I'm just like him."

"Does he go out without you?" Hallie demanded.

"If he wants. I'm not saying it's easy; I'm saying it works."

"So did slavery!"

Bonnie's eyes narrowed. "Hold on a second." She pushed back
her chair, got up, opened the door that led to the rec room downstairs, and was gone. Hallie heard the slide and then the slam of
a drawer, and then Bonnie was back. "I knew I still had it," she
said. "Now listen to this—this is from the *Ladies Home Journal*.
You don't think they're weird, do you?" She looked as smug as
when she'd quoted from the Bible.

" 'Dr. Theodore Rubin on What Makes a Woman Lovable.' "
Bonnie cleared her throat and squinted. " 'A woman will consider
her man the most important person in her life. She will value
him above all other people—including herself.' "

Megan picked up the article and studied it.

"As if men," Hallie said, "by virtue of their sex, are pure good,
pure wisdom, and we're mindless. What about selfish men? Vi-
cious men? Murderers?"

Megan looked up from the article and once again seemed to be
waiting for the secret password.

"What about plain ordinary fallible men?" Hallie rhetorically
asked of the wide-eyed juror. "What about rotten men who hurt
women—what about those wives?"

Megan's eyes shifted to Bonnie, waiting for a rebuttal.

"Their wives should search their hearts to find out why they
drive their men to meanness," Bonnie said serenely. "Why their
men have so much anger. What makes them feel they have to
teach their wives lessons the hard way."

"For God's sake!"

"Exactly," Bonnie said softly. "For God's sake."

"It's a setup! No matter what happens, it's the woman's fault."

"Women create the atmosphere. If you can't follow God's will
and understand that a woman should be ruled by her husband,
you shouldn't marry. Speaking personally, ever since I've been

on the Completely Female program, even my, ah, intimate life has improved one hundred percent. My carrying on turned him off. I don't want equality—I want to be loved."

"Equality is not a dirty word!" Hallie felt heat stain her cheeks. Bonnie made her strident, a caricature of the women's movement, the screaming man-hater. Which she was not, no matter what Ted sometimes said.

So Bonnie's sex life had improved and Hallie's had become a tricky battleground where the day's struggles too often echoed through the night. That didn't invalidate the truth. Everybody wanted to be loved, but for herself, not some subservient slave-self.

"I'd love to read more about the Completely Female plan," Megan said.

"Are you serious?" Megan used to be smart, funny, and now she was a sparrow creature, pecking her sister's stale crumbs.

"No offense, Hallie," Megan said softly, "but Bonnie is the only woman I know who is really, truly, happy."

"I'm happy, too!" If the pebbled blue glass had been crystal, it would have shattered. Hallie's cheeks felt on fire as a harpy voice coming out of her throat screeched that she was blissful while tears of frustration pricked her eyes. "I am *so* happy! *Extremely* happy! *Incredibly happy!*"

Then she was finally loud enough to hear what a fool she had become, what a pathetic argument for happiness. "But not serene, I admit," she added. She giggled, couldn't stop herself, and Megan and Bonnie, after a moment of shock, caught the bug as well and they were able, once they calmed down, to have Harvest Apple Cake and converse about recipes, decorating, and diets. To pretend that nothing serious had happened, that they were all three definitely, thoroughly, completely, female.

Tests and Transitions

1973

Marriage.
The beginning and the end are wonderful.
But the middle part is hell.
Enid Bagnold

1

TED peered through the wet windshield. The conference center, Victorian turrets pressing the night, looked more like a horror movie set than a place where contenders for upper management battled it out.

The official word was that all attendees were exceptional and everyone could pass. But year after year, fifty percent of the men who came to Tarkington Retreat were tapped for senior management and fifty percent were knocked out of the running. Ted hauled his suitcase out of the backseat and apologized to his sleek little car for leaving it unprotected in a storm. The I-don't-do-toilet-training buggy, Hallie called it, after he'd confessed. They'd actually laughed about it, which delighted him almost as much as the car itself. He walked across the gravel lot, up the wide wooden steps, and into an entry paneled in carved and scrolled dark wood. "Relax," he told himself again.

Every fifteen minutes of the five-hour drive to this backwater, he had advised himself to relax. Only games, he'd say.

The problem was, he knew he was lying. It wasn't a game. It was a forty-eight-hour test determining his entire future.

He resented G.T.U. for insisting on his formalized assessment, even if they said that here, the bright hope of Detroit, the hotshot from Pittsburgh, and the star of Atlanta could be more fairly judged than in their home offices. Tarkington found the common denominator, weeded out favorite sons and weaklings.

"Hello. Theodore Bennett, isn't it?"

Ted wasn't wearing I.D. and had never seen the man before. Obviously, the man had studied up on him. *Relax!* He shook the man's hand, read his badge. "Mr. Halliday," he said.

"Bill. No formality, please."

"No formality Bill" wore a perfectly tailored blue blazer, red tie, and gray flannel slacks. His face and hair looked incapable of informality.

"And I'm . . ." Jerk! Halliday knew his name. Probably knew he stole baseball bubble gum from the five-and-ten in fourth grade. They walked past a large room with a wall-length stone fireplace. There were about a dozen other blue-blazered executives and about as many hopefuls. It was easy to tell the varieties apart by the sheen of nervous perspiration on the latter.

"Friday night's loose," Bill said. "Nothing starts till tomorrow. Tonight, settle in, then join us for cocktails."

He was shown to a small, spare room with twin beds, utilitarian dresser, and a flat, fake Oriental. No phone. A cell in which to contemplate my failings, he thought.

An information packet lay on the dresser. He clipped on the name tag and scanned the list of assessors. William Halliday, V.P., Director of Home Appliance Sales, Midwestern Division, was the fifth name down. Another page listed candidates. There were twenty Hallidays observing eighteen Teds.

He felt the fly-buzz of anxiety again. He was a bug under the microscope, an attraction at a rarefied zoo. What precisely would they observe? What exactly did they want?

The impossible, he assumed. Someone aggressive but cooperative. Dynamic but compassionate. A leader but a team player.

An authentic individual but a company man. Your basic contradiction in terms.

Downstairs, Ted nursed a Scotch as he checked the competition. His assessors tried for clubby sociability, as if they had flocked to the leather and oak room for a good time. "Be yourself," they said. Sure.

He didn't believe that scrutiny didn't begin until dawn. Specimens were specimens, eyes were eyes. He drank little and conversed carefully, commenting favorably on the roast beef although he had no appetite, rehashing the Dolphins' Super Bowl victory and the Frazier-Forman bout, raving about Brando in Coppola's new movie, and talking cars after somebody complimented his XKE.

He was glad that he and Hallie had decided against phone calls until it was over because he wouldn't have liked to explain—even, perhaps, to acknowledge—the way he was calculating every breath. Or to admit that nobody once mentioned the two topics that consumed most people they knew—the end of both the Vietnam war and abortion bans. This place was its own world.

By bedtime, Ted was wired tight with tension, a punch-drunk fighter dancing around the ring. He was positive he would never sleep again, terrified he would spend the next two days exhausted, mortifying himself.

He wished he had packed a joint, some of the dope Vicky sent now and then along with her incredibly good bread. But for all he knew, his luggage had been checked while he was eating, so legal insomnia was the safer option.

Dry-eyed and hyperalert, he had a moment of undiluted loathing for who he was becoming—and for how eagerly he put on the mask.

"Gentlemen, for the next hour you are cabinet ministers of the imaginary country of Stornia, determining your budget. Your packet contains information about geography, economics, and population. The country has $100,000,000 to spend. Unfortunately, your separate budget requests total $350,000,000, so compromises are necessary."

Six men sat at Ted's table surrounded by six assessors.

Ted studied his packet and clenched his jaw. His stinking luck to be assigned Minister of Tourism. *Tourism!* How the hell could it compete with defense, or transportation, or social welfare, let alone education and the interior?

This was the third exercise of the day, and he would never call them games again. The thing was to keep in mind what they were testing. Obviously, this one demanded cooperation. To a point. If you were too amenable, you'd wind up a loser with no budget. The real game was to look cooperative while you convinced the other players that your needs were theirs as well. But everybody was hungry for personal victory, so who would give his share to Tourism and commit hara-kiri?

"There are," the assessor said, "two other tables with the same problem. The first of you to solve your budget wins, and there's no second place. Begin."

"I'm sure we agree that Defense is a nonnegotiable imperative." The patrician voice sat on Ted's right.

Defense pushing into first place. Instant leadership. Damn. Nicholas Talbot's face, slouch, and accent proclaimed that he was the end product of expensive genetic strains and schools. But an asshole, because nobody sane tells a group of sharks that his supremacy is a given, that he gets to gobble their fish.

"I don' know." The voice was slow and Southern, and Ted reminded himself that speed and accent did not correlate with I.Q. "From what I see, Stornia has itself a transportation problem, an' if we can't get ever'day traffic movin', how we movin' tanks and men? Got us some heavy terrain here. Hell, those mountain villages are closed off half the year. Poor kids can't get to school, let alone fight a war if we have one. Don' be short-sighted and doom our future ignorin' somethin' basic as roads." Russ Walsh shook his head sorrowfully, completely into his role. "Transportation's requests are rock-bottom minimum and urgent," he said. "An' I mean to announce we aren't givin' an inch, gentlemen."

They had established a pattern of moving to the right. Ted would be last. Around they went, with a rousing plea for education from Perry Middleton. "Gentlemen," he said in a flat Midwestern twang, "Stornia's illiteracy rate is the highest outside

Afghanistan. Who will man our tanks or drive our trains if nobody can read instructions? This is our number-one priority."

A mortified Minister of Social Welfare mumbled about poverty and joblessness. A citizens corps or training program had to be funded immediately, he said with no conviction. Portrait of a right-winger prostituting himself, preaching the enemy's social welfare gospel for personal gain. Ted would have to remember this for Hallie.

The Department of the Interior was more eloquent. He spoke of natural resources, of areas needing preservation and protection from outside exploitation. Ted's mind whirled, sorting the ministers' requests, the grand tally, and monitoring the gruff buzz of the other teams, gauging their level of accord or dissent, weighing their speed and progress.

The Minister of the Interior stopped. Ted's turn. "Gentlemen, as needy and deserving as each department is, we are not going to be able to fully accomplish our separate goals this particular fiscal year." He waited for somebody to ask who'd anointed him He Who Sees the Whole Picture.

Nobody asked. He continued. "I suggest combining into an interdepartmental cooperative, investing in our national future. Gentlemen, Stornia's tomorrow lies in . . . skimobiles."

"*Skimobiles!*" Nick Talbot's jaw dangled. Russ looked as if he might burst out laughing, and Social Welfare actually did.

"Think," Ted said. "We're landlocked with no coastline to exploit during our brief summer. No art or culture to pull them in. Our cuisine is . . . you know. But we have mountains. We could have resorts. Bring in tourists, bring in revenues, and train our people to man those lines and lifts and lodges. Jobs, gentlemen. We invest in skimobiles, which take the little children of the mountain back and forth to school all winter long. Skimobiles don't need roads, so think of the saving! During school hours, the skimobiles are rented by the tourists. We train paramedics to ride them so that the villages finally have adequate care."

"So all our transpor—"

"No, no. We build a better airport as part of the plan. Ours can't accommodate the modern world. We put heliports at the resorts."

"Next you'll say skimobiles are better war machines than

tanks." Talbot's sneer was less assured. He'd assumed some good-fellow rule obliged them to complete the circle, come back to him before beginning an internal debate. Now he'd lost the reins and he was infuriated. "Or perhaps you believe skimobiles can outrace an H-bomb?"

Ted chuckled. Hail fellow well met and up yours, buster. "But skimobiles could transport troops quickly in an emergency. Carry supplies through our notorious terrain." Stornia's geography, as per their packets, wasn't as impossibly rugged as he was presenting it, but nobody challenged him. "Our enemies have to come over these mountains. If they're large and clumsy and we are swift and mobile, won't we have an edge? And for the tallest peaks, I suggest that our helicopters plus small planes fly our visitors directly to their mountaintop retreats—and, of course, to be on hand for emergencies. If we prosper sufficiently, perhaps somebody will actually want to invade us. At the moment, what are we defending?"

He couldn't get over himself. He should have been a politician. He *loved* this bullshit.

"I don't get it," Education said. "You seriously want us to spend the national budget on ski resorts?"

Ted nodded. "Stornia could be the next Switzerland."

"Our mountains are lower and uglier," Talbot said. "Our weather is less predictable. Our snowfall is erratic and there already is a Switzerland, so we don't need a next one."

Ted shook his head. "Negative thinking isn't a solution."

"But what about education?" Perry Middleton sounded honestly concerned for the imaginary children of Stornia. "I see how the kids can get to school more easily, but we have so little money, there aren't buildings for—"

"Important point. A set percentage of the tourist tax goes directly to the schools." In his next life, he'd definitely be a benevolent dictator.

"You're right that the one thing we have is mountains. But your plan will destroy them." Shit. The Minister of the Interior was taking his mandate too seriously.

"We'll . . . we'll set aside sanctuaries. Eden recovered, a model for mankind. Starting with nothing but very tall rocks," Ted said, "we'll be an example to the world, building ideal environments, protecting and preserving the God-given ones."

He let his eyes slide sideways so that it was obvious he was listening to the other tables. The noise level was high, negotiations in full force elsewhere. He looked back at his table-mates, every one an instinctive competitor. "I suggest we form the Greater Stornia Development Association," Ted said.

"Wait a minute! We need a unanimous decision, remember?" Talbot's face was mottled.

"Sorry. Do you have an alternate plan?"

"We should talk it through."

Ted smiled as he glanced at his watch, then scouted the room again. "Anybody?" He waited before leaning forward. "This plan's not perfect, but it can work. We're a team and everybody wins this way."

"Only *some* people win a little more than other people, don't they?" The money spent on Talbot's breeding and manners had been a poor investment.

"Ah make a motion we pool resources." Russ spoke as swiftly as his Southern slur allowed, ending the impasse. Ted was relieved and grateful. The only other solution seemed punching out Talbot's lights, which probably would lower Ted's score. "We develop resorts," Russ said, "and sanctuaries—buy skimobiles and helicopters and form the Greater Slobovia—"

"*Stornia!*"

"I second the motion."

"All in favor?" And all were. Ted turned, his favorite, happiest song in his ears. I won, I won, I won. "We win," Ted told the assessor behind him.

Russ pushed back his chair. "Not so much we won as they lost."

"It's the same thing."

"You're real smart, but you've got some things to learn, maybe." And then Russ smiled his good-old-boy grin, so don't-take-me-seriously that Ted wasn't sure whether it, or his words, were the thing to consider.

"The idea is, you're subbing in this office, called in on an emergency. You flew in on a red-eye, and this is your in-box. Prioritize the items."

Yesterday, he'd actually gotten a major charge out of "winning" the budget of Stornia. Nothing could elate him today except leaving. Thank God this was the end. He couldn't take much more claustrophobic scrutiny.

Be yourself, they said, but his self wanted to turn off his brain, watch TV, drink beer, and belch. His self wanted to curl up with a soft, warm woman. His self wanted anything but another interrogation.

This one seemed easy. No teammates, no negotiation or show of wills. Just an in-basket full of crap.

He flipped through a message from their biggest client that a shipment of radios hadn't arrived for the Presidents' Day Sale. Newsclipping—a gossip column with a highlighted item saying, "A mega electronics company's sexy Christmas party should result in a major lawsuit." A confidential memo about a warehouse with an exceptionally high loss rate; a list of employees who might be involved; some time requested by a man with ideas about the new area of computer games; a reminder of an urgent meeting with the employees union; a phone message from his wife, saying their son was ill—they thought of everything, didn't they? A note from his secretary saying she'd heard that his top project manager was being seriously courted by a competitor.

There was notice that the revised Standards and Practices manual was ready to check, news that the corporate art consultant had three possible paintings for his office, a reminder that he had not yet finished his employee evaluations, and the message "Call. Urgent," nothing else, from the manager of the Central Plains Division.

It was hard to think, irrelevancies bouncing through his brain like Ping-Pong balls. Will this end? Concentrate. How do I sort these? Art consultant last. Good. One thing done. Easy.

Missing shipment, big client—first.

What could this Christmas party business be? What could anybody do these days that would prompt an eye-blink, let alone a lawsuit? Had to find out more. Put it . . . midway.

Hallie after that. Don't want the assessor to think I'm tied to her apron strings. Anybody still wear aprons with strings? Aprons?

Warehouse disappearances—second? So far we're losing clients and materials, but, if this inventory failure had been going on for a long time, then . . .

Computer games. That fellow in California who invented Pong made Ted feel the fool. Every MIT grad who played their Space Wars game a dozen years ago should have thought of it. The guy was going to be a zillionaire. So. Concentrate. Is it too late to jump on the band-wagon? Schedule it. Trust your gut. Make it third. Second?

And who's next? The defecting manager or the union rep? Who designed this, Karl Marx?

He pushed and slotted and rearranged until he'd made as much sense as he could. He handed it over to the assessor and rolled his head back on his neck. The weekend from hell was over.

The assessor pulled a thick loose-leaf book up from under the desk and opened it, running his fingers down its tabs until he found the one he was looking for. "I see you made the threat of a lawsuit—a rather nasty, public one that is capable of doing great harm to our image as a family-oriented consumer-goods firm—number five. Why?" He read the question word for word, from the book.

Goddamn. He'd thought it was over. And why indeed had he put the party there? Who cared? Say anything. "Because, ah, the newspaper can't retract until tomorrow morning, so I thought I'd put out the raging, immediate fires first. And meantime, have our counsel advise me so I'd be informed when I got to that issue."

Did that make sense? Look at those tabs—there must be a hundred. No matter how he'd answer, no matter which item got priority, the tabs had questions to ask about that choice at that position. There'd have been a question if he'd placed the party last. Or first. Or anywhere.

"And you feel the missing shipment is top priority?"

"Well, sir, we're in danger of losing our largest account if we screw them during a Presidents' Day Sale. Without customers, the rest of the agenda is pretty irrelevant, don't you think?"

The assessor didn't think. Didn't smile, didn't frown, didn't yawn, didn't raise eyebrows. Instead, he wondered why union problems were being given short shrift. It was possible that the assessor was a robot.

"Do you honestly consider computer games more urgent than your own family?" he asked next. "I notice you aren't returning your wife's call—and your child is ill, Bennett. Why is that?"

133

And if he had put her first, would the book have asked, "How long have you been pussy-whipped, Bennett?"

"That's a two-part question," Ted said. "First, the issue of computer games, which I do think is an extremely important area for our industry. Atari—a Japanese name, but it's American, you know—is selling Pong way beyond expectations for twelve hundred dollars a clip. My kids are crazy for it—there's one at the pizza place near home. I definitely think G.T.U. should consider the area if we're going to stay a leader in electronic entertainment."

He felt like a suspect in a lineup. This wasn't about priorities, it was about being able to defend them, think on your feet. He couldn't. He couldn't remember anything anymore and he hoped the robot didn't ask him his name.

"And the second part of that question?"

"Excuse me?"

"Your wife."

What about her? Oh. Why hadn't he called her sooner? Because his kid's ailment was imaginary? As was the message? And this whole stupid-ass game? G.T.U. was family-oriented, so had he screwed up? Was Hallie really low priority, the way she said?

"My wife." Hallie the hypothetical test problem seemed as unfathomable as she too often did in the flesh.

"Yes, Bennett, your wife. And your sick child."

"My wife called from home, fifteen hundred miles away. She knows it, I know it. Whatever has happened with my child, I cannot help him from this distance. But she is an exceptionally competent woman and I know she's already taken every necessary step." What else? What else? The guy didn't look impressed.

He could hear the exceptionally competent woman's voice. "Want to turn a man off?" she'd said. "Use the word *emotionally*. Want him to approve? Use the word *realistic*. *You* know, the male view of the world is *realistic*, but women, poor dears, operate emotionally." What a quarrel they'd had about that. But maybe she was right.

"Um . . . if I followed my *emotions*, my *impulses*," he said, "I'd call my wife first, but we can't *realistically* run a business on *feelings*, can we?"

And damned if the assessor didn't look less dead. Almost sympathetic. Ted hammered it home. *"Realistically,* there are problems I can work with and others I cannot alleviate long-distance, like my son's illness. If my wife needed vital information, she would have said so. So I know, from the message, there's no emergency and I should call when it's possible."

The assessor raised an eyebrow. "Good job, Bennett. And here's the best news—it's over. Nothing left to do but eat, drink, relax, and leave." He shook Ted's hand.

Free at last, Ted thought, when he was outside the door. Free at last—Great God almighty . . . that speech, that weekend when Megan and Daniel visited. Griselda, a great fuzzy pup. They'd all seemed so on the verge. Unknowns beckoning, high excitement.

No babies born yet, nobody assassinated, and the war not an issue. Tidal waves of changes ever since and only now, finally, he was truly on the verge. Maybe.

The paneled hall smelled of a crackling fire and dinner preparations. He felt hungry for the first time in forty-eight hours.

"So we are finally done." It was Russ, the good ol' boy with the grin. "I have been tastin' that bourbon all day long," he said. "My cranium has never, ever, been this tired. Let me buy the first round in honor of the heroes of Slobovia." He exhaled mightily and headed for the loud and crowded bar.

"Cheers." Russ handed over a glass. "Figured Yankees drink Scotch."

"Figured right. Cheers."

Russ drank his greedily, nonstop, then sighed. "Just as good as I thought it'd be," he said.

"I wonder how much gets downed per minute at the end of these marathons," Ted said. "I'll bet—"

"What?" Russ asked. "How's that?"

His body flashed with heat and his armpits sweat. *It isn't over till it's over.*

The dry and sober assessors were still watching. And he'd nearly bought it.

This was the last game. The slaughterhouse and the sheep. Flunk by believing. Drink too much, say stupid things, and die.

He almost warned Russ because the guy was nice and all, but

they were competitors and the contest wasn't over. Survival of the fittest never was. He bought the next round but barely touched his, and he watched with an unhealthy interest as all around him too much was downed too quickly. He felt like a spy, like a traitor.

Halfway through dinner, after multiple screwdrivers, Talbot the uppercrust asshole forgot he was talking to Mark Bernstein, one of the only Jews who'd made it to senior management. Talbot's ancestors had forgotten to breed for brains. "Damn civil rights crap," he whined. "Nowadays, anybody white can be a guest at the club. Of course," he added with a boozy reassurance, "there are still standards about who can belong, for which we are grateful."

"Is that so?" Bernstein said mildly.

Talbot would never know what axed him.

Be yourself, they said, and the asshole believed them, so maybe there was justice in these fool games.

Only thing was, Ted wasn't sure if he, too, had been himself. And if so, which self was that, and why did it feel so foreign and uncomfortable?

2

Her station wagon idled as Hallie stood at the mailbox, mittened hands clumsily sorting magazines, circulars, catalogs, letters to "Occupant."

Finally, shivering, she saw a long white envelope with a scarlet emblem. For better or worse, a piece of her future was in her hands.

She returned to the car. Inside, she pulled off her mittens and sat clutching the white rectangle. It seemed thicker than was warranted for a rejection letter. She squelched the thought. No point speculating.

She reminded herself that there were other schools, that applying to this one had been a wild, throwaway gesture. She would not be crushed by whatever was inside.

She opened the envelope with her eyes closed. Finally she

looked. And read. And then she read again, her head light to the point of faintness.

Accepted to Harvard Law School. She covered her mouth, uncovered it, and laughed out loud. She closed her eyes, reopened them, squinted, reread, and yes, they still accepted her.

Dazed, she put the letter in her purse and the car into gear and, grinning like a fool, pulled into the garage.

The house was bedlam, as usual. In the family room, the TV made Saturday noise. In the kitchen, Ted showed Andy how to play the banjo while the radio blared behind them. Andy strummed. "I don't know why they call it a fly," he sang, "it's a pip of a zip, so why . . . do they call it a fly?"

"Your own composition?" Hallie unpacked oranges and bananas.

"Why do they call zippers flies?" Ted asked. With great dramatic gestures, so she'd notice what a liberated male he was, he put the Cheerios in the pantry.

Andy wandered off, strumming like a minstrel. The radio droned news. The first POWs were coming home. Judge Sirica had revived the Watergate inquiry. Six killed in Belfast. "Could we turn that off?" she said. *She* had news.

Ted looked surprised, but complied.

"There's something I've been . . ." A stupid way to put it. "You know how I've always talked about being a lawyer?"

He flipped through the mail, nodding acknowledgment.

"And with Sarah in kindergarten this fall . . ."

A more impatient nod. "It's twelve years since I first wanted to go."

"Uh-huh." Absolutely no interest.

"Something bothering you, Ted?"

"I'm fine."

"You sure? You seem distracted."

He tossed down the mail. "My mother called. She's not well. He's not well. She got to me."

Hallie clenched her fists. His mother always got to him. That was her talent and vocation.

"I said see a specialist, but she'd rather complain."

Surely he'd remember his wife had been in mid-story.

"I said I'd pay for the doctor. She told me how little money my father made and that they can't come here for Passover, so they invited us to Johnstown instead."

He knew they couldn't go, even if anybody wanted to. Sylvia and Ivan were driving up. His dreadful mother knew that, too. Knew the only way Hallie could keep the peace on holidays, secular or religious, was to visit neither set of parents, but have everybody at her home, which pretty much ruined every such event for her.

"Oh, what the hell." Ted checked the mail again. Hallie waited. Ted finally looked up. "You were saying something?"

Hallie opened her pocketbook. Forget verbal foreplay or dramatic buildup. She passed him the letter, then stood with hands pressed against her heart.

"Harvard Law." He looked at her, then back at the letter. "Accepted to Harvard Law."

He had read the same words she had. It was for real. She could no longer be sedate. She pirouetted and bowed. "Two Bennett Harvard graduates. A matched pair." She couldn't find nearly the right words. Overwhelmed with pride, relief, and some terror at the challenge ahead, she made incomprehensible wheeps and skipped around the room.

"She flip out?" At ten, Erica was long legged and constantly, vaguely, hungry.

"Mom just got very good—"

"Great, not just very good!" Hallie grabbed Erica and whirled her around. "How'd you like a mom who's a lawyer?"

Erica pulled free and opened the refrigerator. "I like you as my mom."

"It'd still be me—but I'd be a lawyer. How'd that be?"

"I don't know." She closed the refrigerator. "There's no jelly."

Hallie counted to ten and rooted through her grocery bags until she found a jar and handed it over. "I was accepted by Harvard Law School." Her words resounded off the birch cabinets, the ivy-patterned wallpaper, the Harvest Gold refrigerator.

"Why'd you buy strawberry?" Erica said. "You know I hate it."

"Mom's done something special," Ted said. "Could you congratulate her?"

Hallie sat at the center island and lit a cigarette, trying to remember if Ted had congratulated her.

"Smoking's bad," Erica said.

Hallie nodded.

"I said your mother has done something very special."

"Congratulations," Erica snapped. "Even though I wish people told me what things mean before they got angry at me for not saying the right things back."

"Can I sleep at Jared's? He's not contagious anymore, and anyway, I had it." Jared, crusty with chicken-pox scabs, entered with Andy.

"Mom's gotten Harvalah," Erica said.

"You're sick?" Andy sounded concerned.

"It's not a disease. It's Harvard. Law. School." Hallie took a deep breath. "Where I'll learn to be a lawyer."

"Oh yeah? So, can I sleep at Jared's or what?"

"Say congratulations," Erica said "Or they'll holler."

"Congratulations about what?"

"Harvalah!"

"How'm I supposed to know?"

Hallie didn't require marching bands or Presidential proclamations, but did every emotion have to be snipped and tucked and re-tailored to accommodate everybody's egos—except hers?

"Getting accepted to Harvard only happens to a few people in the whole world and Mom's one of them. Congratulations are definitely due."

"Congratulations, Mrs. Bennett," Jared said.

"Thanks. Andy, you can sleep over. Erica, use honey. Now— is Sarah waiting in the wings with a complaint?"

"She's out." Erica opened a cabinet in search of honey.

Hallie put away groceries until the kitchen emptied of children.

Ted rolled down the sleeves of his plaid flannel shirt, buttoned the cuff, looked at his wrist, and rolled his shirtsleeves back up again. "Getting accepted is quite an honor," he said.

She sat down across from him, still clutching a mustard jar. "But?" There was definitely a kicker.

"But what were you thinking of when you applied?" He had a way of realigning the muscles of his face so that his handsomeness became menacing.

"About going to law school."

"Why were you sneaky about it?"

She caught herself twirling her wedding band, a new habit. Ted had suggested she was testing how quickly she could whip it off in an emergency. "I needed to protect myself. From embarrassment. I'd talked about it for so long that I was terrified to put up or shut up. If it hadn't worked out, I'd have told you, of course—but after I felt okay about it. This way, it was almost not really happening. I felt more in control. Can you understand?"

He pushed his chair back, topaz eyes narrow and chin set in concrete. "All the same, you *knew* I was trying to get into Tarkington. You knew I was trying for the assessment program."

"Yes?" Above her ears, knives cut through the shell of her skull into the soft center of her brain.

"Yes, what? Did you take it for granted that I'd flunk?"

"Of course not. I'm sure you passed." Almost two months after the Tarkington weekend, the results still hadn't been announced and Ted was worn wire-thin with the waiting, although he denied it.

"Then what was the point of applying to law schools?"

"I had to decide a long time ago." Life with Ted Bennett meant there were always factors pending, decisions looming. Last autumn there'd been the unresolved issue of whether he should push for senior management. And then, whether he'd get into the next Tarkington assessment group, now whether he'd passed, and soon whether he'd like the job they offered him. Endless Ted-orchestrated breath holding.

Times like this she saw, with painful clarity, that Ted was capable of forgetting her. She feared that when they weren't touching, weren't pouring into each other's bodies, she dissolved into a concept, words to fill in a form under "Spouse." He knew her Social Security number and mother's maiden name, but didn't know to ask about her dreams or frustrations. *"Harvard!"* The word grated over her building rage. "Aren't you happy for me?"

"What if we have to move? You know we discussed that."

Discussed was not the precise word. She had been informed that the possibility existed. But weighing against possibility was reality—applications to make, tests to take. Her own life to live.

A dozen years ago she'd put this on hold. How much longer did a good wife defer because her good husband wanted something else? They were right, her women. The personal was political and it was all about power and she had none of the kind that mattered. "I want to go," she said quietly.

"And I want you to. But what if you can't? I'm not a Neanderthal. I'm not upset by the idea of your success, only by your timing."

Damn him! She'd gotten into *Harvard*, and all he thought about was what it meant to his career! She enunciated carefully. "Isn't it true that since headquarters are here, relocation is only one possibility?"

He nodded.

"Then, *when* you find out you've passed, *if* they request a transfer, say you'll do it—in three years."

His face went slack. "You're kidding."

The knives minced her brain. There was no way to explain herself. He'd say he understood. He'd *think* he understood. But he had no idea.

Her expression must have given him a glimmering. "You're right," he said. "The future's theoretical; the present's real. Why worry? Let's celebrate my wife the Harvard student."

They'd file the real issues under the rug.

"Tell you what," Ted said. "Sit and savor your triumph. I'll call the sitter."

She smiled feebly. He'd call the sitter for the first time in recorded history. Wow. True equality.

When is it my turn? The voice was cold and familiar. *When, when, when is it really and truly my turn?*

Ted came over, bent down, and kissed her. But as close as he was and as ear-splitting the din inside her, she knew he didn't hear even a whisper of it.

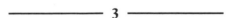

3

Hallie looked out her window on a scene so beatific, it had to be artificial. Celestial arm-twisting. God's way of insisting she be ecstatic about this move.

The plane glided beside a cloudbank. Pristine poufs floated in an intensely blue sky. Ted had undoubtedly arranged this with the Lord.

Her husband was all exclamation points lately. They were going to be so happy! Hallie would love their gorgeous new home! The Golden State! Sunshine! Lemon trees! The Pacific! He was personally proud of California, embarrassingly jubilant, wired with the double thrill of validation and challenge, indistinguishable from those smiley-faced HAVE A NICE DAY buttons that were suddenly everywhere.

Off to the good life! he repeatedly said. Except she thought they already had it, so what were they so desperately pursuing?

She'd always been attracted by Ted's abundant confidence. His overflow buoyed her except recently, when it drowned her. At the thought of him, her muscles contracted, defining her limits.

Except. Last night, after packing for this unwanted trip, after falling asleep angry and depressed as far as possible from the man, she'd had a wordless, imageless nightmare, weights sealing her lungs. Death, and she couldn't even gasp a call for help.

And then Ted's hands rubbed her back. He cradled her, spooned around her, shushed and assured her that all was well, until it was. Half asleep himself, he'd instinctively saved her.

Things that fragile shaped her life, shored its wobbles. The unstable edifice stood, but now they were moving it onto a fault line.

Silicon Valley. Eden, according to Ted. A crater on the moon, according to Chloe Wister. "Sounds crackly and gray," she'd said. "Uninhabitable."

Hallie had wanted her weekend in New York to be a sophisticated and bittersweet send-off, but instead it was filled with dissension. Chloe had no interest in Teddy's being the number-one assessment candidate or his plum assignment heading the brand-new personal computer division.

"Do not go." Chloe had a small, running part in a soap opera, and a steady income made her more opinionated than ever. "Harvard, for God's sake. Have what you deserve and want."

"I want my marriage, too."

"Why on earth? You've had your children. This is patriarchal whither thou goest mind-fucking crap."

"But—"

"The system stinks," Chloe said.

"I know."

"But?"

"I like him."

"Now? Still?"

"Mostly."

Chloe put down her fork. "Then commute. He can live out there and you can live here and go to school."

Hallie shook her head. "That's trendier than I am, and it doesn't sound like marriage to me. And what about the kids?"

Chloe was vastly annoyed.

There were three women lunching at the table next to theirs, fifteen to twenty years older, in their late forties or early fifties, and elegantly maintained. They weren't debating the social order or trying to upend it. They didn't consider themselves political prisoners, but privileged, pampered, adored, and lucky women.

She should have been born sooner or later. Her daughters would know what to do. Her mother had always known. But Hallie's generation was a practical joke. The clown who amuses the audience between acts. 'Tweeners, somebody called them, the last traditional generation now hanging in space, the rug pulled out from under them, suspended between history and the radically altered future. She was the calm, dead center of the storm. Nowhere.

The memory of that lunch full of unresolved issues was displaced by a sudden awareness that the man in the seat next to hers was leaning close. "You don't see a show like that too often," he said. "Mostly, you go into the clouds and don't see anything except gray."

"It looks fake," she said. A Disney vision of heaven.

"It is. Part of California's never-ending PR campaign. You live here?"

She shook her head. Not yet. "Do you?"

"In L.A. But my children live in Santa Cruz with their mother, so I spend as much time as possible up here."

The new circumlocutions depressed her. "My children's mother, my son's father," surgically unmade prior fusing. She preferred the good old days when the woman who had mothered a man's child was known as "my wife." She liked the words *us* and *we*. They live with us. We have three . . . "Sounds complicated."

"You must be part of an intact family."

Another new hairsplit. Intact. You could hear the unspoken "still." As if marriages were prehistoric fossils and an unshattered one was an astounding find.

"Thirteen years."

"Amazing. First, second, or what?"

"First."

He shook his head. "What's your secret?"

"Who knows?" What was his? He seemed like a nice fellow, with his deeply creased face and easy smile and attachment to his kids. What had gone wrong? Had he been transferred to L.A. and had the friends of the mother of his children told her she was a wimp, a sell-out, an unliberated failure if she sacrificed her dream for his, and had she listened?

The man leaned in front of her to get a better view of the panorama, and she inhaled a citrus after-shave. And then, within seconds, their altitude changed and the brilliant cloud show dimmed. He settled back in place. "Out on business, then?"

That question, to a woman, was pretty new, too. "We're moving to Los Gatos in three weeks." The name sounded as silly as Silicon Valley.

"Did they send you ahead as a scout?"

"The house needs minor tending." Expert on the insignificant. Here's my card. "Leaky faucets, bad grouting, telephone installation, the great pediatrician search." Advance wifing. I was supposed to enter Harvard Law in September, she wanted to say. I coulda been a contender.

"Los Gatos isn't far from Santa Cruz," he said, "and unless you have an unusual repairman, he won't work at night. I'd be happy to show you the area. There's a restaurant with an ocean view in Half Moon Bay." He had an inviting half-smile on his lips.

Through the sudden flush in her head and the beat of an accelerated pulse, she tried to determine what, conditioning aside, she actually felt.

Flattered, she decided. She should be annoyed at being a sex object, a stranger's playmate, a one-night stand, but she wasn't. Frightened. Life was complex enough without geometrically increasing its convolutions. Tempted. Nothing would matter or last, and nobody would know. Maybe they'd never tell each other their names. And Half Moon Bay . . . she had an unmet craving for such sounds. And for knowledge. She had known only one man, and that had become embarrassing, like being illiterate.

Disappointed. Very. The rules were so bent, he could praise her rare intact marriage and yet assume it included hanky-panky.

Of course, the old saw held that marriage vows didn't cross state lines. But there again she was out of step. She believed in boundaries, geographical and otherwise. My beloved and no other.

She looked down, considering, and saw her hands, a wedding band on the left, and on the right, a blue and orange Fred Flintstone ring, a gift from Andy. Not the hands of a fling-haver.

"Thanks. I can't. My sister's in Sonoma. She's—we're spending the evening."

He grinned. "Monogamous, aren't you? Married with a capital 'M'?"

"Terminally so." She tried for a wry smile, while her hands were at work, twisting her wedding band.

The plane touched down.

"You're refreshing," he said. "Unique." He smiled winningly, and she was afraid he was an experience she should have investigated, information she should have gathered. He unbuckled his seat belt, stood, and retrieved a raincoat and briefcase from overhead storage. "I'm glad we met," he said. "You've got me believing again."

She wondered what it was he now believed in—marriage, fidelity, or home repairs?

4

"It's not easy generating sympathy for you," Vicky had said. "Forced to live the easy life with a successful, happy husband and three healthy kids."

They'd been dangling toes in the black-bottomed pool cleaned by a boy who hummed to himself the entire time. He, the floor-sander, the electrician, and the grout man had all been California stereotypes, sun-bleached and muscled. She wondered where they hid the pale, flabby folk, and whether her body might, if untended, break a local ordinance.

"This is progress," Vicky said. "Our grandparents lived above their store, we live above our means."

"It scares me. How do I not become this kind of person? I mean for real?"

"Oh, hell. Take a stand. Live up at my farm and bake bread. We're short on help. Low pay, bad hours. Crumbling house. You'd be underprivileged and guilt-free for once." She ran her hand through the clean water. "You know, Wyatt Earp isn't the law here anymore. You're a stone's throw from Stanford and a couple of stones from Cal. Lose a year, gain a tan, and still get to change the world. And may you do better at it than the rest of us did."

The conversation still reverberated days later, even with Vicky three hours north in Sonoma, baking bread, hauling wood, and touching life in an honest way Hallie was afraid this house and life wouldn't sustain.

She sat on a newly sanded and waxed floor and stared through the siding glass doors, over the redwood deck, past the pool to fluorescent flowers still thriving on the last owner's T.L.C.

She thought about her first apartment's sun-craving yellow walls, and about the house in Waltham when gray winter pressed against narrow, multipaned windows, and she tried to appreciate this gift of space and light, the fact that even the back of her house looked like none of its neighbors. Grow up, she told herself. Stop whining. Do something.

She wasn't scheduled to leave for three more days. She could go back to her motel room TV and watch good wife Maureen Dean watching her husband testify at the Watergate hearings. She could switch her ticket and go home early. She could stay and explore San Francisco, or visit Vicky, who'd left precise directions.

It was good being easy with her sister after years of seeming too impossibly different to coexist. Lucky, too, since Vicky, though not exactly around the corner, was nonetheless the only friend she had on this edge of the country.

Except for Megan, five hundred miles south in San Diego, if she could still count her a friend. Almost a year after the lunch in Philadelphia with Bonnie, Megan was still uncommunicative.

Hallie looked appraisingly at her new beige phone. What the hell. This was the West. People settled standoffs out here. She dialed, automatically reaching for a cigarette, then remembering, again, that she was not smoking anymore.

Talking on the phone was nearly impossible without nicotine, and this particular call unthinkable. She could as easily call from Waltham. Later. When her cleaned-out system was more relaxed. She took the receiver from her ear.

Coward. She brought it back up. It took seven rings before she heard an unfamiliar voice. "Lo?"

"Is Megan Farr there?"

There was an asthmatic wheeze.

"Could you ask Megan to come to the phone?"

"*Ahmuggin.*"

Ah Muggin? Ahm Muggin? Megan? "*Megan?* Is that you?"

Like a dull banshee, a wail that, with a stretch, was "Hallie?"

Drunk. In the morning. Jesus. That explained the evasions, the short, tense conversations, the aura of secrets these past few years, but still, it was incredible. "You sound—did I wake you?"

"Uh-uh."

Hallie sat straight against the wall and enunciated. "Well, then, greetings from a beige touch-tone in an otherwise-empty house in Los Gatos." She couldn't control her dreadful nervous perkiness. "I'm about to become a Californian. I wrote you about it, but you didn't answer, and when I called, Daniel said you'd call back but you never . . ."

You never call, you never write. She sounded like a goddamn Jewish mother cliché. "Hello? You there?"

"Uh-huh." Dully, with no enthusiasm.

Hallie dropped the merry-caller routine. "Listen, I called because . . . you've been so . . . Did I do something wrong? I'm so jittery. Afraid to talk to you! But I haven't smoked in five days, so maybe it's no more than a psychotic break."

Hallie thought she heard an intake of air. A laugh? A sob?

More like nothing. "I've been feeling sorry I have to move," she continued, "thinking about 'for better or for worse' and realizing it also applies to friendship. So I'm calling. I'd love to see you. My motel has lost its charm and my return ticket isn't for three days. How about it?" Her palms were wet, as if she were Andy, asking another second grader to a party.

Thick, incomprehensible syllables. Sah Eee? Hallie shook her head, then suddenly heard it. Sorry. Megan's password. About what? Regrets about the potential visit? Like that, without explanation or warmth? Hallie hadn't realized how much it hurt to be surgically removed by a friend. "It seemed worth a try. I'll never know how I got on your shit list, but—"

More garbled sounds.

"What's wrong?" Hallie asked. "You sound . . . Are you well?"

Silence.

"You sound sick," Hallie said. "Is there somebody there to help you? Megan, what's going on?"

That choked breathiness again.

"Megan? Okay, Megan, you're scaring me. I have to ask. Are you drunk?"

Another sobby gulp and a click as Megan hung up.

Hallie's skin turned hot, then icy. She stared at the dead receiver, mouth agape, feeling as if she'd been punched.

If Megan were here—if she could say what she thought—

She stood up and brushed off her jeans, then locked the sliding doors that led to the deck and checked the windows. Not that it would rain until next winter in this bizarre country, and not that there was anything to burgle, but it gave her something to do besides berate Megan out loud, saying what she should have said on the phone. "Friends for *twenty-three years*! Friends when we got our periods. Friends even though Bobby McKenna took you instead of me to the Soph Hop." What hadn't they shared, long distance or up close? They'd spanned pimples and breast pumps, and now Megan wouldn't talk to her.

Hallie locked the front door and went to her car, and once inside it, was filled with a pervasive despair. She backed up, careful not to trample the African daisies lining the driveway. Save the flowers because she was already losing too much. Waltham. Comfortable routines. Friends. Her women's group. Harvard.

Dammit, she wasn't losing Megan, too. Not without a last try. This would be a good test of her new assertiveness.

She wasn't any damsel in distress, waiting for a rescuer. She was the rescuer, remember? Megan was an hour away by air, and Hallie was a liberated lady with three free days and a credit card.

"Is your mother home?"

"She's busy."

Megan's neighborhood was quiet and leafy and the white stucco bungalow small but shiny bright, the front yard manicured with a redwood tub of petunias near the dark Spanish door. So Megan's coldness didn't stem from shame of how she lived. And it wasn't that there was something wrong with the kids. Stephen was adorable in the gawky, sweaty way of eight-year-old males. He made her homesick for Andy.

Mike, playing with a hot wheels set, eyed her through the screen door. She wondered what on earth Megan was thinking of dressing the boy in a long-sleeve polo on a hot August day.

"Hi," she said.

He looked at her wordlessly, his mouth set.

Hallie hadn't seen him since he was a baby, but his face was immediately familiar. The other Michael at his age. Megan's brother. She shivered in the heat.

"I have to see your mom," she told the boys.

"She doesn't want to be—"

"Megan!" Hallie shouted. "Tell your kids to let me in!"

This produced wide-eyed stupefaction on two young faces.

"I didn't fly five hundred miles to stand at your door, Megan Miller!"

Mike stood and disappeared into the back of the house.

"Our name's not Miller," Stephen said. "You have the wrong house."

"Megan Mary Miller Farr!" Hallie shouted.

Mike reappeared. "My mom says please don't shout. The neighbors."

Hallie was admitted. The shades were drawn, but even in the dim light, it was obvious that the living room was spotless. You wouldn't know the family included children, aside from the hot wheels track on the rug. Megan hadn't lost her fastidiousness.

Mike led her to a small hallway behind the living room. "Megan?" she called out. "Don't be mad, okay? I had to come. I couldn't let it end like that."

Her words hung in the air as she opened the door and Mike went back to the living room. It took her a moment to realize that Megan, on top of the covers, was fully clothed, not napping. "Why are you in the dark?" Hallie asked softly.

Megan held one hand up, palm out, hiding her face.

Hallie was suddenly ashamed of intruding. "I'm sorry." Her eyes slowly adjusted to the dim light, taking in royal blue drapes, closed against the day, a dresser with neatly arranged brushes and change dish. And, finally, the woman on the bed, nobody she'd ever seen, face distorted, one eye sealed shut, nose taped, lips thick and broken by a black line of stitches, a green-purple bruise like half a beard, and a peculiar angle of the torso, as if her side needed protection. "Jesus!" Hallie whispered. "What happened?"

A tear snaked down the unfamiliar contours of Megan's face. Hallie felt dangerously light-headed.

Megan made muted, unfamiliar sounds that Hallie strained to understand. "Alked." Walked. "Innaduh." In a door? Walked into a door? "Can oo b'lieve?" One of Megan's eyes opened wider. Half her face joking about the other half.

No. Hallie couldn't believe and didn't. Doors were flat. How could one slam into so many different parts of her? Had she backed up and walked into the door again and again?

But why say something that stupid unless the truth was worse? Being mugged was awful, but why lie about it? Likewise for a traffic accident. Had she been drunk or on drugs? In this immaculate house with the clean little boys, that seemed less believable than ever. So how had this happened?

Megan, who moved with swift and graceful precision and organized, tidied, things, could never be called clumsy.

But she had. Before. A year earlier, in for her mother's birthday with a broken wrist.

Then Hallie remembered the reunion, the black and blue marks. How Daniel couldn't remember his own strength.

Impossible. Just because Hallie didn't like Daniel didn't mean . . . It couldn't be true. They were respectable people with polite children and clean houses. People like her, not the kind who . . .

She heard her own argument, her revulsion, the way she was backing off, and she understood why Megan had lied and avoided her and why she now sat, head bent, wringing her hands as tears oozed from her good eye. Hallie was horrified and ashamed of herself, of her stupidity. She hadn't caught on because she hadn't wanted to.

She sat down on the edge of the bed, but Megan winced, so she stood up again, unsure of what to say. She heard voices so deeply implanted they had no origin in her mind, voices advising her to say nothing. To never interfere in somebody's marriage. She shook her head, the voices, off.

"So ashame'," Megan said.

"*You* shouldn't be ashamed!" For the first time, she understood the expression "seeing red." There was a furious roaring between her ears and blood beating in her eyes. "How could he!"

"Doesn' mean to. Drinks. Cries. Always upset after."

"*Always?* Since when? How often?"

Megan looked down at her hands.

"It has to stop," Hallie said. "Now. People who hurt people go to jail!"

Megan looked out from one golden brown eye. "Not husbands."

"We'll call the police."

"Did. Las' year." Hallie listened, translated, worked to understand. Stevie had called. Daniel had jollied the police off and then beaten Stevie, too. "P'lice don' get involve 'mestic pro-lems," Megan said.

"*Laundry* is a domestic problem! *This* is assault!" Hallie's hands were fists. "Okay," she said. "Okay. What'll we do?"

Megan shook her head. "Go home, Hal."

"I can't leave you like this."

"Have to."

"No. He can't hit you again. Ever."

More slow tears.

"You have to get away."

"No money."

"I'll give you some."

"Go where?" Megan put her legs over the edge of the bed and winced. "Ribs," she said. Tiny and thin as she was, quick and agile as she'd been, she stood up, heavy as a boulder. She seemed beaten slow and thick.

"Sesame Street" 's happy theme song played in the living room.

Megan smoothed the comforter. "Daniel . . . home two hours. Stay till . . . but . . . doesn't like visitors."

"Doesn't like witnesses!" Years of conversational snippets flooded her. Daniel's privacy. Daniel's jealousy. Daniel bricking Megan in alive.

"Hurt Mike." Megan reached for a tissue. "Said he'd never—"

The long-sleeved polo in the heat. Megan's high-buttoned nun look the last few years.

"He's only five!" It came out of Megan's thick and broken lips like a banshee wail. "Said 'Daddy, don't hit her' an'—" She breathed rapidly, holding a hand to her side, the good eye blinking furiously.

The past, the missed clues, pressed on Hallie until she felt sick with her stupid ability to not truly hear Megan's frightened questions about husbands, to misinterpret every pull back and attempt to hide as a personal insult. "Does your mother know?" Hallie asked. "Bonnie?"

"Pretend not to. Made my bed. Have to sleep in it."

Bonnie's gospel of submission. If a man was angry, you made him that way. She remembered how desperately Megan had listened to her sister. "Come to me. Come to Waltham," she said.

"He'd find us." Megan moved stiffly, out of the room, into the hall, into the kitchen.

Hallie followed, sputtering. "So what? We'll—I'll—we'll take care of that then. You have to get out! For the boys, too!" She tried to imagine squeezing three more people into her house—and what about when they moved to California? Well, she'd worry about that then.

"Has a gun." Megan's kitchen was as spotless as the rest of the house. Four potatoes and a bunch of carrots lay on a cutting board. "Said he'd kill if I ever tried."

With difficulty, Hallie pushed down her cowardly—or realistic—response to the image of Daniel Farr, armed, at her front door. Megan picked up a potato. "You're making dinner? As if nothing's happened?"

Megan looked momentarily startled, then she dropped her eyes to pare and slice and Hallie could see, like silhouettes behind her, shadows of other afternoons when she prepared well-balanced meals for the madman who'd broken her bones and split her skin.

And she saw something else. The way out. "Megan!"

Megan dropped her peeler and looked terrified.

"I know a place, and I can take you there. *Now.*"

Megan put the carrots back on the board and leaned on the counter rim. "He'd . . . find . . . kill us."

Hallie felt Daniel's brute power scaring her into inaction, making her forget all she needed to believe she was, and she understood how Megan, how anybody, could be mutated by fear until the original person barely existed. "He won't kill anybody." She hoped Megan was convinced. She wasn't. "He's a bully. Besides, he won't be able to find you. We'll take my car. He can't track my rental. What the hell—unlimited mileage and I have to get used to your freeways sooner or later. They terrify me." She smiled. Without some levity they were going to sink through the kitchen tiles.

Megan looked blank.

"Vicky," Hallie said. "Daniel doesn't know she exists. He won't know I was here. Her place is perfect. A farm in the country. No phone, no address—just a P.O. box. Absolutely no way he could find you. And she has space. Probably even a job."

Megan fumbled for the cutting board as if she'd gone blind. "Really?" she said. "Really?"

"*Really.* Hurry!"

Megan reached out and touched her arm, as if making sure she wasn't an apparition. "Friend," she whispered, as if she had just learned a foreign word.

Kludge

1974–1977

All marriages are happy. It's the living together afterward
that causes the trouble.
Raymond Hull

1

"HMMM," Ted said, in the cryptic code of a parent
trying to communicate without alerting the children.

"Hmmmm," Hallie echoed. All five Bennetts were
cramped into a borrowed Volkswagen. "Doesn't look
good."

"What doesn't?" Erica was reading Nancy Drew but monitoring every word her parents said.

"The weather," Hallie said quickly. "It's raining."

"Mom! It's been pouring all day."

Oh, what a tangled web we weave. What hadn't looked good
was Vicky, whose farmhouse they approached. She was quarreling with a tall man in a yellow lobsterman's slicker. After much
arm-waving, the man got into a van and drove off on a newly cut
road. Vicky, in jeans and a blue shirt, ran and slipped on a
mudslick.

"Look at those houses, kids," Ted said too enthusiastically. "Mom says this was all farmland last summer, when Megan moved up. But the owners sold it to a developer, except for the house and barn Vicky bought. And now . . ." Nobody was listening except Hallie, who leaned over and kissed Ted's cheek. "I love you forever for trying," she said.

"Hey, there's Aunt Vicky," Erica said. "Honk, Daddy."

At the sound, Vicky, muddy and drenched, wheeled around and seized her chest, as if she were dying of fright.

"It's only us!" Hallie called out the window.

"Oh, God," Vicky said. "I didn't recognize the car. I thought he'd found us!"

Daniel had found everyone except his wife. He'd terrified Hallie with threatening phone calls. He'd called Sylvia Saxe and Kat Miller and Megan's cousin Grady and presumably any name found in address books or Christmas card lists.

"What brings you—"

Hallie signaled silence. The family piled out of the cramped car. "We borrowed the VW so we could make it here on our two-dollar gas allotment." They all ran to the open door of the shabby farmhouse. "If the damned embargo doesn't end soon, we'll never be back."

"Make yourself comfortable. I'll be one sec." Vicky took the stairs two at a time. "Megan made the slipcovers," she called down. "She can do anything with a sewing machine, can't she?" She banged drawers and doors.

They settled onto weathered, lopsided relics covered in fresh purples, periwinkle, and forest greens.

"She's painting the walls next. It's great having a wife." Vicky loped back down in dry jeans and flannel shirt. "Staying a while, I hope. Megan and the boys should be home soon. How 'bout some hot mint tea? I think there are cookies, too."

"Cookies, yeah." Andy deposited comic books on a table whose curlicued excesses had been painted and highlighted whimsically.

"Megan did that table, too," Vicky said.

"Ooooh," Erica said. "Look! A cat! Soooo pretty!" Erica emphasized every word, through a need to get her tongue cleanly around her braces.

"Her name's M.B.," Vicky said. "Short for Mouse Breath. She loves being petted."

"Sooo pretty!" Andy mimicked. He had his sister's squeaky love sounds down pat.

"Let me pet her!" Sarah shouted. "Give her to me!"

"I saw her first."

Hallie left Ted to handle the fray and went into the kitchen with Vicky. The room was rustic with a potbellied stove and ancient iron range, but it bore no resemblance to the charming, affluent country kitchens in vogue. "So who was the guy outside?" she asked.

"You know, I want a kid, but not one with sideburns."

"He won't be my brother-in-law, is that it?" Hallie jiggled lopsided drawers, looking for spoons.

"Nobody will. I want a kid, not a husband." The kettle whistled. Vicky poured hot water into a teapot. "Except." Her voice constricted. "Doesn't much matter what I want. Turns out that butcher ruined me." She avoided eye contact and sounded as if she were telling somebody else's not completely comprehensible story.

"Oh, Vick." Hallie sat down at the scarred kitchen table. "Damn. I'm so sorry."

"At least now it's legal and safe. If it happens to Erica, or Sarah, they won't wind up like me. They'll have their lives and their choices and their babies when they're ready. Everything's a matter of timing, isn't it?" She rubbed her arm against her eyes, then opened a round tin and took out gingerbread cookies. "I'd adopt, but I'm single. I don't qualify. Ah, who cares?"

"I do."

"I know." A sad smile flickered. "Enough. Tell me why you drove through the year's worst storm, when they're rationing gas?"

"If you had a phone, I wouldn't have. Can't you get one now, with all the new construction up here?"

Vicky brushed the question away. "Doesn't matter that I support myself. I'm a single woman. They told me Dad had to secure my checks. I told them to fuck off." She poked Hallie with her index finger. "This isn't about phones. Why are you here? It's Dad, isn't it? What happened to him? Did he—"

"Daniel's dead."

Vicky frowned as if she couldn't remember who that was.

"Killed himself last week. On Valentine's Day."

"Daniel." Vicky's hand froze on the lid of the honey jar. "How do you know?"

"It's involved. A neighbor heard the shot and called the police. Somewhere in his personal effects they found his work number and there, a form listing his mother as the relative to notify."

"His mother? But she's dead."

Hallie shook her head. "Daniel said so, but she's alive. A piece of work who walked off when he was seven. She hasn't seen him or his father since."

"I thought his father was dead, too."

"We all did. He's a drunk, but breathing. Pathetic, isn't it? I wouldn't have believed I could feel a moment's pity for Daniel until I heard that every Mother's Day since he was seven, he sent that woman a card and letter. She never answered, but that's how she knew he was married, knew about Megan and the boys, and knew that maybe Kat Miller should be notified. And Kat told Bonnie, who called me last night, hoping I'd know what to do. We came today because the gas stations are closed Sundays. Damn Arabs. Damn embargo. I didn't mean to be cryptic, but we didn't tell the kids yet. I was afraid they'd say the wrong thing at the wrong time." She put cookies on a plate.

"Why?" Vicky said. "Why now, six months after she left?"

"He's been getting crazier, drinking nonstop." She put spoons on the serving tray and felt ludicrous, discussing a madman's suicide while preparing a tea. Or perhaps they needed to be reminded of small civilities. Perhaps that was the rationale for all domestic routines.

"He really, truly, couldn't live without her." Hallie lifted the tray. "Maybe he always knew that. Maybe that's what enraged him."

*   *   *

"He's gone," Megan said again. The rain had stopped and Ted had the children, including Megan's sons, out on a mud walk. "Dead." She sat in the kitchen on a battered rocker with bright blue-violet pillows. "Gone. Death did us part."

"Are you okay?" What a stupid question. Hallie felt useless and knew Vicky felt the same. Both of them hovered, did busy-work, flapped their arms like nest-bound fledglings.

"One morning when we were in Philadelphia for my mother's birthday," Megan said, "I looked outside and there he was, laughing and tossing a rubber ball to his sons, his Navy sweatshirt riding up." Her voice was dreamy and slow. "It was November, and cold, and when he laughed, it smoked the air. He looked so right, the way I'd always imagined." She rocked herself back to a normal position. "Why is that what I remember? That and the clean midshipman who was going to put my life in order."

Who knew what photos anybody kept in her heart, or why. What Hallie remembered was Megan's face six months earlier. She wondered what she herself would see if Ted were suddenly gone, and was horrified that the immediate, unsummoned image was of a year ago, locking horns in the Waltham kitchen, the acceptance from Harvard on the counter between them. Why that out of everything? Even out of today when he'd been so willing, so understanding? She mentally apologized, confused.

"The boys can use their real names at school now," Megan whispered. "I can pay Social Security, buy a car, make friends. Join the PTA." She rocked in silence for a moment. "I thought we'd be running from him the rest of our lives."

Hallie sat down on a wobbly ladder-back and leaned elbows on the kitchen table. "You sure you don't want tea?"

"I'll have to lengthen Stevie's pants. For the . . . hard to think of him dead. In a box in the earth." She shuddered. "He said he was an orphan." Back and forth, slowly, the old chair and floor-boards creaking with each move.

Vicky had baked fresh gingerbread men. Now she brushed on a sugar-glaze, and carefully placed buttons and raisin eyes.

"Who was he? What other secrets did he have?" Megan's voice grew thin, as if stretching to capacity. "He was so *big*." She put her arms up and spread them. "He always *loomed*."

Vicky stopped brushing and stood at attention.

"Thirteen years of looming and nothing's left of me," Megan whispered.

"No," both Hallie and Vicky said. "No."

"All I had left was fear. That's kept me going. Now he's dead and that's gone and nothing's left."

"You're still there," Hallie insisted. "You've been hiding."

"Dead and buried, and good riddance. I was a pretty pathetic specimen, anyway." She sounded remote and bemused.

"We make ourselves up all the time," Vicky said. "There's no other choice. A new version starts now, but you're still you."

"So horrible." Megan brushed away a tear. "The one, the only kind thing Daniel did for his family was kill himself and set us free. So sad."

The silence, fragrant with spicy ginger and the woodsy glow of the pot-bellied stove, was broken only by the squeal of Megan rocking, eyes focused ahead, on nothing.

2

"And that's the grand tour," Ted said. "Full circle." He led his old friend James back into his office. THEODORE BENNETT, V.P. SPECIALTY INDUSTRY SALES was engraved on a brass plaque beside the door, and every time he entered, he had to control the urge to touch it for good luck. "A drink?"

James nodded.

Having a bar and refrigerator in his office still seemed glitzy, a little shocking. Much as he hated to admit it and much as he fought it, he still had traces of being small-town, Simon Bennett's son.

"What's this?" James stood in front of a console table, on which a monitor blinked.

"Game prototype. Pro-active football. Players call the plays, intercept the ball. We only wanted their monitor work initially, but now we're trying to buy a piece of the company itself. Of course, by the time G.T.U. approves, the Japanese will have snapped it up." Working in the fastest-moving part of the world for a slow-moving company was pure frustration.

Each holding a Scotch on the rocks, they settled on leather club chairs that ringed a squatty glass table. On the wall above was a framed print of a G.T.U. monitor reflecting a shot of Earth from space.

"To further success," James said.

They drank and spoke, refilled and spoke more about the consulting work that had brought James to the Bay Area and about Ted's attempts to make his whale swim as quickly as the Silicon Valley sharks, particularly now. Nineteen seventy-five was not starting well here. Ted told about a friend instructed to lay off his group. Ten minutes after he did so, he himself was laid off. An hour later, the boss who'd canned him was kissed off. Dominoes were falling that fast.

You had to move or die. One month's advantage could be the difference between success and oblivion. G.T.U. didn't comprehend that. G.T.U. was committing hara-kiri.

The January sun set early and crimson, a persimmon ball over the flat roofs of Cupertino. Yellow lights appeared in boxy office windows and far up the hillsides. An hour later than intended, they went to Ted's car, the I-don't-do-toilet-training Jaguar. Ted turned on the ignition and the radio blared into "Having My Baby." He snapped it off.

"You sure a surprise dinner guest's okay with Hallie?"

Did James think he was henpecked? "Sure. Besides, you're not a surprise. I left a message with Erica, and she's good about that. Has to be. Since Hallie started law school, that's how we communicate."

"These new ambitious women are difficult," James said.

Ted agreed, but silently.

"A lawyer!" James said. "Since the divorce, I can't even afford to say the word."

"Saw Veronica's picture in the paper with some producer."

"Serves him right. She's like those female giraffes who are so uninvolved and uninterested in sex, they wander away while in the act. The male goes splat, down onto the ground."

Ted chuckled.

"Hey, splatting hurts! Nowadays, if I like somebody, I never call them back," James said. "I'm not getting involved again."

"Until the next time."

"And you? How long is it now?"

"Fifteen years in March." You could murder somebody and get a shorter sentence. He tried not to think of the fifteen years' worth of women and adventures James had known, but did wonder why he'd felt compelled, so young, to be married. Had a wife been the final requirement for a B.S. in Grownuphood?

What would it be like to be single, driving his old pal to a hillside hideaway staffed by a housekeeper paid to welcome him graciously no matter the hour or condition? Think of the money he'd have without braces and gymnastics and summer programs and baby-sitters and law school tuition. The mental peace without a pubescent daughter singing "Having My Baby." The women, the infinite possibilities, the . . .

No. Don't. The secret of staying married was in keeping the imagination impoverished, in not thinking.

"Be honest," James said. "No offense, but don't you ever roll over in the morning, take a peek and gasp, 'Not her again!'?"

Ted gripped the steering wheel more tightly. "Married is a different trip. I can't explain." And wouldn't if I could, because there's no way to make it sound better than dull, because maybe it isn't. Compared with James and two women in the Caribbean. James on a yacht with the wife of his host. James and the fla- menco dancer.

"Remember that night in Boston?" Ted said. "Five, six years ago when I went home and you didn't? I've thought about it a lot. Always meant to ask how it turned out."

"Boston?"

"Girls—Sabrina, or Daphne. Something overdone like that. T.G.I.F. party in a bar near my office."

"Sorry. Mind must be going."

Why should the man remember any one set of girls, one party? The car lurched as Ted accelerated too heavily, as if squashing something loathsome under his gas pedal.

*   *   *

"—inconsiderate!" She hissed the word. He had left James downstairs with a fresh drink and Andy's inept magic tricks for entertainment.

"I called," Ted said. "And it's not like he's a stranger. He's one of my oldest friends. And yours."

"Beside the point." She pulled on boots, talked in rushed clumps. "Say you support me, but when push comes to—"

"I'm going back down. This is rude. Are we going out or eating at home?"

"House a mess. Bad enough getting them fed—and you an hour late! I've had a stinking day—race from school to pick them up at Hebrew School and find out Andy's cut the last three classes, and besides, it's Sarah's Back to School night."

He'd go nuts with their schedules and the interminable demands he was supposed to fully share. Sometimes divorce seemed the smart way to see your kids and wife in nonlethal doses.

"Forgot, didn't you?"

"I'm really sorry." Home, home in the kludge. He'd been proud to usher James into the living room with its Chinese porcelain colors and three pretty children. Gold seal of approval. But it was still kludge, the tech's word for machines with their guts hanging out, wires loose, pieces taped with duct tape. Inelegant messes, whether or not they ultimately worked.

"I'll go alone," Hallie said. "Again." She frowned into the mirror. "And I *love* seeing playboy James, who only dates Miss Universe candidates, when I haven't slept and I'm getting a cold and I feel like shit."

"Are we eating here or—"

"Eat wherever you want!" The tendons of her neck stuck out like a harpy's. "I'll be at Sarah's Back to School night! And then I have to read a case for—"

He put his hand on her blouse, wishing she were as soft as its powdery color suggested. He thought maybe she once had been. Now she seemed ready to shrug his hand off. "Just—please— while he's here, pretend," he said.

"What are you talking about?"

"*Pretend!* I want James to think we're happy!" His words shocked him, but he didn't retract them.

And for once, his wife, his partner in the kludge, the one he loved—although not all the time—the one who drove him crazy and depressed him—although not all the time—didn't challenge him. Instead, she stood, unpainted mouth open. And then she bit her bottom lip, nodded, applied lipstick, and walked downstairs with him, her newly colored mouth in a wide smile.

--- **3** ---

Megan was late and Hallie was annoyed. But a lot of things annoyed her lately. She was living at breakneck speed between law school and family, giving each side half, leaving nothing for herself. The new woman felt extremely old.

Not that coming into the city from Berkeley was a big deal, or that meeting Megan for dinner was a bad idea. Nothing was bad, only too much, including guilt over everything un- and half-done.

It was this too-muchness, hers and Megan's, that had kept them from seeing each other for at least half a year. Since back before law school. Hallie checked her watch again and frowned. She sipped wine. More guilt. She had to lose ten pounds, and wine was pure calories. But calming.

"Sorry. Damn! I'm trying not to say that anymore." Megan pulled out the chair across from her and grinned. "Since when do you wear glasses? Are we getting old?"

"Not you. You look terrific." The fact was, Megan had a glow that Hallie knew contrasted with her own saggy, puffy pallor.

Megan balanced on a wobbly chair. "It's good to see you." She poured herself wine. "Been too long. Bring me up to date."

Hallie cocked her head. "Let's see. A boy gave Erica a Pet Rock and we aren't sure if that means she's engaged. Sarah is trying out for Little League and Andy calls himself The Great Amazingo and wants to be a professional magician. Ted is busy working and complaining. Not happy with G.T.U."

"And you?"

"Me? I love school. It's exciting being ready and sharp, thinking of every angle and counter-argument. But the rest . . . It's hard managing everything, so . . . I'm not. I'm doing it all middling well, trying to survive. Don't look for me as either the Happy Homemaker or on Law Review." She sipped more wine and sighed. "I have this recurrent fantasy of a one-room apartment. A refrigerator, a hot plate, and one hook for clothing. When I need my family, I'd invite them over."

She drew a line on the paper place mat with a chopstick. "Griselda's fine, too. Arthritic and creaky but hale. And that's us, except for Andy's fish, which are too dumb to have problems."

A reedy hostess deposited plastic-covered menus.

"It's sad," Megan said, looking at the Vietnamese specials of the day. "In the end, the only change the damn war made was a lot of dead boys and a new cuisine stateside." She pushed the menu aside. "Sorry," she said. "Don't mean to be glum. Don't mean to say sorry, either."

"Your turn now."

Megan blushed. "The good news is, I'm in love. The bad, he's twenty-four. I'm eleven years older." She giggled nervously. "At least, I couldn't have given birth to him—that would be my bottom line."

"Well," Hallie said carefully, "it's certainly past time for you to have fun. Daniel's been dead a year. Not that you had fun while he was alive."

"I had decided never to date again. Didn't want to hear any more stories about what was wrong with the exes. The one who told me aggressive women gave him a soft-on. The one who had a custody fight for his Persian cat."

Hallie smiled sympathetically.

"The last straw was when I told this date I was a widow with two small sons and he pushed his chair out and said, 'I subscribe to Nelson Algren's adage'—pompous ass!—'There are three things a man should never do. Never eat at a place called Mom's. Never play cards with a man named Doc. And never go to bed with a woman whose troubles are greater than your own.' Stands up. End of date—before we had dessert. Remember all the creepy boys? They're creepy men now. Not worth the hassle."

Hallie shook her head. "At least they weren't tough acts to follow. Now—who is he?"

"Eddie. He's working his way through Sonoma State. Studying biology. Going to save the planet. He waits tables at a place where I deliver bread."

He sounded woefully ordinary. But Megan continued to glow.

"He—he pursued me!"

"Why so surprised? You're so *now*. A terrific-looking female truck driver!" Meanness, a desire to snipe, was too close to her surface, and she felt even nastier knowing she was envious.

The hostess requested their choices in a voice silky as her tight dress. They ordered roasted crab, lemon grass curry prawns, and another carafe of wine. Thanking them, she wafted off.

"Tell me more. What is it about your . . . lover?" What a word. Spanish balconies, daggers, swoons, and darkly veiled women.

"He's so . . . well, he's gentle, but not, you know, weak. Self-assured, bright, but nonthreatening . . . and, um, sex is, well, like it never was. With Daniel, I was convinced I couldn't. That I was deficient."

"God, that man makes me angry. Even posthumously!" And Megan—Megan feeling so good, made her feel what?

The waitress arrived with their salad and wine and Hallie poured both of them a glass, then raised hers. "To you. Plural."

"The cradle robber, the dirty old woman."

Hallie shrugged, remembering the times she'd found herself speculating about a young classmate, about what it would be like to have no history, only shared sensation.

An emaciated teenaged boy placed the crab and curry on the table, next to the largely untouched salad. "Think of the French system," Hallie said. "Old courtesans tutoring young men. They pretended it was for the young men's sake, but I'm sure it was a reward, like a pension plan. Put in time with the tired old men and you get to tutor fresh stock with unlimited energy and curiosity. Teach them exactly what delights a woman. Practice over and over. If that isn't happily ever after, what the hell is?" She smiled, her good humor restored. "Enjoy it, Megan. He isn't a problem, he's a gift." Hallie broke off a crab leg and sucked out the meat, then she stopped and looked concerned. "You marrying him?"

Megan shook her head. "I already did marriage enough for this lifetime. Which reminds me—my cousin Grady's open marriage is all the way open. Kaput."

Hallie wasn't surprised. Marriage was a choosing, a closing the circle. You could no more open it and stay healthy than you could a vein. The wraith passed their table carrying steaming platters. "I always hope eating their food will make me look like them," she said.

"You look fine. Anyway, Christina thinks we have a lot in common as what she called 'single women rediscovering ourselves.' "

Hallie didn't see the point of talking about the twit. "So, then. If you're not marrying Eddie, there's no problem."

"It can't last."

In some ways Megan was still a child. "Nothing can," Hallie said as gently as possible. "Nothing stays the same. Certainly nothing to do with men and women. Sooner or later, the milk gets spilled. Why cry over it in advance? There's always time later."

Megan pushed food around her plate. "You give me the willies." Then she exhaled. "Or maybe I just can't stand hearing the truth. I know I'll end it, and it makes me sad." She looked skyward, as if her answers might be on the stamped tin ceiling. "He's too enthralled with my history, my experience. He just plain doesn't have enough of his own. I'm already a little tired of being fascinating."

"Forgive me," Hallie said. "I don't get it." Her life seemed all routine, pragmatic distractions. Love was the unseen underbelly of the whale, too often lost beneath turbulent waters. Being fascinating, feeling fascinated herself, sounded delicious.

"Sometimes I feel like I've swapped one act—the meek, invisible woman—for another, which is more gratifying, but still an act. Eddie doesn't really see me. He sees someone better, brighter, wiser, and sexier. The older woman, the experienced other. It's sometimes exhausting being his image."

"Maybe nobody sees anybody." Lately, Ted seemed to spot an irritant when he looked her way and she too often noticed an interruption when she looked his. "There must be a reason they say love's blind. Don't look too far ahead, Meggie. There isn't any problem. You're entitled to feel good. You're entitled to be loved. We all are," she added emphatically, as if someone had challenged her.

4

Hallie sat next to Ted on the *bima*, the raised platform at the front of the temple, watching her daughter read the Torah. Above them, torrential winter rains pelted the synagogue roof, but under it and inside her, all was light.

"Why?" Erica had demanded. "Why do I have to learn that old stuff and do this? It's not even traditional," she had logically protested. "Girls didn't used to do it."

"They weren't allowed. We don't need to repeat history," Hallie said. "We need to make it."

In the end, thirteen proved too young to understand the attraction of tidying the chaos with patterns and rituals, so Hallie had simply insisted that important birthdays were to be celebrated. The country had done it for itself this bicentennial year, so why wouldn't Erica?

Hallie wasn't sure if her feelings had anything to do with religion, or if they were the essence of it. She was uncomfortable with second-hand prayers and preferred forging her own petitions and thanks. But there was much to be said for words that reverberated with several millennia's repetitions. For ceremonies that reaffirmed the strength of human bonds. For the gathering of the clan.

Her daughter chanted in a clear voice and Hallie, embarrassed by the fire of her pride, looked beyond the *bima* at the faces of her life.

Movement in the front row took her to Sarah, who, with a strand of light brown hair pulled across her lip like a mustache and a cross-eyed grimace, was attempting to derail Erica. Hallie intercepted her glance and Sarah, surprised, let go the hair and beamed. Joy was her natural state, at least at nearly nine, at least this week. Children had good phases, too. She had to remember that.

Through the fine upturned features of Sarah-now, Hallie saw Sarah-then, the toothless grin at dawn, the soundless laugh.

It hurt understanding that life was mostly memory, slipping away as you clutched it.

In little more than a year, it would be Andy's turn. Poor larval man, lurching along in the shadow of his bossy big sister, growing in odd spurts and directions, hands too big, neck too skinny, knees everywhere, cowlick an exclamation point on his head. His latest passion was tropical fish, the odder, the better. He was encyclopedic about Blue Damsels, Black Crappies, and the One-Spot Fringlehead, his taunt at Erica when she had a pimple.

But while her son expanded, her father dwindled. Ivan Saxe's skin hung like a poor-fitting hand-me-down.

Her mother checked him every few moments, as if afraid he might have disappeared, and both her dedicated agnostic parents nodded and dabbed at their eyes as Erica chanted the ancient words.

She heard hissed, sharp notes and then a loud "Shush!" Simon, happily whistling "Don't Sit Under the Apple Tree." Miriam Bennett had suffered a mild stroke a year earlier. Her hands trembled and her speech was halting, but she was as dictatorial and crabby as ever, only slower at it.

Hallie's glance crisscrossed the chapel. Friends from law school. California neighbors. Ted's division heads, his administrative assistant. Erica's favorite teacher. Two women from the CR group. Philadelphia and Johnstown relatives. Lives braided together, inseparable at the points where the same memories pulsed in each of their minds. And now they'd have today, too.

Vicky, the strong and weathered pioneer woman. Megan, with her handsome sons, but not Eddie. After a year and a half with him, she called and said, "I've given up my child." A poor joke that didn't mask her audible pain.

Eddie had been a good usher, guiding her from one place in her life to the next.

Hallie's eyes traveled to James Harris, with his new fiancée, a stunning Eurasian in sable. His second marriage, to a Brazilian beauty, had lasted the first forty days of 1976. Chloe, either ignoring the odds or understanding them, brazenly flirted with him.

Erica's eighth-grade friends sat in a clump, self-conscious and awkward boys pretending to ignore a row of girls giggling through bulgy braces. Many things were as much forever as the words Erica chanted.

I am so blessed, Hallie thought. She felt the heat of Ted's hand on hers and turned and saw her own thoughts reflected, her mirror. *Look what's become of us and our love. Look what magic we've created.*

Remember this, she told herself. Hold on to this for all the times you trip over details, resent love's irritations, for when you run too fast to stay connected, thinking it'd be easier or better to break free.

Remember how sweet it is to be part of a family and feel yourself fit into the chain of life.

She held on to his hand, on to all of them, all of it.

5

She was half-asleep, still deep inside herself, dreamily accepting the pleasure floating on the ends of her nerves.

She turned, adjusted more of herself over to the delicious wash of feeling. "Mmmmm." A soft hum tickled her vocal cords, deep in her throat, echoed in her ears. "Mmm," she dreamed again, absorbing the pleasure, enclosing it. She shifted her knees to pull the pressure deeper.

"Good morning." Teddy, gold as the new day itself, smiled down at her. He moved slowly, easily, confidently, in and out, teasing. Each time, her body was surprised, but her legs encircled his and the parts he'd touched and warmed shared his rhythm.

"That was lovely," she said later, "even if I missed most of it."

"You were there when the fat lady sang."

"I *was* the fat lady who sang."

He turned off his alarm. It hadn't rung yet.

She lay in his arms, heavy-lidded and -limbed. "We need to go away," she said. "Somewhere romantic. Big Sur, Yosemite, Mendocino. The two of us, alone."

"Sounds great." He kissed her, disengaged, sat up, stretched, and left the bed.

"When?"

He was halfway across the room, thin early light letting her enjoy the sight of his body, which, if no longer a youth's, was still defined and muscular. She liked the signs of age, of time lived, even though they made her sad with their clear intimations.

"When what?" He rummaged in his underwear drawer.

"When can we go away?"

"Dunno. I think we're close to signing, but who knows?"

"What happened to your mushroom theory of management? Keep 'em in the dark, feed them shit, and let them grow. Isn't that how it went?"

He grinned. "It isn't only my theory, and it doesn't apply to contract negotiations."

She couldn't remember when they'd last been alone. Except asleep and for moments as short, if sweet, as this morning's. She was as much to blame as he, as much consumed by her life. Now that she had just about gotten her separate identity straight, their couplehood was in danger of atrophying from lack of exercise. "A weekend," she said. "Friday and Saturday night. I might even accept one night. But two full days," she hastily added.

"Sounds nice." He whistled an off-key tune, a sure sign his mind had left the room before his body had.

Seduced and abandoned.

Her alarm blared and she slammed it off. She forced herself out of bed and listened for signals that the rest of her clan was also rising. She was sure her mother was already downstairs, making coffee and oatmeal and playing Super Grandma as she had done since day one of the Bat-Mitzvah-to-Thanksgiving visit.

While Teddy lathered his face, Hallie showered and considered the day ahead. Tuesday, time again for the cleaning woman and Sylvia Saxe to face off. At least it was no longer Hallie on the carpet for bad housekeeping, or the last century when, as Ted had pointed out, a woman could be put in the lunatic asylum for refusing to do housework. Nowadays, only trying to do it and everything else put you in the asylum.

Mati, the cleaning woman, was a surrogate incompetent, a smiling Salvadoran refugee supporting one husband, five children, and at least a dozen relatives, and therefore as unfireable as she was inept.

"Could you pick up film before Thursday?" Ted asked. "This time I promise to photograph everybody before they fall asleep and the turkey before it's . . . oh, sorry! *I'll* get the film myself. Old habits die hard." He picked up his razor.

"Hey!" Hallie said. "I have it. My folks are here through Monday, and Mom always offers. This is our getaway. A weekend of us instead of leftover turkey."

He'd been whistling between each stroke of the razor, but now he paused. "This weekend?"

She stood behind him and wrapped her arms around his middle, pressing her naked body into his. After all these years, she still yearned to get hold of Ted Bennett.

He shaved intently, his chin skyward in search of renegade whiskers.

"Alone together all day, all night. Finally." She brushed her lips over the top of his back, traced his spine with her fingertip.

"Sorry."

She pulled away. "What could happen to contract negotiations over Thanksgiving weekend?"

He rinsed his face and patted it dry. "It's not that."

The Theodore Wall. Not as well known as the one in Berlin, but equally impervious and divisive.

"What am I?" she demanded. "Muzak? Explain yourself. If you don't want to be alone with me, say so."

He sighed, then put a towel on the bathtub rim and patted it. "Have a seat," he said.

That was kind. She was naked and bathtub rims were cold. Put that on the plus side of his ledger.

"I didn't want to say anything," he started. Her heart plummeted. News of impending death or pending lovers started that way.

Or a mid-life crisis. The hot new plague of choice.

She remembered his healthy body inside hers a few minutes earlier. How could anything be seriously wrong? All the same, he was tense, definitely not himself lately.

"Something's happened," he said. "Something I have to deal with. I didn't want to upset you before I had a better handle on how I feel. What I want."

She couldn't believe she'd get the news bare-assed on the edge of a tub.

"It involves you, of course, but at this point . . ."

Forget I asked. Rewind the film back to where you were whistling and I was bathing, and let's skip this scene.

He took both her hands. Very, very bad. "It's not like I went out looking for this to happen."

A woman, then.

"But I have an appointment Saturday afternoon."

So maybe not a woman. But wait—an appointment with a physician? A divorce lawyer? A psychiatrist? And why wasn't she certain which she hoped it was?

"It's Fritter Marks."

A health problem, then. "What are fritter marks?" She skimmed his body for signs of them.

"Come on—even you must know who he is!"

"A person?"

"You're kidding, right?"

Okay, she told herself. He wouldn't react this way if this Fritter Marks were about to operate on him or on their marriage. She shrugged and made a face, her hands still in his, to acknowledge ignorant dummyhood.

"Fritter Marks." Ted said the name reverently. Fritter Marks had probably found the cure for cancer. "Fritter Marks is picking up where Nolan Bushnell—you know who he is, right? Pong, the game?—where he leaves off. Where Atari hasn't yet gone. Fritter Marks is the world's best toy maker."

Toy maker? Who was Ted? Pinocchio seeking Gepetto?

"He's opening a company called The Fun Factory. He's been based in Phoenix until now. A multi-multimillionaire already, but he understands that the next step's electronic games and he's taking the leap. Using his own money, owning it fully. Christ, it's all anybody's talked about for weeks. How could you miss it?"

It hadn't been all anybody talked about at law school. Normally, she would challenge such insufferable egocentricity, but she needed to know whether Fritter Marks represented danger or opportunity—and, if the latter, whether the Bennetts could survive much more opportunity. "About that appointment?" she prompted.

"This head hunter calls a few weeks ago, takes me to lunch, interviews me intensely, and I guess I checked out because Marks wants a meeting Saturday at his home in Woodside. He's a creative genius, a visionary, but a lousy administrator. He needs a professional manager. He's offering a piece of the action, eventually."

She ran her fingertip over a scar on his thumb. "And so?"

Ted stood and walked out of the bathroom, Hallie following. "He needs somebody who can talk to tekkies." He pulled on his pants. "Who knows computers and entertainment—TV, radio, et cetera. With marketing and sales experience."

Ted's resumé, except for Army reserves, wife, kids, and dog.

She made the bed, poked legs into jeans and torso into a long blue sweater. He transformed himself from her sleepy lover into generic corporate man. "There's risk," he said. "These companies have a way of flashing in the pan and disappearing."

"Meaning what? For us, Ted, meaning what?"

"That I'm having lunch with Fritter Marks. That's all."

"But would you—if he—"

"That's why I didn't want to mention it."

"But if he offered—"

"Are the kids ready?"

She had to abort the discussion and check her tribe, or risk driving three lazy children to their various schools and being late to her own classes.

She marched down the hall shouting warnings. The more distant future would have to take care of itself.

—————— 6 ——————

"Nice evening, wasn't it?" They drove away from what she now thought of as Fritterland.

Nice? She glanced at Ted sideways, checking for a hint of humor, but found none. *Nice* was not the word for it.

Ted's warnings had not prepared her for even the sight of Fritter Marks, six six, barrel-shaped with a moon face and a head shaved clean by his personal barber every morning. His ego was even larger than he was. Humpty Dumpty without the thin skin.

It had been an evening of faking enthusiasm for the boss, for all things Fritter. "My sixth-grade teacher told me I wouldn't amount to beans because I frittered my time on games," he'd said with a guffaw, touring them around a living room the size of the Titanic.

She had praised the architecture that dwarfed them. She had praised his collection of antique jukeboxes and the life-sized stuffed animals lolling about. "Fritter's Critters," he said. "Made me my first million. I owe them."

She felt sorry for his pint-sized bride, his third, heroine of a love story of the newest sort. Lucy had been an office temp in Fritter's Phoenix operation. They'd both had to defy their families to be with one another. Almost Romeo and Juliet, except the families weren't Capulet and Montague parents, but wives and husbands and, in Lucy's case, children.

From the stories she'd heard, Hallie had expected a fiery, dramatic woman, a properly defiant and to-scale heroine. But Lucy Marks was tiny and plain, a planet revolving around Fritter's sun.

Fritter said he'd built the house for Lucy, but he'd built it to his scale. Hallie could imagine his wife sinking into one of the enormous sofas, disappearing, her peeps and squeals unheard in the cavernous room.

Fritter told Hallie to stop hitting the books, forget about becoming what he called a "lady lawyer." She didn't need to, he said, because being part of The Fun Factory family would make them rich. "You're about to experience the American dream," he said. "The American wet dream." Hallie smiled politely.

She didn't want to be part of his family. Didn't like him or his humongous house with lamps like redwood trees and great overflowing platters of food and a bouquet of tampons for the little ladies, each festooned with a silver bow, in the powder room and me, me, me the pattern on the wallpaper and the theme of the evening and Fritter Marks's life.

But Ted bought it all.

"All my life," Ted had said two months earlier, the day of his first interview, "I knew something big would happen someday. A chance. A major risk. And I've hoped I'd take it. That I wouldn't be too afraid. This is it. Do you realize the possibilities? Do you know how many millionaires happen overnight in this Valley? And *Fritter Marks*? This is day one of the rest of our lives."

At the time, she'd been trying to unravel a case concerning a man whose inventory was eaten by a rare form of beetle, and she'd barely responded. She apologized, then realized he hadn't noticed her distraction. That's how it had been ever since day one of the rest of their lives.

On the surface, he could pass for normal. But she knew him so well she felt the crackle and pop of craving in his blood, the dizzy spin in his brain. She tried to ignore it because he loved his high like any junkie would and because it was easier on her emotions if she didn't monitor the nuances of his. The one time she suggested that they were already lucky and privileged and that nothing was worth several years of exhaustion and risk, Ted went into heavy withdrawal.

"There's nothing immoral about getting rich!" he'd shouted. "It's the goddamned American way! You're the only woman I've ever heard of who'd be happier coping with poverty. You have no dreams, no capacity to think big. Go ahead and save the world, find a way to be the only poor lawyer in California, but don't tether me."

Her husband was in love with who he'd decided to be. She'd been too busy to notice. But then, the wife always was the last to know.

She wanted to tell him about the tampon bouquet, but she wondered if he'd laugh or consider it a sniper attack on his hero, his love, his future. She wanted to tell him how her after-image of Fritter was of an enormous open mouth, eating, eating, eating, and that it made her nervous to think of somebody she loved anywhere near those teeth.

But she wouldn't. "Yes," she told her husband. "A nice evening."

She wished he knew she was lying. It would make all the difference.

7

Through the sliding doors, Hallie watched Griselda sleeping on the deck. In and out went her rib cage, its outline visible beneath the thinning coat. Hallie could almost hear the effort needed to suck in air one more time.

It was no good, Ted had said. He'd held Hallie close, whispering into her hair. She thought maybe he was crying, as she was. No fair prolonging the misery. Selfish to keep her alive. There was a tumor, pain, the true meaning of doggedness clear as Griselda staggered through her obligations, falling as she squatted, needing assistance to unclench the bones and stand upright again. Insisting on her dignity. Hallie spread paper inside, begged the dog to use it, and for the first time in her life, Griselda looked offended. Then laboriously, she dragged herself outside.

Oh, doggie, if I ever need to be . . . Hallie corrected herself. Nobody got out free. When I need to be, let me be as brave as you.

I'll miss you, dear creature. The glass in front of her mouth fogged. I love you. I'll hold you all the way, won't make you take this trip alone.

She glanced at the clock again. They were due at the vet's in two hours.

Just yesterday Chloe brought them the puppy. Just yesterday when they lived in Boston and Hallie was pregnant with Erica, and Ted was in grad school, and they were so poor and worried and at the same time happier than they could ever be again because everybody was young, everything was about to happen.

Now it was the Me Decade. Ask nobody what they can do for

anybody. Except for Griselda, and Griselda was going to die this afternoon.

Hallie sighed and turned from the window. Soft kitchen noises pressed on her. The hum of the light fixture, the muffled ticks of the oven clock, the sighs of the refrigerator as it, too, aged.

She needed distraction. Anything. Her high-school reunion newsletter was on the kitchen table, along with the morning paper and an untouched turkey sandwich. Her eyes wandered back to Griselda. The balance of the family and its constancy were going with the dog. There would be no one left to hold. Once, there'd been flesh all over her days. Hands, arms, cries, kisses, baths, and pleas to be held. And Griselda, pushing in to give a kiss and have her head scratched.

And then, overnight, only Griselda. Sleeping on Hallie's feet while she studied. Greeting her every return. Uncritically approving of how she looked, what she chose to do, who she was, no matter what.

Erica and Andy had spun out of grasp into their own adolescent lives and even Sarah, rushing at top speed, begrudged time spent on kisses and hugs. Her husband was so far out in hyperspace they had to communicate by satellite. There was only Griselda.

Hallie had been surprised and touched when Ted volunteered to go with her to the veterinarian. Sometimes she forgot what a good and decent man he was. And then she wondered if, God help them both, he too felt that only Griselda blindly, passionately, irrevocably loved him.

She checked the clock again. Three minutes had passed. She had to fill time. The newspaper shrieked about Elvis, the drought, and the lunatic murderer, Son of Sam. Dead singers, murdered people, dying land. She pushed it away and took up the stapled pack of pages. She'd missed her twentieth reunion and had forgotten even to read the newsletter sent afterward.

It appeared they'd grown up and gotten old. Earlier newsletters had been about futures. Weddings, babies, promotions. Then the losses started. Misplaced spouses, firings, less than ideal children, frightening diseases. And, whistling by the graveyard, perky announcements of second chances, re-enterings and re-trainings. They bumbled around, messed up, but the one skill they all had was burying unpleasant truths more efficiently than old Griselda had ever buried a bone. Nobody was unemployed; they were "consulting for a while." Nobody mentioned divorce; they were exploring new options, or the husbands whose careers they used to proudly chart were no longer mentioned, or the men listed children a generation apart. No explanations offered, none demanded.

What if, just once, she wondered, we admitted being human, screwing up, being scared, getting older?

Even Megan, who insisted on honesty in her new, sometimes overly fierce independence, had found it necessary to sanitize her life for the alumni association.

Three years ago, I was widowed and it seemed a good time for a change. So now we're living in Sonoma, near Santa Rosa in an old farmhouse, and I work for Real Bread, a whole-grain bakery. I'm back to my hobbies of painting and sewing and I'm doing community volunteer work. My sons are thriving in the country atmosphere. Stephen (12) is starting junior high. He tolerates schoolwork only so he can play baseball, and Michael (9) is a video-game addict, so . . .

Wouldn't it be lovely, perhaps even freeing to somebody reading it, if Megan had made it clear that her volunteer work was helping start and maintain a safe house for battered women, that she herself had escaped from abuse?

But Hallie knew herself for a judgmental hypocrite, because, in fact, she hadn't come any closer to the truth.

. . . in California for the last four years and thoroughly enjoying it. Husband Ted left G.T.U. early this year to become President of The Fun Factory, a new video-game company. As I write, I'm completing (I hope) my second year of law school (U.C. Boalt Hall), fulfilling a long-time ambition. My new ambition is to sleep all summer. I'm sorry to miss the reunion, but Erica (13) graduates from Middle School that day. Andy (12) and Sarah (9) keep . . .

She glanced outside again. There was a drought in golden California and the desert was growing and neither dogs nor humans were given a fair life span. Her husband was self-absorbed and her skin was drying and her older daughter's hobby was cataloging her mother's faults. The twenty years since high school blurred into a string of kids, diets, shopping lists, and calendars with circles around one day each month.

Maybe so little truth floated on these lines because nobody, including herself, knew what it was.

. . . still mostly making background music, but I did receive an Emmy nomination for an episode of "The Waltons." Can't be at the reunion because of a . . .

Craig Forman. She was oddly pleased, since she hadn't been at the reunion, to learn that neither had he.

She read on. The boy who was going to be the next Hemingway was writing for a weekly paper in North Carolina. The boy who was surely going to jail was a computer scientist. Chloe made herself sound like a bicoastal star, but she had called recently, drunk and in despair. "Twenty years breaking my back," she'd said, "for what? Now if I'm lucky, I'm the mother who washes out stains in laundry ads."

Movies and books lied. If you wanted something enough, they said, if you had a dream and worked hard, you were rewarded. Thundering applause, rave reviews, all your fantasies come true.

You found your one true love, checked off a multiple-choice quiz—this is who I'll marry, who my children will be, where we'll live, what I'll do. Done. Your life snapped in place and you glided into the happily-ever-afters.

Nobody mentioned that there would be daily revisions of the test and that the answers would keep changing.

Twenty years and ten minutes used up. She pushed away the untouched sandwich and the newsletter and went outside, where there were no clocks, where she could sit with her old dog and speak to her of love and life, of dignity and indignities. And listen, too. And learn. If there was time.

The Men We Wanted to Marry

1978–1980

Then it's a mistake to get married.
It is, my dear, but it's a much bigger mistake not to get
married.
George Bernard Shaw

———————— 1 ————————

YOU feel so good," he whispered, his breath warm in
her ear.

Saturday morning. Outside, low clouds smudged a
slate sky and inside, only them. At four-thirty A.M.,
Hallie had forced herself awake to ferry three children to the ski
club pickup point. Her reward was a rare and special day alone
with Ted. She had climbed back into a warm and waiting bed
dressed in a rainbow-silk confection Megan had designed and
made as a birthday gift.

Now, with the silken gown a prismatic puddle next to the bed
and her husband in her arms, the telephone rang.

She pressed up. "Don't answer," she whispered.

The phone rang again.

"Don't," she repeated, releasing, then pressing. The first Saturday in six months that Ted wasn't working.

A third ring. "Teddy-Teddy-Teddy," it sang. "But what if something . . ." he said. For fifteen months, "something"—a large, bald something—had invaded whatever time they had.

"The machine will pick it up. Make love, not phone calls."

"Make both," he said. "Watch." He braced himself on one arm and reached for the receiver on her night table, still joined to her from the waist down. The two-headed hydra, she thought. And here comes Hercules to kill us.

The receiver boomed. The love object. The drug of choice. She closed her eyes, trying to block out all sensory data except the feel of Ted inside her.

She heard him reassure Fritter that he hadn't awakened him, his voice absolutely natural while he withdrew, then slowly reentered her. She opened one eye and peeked. He raised his eyebrows, grinned, and repeated the smooth motion.

"Sinful," she murmured. "Furtive."

He winked. "About what time?" he asked Fritter.

She closed her eyes and waited, moving subtly to keep the pressure of him. There was a lot to be said for sin. A pity it was so difficult to manage in these tolerant times.

"That could turn into something." He was excited. By Fritter. Not by her. Definitely not by her. You could not keep a man prisoner this way. He was escaping emotionally and physically, part by part, top to bottom. His mind first. His heart soon after. And now . . .

"You think they'd— Then show them Fever Demons. Phelps knows how. Sure, but Bopple doesn't have the resolution."

And he thought of that baby talk as the real world. She wanted to roll away, reclaim herself, but Ted's weight was on her, with Fritter's added to it.

"Seems I lost my place," Ted said when he hung up. "Guess I'm not the man of steel I imagined."

She said nothing. Let him blame her silence on unsatisfied lust. Let him think this was about sex because that was safer territory than loneliness and a terrible creeping chill.

They were becoming an arrangement, not a marriage. A convenience.

"I have to go in to the office."

Did he really think she was surprised?

181

She didn't argue or protest, even though for once, she could have without worrying that a kid would appear the way Andy had, two weeks earlier.

"You're getting divorced, aren't you?" His voice had cracked and wavered.

"Divorced! No! Why?"

"I heard you."

"We had a disagreement. People do."

"That's what Brad's mom and dad said, too." He shrugged and turned to leave and she had to almost wrestle with him, to give him the hug and reassurances he required.

Her childhood had been safer. Her parents screamed and threatened and slammed out—but it was a given that they were in it together, forever. That's how it was with grown-ups back then. Andy didn't have those assurances. Neither did Hallie.

Brad's mom had an M.B.A. "When you have your degree," she'd said, "you don't need this shit. The only justification for men's existence is that vibrators can't move furniture."

"I know we were supposed to spend the day." Ted stood and stretched. "But a fast-food chain in the Midwest wants our games as an incentive. They'd buy units for all their stores, run special ads—two Cokes, a superburger, and a game at one-third retail. This is the only time they can make it, and Phelps, who could show them the games, has the flu, so . . ."

Ya-ta-ta-ya-ta-ta. Who cared which words he plastered to the simple truth that he was out of here, that they wouldn't have their day, and she wasn't sure what it was they did have, besides three children, a mortgage, and a not totally extinguished lust, given half a chance, which it seldom was.

"Love you," he said.

Oh, yes. That, too. She yawned and turned her back.

--------- 2 ---------

You never.

He wouldn't listen, wouldn't participate, not this time. He was damned tired of her sniping.

No matter how many times I—

Worked his ass off to give them a better life than he'd had. His family didn't have to agonize over every penny. Didn't even understand how it felt.

Why can't you—

She created her own burdens, like law school on top of three kids, and then she bitched about the unfairness of what she was carrying.

I always.

Women! He was as liberated and understanding as the next guy, but Freud was right, and what the hell *did* they want?

I thought we'd—

Bitch, bitch, bitch. He could phone in the goddamned quarrels, they'd become so routine.

You've changed.

He'd changed? That woman had changed from a lovable, funny, bright girl into a goddamned harpy!

Materialistic, superficial, excessive.

So she wanted to take care of humanity. Great. Work with low-income women. Terrific. His sweat, his lifetime of taking care of this portion of humanity, had *given* her the luxury of a low-paying liberal knee-jerk job, so she could get off her high horse and stop sneering at him for entertaining the world, not saving it.

I don't know what you want!

"I want everything!" he'd shouted, breaking his promise to stay out of this one. "*Why the hell not?*"

She looked like he'd shot her. "Oh," she said softly. "Well, then. That's it. You see?"

No. He did not. He absolutely did not. He only saw her, too often angry, always unfathomable.

———— 3 ————

Love and money, money and love. They shared variations on those themes along with an appetizer of Caesar salad and a bottle of wine. By the main course, having at least temporarily exhausted money woes, they switched to love in the person of Megan's ex-cousin and former classmate, Christina, who still kept in touch.

"She's enrolled in every self-improvement course and workshop in the mid-Atlantic states," Megan said, ticking items off on her fingers. "Marathon encounters and primal screaming and floating in silent tanks and Rolfing and that thing where you can't pee and even something called P.O.W. I thought it had to do with Vietnam, but it was for pre-orgasmic women. They teach you how."

"How what?"

"How not to be pre. She claims she was accompanying a friend. Anyway, she also took an adult evening course and wound up marrying her fifty-eight-year-old professor."

"Some man's magazine said a woman should be half the man's age, plus six," Vicky said. "Chris, at thirty-eight, is a little old for her new hubby."

"That's the formula for trophy wives," Megan said. "Not us."

"Show me a sign of progress between men and women," Hallie said.

"Grady says the professor's a drip," Vicky said. "He visited us. Lives in L.A. now. Cute man and a great lay."

"For Christ's sake!"

"Still a prude," Vicky said. "He was a good antidote for McNaughton the shit." Her nonchalance abruptly disappeared. She became engrossed in fluffy bread crumbs that she rolled into a ball. "So—you're a lawyer. Could you help me with something?"

Make it simple, Hallie telegraphed. She'd been a law school graduate for all of six days. She hadn't yet taken the bar.

"McNaughton the shit has a kid. Polly's six. She was with us the whole five months. Her mother's a junkie, if she's still alive. So one day, McNaughton's gone, but Polly's there with a note pinned to her blouse, like Paddington Bear. It says 'Take care of her.' Unsigned. So, can I keep her?"

"You sound like Sarah, when she brought home that stray."

"I am. I'm exactly like her."

"Are you sure you want full responsibility for a six year old?"

"I've been responsible for her for a long time. I'm sure."

"I'll find out what to do."

Vicky beamed.

"Her father walked off? Like that?" Hallie asked.

Vicky's smile died. "Typical male scum."

The enraged kneejerk was everywhere and automatic, a new female secondary sex characteristic. "Please, could you for once not trash the entire sex?" Hallie said.

"We are having a nice, civilized ladies' lunch," Megan said. "Couldn't we keep on—"

Vicky interrupted. "Hallie is still in awe of men. Stuck in that Fifties crap that love, which of course to her means marriage, is the answer to everything."

Hallie knew how vulnerable her position was. All alone on the planet, without reinforcement and despite hard evidence to the contrary, she defended the crumbling institution, insisted that coexistence was possible. Perhaps she was delusional.

"You should be Bonnie's sister, not Megan." Vicky twisted a forkload of linguini.

She certainly wasn't an evangelist for marriage at all costs, but the choices were the love 'ems or the leave 'ems. In between, where Hallie was, there was nothing.

"Have you heard her show?" Now even Megan looked glum.

Hallie was relieved to have the conversation shift direction, although remembering the night when she'd heard Bonnie's radio program made her uncomfortable again. Andy and a friend had been caught shoplifting at a local convenience store. Ted was at a business dinner when the call came. She had gone to retrieve her son in a rage, a large proportion of which was directed at her missing husband.

Child-generated fights had become a squabbling subcategory. Spats over how to establish, maintain, or measure degrees of freedom; over children's wardrobes, vocabularies, and love objects; over academic apathy and peculiar associates; over slovenliness. They bickered about the dire effects of what the other hadn't said or done or thought of, about over- or under-reacting. They parried and thrust with "too lax" and "too rigid," but in truth, neither had any idea of what the current norm was or the rules should be.

The kids bounced on to provoke new crises. Ted and Hallie, exhausted and divided, seemed the real casualties.

She thought of that night, of Andy, scrunched low in the back-seat, arms folded over his chest, baseball cap tilted to hide his face, his voice cracking between surly defiance and abject misery. And of herself, ashamed to have faced the manager of the store—I am the mother who so poorly raised this wretch—driving silently, furiously, turning on the radio and hearing Bonnie twinkle mind-less homilies on subjugating yourself to your man.

"It depresses me to think she found enough listeners to keep her first show alive," Megan said, "let alone become syndicated."

They were interrupted by a stocky, middle-aged woman in a pink sundress. "They said you make the bread this restaurant serves." She folded her arms across her belly.

Vicky paled and nodded, and there was fear on Megan's face as well. Everybody ran scared these days, and Hallie's newly acquired profession was at least partly to blame.

"They say it's only sold to restaurants." She sounded tried beyond endurance. "That I can't buy it."

Vicky nodded.

"Not fair. Not smart!" She had raisin eyes in a face as puffy as unbaked bread. "Not good business."

The owner of the place, wiping her hands nervously on her apron, approached. "We don't want their lunches getting cold, Mrs. Trapper. I'll sell you one of my loaves." She led her away.

"The awful part is, she's right." Vicky's expression darkened. "I need retail outlets to make this work, but we're at capacity at the bakery, and my rent already eats up the profits, so I can't afford more space, even if I could find it." She shook her head, her long braid swinging like a metronome. Hallie hadn't seen her sister look defeated in over a decade, not since the day of the abortion.

"A court won't give me Polly if I can't make a living," Vicky said. "I put the barn up for sale, so maybe a developer will bail us out—but for how long?"

"Money," Megan said. "Money, money, money. The only problem worse than men. And kids. Money and kids."

Megan was so determined to weigh out Daniel's violent legacy that she sometimes didn't apply necessary limits. On the other hand, Hallie thought she herself did, and even so, Andy still wound up shoplifting. Nobody had the answers.

"We're stretched as thin as possible," Vicky said. "Megan makes all the clothing. We grow vegetables."

Hallie's mind had wandered. They were still talking about money, while she had the luxurious ability to forget an issue as vital as lifeblood to these women.

"Even with Prop Thirteen, even with the tax cut," Vicky continued, "we could lose chimp central."

"I won't ask what that is."

"Us. Megan and me. Lady chimps and their kids live in communes. The guys periodically raid to mate and kiss good-bye. And some people deny that they are our ancestors."

"To think I once memorized where to place calling cards and when to wear white gloves. No more money talk, okay?" Megan said. "We have this conversation every night. Maybe a developer will pay a fortune for the barn. Maybe an unknown rich uncle will appear. Meanwhile, was Ted upset about your going off alone?"

These women had written off all binding arrangements with men and didn't understand the ambivalencies of marriage. Hallie was their specimen wife, afraid that with complete honesty, she'd confirm their misgivings about the institution. "Not exactly," she said carefully, poking her fork through the side of her frittata.

Vicky twirled linguini. "High time you found yourself."

"I'm not lost. I hate that expression. Besides, the only place anybody seems to look for themselves is between somebody else's legs. I'm not interested."

Vicky looked skeptical.

"He said he'd be able to get away in a few months—*probably*. Wanted me to wait, but by then, I can't go anywhere. I start at the Law Center next week, and I'll be studying for the bar. I'm just not very high on his list." Hallie felt teary prickles.

"You're spoiled." Vicky's tone was as frigid as ice water. "Nothing bad ever happened to you. You're protected and coddled and you've never been tested, so you complain about trivia! So what if he can't vacation with you? Your life's too easy."

Hallie swallowed wine, blinked hard. "There are problems besides money, or even kids," she finally said. "Tests like staying married. Really married, not just legally. It's not pure inertia, the way you make it sound. And nobody helps. Nobody thinks it's worth the effort. People like you say you know about the world and men and pain and adventure and life and I don't. Because I'm still married. A sexual reactionary. A foot-dragger. As if I copped out of life because I haven't left Ted. Haven't *grown*, for Christ's sake!"

"Listen, Hal," Megan began.

"I'm sick of being told marriage is dead, the nuclear family is a relic. Stop sniping at me!" She cross-hatched her frittata with her fork tines.

"I'm sorry." Vicky's voice sounded like it had weights attached. "I get jealous. I want to keep Polly and make a living. It has nothing to do with you."

But Hallie still scowled. "And I hate when you go on about what jerks men are. I know there are assholes, but you talk about who's a good lay and the whole scummy sex and you sound just like the creeps on the street corner used to. We're not only becoming the men we wanted to marry, the way Steinem said, we're becoming the men we *didn't* want to marry, too."

"I have an idea," Megan said. "About that lady who wanted your bread? Maybe the restaurant could have a special rack near the door. Real Bread Retail."

Vicky raised her eyebrows and looked at Hallie. "Shall we let Mary Sunshine change the subject and make peace?"

Hallie managed a tight, tense smile. "Didn't mean to rant."

"Megan," Vicky said patiently, "like I said, I can't bake more bread without more ovens, and I can't afford more ovens."

"I'd lend you money," Hallie said. "You know that."

"Don't be nice right after I've been rude. It's disorienting. Besides, I'm not comfortable with the lady bountiful bit."

"I'm spoiled and untested. Teach me reality. Take some of my unearned riches." She looked heavenward. "Or don't. Starve. Lose Polly. Make your strident superliberated points."

"I can indeed be a creep," Vicky said. "I don't know what came over me. I want you to be happy, I swear."

"Now, again—what'll you do on your solo trip?" Megan asked. She looked wistful. Or maybe it was only her new, almost determined plainness. Her black hair was graying and she didn't color or style it, simply pulled it back and secured it with a rubber band. Megan, who'd won a Tri-County design competition in high school, who'd crafted and sewn her prom gowns and her own and Hallie's wedding dresses, now stitched herself the simplest of shifts. Megan thought it was about making it clear that she was no longer interested in pleasing men. That she traveled solo and was strong. But she was also unnecessarily drab.

"All I plan to do in bed up there is read and sleep."

"The best-laid plans and women," Vicky said. "Did you pack that stunning nightgown Megan made you? Just in case?"

Hallie sighed. "It scares me to think I might die having slept with only one man, but it scares me more to risk that same one man. So no, I didn't pack the beautiful birthday nightgown, but thanks for reminding me, because I want another one. A peignoir set this time."

Megan gaped. "I'm glad you like it, but . . ." She hesitated over each word. "I'm really pressed for time." She smoothed a crease on her napkin until the pink linen square could have passed a military inspection.

Hallie belatedly understood. "Not a gift! I want to buy one, give one of your creations *as* a gift. Fritter's niece. Lucy's giving a shower for maybe a hundred women. Please. The best fabric, your favorite design, and charge a fortune. Teddy won't begrudge any offering at Fritter's shrine."

"It's one thing to sew for you, but for somebody whose taste I don't know . . ." She shook her head.

"Take the dare and the money." When Vicky made her voice hard, it could saw through brick. "Stephen needs braces."

"I'd be embarrassed to have strangers judge me. Don't look at me that way. Those were kid dreams and we're grown-ups now."

"Obviously, we're all only brave about what doesn't matter to us," Hallie said. "Do it. And make a label, too."

"A what?"

"Label. Brand name. As in designer sleepwear?" Hallie leaned across the table. "The spoiled, coddled, overprotected, over-rich wives of Silicon Valley—women like me, okay?—are going to pass that nightie around and wonder if it could make the old man pay attention to them instead of to integrated circuits."

The murmurs of voices and chinks of silverware and china were hypnotic and comforting.

"Your initials might be nice," Vicky said. "M.F. Appropriate, don't you think? I'd like a label myself. If my bread was for sale in its own wrappers. And rolls and baguettes and muffins . . ." She looked up at the ceiling, her mouth ajar.

"Coffee?" the waiter said.

"That's it!"

"Right away!" The waiter wheeled around.

Vicky snapped her gaze back down, but it was still unfocused. "It would work. A café, with coffee and Real Bread products baked on the premises. Real Cookies. Real Croissants." She looked feverish, flushed, happy, and worried.

"But," Megan said. "The cost. I thought—"

"The barn. If the zoning—"

"The barn!" Hallie echoed. "It's perfect. Near the road, big enough—too big?"

"I'd stop renting the bakery. The barn has room for tons of ovens. I could get a loan from the bank, I'm positive. I have a track record now."

"If you need a cosigner, I'll—" Hallie began.

"Thank you." Vicky's new zest was contagious. Megan also looked less frayed and drab.

"To brave new women." Hallie poured the last of the wine.

Megan looked down at her uneaten lunch and shook her head. "I don't know. I mean a label for a one-time thing—*if* I even do it that one time, that is. Silly. Scary."

"We're getting too old to postpone things that scare us," Hallie said. "Maybe silly things, too." She pushed back her chair. She had to leave. The truth was, the winding drive ahead made her nervous, as did the entire trip. She was in her late thirties, taking her first solo voyage at long last, needing to find her legs, learn how to be alone. This trip was like a vaccination—a small dose to prevent the full-blown disease.

"There's no rush," Vicky said, putting her hand on Hallie's arm. "It isn't too far."

"Too Farr!" Megan nearly levitated. "Gone Too Farr!"

"I have?" Hallie asked. "Me?"

"I'd do a label if it said 'Gone Too Farr.' Isn't it perfect? I always wanted to go too far, back when it was still possible." She lifted her empty wineglass in a salute.

Hallie looked at them, each facing something new and important. "You know that point in *Peter Pan* when Tinkerbell can live if everybody will believe in fairies?" she asked. "I think that just happened for all three of us. We're going to live."

-------------------- 4 --------------------

A stretch limousine, looking like five cars glued together, waited on the Tarmac when the plane touched down. Its driver transferred the luggage while everyone but Fritter, who was still with the pilot, seated themselves.

At eight A.M., Hallie had been talking with a client on food stamps, figuring a way to get the support her husband owed so she could find a minimum-wage job. At nine A.M., she'd been drinking champagne on a private jet. Real schizophrenia might be less disorienting.

They settled onto the leather upholstery. "God will not condemn you because you skipped the normal inconveniences of flying, will She?" Ted found feminism amusing. He was loving this trip. "A party in L.A.," he said. "Harry Bevan, the film mogul. Fritter's pal."

Fritter wanted rights to big-action films. Wanted to base games on Hollywood's hottest heroes. It was assumed that dancing at the mogul's charity ball would make them blood brothers and close the deal.

She hadn't wanted to shop for clothing, arrange for sitters, rearrange her schedule. She treasured and required weekends for recuperation. Besides, tomorrow was their twentieth anniversary, and she wanted to be alone with Teddy, remember who they were supposed to be. She daydreamed about the ugly green motel room in Cape Cod where they'd spent their tenth anniversary and even thought of flying back there, for fun, for this one, but hadn't told Ted, who'd no longer understand.

She could barely find traces of the young engineer she'd married, the scholarship boy who was going to change the world. Or maybe she hadn't heard him right. Maybe all he'd ever wanted to change was *his* world. Which he'd done. It was a long way from his parents' house in Johnstown to a serious Hollywood party.

Fritter bulged into the car. "That cockpit's the click-and-whir center of the universe! Gave me a great idea for a game." Everything—good, bad, or disastrous—did. Even Three Mile Island sparked a nuclear meltdown concept that was, happily, squelched.

Fritter filled a space designed for two normal men, patted Lucy's knee, asked if anybody wanted a drink, itemized the contents of the limo's liquor cabinet and directed the driver, all at once.

"Do we have to go have more fun again?" Hallie's feet still ached from an eye-popping blitz of Rodeo Drive. "All I did was buy things for the kids they could buy at home for less. I'll leave the price tags on so they'll know it's from Beverly Hills."

"Yes," Ted said.

"Yes? Leave them on?"

"Yes, we have to go have more fun. Now."

"Where are the homely people?" Hallie whispered.

"In graves. They shoot them. It's considered an act of mercy."

They certainly weren't at this party. Hallie stood on a grass and flagstone patio searching for imperfection, but the humans were as carefully groomed as the landscape.

The women didn't have the hard-edged chic of Easterners. They were, instead, artificially natural, sculpted, scalpeled, pumiced, and pummeled into a glow of youthful perfection, and the scars, the effort, the workouts, the diets, and the paint were invisible.

Up to a point. Or an age. One grande dame's false eyelashes brushed like black palm fronds against eyebrows lifted too often and too far. Nobody else looked past thirty. Except Hallie.

I grow old, I grow old. And she had really tried. Experimented with a rinse to hide the squiggles of gray. Bought new blusher and polished her toenails. Still, she felt dumpy in her flowered challis skirt and loose cotton sweater. But since she couldn't squeeze into a stretchy, skintight jumpsuit, or bare her midriff like these trampoline-stomach women, or get away with a long open vest with no underwear except a leopard bodystocking, she resigned herself to mid-life mufti.

The men were equally gorgeous, a peacock gallery of fit bodies in crayon-box clothing topped with luxurious heads of hair.

Golden Teddy, skin tight across classic features, trim in his turquoise sport shirt, belonged, but Hallie was an interloper from a Homes of the Stars' tour bus.

She suddenly thought of Craig Forman. In high school, he'd been dopey-looking. Ten years later at the reunion, he was put together and sexy. He'd been L.A.'d. It was a matter of geography, or perhaps a side effect of smog.

Craig. A potential opportunity, a life experience, ignored. For thirteen years, whenever she used the evening bag, she was surprised to find his card still in it. And then less surprised that when she put the bag away, she left the card in it once more. But now, unwilling to keep a fantasy so old it was senile, she'd donated the bag and tossed the card.

She'd missed the sexual revolution, and it was too late to join. Her ticket had expired. Nowadays, fidelity was preserved by the aging process and fatigue. Forty. Droopy, saggy, lined, and shop-worn forty.

She silently toasted all the Craigs she'd never know.

If only she didn't feel like a toad. If only the renunciation of the Craigs felt voluntary.

"Andy told a buddy this was our twentieth anniversary," Hallie said. "I think the point was to brag about this party."

"Hmmm." Ted was excessively enjoying the limo ride back to the hotel. If the windows hadn't been tinted so that the peasants couldn't see in, he'd have waved and nodded at the passers-by in the manner of the Pope.

"The kid said it was gross."

"What's that?"

"The kid thought being married this long was sick." She

waited. "What's happening to the world if kids think staying married is aberrant?"

Ted wasn't listening, but he heard her questioning tone and pause, and he shook his head in fake sympathy. The limo hummed past the Bel Air gates, up into a road of Americanized chateaux, villas, palazzos barely visible behind fences with warnings about armed responses. They glided past the swans, toward the canopy of the hotel. "Not to worry," Ted said. "The world's just fine." He patted her hand.

She checked out his profile. He looked like a glossy coat of paint and about as weighty. She felt his patronizing hand. Gross, she thought. Positively gross.

"A ball. A genuine ball." Not a dance, not a hop, not a party. Hallie stood in her luxurious hotel bedroom, smitten by even the semantics of the evening.

"Just like Cinderella's," Ted said. "Which is fitting, because you are straight out of a fairy tale tonight."

"Not the evil old crone, I hope."

"Oh, Hal. You're gorgeous, and you know it."

She curtsied, head down, holding the flower-petal chiffon skirt, hiding her flush. Ted was never generous with praise. Sometimes she thought it was the beautiful man's handicap and sometimes she thought he was still Fifties cool, or afraid to acknowledge vulnerability. And sometimes she thought he was just plain inconsiderate.

In any case, it had been an especially long time between compliments, and she felt like a frostbitten person approaching a fire, adjusting gradually. "My fairy godmother finally showed up," she said, only half joking.

Still in her stocking feet, guilty about relishing this opulence, she nonetheless strolled into the living room of their suite and savored its fine silks in the colors of Monet's water lilies, the collection of blown-glass bibelots, the cryptic, contemporary Japanese art on the walls.

The coffee table supported an extravagant arrangement of white roses and greenery next to a spun silver basket containing enough fruit to prevent scurvy for a year. A refrigerator, fronted with rosewood, burst with gourmet delicacies. And, lest Hallie and Ted be reduced to drinking the brandies and liqueurs already stocked, Harry Bevan the film mogul, whose name was never abbreviated to anything less, had provided Remy Martin Louis the Thirteenth Cognac. "Five hundred dollars a bottle," Ted whispered reverently.

Now Ted came into the room and watched her appraisingly. "I always knew you had a price," he said. "I just never suspected it was this high." He took her in his arms and she felt the jolt of the new. There was nothing familiar about his lips or their kiss. Everything was reborn in the scent of tuxedos and white roses.

They entered a brick warehouse now transformed into a rain forest, except for humidity, poisonous snakes, and animal droppings. The walls were lined with the jungle sets of a hundred grade-B movies. Foliage rich with brilliant flowers filled three corners and encircled a lagoon in the fourth.

"This is how God would entertain, if only He had Harry Bevan the film mogul's budget," Ted said. She could barely hear him in the din of a thousand party goers, the metallic beats of a calypso band, and periodic outbursts from electronic cockatoos and monkeys.

They poked each other upon sighting Famous Faces.

"He's so tiny!" she said. "He looked tall in that movie. Everybody else must have been on their knees."

"They must shoot her through gauze," Ted whispered of an aging and overdone sex goddess. "She needs some now."

"Odd to see him laughing," Hallie said of an elegantly tailored man who played psychotic killers.

A woman in fussy brocade clutched an old-fashioned glass and made her way around them, murmuring, "Excuse me," with each step. Then she swiveled back, raised a wrist laden with sparkling stones, and pointed at Ted. "Aren't you somebody?" she asked.

He looked at Hallie.

"Wait!" the woman said. "You are—you definitely are somebody. Don't tell me—I have it—it's on the tip of my—that movie about—the wild, the wild—I'm right, aren't I? You're him. My God, I never dreamed I'd actually talk to you!"

"The fact is—"

"I saw your movie five times with my friend Doris back in Duluth. She'll die, that's all, when I tell her."

"But actually," Ted said, "I'm not—"

"He's hoping to keep a low profile tonight," Hallie said. "The spotlight must remain on skin disease."

The woman nodded solemnly. "Hope you'll forgive me." She waved her old-fashioned glass for emphasis. Hallie stepped back, out of the orbit of bourbon spray. "Thrilled, absolutely thrilled to have met you," the woman cooed. She lifted her right hand to wave farewell, and Ted took and kissed it.

"Thank you for your support," he said. "Where would I be—indeed, who would I be—without you?"

"Ohm'God." The woman backed off, eyes on Ted until she bumped into a man who was not amused and was probably not even somebody.

"You missed your true calling," Hallie said.

"What are you talking about? I was terrific in that film *The Wild, the Wild*. I am definitely somebody."

"Poor star-struck creature." They moved through the crowd. "Imagine how bleak her life must be. Worshiping celluloid heroes, play-actors. Sad to have make-believe so significant, to—" She delivered a sharp elbow to Ted's ribs. "Over there," she whispered. "Look. Over there."

"Why? What are you—"

"Cary Grant. Cary Grant and he's smiling, do you see? Oh, look, Ted, he's—" She sighed, staring openly. "I can't believe I'm in the same room as Cary Grant."

"This is sad."

One of the department head's wives, Vivian, suddenly materialized. "Anybody seen my husband?"

Hallie shook her head. "Our most recent sighting was Cary Grant. Next to that hibiscus. He just walked away."

However Vivian felt about Cary Grant, her husband worked for Hallie's husband, so she paid homage to the empty space. "Some party, isn't it?" she said. "The dresses, the jewels! I can't stop gaping and drooling."

The gowns were, indeed, spectacular. Hallie's hand-painted

chiffon had seemed both lavish and subtle, but now felt like a housedress in this sea of sequined, beaded, jewel-encrusted, hand-carved bodies.

"In the olden days," Hallie said, "you could tell a guy's status by his clothing. You didn't confuse a king and a serf. But now, with democracy and everybody in jeans, it's too hard to flaunt, so they have these charity balls." She toasted her theory with champagne offered by a waiter wearing a loin cloth.

"Then why do men all wear exactly the same thing?" Ted asked.

"Easy," Vivian said. "Men are executives. They have other people flaunt for them. If women ever achieve true equality, we'll dress our honeys in gems and satin. Speaking of which, I'm off to find mine before some movie star snatches him."

Vivian was a thoroughly modern woman in a thoroughly modern remarriage. She had old children and new step-children plus ex-step-children from her first marriage to a man who'd been married before. Her husband had the same. Perhaps to keep one constant in all the shifting, Vivian retained her maiden name. Children of this marriage would be hyphenates until, perhaps, another partner shift took place.

Confusingly modern and overpopulated or not, Vivian's marriage was brand new, and she hovered around her painfully plain husband and hung on his words in classic old-fashioned style. Hallie gave this stage another week. Uncritical adulation had a short shelf life.

"Chow's on!" The voice was unmistakable, as was the bald bulk approaching them. They followed him dutifully to the table. Harry Bevan the film mogul's table was in the center of the room, the bull's-eye heart of the jungle, and guest tables radiated out, all the way to social Siberia near the entrance. Fritter had a power table next to the mogul's.

"Yes," Fritter said, settling in. "This is where you'd put somebody you wanted to give a license to, somebody who was going to make lots of money along with you."

Hallie was more intrigued by the table's decor than by its strategic placement. In the center of a green satin cloth stood a tall and heavy spun-glass palm tree. Crystal parrots and monkeys swung from twisted transparent vines creeping up its base. The icy tropical tree glittered in the light of dozens of votive candles on lakes made of mirrors.

"One hundred trees. One for each table." Lucy Marks sounded sad, but looked expensively elegant in a black and white gown and onyx and diamond necklace.

Hallie lifted a dark green shopping bag off her seat. It was filled with beautifully wrapped parcels. "What's this?"

"Party favors," Lucy said. "Your reward for being so charitable."

In the three years since Hallie had met her, Lucy had studied what Ted called "Wealth 101." Her weekly schedule included a personal trainer, a skin expert, a masseuse, and a cosmetologist. She visited spas. She hired wardrobe consultants. Her hair was highlighted and sculpted and she wore tinted contacts.

She had replaced the quiet waif aura with high gloss and increasing desperation. "All the things I was good at," she'd once told Hallie, "I don't do anymore. Cooking, cleaning, typing, filing, budgeting . . ." Her voice had dropped to a whisper. "Raising kids. And all the things I didn't have an idea of how to do are what I do all the time now. Entertain, dress right, be on committees." The strain showed.

Hallie couldn't imagine how Fritter and Lucy were making a marriage. Even ordinary, generic marriages were weighted with so much cargo, enormous and piddling, it was a miracle when they flew. How, then, did you manage when it was imperative to be constantly ecstatic, to strike a fair exchange for lost children and normality?

The evening progressed in a haze of fillet and fois gras, spun-sugar baskets and chocolate mousse, almost all of which, Hallie was sure, wound up in the garbage because these willowy creatures couldn't eat that way and be admitted to the next convocation of the absolutely beautiful people.

The meal was punctuated by dance breaks provided by two orchestras, no waiting, a rusty but earnest performance by Sinatra himself, and brief speeches on behalf of the skin foundation by aging television stars and hopeful politicians.

Five actor-speakers told what was essentially the same bad joke about malfunctioning organs whose punchline was that the organ they meant was the skin. Hallie tuned out. During speakers three and four, she realized that of the six women at her table, only she was roughly the same age as her husband.

The same was true of the entire room, unless a lot of the young and gorgeous female consorts were on-duty geriatric nurses.

She shivered. "First wife" was right up there with Siberian tigers on the endangered species list.

During speakers four and five, Hallie investigated her boodle bag, finding a crystal pin box, a flacon of perfume, designer chocolates, a sports watch with Harry Bevan's logo on its face, and a silver picture frame.

Next to her, Ted pulled out cologne and aftershave, a man's version of the watch, miniature brandy bottles, a silver-plated corkscrew, and a travel alarm.

Yet another semi-faded comic praised them for being generous and told them that skin was important.

"Lucky we came," Ted whispered. "I was about to throw away my skin, but they've turned me around on that."

Finally, Harry Bevan the film mogul announced that he was donating a million dollars to the cause. "What if," Hallie whispered, "everybody stayed home and mailed in the amount their dress and hairdo would have cost? Don't you think they'd come out with a bigger profit?" Ted didn't smile. He eats this up, she thought as he propelled her onto the dance floor. The superficial asshole thinks I'm drab, a provincial creep.

She'd vowed to be true through better and worse and had meant it, thinking the trick was riding out the hard times. But they'd done that with reasonable grace and here she was with an excess of "better." Rich enough to choke on. The betters were turning out to be the worst.

An ancient film idol creaked by with his child-bride. His skin had been so tightly pulled and snipped, his thin face looked like a death head. "He doesn't have enough left to frown with," Hallie whispered. "Has to smile forever, like a 'Have a nice day' button."

"Incredible, isn't it?" Ted said.

He loved it. She knew, with a great sag of her heart, that they were not going to last.

"The epitome of excessiveness," he said. "I wish your father were here. How he'd love hating it."

And suddenly they were back in alignment, synchronized in more than dance steps.

"Had enough?" he asked.

"Of this party? Definitely."

"How about of excessiveness? Because, inspired by the night, I have some interesting ideas."

"If they involve sequins, I quit now," she said. But all the same, they left, hand in hand, laughing.

"Hal? Where are you?"

"In the living room! Good morning!"

"Ready?" he called. "Brunch starts in twenty-five—"

"Close your eyes."

"We'll be late for the—"

She heard the bed squeak softly, as if he were leaving it. "Wait!" she called.

"I have to shave."

She pulled open the wooden doors that separated the rooms. "Naked girl-o-gram!" she said, her arms to the sides, one hand on each of the folding doors, and HAPPY ANNIVERSARY written across her breasts and midriff in cream cheese. Her nipples and belly button, along with the *H* and the *A*, were outlined in caviar, thanks to the largesse of the rosewood refrigerator.

Teddy, laughing, sat back on the rumpled bed. She walked toward him, kicking clothing aside with her bare feet. His tuxedo shirt. Her gossamer dress. A pair of stockings. One patent leather man's pump.

"I've been waiting for you to wake up. Trying not to stain the living-room furniture," she said.

"Your *n*'s are backward," he said. "You didn't compensate for the mirror."

"Haggling over penmanship?" She walked very close to the bed and pushed a hip with a caviar heart tattoo close to him.

"Weren't we sufficiently excessive last night?"

"Are you kidding?"

"I'm not a young man anymore."

"Hey, fella, I know you."

"But brunch!"

"You're looking at it." She passed him the phone.

She waited, looking merry and, she hoped, sexy and, she hoped even more, not as anxious as she felt. More than she cared to acknowledge at the moment had come to hinge on his decision.

"But he planned this meal, reserved a private room at—"

"Ted, I planned this meal, and this room is as private as it gets. And more important, this is our anniversary, yours and mine, and Fritter has no right to plan that."

Choose me. This is not a test. This is an actual emergency.

He clamped his mouth, then he looked at her.

"Trust me," she said. "I'm more fun than a bagel."

When Ted finally dialed, she lay back on the sheets—carefully—and listened with pure pleasure.

"Fritter?" he said. "I hope this won't interfere too much with your plans, but Hallie and I, we're . . . eating in the room."

"Oh, Ted," she said when he hung up, "I would marry you again in a flash. I do right now. Happy Anniversary. I now pronounce us man and brunch."

He licked cream cheese and caviar from her nipple. "Delicious," he said.

There was a chance they'd make it. Even through the betters.

Tremors

1981–1982

If you are afraid of loneliness, don't marry.
Anton Chekhov

---------- 1 ----------

SHE stood at the kitchen's center island, tapping her nails on the side of a picnic basket from which a bottle of wine protruded. His muscles tensed. "I heard the phone," she said.

"The prototype arrived."

"And if you don't test it today, July Fourth, the very fabric of our society will rip asunder."

He popped a water cracker in his mouth. "I won't be long."

She pushed the entire picnic basket inside the refrigerator, her movements rough and jerky. She looked so defeated, so wretched, he moved toward her, arms out, but she shook her head, and he stopped and left her untouched. "Why do you make life difficult?" he demanded. "I love you and being a success. Why should that be an impossible combination?"

Her expression looked like a nail on a blackboard sounded.

"Why do you jump when he snaps his finger? Why do you measure success in dollars?"

He felt for his car keys in his pockets, but couldn't find them. "I'll be back as soon as I can."

"I won't hold my breath."

"Make sure your second husband has a nine-to-five job and a low salary, okay?" He checked the hook on the wall, then searched under the newspaper, the student bus tickets, and the tennis shoe littering the kitchen desk. Her house was as much a mess as her priorities. They'd been mismatched from the git-go.

He left to see if the keys were on his night table, just as the phone rang again. By the time he returned, keys jingling, Hallie had hung up. "Chloe," she said. "Chloe Wister. She's in town for an audition. Leaving tomorrow. I invited her over."

"Here? Today? It was supposed to be the two of us today."

"Yes," she said. "It certainly was."

Chloe sat on the deck and waved expansively at the surrounding hills as if blessing them. The sun hung low, hot and heavy, rouging her white wicker chair. She twirled her glass so that the pink light caught the crystal facets. "When's Ted due?"

"I'm not sure." Two, three hours ago? Chloe had once said a shared life was a half-life, like what radioactive waste had. Maybe she was right, after all.

They sipped wine and talked softly as the sun melted into the horizon, burning the treetops bright lime, their bottoms, a chilly purple. Twilight made Hallie think of her scattered children, instinctively ready to gather them to safety for the night. But Sarah was away at sports camp, Andy was at Tahoe for the weekend, and Erica was working in the city. In September, she started college.

This was the hour of letting go.

Chloe, silhouetted against a scarlet-streaked sky, poured the last of the wine and Hallie went to get more. She checked the kitchen clock.

Fucker forgot about me again.

Wrong. He hadn't forgotten anything. He was demonstrating manly autonomy.

She wondered if there was such a thing as womanly autonomy.

She lined a wicker basket with a napkin and filled it with chips. Hungry all the time, ready to peel the plaster off the walls and stuff it down her throat. Her skirt bands were tight, her skin loose and puffy.

She pulled another bottle of wine from the refrigerator and returned to the deck. What the hell.

The sun was altogether gone now. Only pearly afterglow remained near the horizon with a dark lid of clouds on top of it. Chloe's skin was luminous in the near-dark. "You and Ted are the only old, original first marriage I know. How come?"

In the dusk, she shrugged. "Used to be, whoever left first had to take the kids. Now that the kids are leaving, we're holding out for the Guinness Book of Marriages."

"Seriously."

She thought, then finally spoke. "So far, the times it stops being fun or good are shorter than the time it would take to undo the contract. The weight of the institution keeps us in place."

"Yes." Chloe's voice was suddenly harsh, almost angry. "It keeps a lot of people in their places. Including me. I didn't come west for an audition. I'm a frequent-flyer bonus on a business trip, except he suddenly remembered relatives, a family party up at Russian River. What better excuse for staying out here over the holiday weekend? He'll be back tonight to fuck me and then we'll leave tomorrow and maybe he'll call me again and maybe he won't."

There was a long silence. Then Chloe laughed, a hard little bark. "I imagined us tragic lovers. Set us to the love-death theme, you know? I was his Isolde, the forbidden love-object, the beloved." Her voice mocked her failed illusions. "There were two Isoldes, remember? The one Tristan adored and couldn't have and the one he married, Isolde of the white hands, who nobody remembers, who doesn't matter. But he remembers her enough to dump me at the hotel and take off for the sake of an alibi!"

Chloe broke a chip into small pieces, then tossed them onto the deck. "I'm an office temp to pay my rent while I audition and hear I'm too old or not the type. I have nothing saved. I'm forty-one years old. I'll never have a child. I've never even lived with a man, and now that I'd like to, everybody's afraid of palimony suits."

"Come on, you're just feeling sorry for yourself."

"I should know better. I've heard this story a million times in my group."

"You're still in the CR group?" Hallie was swamped with nostalgia, sorrow, and jealousy, remembering the closeness she'd had with her group in Boston.

Chloe shook her head and filled her glass again. "A support group for other women."

"What other women?"

Chloe laughed. "The plural of *the* other woman."

Hallie sat back further in her wicker chair. Oh Brave New World that has such broad-based empathy.

A great many of Hallie's clients were what was now called "displaced homemakers." It was hard to listen to their stories, hard to be a rapidly aging, first, training wife herself and feel compassion for the predators. Andy had told her about the hagfish that rasped its way into another fish and consumed it from inside. She couldn't get past the sense that the Chloes in that support group were hagfish.

"Why so silent?" Chloe asked. "What are you thinking?"

"Honestly? Not everything should be supported. If you willingly put yourself into a grief-filled situation, and in fact help create it, then expect and endure the emotional fallout."

"Not everything's so cut and dried. It happened. I couldn't help it."

"You're too taken with your myths. You didn't drink a magic potion. You're in control of your own actions."

"Well, I didn't start it. Why was the guy looking, if there weren't already problems?"

"There are always problems. But there's nothing like another woman to make them insurmountable." The night felt heavy and dense, broken only by the creaks of the wicker chairs.

And where was Ted?

"If you don't like your life, change it." Hallie's tone was harsher than intended. "Why stay with a man who doesn't care enough about you? A man who left you stranded today?" Her words punctured the night air, and echoed. She was glad it was too dark for Chloe to see and question her shocked expression.

"I'm home! Wait till I tell you. It's fantastic, the game to end all games. Sorry I didn't call."

He did a soft-shoe through the foyer, into the living room. Every kid in the universe would want this one.

Andy and Sarah could be the first to play, the envy of their peers. Erica was too terribly sophisticated, but maybe he'd twist her arm. He felt expansive, a beneficent father bringing his children treasures.

The house was dark. It was much later than intended. He'd say he'd wanted to wait until Chloe was gone.

"Hello!" he called, flicking light switches. He half expected Hallie to leap out brandishing a rolling pin, like in the comics.

He felt woozy and didn't know why. Only one celebratory drink with Fritter. He'd *had* to stop by after seeing how it worked, whether or not Hallie understood.

Ms. Compassion was uncharitable about Fritter. Sure, the man was crude, insensitive, certainly not up to date on politically acceptable nonsexist jargon. But he had his own genius, a kid's-eye view of the cosmos combined with an adult's ability to make it real. "Hallie?" Nothing.

He walked from dark kitchen through dark dining room to dark family room up to dark master bedroom. The quilted, puffed spread was smooth, neatly tucked under the pillows. Untouched. He walked out and examined the remaining bedrooms, lighting them as he moved, feeling like Goldilocks. Nobody sleeping in Sarah's room. Or Andy's, where the aquarium glowed blue and eerie in the dark. He turned off the light, let the gouramis sleep. Nobody in Erica's or the guest room. Nobody in the bathrooms.

"Hallie? Where are you?" He didn't like how frightened and childlike he sounded.

She was gone.

He remembered her tight, unhappy face. He acknowledged the fact that she was independent now, made a living, albeit a pitiable one. She didn't need him for that anymore and she'd been saying, in many ways, that she wasn't getting what she did need.

He sat down at the top of the stairs. Everything could have waited until tomorrow. Why did he always buy into Fritter's emergencies? Was he really a yes-man, a well-paid lackey?

They could have climbed the hill to the lake and had their picnic and watched the sunset together the way they'd planned. It wasn't much of a demand and it was what he'd wanted, too. He wanted her. He could have given her that much.

But he hadn't. He'd put the next-to-last straw on the camel, and instead of waiting until its back broke, his camel checked out.

He put his hand on his chest and forced himself to inhale, then exhale, and when he walked downstairs, he held tight to the bannister.

He carefully retraced his route, as if Hallie were something he might easily have missed. "She left me." Guys said it and you thought that kind of thing could happen to them, but it was unimaginable in your life, with your wife.

This time, he spotted it, a note on the kitchen counter. He stood across the room, not touching it. Nothing counted, nothing was real if you didn't read it. Finally, he forced himself across the tile and picked it up, feeling feeble.

Teddy—
   Chloe had too much to drink and is in no condition to drive to the city. Her rental car's in somebody else's name and it has to be returned. Besides, she's flying out first thing tomorrow, so I've driven her back. (over)

He laughed with relief. An ordinary, even boring, note. His pulse began a descent. He turned the note over.

   Since there seem to be no binding commitments at this address, I've booked myself a suite at the Fairmont until further notice. If you need me.
   Happy Independence Day, Hallie

He grinned. Hallie threw the gauntlet, not a rolling pin, and she didn't come cheap.

But she hadn't left him, although he now knew, with certainty and for the first time, that she was capable of doing so.

But not quite yet. She was offering a lifeline and an oh, so polite warning.

He pocketed the note, his passport and ticket of entry to that suite at the Fairmont.

I do need you, he answered it. I definitely need a hard-headed woman who's still a sucker for semi-lost causes.

———————— 2 ————————

"We used to call underwear foundation garments." Sylvia Saxe lifted a royal purple bra and bikini brief. "But nothing here holds anything up or in. It just decorates it."

Sarah, mouth pouty over braces, smiled.

"So what do you think of Gone Too Farr? Despite the lack of corsets and girdles." Megan Farr, purveyor and creator of erotic fantasies, was justifiably proud of every detail of her small store. While she spoke, she smoothed a teal nightgown, then straightened a lacy bulletin board with a rainbow of bras tacked on it.

They had already toured Vicky's bakery and café, and its yeasty imprint was in this part of the barn, too, in the cinnamon-scented air. "I'm wildly impressed by both you tycoons," Sylvia said.

Megan's smile had always seemed larger than her entire frame, and its frequency had escalated in the last two years, correlating perfectly with the opening of Gone Too Farr. She had also re-sumed wearing bright colors and her hair was cut and shaped. "I'm only a tycoonlet," she said. "Although anything's possible. I'm working with a consultant now about catalog sales." She took a deep breath and grinned again. "You and Sarah are staying for dinner, aren't you, Hal?"

"Wish I could. Entertaining clients."

"Yours?"

"You have to be kidding." She lifted the corner of a black and white satin kimono designed for somebody fifteen years younger whose parts did not flap. "Some South American muckety-muck with a new way to retail games. His wife and I will smile and compare offspring while the men talk business."

"Don't be modest." Megan refolded a half-slip the color of new grass. "You'll eat pâté somewhere elegant while we slop spaghetti in the farmhouse again."

"They could never have called the old corset stores Gone Too Farr," Sylvia said. "It was impossible to go anywhere in that latex armor. Or to get out of it."

Sarah giggled. At thirteen, she veered between innocence and world-weary sophistication.

Sylvia checked her watch. "I'd best be going."

"Dad's napping. And Polly's with him." Her father was on fast-forward, aging at an escalated tempo. The most alarming evidence was his new placidity. Now, when Sylvia said something, instead of the traditional, reflex argument, Ivan shrugged and picked up a newspaper. His family had come to miss what he once insisted were "only discussions."

"Um, where are, um, the boys?" Sarah's voice was so studiedly nonchalant, Hallie bit her lips to hide her smile.

"Steve had a softball game in Petaluma and Mike's . . ." Megan glanced at her watch. "He'll be at the house any minute."

Sarah dragged her finger through an entire rack's price tags. "So, um," she said, "guess I'll walk up there with Grandmom." She was ready to leave when Michael Farr and a thin man with a long, weathered face walked in, so she repositioned herself in a casual pose Hallie had seen her practice at home.

"Michael! What's wrong? Why are you here?" Megan's worried glance spun from her son to the man to Hallie.

"Ben needs to know about next Saturday," Michael said.

"I have tickets for a Giants game." The newly identified Ben had a comfortably serious voice and face. "Is it okay?"

"Sure," Megan said, too quickly. "No problem."

Hallie wondered at the terseness, the failure to introduce Ben, the nervously flitting glance.

"See you ten-thirty, then," Ben said before leaving.

Megan nervously refolded a camisole.

"You leaving?" Mike asked. He was gawky and slight and seemed more than six months younger than Sarah, but there was a dark sullen beauty, the alluring aura of an unpredictable bad boy. Hallie sighed for Sarah's sake.

"Oh, I thought I might," Sarah said.

"Well, me too." He opened the door.

Sarah shot her grandmother an anguished look.

"Don't wait for me, kids," Sylvia said. They didn't. "Hormones," she muttered. "I'll walk slowly."

"Who was he?" Hallie asked.

"Who?"

"The guy. Ben."

"Nobody." Megan opened a door marked PRIVATE and flicked on a light. The room was lined with cartons, gowns on layaway, walls full of lingerie ads. "A thousand and one ways to decorate tits and crotches. What a business for a celibate widow-woman." She lifted two cartons off a ladderback chair. "Sit," she said. Then she flipped through papers on her gray metal desk. "A guy wants me to stock a line of maternity lingerie called Mother Fuckers, can you believe it?"

"What I can't believe is how evasive you are."

"I might be featured in *Cosmo* this spring. An article about seduction. My own design, not the other stuff I carry, but I never answered. . . . Ben Madera, okay?"

"But, still, who is he?"

Megan started wringing her hands. Hallie hadn't seen that since San Diego, eight years earlier. "The school felt Mike needed . . ." Megan breathed deeply, sat down at her desk and put a hand on each knee, her eyes downcast. "It's humiliating. A male role model."

"That's no reason to be so upset."

"Michael's not meek like I was, thank God, but schools don't know what to do with kids who don't fit the mold." She scratched her forehead, pulled at her earlobe, touched her fingertips to her lips, then, seeming to reach a decision, she opened the desk drawer. "The eighth-graders had to find poems that meant something to them, and he picked . . ." She passed over a sheet of lined notebook paper, handling it gingerly, as if it were contaminated. "He had to look hard and long for this."

Hallie read:

> *They fuck you up, your mum and dad,*
> *They may not mean to, but they do.*

The poem continued in a similar vein. When Hallie looked up, Megan, hands in fists, was biting her bottom lip. Her nose was bright pink.

"It's only a poem! It has bad words to freak his teachers," Hallie said. "He wasn't talking about you. Shock value, that's all. Everybody else probably brought in little cats' feet or Emily Dickinson. He's creative."

"I try so hard. It's the only thing that matters to me. I want to make it okay. Make up for. Why that poem?"

"Because he's thirteen and it has to be one of the only legitimate poems he could find that says 'fuck.' "

"Then they said he lacked discipline! If they only knew how much discipline he once . . . And then sneered at his untraditional household. That's what they called it, because we're two single women. But this kid in his class, Shazam? He lives in a yurt and has three communal fathers, a birth mother, and four yurt mothers. Why pick on Mike?"

"You're taking a call from school too seriously."

"They made me feel like—like the poem was right. Like I couldn't save him, he was doomed. If they knew how it was when he had that so-called normal home, when I was properly married!"

"Come on, this Ben whoever, Mike's counselor, seems—"

"His Big Brother. Sounds like Father Flanagan's Boy's Town. Makes Michael . . . needy. He's not heavy, he's my little brother."

"Ben seems nice."

"So what? *I'm* Michael's parent. Ben takes him for special outings like Santa Claus. I can't afford to take off next Saturday for a baseball game. So I . . . what's my role?" She tried for a smile.

"Except, of course, my specialty. The fucker-upper. I did not mean to, but I did."

— 3 —

Hallie filled the pots with soapy water and turned off the faucet.

Ted emptied an unfinished bottle of wine into two glasses and she gladly accepted one. "Went well, don't you think?" he asked. "Considering."

"Considering. I used to think nobody entertained anymore because we were too busy with work. Now I think it's because we've had too much time to screw up and screw around so that it's dangerous to risk untried combinations. We need dinner party matchmakers. You'd fill in a questionnaire and buy no-friction matched sets."

After it was too late to change her guest list, she'd found out that David Strong's date for the evening was the bitch who'd broken up Missy Parkins's first marriage and that Peter, Missy's current husband, was Penny George's shrink and that David Strong and Charlie Meyerson were in litigation about a property line issue and that Charlie Meyerson had been much too successful as Bill George's first wife's divorce lawyer.

And even though the inertia of civilization and half the wine cellar kept the tooth-grinding, the feudin' and a-fightin' to a minimum, there were other, equally daunting pitfalls.

Peter Parkins was carbo-loading for a marathon.

Missy Parkins ate no red meat.

David Strong, perhaps because of his house-wrecking bedmate, had suffered a mild heart attack and was on no-fat, no-salt, no-sugar Pritikin.

The house-wrecker's nutritionist had sworn her off grains and dairy products.

Penny George was on a protein-sparing fast. She brought her milkshake mix and personal blender, requiring six ice cubes to thicken the mix.

Bill George was strictly meat and potatoes.

Charlie Meyerson was a recovering alcoholic with a shellfish allergy.

Kitty Meyerson shunned inorganic produce, nonunion grapes, and politically incorrect veal.

Nobody could tolerate caffeine; everybody wanted to lose weight and life had become too complex for dinner parties.

Hallie put away the washed crystal. Up on a high shelf sat a set of individual ashtrays, from pre-history when good hostessing meant providing easy access to between-course smokes.

"Once upon a time, food wasn't scary," Ted said later, upstairs in bed. "Remember?"

Hallie nodded in the dark. "Real cream in your coffee," she murmured.

"Real coffee!"

"Bacon." She put her face near his and whispered, "Crisp, wonderful bacon."

"Cheese. Brie and Camembert and St. Andre."

"Sweet butter slathered on bread." She sucked on the soft lobe of his ear.

Ted groaned and shifted his body so that he faced her.

"Eggs," she murmured. "Sunny side up, cooked in bacon grease."

"Barbecue. Big fat ribs."

"And rib roast with the crackly wall of fat around it."

"Oh, God, when you talk that way—and fried everything! Chips and chicken, and remember when fish was always fried? Fried oysters, fried zucchini, French fries, home fries—"

"Desserts. Eclairs. Doughnuts. Oh, Lord, I can just—"

"Oh, oh, me, too." His hand ran up her thigh.

"And liquor. Hard liquor. Scotch and bourbon and Harvey Wallbangers and Black Russians and—" She moved her hip against his, pressed.

"Egg salad sandwiches." His lips were on her ear. "Sausage." His hands all over her, then his mouth.

"Rocky Road ice cream!" Her hands cupped his buttocks, she pulled him close, then closer.

"Cream sauce!" His breathing was rapid and shallow. "Garlic butter! Hollandaise!"

"Yes!" they said. "Oh, God, yes!"

4

"You're my only client selling a house without a court order." Paula the realtor was in her early fifties, short and chunky with a fluff of blond curls and a nonstop mouth.

"I'm not selling or buying. Only looking," Hallie said.

Paula nodded, humoring her.

Ted wanted bigger and better, his worth demonstrated in mortar, so week after week, Hallie looked, hoping not to find. They needed less house, not more, with the children leaving and both of them at work all the time. Nobody needed or would use a yard except Spot, the white mutt Sarah had brought home. It was insane to househunt for the dog.

At least Paula was amusing, offering opinions on everything. At the moment, as they cruised past the OPEN HOUSE signs, Paula discoursed on the value of workouts.

"I don't lose weight. I don't get firm, but I see naked women," she said after Hallie vetoed an Italianate monstrosity. "When we went to school, girls had to be modest, am I right? Towels pulled around us. The only nude women I saw were in *Playboy* and I always felt like a mutant. Then, at the gym, I see that when they aren't airbrushed, women have hair and droops and veins and I'm not abnormal." She slowed down and pointed.

"It looks like a grain silo," Hallie said.

Paula sighed and accelerated again. The silo's driveway was lined with boulders. Hallie envisioned its occupants shivering inside their bleak domicile on this wet February Sunday.

"See that?" Paula pointed at a Dutch Colonial. "My ex lives there with snookums. She won't let his kids—my kids—in her house, and he's such a yutz, he goes along. For Father's Day, he met them on the driveway, took their gifts, and went back inside."

Hallie shook her head sympathetically.

Paula sighed. "No fault. It was like an Arab divorce. He walks around me saying, 'I divorce you,' and I have as much to do with it as a piece of anthracite. Then I have to sell the house so we can split our assets. The judge says that since I put the yutz through school as a typist, I am obviously capable of earning a living. So I wind up with no house, four kids, and a year to find that living I'm supposed to be able to make. I finally find it selling other no-fault divorcees' houses. This is why I love America."

"The adversarial system was worse."

"Nah. I *like* fault. You catch your husband with his balls hanging over your best friend and you're supposed to say hey, we've outlawed blame? Forget the Judeo-Christian tradition—there's no more fault. Who are we kidding?"

Hallie wondered in what century the realtor's divorce would truly become history and stop hurting.

"Used to be, he paid for fun through the nose. Remember that saying 'The screwing he gets for the screwing he got'?"

"Hey," Hallie said. "Look—up there." In the sky above them, half a dozen small brown birds pursued a raven, around him, behind him, like a cloud of gnats.

"It's called mobbing," Paula said. "The crow threatened the nest, so everybody gangs up and drives him away." She slowed to a halt and they watched the attacker retreat. "Some nerve to call them bird brains. We should only be that smart about housebreakers." She put the car back in gear.

"So," Paula said after Hallie had declined to inspect three more houses. "You know how to tell a first wife from a second? The first wife has fake jewels and real orgasms." They were on a cobbled circular drive with a Bentley near the front door. "Don't like this place either, right?"

"This isn't a house, it's a bank statement."

Paula looked at a list on the seat between them and put her car in reverse. They backed onto the blacktop and left. "The son of a bitch who owns that place looks like Albert Einstein with a blow-dry hairdo. He installed twenty-year-old twins in the master suite and told his wife she had no understanding of the male condition. Prime candidate for Camp Asshole."

"Do I want to know what that is?" Hallie was becoming homesick.

"A business idea. Summer camp for mid-life men, subsidized by first wives. Nobody but twenty-six-year-old bimbos, who also do the cooking and cleaning. Barbed wire and a minimum two-month stay. They can screw till their cocks fall off, but they can't talk to grown women till they serve their time and beg for it."

"Aren't you afraid it'd backfire and they'd want to stay?"

She shrugged. "Let them. Thin out the herd. Listen, there's one last place. Spacious but not splashy. Asking eight-fifty."

Hallie slumped in her seat. Falling up was very odd.

"Your husband's president of the hottest company in the Valley," Paula said softly. "It means you live a certain way."

Dressing for success included houses, even though, until the company went public, Ted had more title than income.

"You worry about him?" Paula asked. "He must meet fancy females. Good-looking man."

"There are good men, you know."

Paula shrugged and pulled onto the highway. "How would I? That house I mentioned? It's got a pretty garden. They're nice people, and it shows."

"Why are those nice people selling?"

"Need you ask?"

How could Tolstoy have thought that all happy families were alike? Only in the way that all miracles were alike. "What if divorce became unthinkable again?" Hallie said. "Like it was. What if everybody had to work things out, or stick them out, the way our parents did?"

Paula laughed. "Civilization as we know it would end." The pink flowers on her raincoat bobbled with each exhalation. "Divorce, not defense or computers, keeps our economy going. That's why nobody supports marriage anymore. Think—unemployed realtors, condo builders, child-care workers, mediators, bar owners, therapists, dating service owners, support group coordinators. . . ."

The drizzly gray around the car made Hallie yearn for a warm kitchen. She could bake today. Sarah would learn to love the chemistry of cooking as Hallie did, the way elements became new things that only happened in combination. It was like sex. Like families. "I feel an irresistible need for home," Hallie said. "My home. Nice people live there, too."

She knew something was wrong the minute she turned the key. No rock music to demand lowered. No squabbling. An abnormal graciousness in the greetings. Andy looking up from the funnies and saying, "Hi, Mom," instead of grunting. Sarah fluttery and anxious.

"I'm sorry," Ted said, holding her. "Very bad news. Your dad. It was quick. He didn't suffer."

Her raincoat was removed, and she was seated. Words kept coming, soothing, bridging the time he was alive, remote but there, and now, filling his newly emptied space.

"Arrangements. Called the airlines. We can—"

Ted sat on one side, arm around her, Andy on the other, Sarah on the floor in front. Even Spot came close.

This is how things happen, Hallie thought. Out of the blue, out of the gray, without warning. While you think your biggest worry is wasting Sunday looking at houses.

My father is dead. The father I hoped to someday know no longer exists and the stories and wisdom and secrets he didn't choose to share are gone. She felt desolate, cheated of possibility.

My poor mother.

My poor father.

My poor me.

She remembered her mother crying long ago because she wanted to be closer, to sleep by her husband until the end.

And Hallie looked at Ted and in his amber eyes saw that when it counted, he understood the difference between the real and the ephemeral.

He held her close and she was sure she'd never cry in a kitchen for being lonely with him. She was sure they'd keep holding for all the time there was, which would not be enough.

Right now, she held on for dear life.

Fritter leaned back in his desk chair, an action that always made Ted nervous, even though the chair had been engineered for its owner's girth.

"They loved them," Ted said.

"All of them?"

"We could have sold your toenail clippings. This was your toy show." The man required endless ego-massaging. Fritter had already seen the figures, tallied the advance orders, understood ·his success, but he had to hear it, and he had to hear it from Ted Bennett. "They said our games had a look, a cleverness."

"Good," Fritter said. "Now we move on. Three things."

Trials or wishes, like in fairy tales.

"First, I want us to be the entire best-seller list. One hundred percent."

They already had the top, fourth, and tenth slots. "We'll come close with these new five."

"Close isn't what I said. The entire list. Make history. Our three, the new five, and two more."

Where was the genie to go zap—two more best-selling games? Fritter had an adult's vocabulary, a king's pocketbook, and a two year old's ability to accept limits. But who was Ted to question the man's genius or desires? The more best-sellers, the more valuable their inventory, the better the price of their stock when they went public, and the richer Teddy Bennett and his descendants.

"Next." Fritter leaned back, chair squealing. "The best architect in the country. Correction. The world."

"What kind of game is that?"

Fritter straightened his chair with a whoomph of leather and a clump of his feet on the floor. "No game. Headquarters. We're building our own Funny Farm. Why stay in this dump? Why pay rent? Apple has a campus. I want one, too. Only my buildings won't look like cartons. I want imagination. I want the *New York Times* architectural critic to come when he sees it. I want awards."

Would he really piss away their profit on his ego?

"Hey! You haven't been home in five days," Fritter said. "A

shame Hallie's so career-minded. She could have gone with you, made it a vacation. Go home and visit. She's okay, isn't she?"

"Hallie? Fine." What kind of campus? What cost? Hundreds of millions? "Depressed about her dad. It's been a few rough months, back and forth to Philly since the funeral."

"Still house-hunting?"

"Not much since February, like I said."

"Well, it's May now. Time to start again. You think Lucy could go along with Hallie? She's kind of mopey." Two months before Ivan Saxe's death, the day before Christmas, Lucy lost her mother. She'd been withdrawn ever since. "You know," Fritter said, "even on her death bed the old fanatic wouldn't talk to Luce because of the divorce."

Ted shook his head sympathetically. "I'll tell Hallie to give her a call." And Hallie will tell me she doesn't work for Fritter Marks and that I can't tell her what to do. And I will remind her that she likes Lucy, and she will insist that it's the principle of the thing. "See you tomorrow, then." He was halfway to the door when he remembered. "There were three things."

"Oh, right. There's this guy, Peterkins. Get him in the family to build a team for voice-activated games. Kid talks to the tube and makes things happen. Hot idea, huh?"

What was wrong with Fritter? "There's no interface technology for talking to the monitor," Ted said.

"Peterkins will invent it! And hire artists, too."

Four. Not even kings got four wishes. "But we already have the best artists in—"

"Not computer-graphics people. Art like in galleries, museums. I want that kind of mind and imagination on my side. Get them with the computer engineers and they'll knock the industry's socks off, right?"

Painters and sculptors? Ted nodded feebly.

"What? No lecture on spending too much?"

Ted roused himself. "Frankly, I don't want us caught in a cash-flow situation. We're already overboard on esoteric research, so I would emphatically advise against adding more nonproductive personnel, and as for a campus—"

"I appreciate your input. We both feel better now."

Ted smiled from the depths of economic necessity. Two, three years. Then they'd go public and he'd be out from under the fattest thumb in computers.

"I'll get on everything tomorrow." His throat felt tight and raw. He wondered what bug he'd caught.

Unrecorded Road Kills

1982–1983

Marriages would in general be as happy, and often more so, if
they were all made by the Lord Chancellor, upon due
consideration
of the characters and circumstances without the parties having
any choice in the matter.

Samuel Johnson

1

"YOU didn't miss much," Megan said. "Middle-aged
jokes about failing eyesight and bad sex and middle-
aged whispers about who's dead or divorced."

Hallie had skipped her twenty-fifth high-school reunion. If she'd felt better about her appearance, she might have
gone, revisited her youth. And Craig Forman, whose memory
and potential still tickled a portion of her brain.

"Some people really changed. Remember skinny Roy? At
least three hundred pounds. And Stan, who was in that commune the last ten years? He's a bond salesman now. I went to
make sure I'd changed, too," Megan said. "The old high-school
measuring rod. I had to feel good about myself in front of
them, and I did."

Their class was beginning to meet the statistical norms and not only in marital casualties. According to Megan, two classmates were battling breast cancer. One had survived a heart attack. It didn't bear too much thought.

They stood on the first floor of I. Magnin's. Upstairs, a few minutes ago, a buyer had—almost—promised to—probably—carry Megan's Gone Too Farr designs.

So despite statistical probability, anything seemed possible on this wide-open autumn Saturday with its drinkable air and a cable car clanging at the end of Union Square. Anything except finding a formal dress for Hallie, who searched with the enthusiasm of an archeologist forced to excavate a cesspool.

They had already exhausted Magnin's racks and salespeople. "I feel like a cow," Hallie said. "Like a grandmother."

"Sally and Martha already are. Grandmothers, not cows," Megan said.

They crossed the square and walked into Saks. "I'll never be one. Erica swears she won't marry. Andy's only interested in fish and baseball, and Sarah is so sick of being ignored by your son, she's petitioning the Vatican to allow Jewish nuns."

"Means nothing. Marriage is no longer required and men are unnecessary. Penises are passé. One of my customers was impregnated by a sperm bank specializing in 'the semen of geniuses.' Doesn't that sound like breakfast cereal?"

They made their way through sweet-smelling cosmetics and up the escalator. Hallie felt like a penitent. Please, somebody up there, make me look nice.

She headed for the heavily beaded numbers chained to their rack, like prisoners. The dresses were so stiffly constructed, they didn't need a body to fill them. They could go out and have a perfectly good time without her.

"Didn't the evil monkey warriors in *The Wizard of Oz* wear something like that?" Megan asked.

"Let's finish and go have a long something cold," Hallie said.

"I, um, have to get home."

"That's the sound of a woman with a date. Who is he?"

Megan found a dress that looked spun of sea foam. "Remember Mike's Big Brother? Ben? He's not bad when he isn't phasing me out as a parent." The whole time she spoke, she searched the rack, pulling out three more dresses. "I'll keep you posted."

"Hope springs eternal," Hallie said once inside the dressing room. "Except in a three-way mirror. I hate this. Spend a fortune to look weird and waste an evening with people I don't like, all for the greater glory of Ted Bennett's career."

"Ah, Hal, why don't you give in to your life?"

Hallie pulled an emerald taffeta confection over her head. "Because I don't like it. I have motion sickness from the speed we're moving, and I don't want to go where we're heading."

"What you don't and never have liked is shopping. You and Ted have the best marriage in the world."

Megan sat quietly, knees together, on an upholstered pouf, holding Hallie's bag. "Some of those parties must be fun." Little Megan Sunshine would never change. "And being mentioned in *Newsweek* and all."

"Ted's mentioned, not me. I look like a wing chair in this. Don't worry, we're not getting divorced yet. He thinks he's going to be rich. I'll wait till then." She smiled to show she was kidding. Probably kidding.

Megan held a black beaded dress out like an offering.

Hallie shook her head. "My grandmother wore that to her fiftieth anniversary party. She looked like a troll with orthopedic shoes. Every day she called my mother to complain about my grandfather, but at the party, when he danced with her cousin Ida, she waddled out and swatted both of them with her handbag—also beaded. Jet beads rolled all over the floor, and Ida fell on her tush, but Grandma skidded around until she'd thrown her husband out of his own anniversary party." Hallie stood in her slip and sighed. "She died a month after he did, and every day in between, she cried that she missed him. None of it makes sense."

She lifted the two remaining dresses. "This pink number reminds me of tissue samples, and forget the blue. My hips haven't gotten smaller in the last ten minutes."

"The problem is not how you look in the mirror," Megan said. "The problem is how you look *at* the mirror."

Hallie closed her eyes. "Reading perky how-to's again? 'Five thousand ways to feel better about yourself? I thought you said you were boycotting magazines until they write the same stuff for men." Megan had made up articles like "Guys! Look Younger," and "Ten Mistakes Fellas Make in the Dating Game," and "Colognes to Enhance Your Manliest You."

"I'm clean, I swear it."

"Then where did that mirror garbage come from? Have you been sucked into the touchy-feely seminars? Next you'll tell me to get my head on straight."

Megan giggled. "That's how Christina talks. Says she's finally getting her shit together. I imagine her with acres and acres, tons of shit she's gotten together by now."

Hallie zipped her comfortable old skirt and pulled on her boots. The rejected dresses twinkled and taunted on their hangers.

"She asked about you."

"Me? Or my husband?" They left the dressing room and Hallie looked apologetically at the expectant saleswoman. This time the customer, or at least the customer's body, was definitely wrong.

"Now that you mention it, she did mention Ted's being in the *New York Times*."

Hallie scowled.

"Okay, I won't talk about her anymore. Can I talk about her ex?" They left the building and crossed the square. "Grady called. His wife, that agent in L.A., had a baby. Twenty-four years between his first daughter and this one. He's ecstatic."

"And I bet he insists that this time he finally knows how to be a daddy and really appreciates the baby." Why was everything, even this relative stranger's fatherhood, annoying her today?

"Yes, why?"

"As if the first family was for training, like the first pancake, made for the tossing. Makes me mad."

Megan looked at her quizzically. "What I was trying to say is that Grady's wife is back to work and Grady's home with the baby. His gigs are at night, anyway."

"A househusband. Christina's probably sick to have her ex trendier than she is."

In Neiman Marcus Hallie again faced merciless mirrors that

accused her of insufficient self-control. Not sexual abandon, because that didn't count anymore. Her sins of the flesh were serious, unforgivable. She was promiscuous about food.

Thou shalt not be dumpy. The only Commandment left.

"I'm moving to Iran," she told Megan. "There's something to be said for wearing body bags while you're still alive. Don't have to pull in your stomach or worry over a few pounds." She sucked in. "What do you think? Hopeless?"

Megan looked dubious.

Hallie felt defeated, and it must have shown.

"Okay," Megan said, "I wasn't going to tell you this, because it's mean and it'll only add to your Christina prejudice, but maybe it'll make you laugh. It happened at the reunion."

I should have gone, Hallie thought. She remembered how he'd held her hand in both of his and how alive and desired she'd felt. She needed to feel that way again, before it was too late, even if he had said his offer had no expiration date.

"Christina arrived alone. Her husband was out of town," Megan said. "But she left with this guy."

Hallie viewed her image in turquoise silk and knew that the emperor's old lady would have no new clothes today.

"This incredibly romantic once-in-a-lifetime thing had happened to her, she said, and, in her words, she couldn't deny her feelings or stifle her growth. Seems she'd just found out that for twenty-five years she'd been somebody's great and secret love."

Hallie's stomach caught on before she did, and pleated in on itself.

"A songwriter. He said he wrote sad love songs based on his feelings for her. He'd come in from L.A. to find her, to see if the feeling still held, and it did."

One wall of the dressing room had a carpeted ledge, and Hallie slid down until she was sitting on it. She was ashamed of the years she'd kept his card as her amulet, her passport. She was ashamed of herself.

"What makes it awful," Megan said, "is that the same guy pulled the same routine on me a half hour earlier, only I was willing to stifle my growth. Why would I leave with a guy wearing colored contacts? You wouldn't even remember him. His name is Craig Forman, and he always was a nerd. But what a routine the guy has now!"

Hallie stood and slowly removed the turquoise dress.

"Poor you. You didn't find anything," Megan said.

Nothing found. But how would she answer if Megan asked whether she'd lost anything?

——————— 2 ———————

"—so trapped by prejudice that the legal system might as well not exist. Do you think I said the right thing?"

"Hmmmm?"

"I can't believe it. Do you ever listen to me?"

Damn. He couldn't remember the topic. What had she been ranting about? Prejudice! Right. "So what about the lesbian?"

If looks could burn, the right side of his face would have been seared.

"*The lesbian.*" She curdled the words. "That's exactly it! Her husband's counting on people like you to tag her that way. That's why he's been able to blackmail her, force her to pay his debts, because people like you call her *the lesbian* and would take her children away if the issue reached the court. Her name's Naomi. She's a chiropractor."

"Don't pick a fight."

"I was talking about a case that really bothered me."

"Sure, but you make it an accusation. Like I'm her rotten ex. Like all men are the same."

"I never said that. If you feel that way, that's your problem, not mine."

Ted knotted his hands around the steering wheel and aimed for San Francisco. She was glib about what was and wasn't her problem, dividing up emotions as if they were property they had to split.

"You're driving too fast," she said.

"So is everybody else!"

"I wish you hadn't said we'd go. Another New Year's with boring famous people and sickening star-fuckers."

She treated his achievements and success as if they were contaminated.

"Remember how much fun we used to have on New Year's? Oh, God, Ted, I liked us so much better then, when we were us. I feel like we're trick or treating as Prince Charles and Lady Di."

If he wanted to, he could zing one back on that score. Nobody would mistake her for Di if she kept letting herself go. There'd been a time he couldn't get enough of the planes and colors of her face, the long, thin nose, the strong jaw, the dark-lashed pale eyes, the mop of brown-blond hair. And soon everything but the hair would be lost in frown lines and fat.

"I don't trust Fritter. Why hasn't he taken the company public yet? What's his real game? It's five years and now he's pissing the money away on a campus."

He hated it when she expressed concerns that he was trying to bury. "Five years since he hired me to find people for a company. Three and a half since we've had anything to sell. Two since we've hit stride. You don't understand business."

He wanted the woman he'd married back. This one had no faith, didn't believe in him. This one acted as if morality meant not wanting, not even having what you deserved, what you had honestly earned. She undermined, made him doubt his own judgment. Said he'd changed, wasn't who he'd meant to be.

He looked at her jaw set with a near-fanatic desire to be a good person. Why did her wish to be her best self bring out the absolute worst in him?

He made a Bogie voice. "Listen, sweetheart, we have to tough this one out. Be brave. Even Gandhi went to parties. If he could stand it and still save India, can we do less?"

"Don't try to jolly me out of a righteous snit."

"Admit it, I'm irresistible."

She smiled, first grudgingly, then for real. "Just often enough," she said.

Ted Bennett sat on a burgundy velvet bench in the spacious mirror-faceted dressing room. He wore an unfastened tuxedo shirt, boxer shorts, and high black socks, and could see his semi-dressed self from almost every angle. When Mr. Scott Porter—he wore a silver name tag—said, "I'm your salesman," he sounded as if he'd become Ted's indentured servant. Right now, Mr. Scott Porter was scouting cuff links. In the meantime, Ted sipped chardonnay from a Waterford goblet.

The luxurious moment snapped when his mother's voice knifed out of an angled mirror, sharp enough to shatter it. "That Waterford and wine they gave you will show up on your bill, believe you me. Some people have lost all perspective. Throwing away money when the same thing costs half in less hoity-toity stores."

Then he heard Hallie's voice rephrase the same message. "This place overstates how understated it is. Why doesn't its hypocrisy bother you? And why on earth do you need a new tuxedo? The old one is fine! They all look alike, anyway."

Jesus Christ—he'd married his mother, just like they said men did, and it was the last thing on earth he'd intended.

Sure, he was wasting money, but it was fan-fucking-tastic that he could. A lot better drinking wine and being fawned over than shopping sales and compromising and making do.

A good buy. A wonderful buy. The best buy. How he despised the "buys" of his youth. "I don't want to hear from your smart mouth," his mother had said when he was fourteen. "These will last the winter. Strong fabric and your size. Real buys." She'd held up two pair of slacks—one the color of a breath freshener and the other of spoiled salmon.

"Of course they're cheap," Ted had said. "Only a blind man would buy them." He'd be a laughing stock.

"So selfish!" she hissed. "Do you know how hard it is to make a penny? They're a wonderful buy."

The hideous pants were the last pieces of clothing she bought for him or paid for. He worked after school and during summer vacations and learned not only how hard it was to make a penny, but also how pleasant and powerful it was to spend one, and not on bargains or good buys. You did that only when you had to.

There was a knock on the dressing-room door. "Links, Mr. Bennett," his man said with the aplomb, and accent, of a British butler. He entered, his offering cupped in his palm. Ted watched the multiple supplicants in the mirrors. "Lapis, gold, and onyx,"

Mr. Scott Porter said as if it were a holy secret. "Handsome. But, of course, we have other designs. Or you may prefer something already in your collection." He pushed the link through the right cuff and snapped it shut.

Ted nodded gravely, as if considering the possibilities of his cuff link collection.

Mr. Scott Porter disappeared after murmuring that the tailor would soon "pop in."

Ted zipped the tuxedo trousers, fastened the black pleated cummerbund, and slipped on the jacket and patent pumps. "Well, Dorothy," he told his army of image-companions. "We sure as hell ain't in Johnstown anymore."

He glanced at his watch. In twenty-five minutes he'd meet Hallie for lunch. He hoped she, too, had found something that transformed her into who she'd always meant to be, although what was that? A bedraggled peasant? A placard-bearing revolutionary?

He preened for the tunnel of mirrors. Nothing like a tuxedo to transform you. Hallie had, on other occasions, in other tuxes, said he looked like Jay Gatsby. Like Redford playing Gatsby. A definite somebody.

Nothing like owning the world's finest, either. He didn't care if the thing sat in his closet for the rest of his life. There was something about having it.

I liked us so much better then. When we were us.

How could she say that? Didn't even make sense.

Another discreet tap, and in walked the tailor, a small man with a goatee and thick black eyebrows. "You are ready, sir, for me?" The accent was generic Middle European.

Ted nodded and picked up his goblet.

The man introduced himself as Hendrik. Tailors didn't get silver badges or full names. Hendrik kneeled and pinned, pinched fabric and marked.

The men in the mirrors sipped wine, blond hair gleaming while midnight-dark tuxedos were microscopically rectified.

I want this. This is who I want to be. Him.

Except that as he shifted his weight for the tailor, the "him" he wanted to be fragmented and slivered, multiplied and reflected back into, through, around, and behind himself. Blond men in black tuxedos and clear crystal in their hands. But which was Theodore Bennett?

Ridiculous. I'm me. They're mirrors.

Me who?

That man playing dress-up, grown-up, Silicon Valley tycoon?

I am. I am for real. Look how they bow and scrape because of who I am, what I've accomplished—isn't that real? I make more in a month than my father ever earned in a year—is that real enough?

Who the hell was he convincing?

Ted perspired, felt himself thin out until he was transparent, and only the tuxedo was left, floating on one of the mirror men, the not-really-Teds.

Oh, God, I liked us better then. When we were us. What made her say that? Who had they been? She was breaking him, destroying his confidence, questioning everything. As if he were an idiot.

He was his own man. Not Fritter's. What was she suggesting? Who did she see when she looked at him?

Who did he see?

Are you Somebody?

"You all right, sir?"

"Why?" He was shocked that an audible, human voice came out of his invisibility.

"Your breathing—I'm sorry, I thought I heard—asthma, perhaps?" Hendrik shook his head and continued.

Ted avoided the mirrors and focused on Hendrik's bald spot. Had the man had another life, somewhere else, where he had a full name with complete dignity?

Ted counted to ten, inhaling on the even numbers, exhaling on the odd. He nearly grabbed Hendrik's head for support. The mirrors were dangerous. His hand could be sucked into them, pulling him after until he was only a reflection.

Hallie. If he knew where she was, in which store, he'd have her paged, have her get him out of this.

How unmanly. How weak to need someone so. A woman. Your wife. For shame.

But she knew which one he was.

Hendrik stood up. "So," he said. "All done. You will bring out the suit at your convenience, sir?"

Ted nodded, pretending to be a functioning, living male. He stood rigidly, afraid at first to move a muscle, further fragment the mirror men. Then he slowly lifted his wrist and checked his watch. Fifteen minutes to go until Hallie. Meantime, he would tutor this impostor, this empty nonbeing. Pull the hand out of the sleeve, unbutton the . . . no, first undo the links . . .

An automaton, but in a few minutes, he'd be with Hallie, without whom, on some elemental level, he did not fully or even truly exist.

He could admit it. He could admit it here in this sumptuous dressing room. He could admit it at last.

But when they were at lunch, Hallie grumbling about the cost and ridiculousness of everything she'd tried on, when there were no mirrors around him, when he'd been revived by the cold winter wind, all he did was laugh and tell her the story of the terrible tangerine and mint green slacks. "The end of innocence," he called it.

────────── 3 ──────────

Hallie pulled her briefcase and a grocery bag out of the car, mumbling as she cataloged responsibilities still unmet. She'd forgotten to buy cinnamon. Wasn't completely ready for her first client in the morning. Owed invitations to everybody. Had to talk with Vicky about what permanent living arrangements would work for Sylvia Saxe without making either daughter crazy. Had to do something about the sloppy paralegal.

Someday she'd be buried still clutching a "Things to Do" list.

The table was unset. Such a little thing to ask of Sarah. Nobody gave a damn about her. More and more often, she retreated into her comforting fantasy of the little white room with a clothes hook, a hot plate, and a thin single bed. One dinner to prepare. One cup to wash. Only her own life to take care of.

She heard a car, his, pull up, a door slam. She smacked boneless chicken breasts onto the cutting board, repulsed by twenty-three years of turning dead meat into meals.

"Halt!" Ted, his honey-streaked hair ruffled from his convertible ride, was followed by Sarah. "We're going out to dinner." He kissed her forehead.

She shook her head. Easier, quicker, to get it over with here, then take care of her paperwork.

"In fact," he said, "we're going out to breakfast, too. In Boston."

"Surprise!" Sarah said. "Happy Valentine's Weekend!" She and Ted wore goofy grins.

"Very funny, guys. Now could you set the table, Sarah? I have an extra-full day at the office tomorrow and I have to—"

"Wrong," Ted said. "You have a lunch date tomorrow while I check out Faneuil Hall. Your CR group from Waltham, together again for your sake. Am I an okay guy or what? Your schedule for tomorrow was a fake. Peggy is my coconspirator."

"Peggy? My secretary?"

"After Boston, we take the shuttle to the Big Apple. Saturday night, we'll see Chloe's play and have an after-theater dinner with the actress herself. The rest of the time *we* play. You and me. It's been in the works for weeks. Go pack."

"Sarah?"

"I'm fifteen. I could take care of myself. But Dad's making me sleep at Beth's, anyway."

She looked at Ted. "You hate New York."

"Correct."

"And you don't like Chloe."

"Correct again. But I like you and I like us and you were maybe forgetting what a good thing we were, what a gem I am. I thought I'd remind you."

"You're very wily," she whispered.

"I thought you'd never notice."

—————— 4 ——————

Nessa O'Brien was possibly the last woman in the USA who used a cloth handkerchief. Flimsy, with a faded pattern of floral sprigs, it had been neatly pressed when she entered Hallie's office. Now it was twisted and sodden.

Nessa's hazel, needy eyes, constantly overflowing, were topped by pink-edged, puffy lids. "We had a good marriage," she said.

It was amazing. Almost all the ruptured marriages she saw said they'd been happy ones. This was the party line because without a recognizable shape and order, there was no story. So first Eden, then the snake. Of course, they would say, almost casually, he pushed me around. We didn't speak for weeks. He was horrible with the kids. He had other women. He took my paycheck, checked the garbage in case I was wasting food. Wouldn't let me out of the house. Drank. Shot up. But we were happy until . . .

Until something almost arbitrary, not necessarily different from the status quo, forced apart the facts and the story. One of his women contacted the wife. One of his rages broke her sofa or her face. One of her spending orgies was one too many. Almost anything, and suddenly, the happy part was in the past tense.

"He'll go off with her," Nessa said, "and what'll I have?"

"That's why we're figuring out about the house and car. I don't mean to rush you, but we have lots to get through."

It was the traditional month of weddings, but all she saw were marital casualties. Sometimes she pictured society fragmenting in slow motion, like a time-release photo. From tribes to clans to families, and now, to why-do-I-think-I-need-anybody-else.

"You seem upset by the idea of community property," she said to Nessa.

"I want to be fair."

"Fair!" Nessa, phlegmatic as stagnant water—the classic "good woman"—made Hallie itch with impatience.

But why rush her? They weren't headed much of anywhere. Hallie could offer only Band-Aids for her critical injuries. Here a form, there a formula, here a restraining order, there a court date, a mediator for a nasty custody battle, a court order for unpaid support payments. Have a nice life.

Nessa had waitressed whenever Jack was fired or simply not in the mood to work. The divorce judge would declare her able to support herself. She'd have to sell the tiny house in which they had almost no equity, so her half of the minuscule profit, if any, wouldn't buy anything else. She'd rent and waitress and down-scale as the cost of living escalated and her legs went.

Nessa twisted the handkerchief. "We need papers, numbers for the house and car," Hallie said. "Ditto for insurance policies, whatever pension plan he had or has. Could you copy it before our next appointment?"

Nessa shook her head. "He'd kill me if I touched his things."

Hallie's office was full of framed cartoons and quotations. She stood, rubbing the small of her back, pushed her glasses up on her nose, and read from a black-framed bit of calligraphy. " 'The perfect wife submits herself with quietness, cheerfully, even as a well-broken horse, readily going and standing as he wishes that sits upon his back.' " She returned to her desk and reseated herself. "That was the seventeenth century. This is 1983. Get him the hell off your back."

"He locks up his papers," Nessa whispered. "I couldn't steal."

Hallie manned the killing grounds of the sexual revolution, too often wondering what, if any, gains the upheaval had produced. Certainly no visible ones for her clients.

One after another, lost women who'd clung to visions of apple pie and Mom sat in that chair still deferring to a "he" who made them miserable. Hallie had to be the heavy, the cynical voice of experience, warning them—gently so that they didn't bolt in ter-ror—that their guts would hang in the dust if they didn't change their style. "There must be a key," she now suggested.

Nessa's hair was a fried brown and her purple lipstick looked as though it had been applied on the lam. Her skin seemed tenuously attached to her muscles. It shocked Hallie to realize that she and Nessa were the same age.

"He's a sound sleeper, though." The worm was considering a turn. "Maybe . . ."

Twelve years ago, Chloe Wister had insisted that marriage was about power. Only now was Hallie ready to agree. Or at least that it was about the perception of power. As long as both part-ners considered the balance scales in alignment, however steep their actual tilt, they were content, but not a moment longer. Nessa was beginning to notice how cockeyed her weights and measures were.

"When he falls asleep, the house could collapse, he wouldn't know." Then she looked up, and her face had further aged. "There was nothing wrong until he was laid off and she flounced in. We had our ups and downs, but you expect that." She shuddered and squared her shoulders. For the first time that morning, her eyes were dry. "I guess when his pants are on the floor I could . . ."

"Now you've got it!"

"What?" Nessa asked sadly. "What do I have?"

His ass, Hallie thought. Ted accused her of becoming hard and vindictive, but she saw what she saw. She was the posse in a lawless world, and she was gonna nail the fuckers. All of them.

The Law Center was in a Victorian house that, like many of its clients, had seen spiffier days.

Hallie tossed her bag onto the passenger seat and pulled out of her spot on the makeshift lot behind the building. Pebbly bits of gravel spit at her tires as she turned her car to face the street. She had to be back promptly at two. A woman whose husband had gambled away their life savings, twelve thousand dollars. And after her, a man, laid off, unable to meet child-support payments.

She shouldn't have promised to meet Lucy Marks today. Hallie shifted into drive and pressed the pedal. She should be catching up on paperwork instead. Lucy was nice enough, but a woman whose work was finding ways to fill time couldn't understand how a lunch date could be pressure, not pleasure.

Halfway down the driveway, a squirrel sat on its haunches, tiny paws curled. She slowed, stopped. "Move," she snarled.

The squirrel darted to the right, paused, darted back, stood up again. Hallie honked.

The squirrel flinched, scampered in a tight circle.

"Idiot!" she shouted. "Get out of the way! Please?"

The squirrel resumed his praying-rodent pose, then broke to the right, clear of the car. Hallie took her foot off the brake and applied gas.

And the squirrel ran back. Under the wheel.

She felt the bump, gasped and threw the car into reverse, fast, cinders spraying.

The squirrel twitched, dragged himself to the right and, finally out of the path of any traffic, convulsed once and grew still. "Oh, you stupid, you stupid, you—" Hallie put her head on the steering wheel and burst into tears.

"I never drink at lunch," Hallie said, "but that squirrel . . ." She sipped wine and poked at a Chinese chicken salad for which she had no appetite.

"I never used to drink at lunch," Lucy said. "But it helps."

"I never killed anything before." Of course, there was Griselda, she thought. But that was different. The squirrel wanted to live. He simply wasn't a match for her machinery. She put down her fork. Flesh was repugnant. "How many creatures die unrecorded, the road kills." It wasn't really a question. "You always see turkey buzzards circling."

"This conversation is not improving my mood," Lucy said.

"Why is it so bad?"

Lucy pursed her mouth. "Because I'm tired of my entire . . . of committees, of luncheons, of dancing for social evils." She grimaced. "Listen to me. I sound like a spoiled brat. Who am I to complain?" She turned her attention to her crab puff.

Hallie understood. Queen of guilt, she never forgot what she wasn't suffering. She didn't live in El Salvador or South Africa or here with a less fortunate skin color or accent. She didn't have cancer. She wasn't on food stamps or sleeping in the street. Her husband didn't beat her and her children were healthy, so how dare she not be ecstatic every minute of every day?

Except that an absence of plagues was not a guide to everyday life and you didn't need a mortal injury to feel pain. Her problems were rarefied luxuries, but they were her problems nonetheless. It was also and ironically true, therefore, that guilt about thinking she had problems was, indeed, one of her problems. "You want to talk?" she asked.

Lucy chewed julienned potatoes, one by one. Her ability to be silent, to think before speaking, impressed Hallie, who had to fight the urge to slather conversational gaps with words, any words.

"When I met Fritter," she finally said, "he was like a tornado. Elemental. I'd never known anybody like him. It was a bad time in my marriage. I was working temp jobs, wanting to be home with the kids, exhausted and angry. My husband is not ambitious. Then Fritter singled me out."

My husband *is* not ambitious? She wasn't talking about Fritter.

"I never would have believed I could commit . . ."

Commit. What an old-fashioned verb. Like adultery, a truly archaic term which Lucy was now choking over. And infidelity, which she could barely say, but she didn't have to, because it was now considered too judgmental a term. Extramarital sex, we called it now, making it sound like a bonus. Eat all your marriage, you can have some extramarital sex. You couldn't commit extramarital sex, you could only experience it.

"To this day, I don't know what it was about." Lucy said. "Not sex, not like in the movies. Not money, the way people thought. Or it was about all of it, because it was this *power* Fritter had. Afterwards, I was so ashamed I wanted to spend the rest of my life making it up to Billy." She shrugged. "Didn't matter. Fritter was crazed. I had to be his forever."

Her right index finger smoothed the cuticles of her left hand. She looked bewildered as she spoke. "I confused possessiveness with passion. Besides, Billy threw me out after Fritter told him what had happened. He said he'd agree to a peaceful divorce if he got to keep the boys. Otherwise, he'd tell my sons what I'd done. I thought we'd live in Phoenix forever and I'd see the boys all the time, but after his divorce, Fritter was uncomfortable there and he moved us here. And then Billy took out that court order, said I'd kidnap the children if I was ever alone with them."

She sat, groomed perfectly for the late twentieth century except for her mind, still cluttered with antiques like sin and scandal.

"So now I have a life as stupid as that vulgar house." She stared at her manicured hands, at her diamond-encrusted wedding band and her large emerald ring. "I have to decide what to do."

Hallie wondered when Lucy would understand that she'd already decided.

"My older son, Link, is graduating from sixth grade today." She brushed her eye and sat rigidly while the waitress cleared their plates. "Fritter's my kid now. A gigantic, selfish, possessive, impulsive spoiled child. He takes care of me, doesn't leave me out in the rain to rust, but in the end, I'm something he designed and manufactured to serve his purposes. Everybody is."

It sounded very much like a warning. If only Ted could hear this. If only he would listen.

Lucy took a quick sip of black coffee. "Sorry I'm such a whiner." She looked into her cup. Her eyes filled and she blinked hard. "Poor squirrel," she said. "Couldn't think fast enough, understand enough to get out of the way."

5

"Okay, six-second pulse count, when I say go, check for your target zone but don't stop moving just—"

Hallie put two fingers on her throat and kept her feet in motion. Through a grid of leotarded legs she saw herself in the front mirror, frizzy-haired with a body designed to withstand famine.

But you tried. You had to, because husbands were rushing off headlong in droves, like lemmings.

Motors revved after dark and hitherto stable married males defected to singles complexes.

Sometimes they left in the classical manner, packing and bidding formal adieu. Sometimes they were baroque, forgetting to return after a vacation, disappearing while the wife was out jogging, sending a change-of-address form to the old homestead.

"Slow down if your pulse was too high, give it more pep if it was too low."

The women speculated. Did it have to do with fallout? Was it biological? Mostly it was their own fault. They'd done something wrong, like age.

Men found new buddies, women who made them feel young. Very dangerous to make a man feel old, so aging wives paid plastic surgeons, diet gurus, mental-health counselors, wardrobe and color consultants, manicurists who glued on plastic nails. Even so, husbands evaporated, leaving half-empty beds all over the Valley.

Bill Haley and his Comets blared. We're gonna rock around

the clock and kick that leg and work that tush, and a one and a two, lift that goddamned leg even though you've put in a full day at the office and still have dinner to make and—

Paula, her realtor, puffed next to her in purple and pink and nodded toward a thin woman resolutely working out at the front of the class. "First, he says she's fat, so she loses weight." Paula was able to exercise and gossip simultaneously. "Then he says she's flabby, so she joins the gym."

The music switched to Ray Charles and "I Got a Woman." Hallie did jumping jacks and envisioned her grandparents visiting the mirrored aerobics class—Morris and Fanny, gape-mouthed as Hallie grunts and gasps. "Sweating like a peasant!" they'd say with horror. "We escaped Russia so you should live *nice*. Live *easy*. What are you, crazy?"

"Then she liposucks the bottom down and silicones the top up."

". . . way over town, she's good to meeee"—half-turn clap, turn back, jump, clap—

"And then he says she's stagnated. Hasn't grown."

Hallie liked that one. Must be a turn-on, that growing. Must be the reason so many left the fully grown for girls so young their brains hadn't jump-started and even their feet were still growing.

"So," Paula said, "she takes classes at Stanford. And then, when she's skinny and curvy and fit and getting A's, he admits he's in love with somebody else."

Hallie shook her head sympathetically and concentrated on the sideways half-jump. "I Got a Woman" didn't used to be this long.

"His love's named Fred," Paula said. "Former linebacker."

Kick, jump, clap. "Smile! This is fun!" the twenty-year-old instructor said. She had wide blue eyes and the kind of body Hallie had never had, plus a middle-aged, wealthy, road-tested beau. His ex exercised elsewhere.

The instructor was vibrant and alive and young, and there were so many of them, their numbers increasing every day. So you kicked, sweat, and jumped to the songs that had raised your pulse years ago, too. Back then, it was for love. Now it was for a tighter butt. Were they really the same thing?

—————— 6 ——————

Ted Bennett's stomach burned. He was old, his systems disinte-grating. Forty-six, nearly fifty, for God's sake.

His firstborn turned twenty tomorrow. The age her mother was when she married. He could be the father of a bride. A grandfather soon.

Old man, and Fritter's campus was aging him faster than any calendar. Every day he visited the construction site. Every day he heard why there was an overrun, more work orders, a revised design concept, an unexpected snag, a delay due to illness, a threatened stoppage. Every day he had to race for a toilet. Even after Lucy resigned.

For four months, Fritter had declared Lucy official "liaison." Ted never figured out what or whom she was connecting, and it was obvious that neither had she. Fritter said the job would snap her out of the blues.

Lucy seemed desperate to come up with something new. Plans were scrapped and redone to indulge her until The Funny Farm was an accurate, not particularly witty, name.

Three weeks ago, the problem of Lucy had solved itself when she announced that her ideas were dreadful and the people who listened to her, fools.

But even since Lucy's tenure, the growing steel-and-glass pal-aces gave Ted a bellyache. They were stunning, no doubt about it, and would probably make architectural history, combining the highest of tech with humor, integrating an efficient workplace with a sense of community. At least that's what *People* had quoted him as saying. Put it right below his photo. A flattering picture, he had to admit, of both him and the finished portion of the Farm.

The budget had gone all to hell several times, but when Ted suggested cutbacks, modifications, or delayed timetables, Fritter had a standard response. "It's my money, Bennett. My company and my call."

When push came to shove, and it did too often, "mine" was Fritter's automatic response. Ted was frightened by the percent-age of their assets that the campus devoured. He wanted to diversify, cover their flanks, find applications for their sophisticated graphics in education and medical imaging. He wanted people hired on a project basis, not given lifetime sinecures in case they someday stumbled over an idea.

Ted wanted, but Fritter decided.

But that hadn't been the deal. They should have gone public a year ago, but Fritter had decided he didn't want shareholders telling him what to do about his campus. "If they had brains and vision, they'd have their own companies, not pieces of mine," he said. "Build it first, then let 'em in."

Ted gritted his teeth until he could take his marbles and leave. It couldn't be too soon for him.

Making it all worse, Hallie didn't want to hear about it anymore. Told him to quit if he was unhappy. Told him to do the research he yearned for. Told him she'd support them now. Said she had her own problems. Said it politely, mildly, but meant it.

Sometimes he thought about how he'd expected it to be. The wife waiting at home, eager to hear about your day, to take care of you, to make you and your family her job. Why had it changed during his turn at marriage?

He left the site, got into his car, stomach aching, and turned on the radio. ". . . zoning laws to obstruct future video arcades. P.T.A. President Stephanie Brandwiler quoted educators on the dangers of electronic adventure games. 'Our children's minds are being seduced by video arcades—' "

Back when the wheel was invented, Stephanie's ancestors had probably insisted that playing with round objects destroyed cave children's minds. Stephanie was beating a dead horse, anyway. The arcade boom had peaked. Home video games were the hot item now, and they'd be even hotter as people bought personal computers.

Which meant that their resources should be pumping up for that, not for building a goddamned FritterWorld.

Ted switched stations until the synthesized sound of "Chariots of Fire" soothed him into the necessary courage for the day.

There was a stack of messages on his desk. "Call Hallie. Very Important (but nobody hurt)." "F.M. wants to see you A.S.A.P."

"Carlos conf. meeting in N.Y. Friday, 10 a.m. Will lv. dir. at hotel." "Tom Wilson wants mtg. today if poss." He thumbed through the pile, then returned to the first two, suddenly remembering Tarkington and the in-box game. "Very Important (but nobody hurt)," he read again, then, as he had in Tarkington, he gave top priority to another message and went to see Fritter.

"Sit down." Fritter's hands were folded on his desk. "Don't want you hearing it second-hand through the grapevine, so . . ." He cleared his throat. "Lucy and I . . ." He unlatched his hands, put them palms up. "Finito."

"I—I'm sorry," Ted said. "Really sorry."

One massive hand rose to smash back onto his desk. "The *bitch!* Did you ever *hear* of a woman given more? She had *nothing* when I met her! *Ungrateful bitch!* Good riddance! Moping and whining long as I can remember, so to hell with her!"

Ted smoothed his trousers and tried to look neutral but sympathetic.

The oversized desk chair creaked as Fritter leaned forward. "Tell you this. She doesn't get a goddamned *cent.* Forget community property crap—I wasn't an asshole this time. A lawyer drew it up, good and proper, and she signed. She gets *nothing.*" He drummed his fingers on the desk, panting and red-faced "If you're smart, Bennett, you'll do the same thing. Now."

"But I—we—it's a little late for a pre-nuptial—"

"Call it post-nuptial, who gives a shit? Christ, yours is a lawyer. You think she's nice, right? They all act nice until they decide to have your balls for breakfast!"

"I'll . . . I'll certainly . . ." His stomach burned. "I'm really sorry, though, about you," he said. "When did—"

"This fucking morning! No warning, just pulls off her rings and quits—like that! Going back to *him!*—the prick, the nobody who threw her out! Crawling back. The fool, the bitch! He forgives her, she says. Like he's the fucking Pope!" He smacked the desk again. The heel of his hand was red when he lifted it. "*Goddamn bitch!* She could have had new kids if she wanted them so bad. She could have stayed!"

This was what Hallie's message had been about. She'd wanted to warn him. Lucy must have called her.

He would have to pretend to be shocked when he called home. Wouldn't let her know he'd put her in second place. Definitely would not let her know that today. "Anything I can do?" Ted asked. "Anything at all?"

Fritter shook his head, the way Ted expected. Fritter gave. That was his power. He couldn't imagine Fritter admitting need. But even if he could, it wouldn't be to Ted. They weren't friends. They were two ambitious men sharing space.

"Built her a *palace*! Polished her, made her something special! She was depressed, I let her run the goddamned project! She was a *shadow* when I met her. I'm the one made her a person!"

His rage was dragon-strength, searing the air, singeing Ted. He took a deep breath. Fritter's personal life has nothing to do with me or my life, he told himself.

"Goddamn bitch'll crawl back, you'll see, but I won't have her. *Nobody* quits me. Nobody fucks Fritter Marks."

Nothing to do with me, Ted said again. Nothing. Nothing.

Impure Bliss, Adulterated Happiness

1984–1985

It isn't whom you lie with. It's whom you lie to.
Frank Pittman

——————— 1 ———————

I SN'T it a nice house?" Kat Miller was connected to a porta-
ble oxygen tank. She paused for breath between each sentence. But she sat in the living room of Megan's new house
and beamed. "When Sweets passed, and I got the emphy-
sema, I didn't know what to do. Both my girls offered, but I
thought I'd go west, like the man said." She wheezed out a laugh.
"Girls today. You a lawyer, your sister with a bread company.
Megan buying a house and Bonnie with the radio and a book."
A copy of Bonnie's *A Marriage Primer* was on the coffee table,
put there by Kat.

Megan looked at her watch. "We're late. Gotta go, Mom."

A Fuckerware Party, she'd said. A learning experience.

Sarah lowered her eyelids, maintaining her pose as one coerced
into accompanying her feeble mother to and from Sonoma. Wild,
bad Michael Farr, the real object of her trip, flipped the pages of
Sports Illustrated.

Once in her car, Megan sat straight, hands tight on the wheel. "Putting a roof over my kids' heads, taking care of my mother all by myself feels great," she said. "I am finally, definitely not the pathetic, good, abusable Megan anymore. I even feel taller." She smiled. "Ben says I'm bull-headed about my independence. That I'm messing up Michael. We quarrel about it a lot."

"Every couple quarrels about children. I hope. We certainly do." She sighed. "It's not the stuff of love songs, is it?"

Megan peered out the windows, checking street signs. "Ben needs to take over, be the daddy, the husband. Make me the little woman. He doesn't admit he wants that, doesn't understand it, probably, but that's how it is, and so help me, it'll never be that way for me again."

She sounded like Scarlett swearing she'd never be hungry again, as if marriage had to be a slave-master arrangement.

"I survived in less than Norman Rockwell traditional," Megan said. "So will Mike. He'll be fine."

There was an etiquette to friendship, an obligatory laissez-faire about child-rearing. You suggested, you hinted, you stated your own beliefs, but you didn't dictate your friend's parenting style. The two women had circled the subject too often already. Hallie kept her mouth shut, but she was glad Kat was chaperoning the kids and wouldn't have brought Sarah otherwise. She didn't really know who lived behind Michael's handsome, angry face.

Megan drove aggressively. "I'm finally independent." Hallie tried to estimate how many times Megan had used "independent" this evening. "Why live together," Megan continued, "or *marry?*" She made the word sound obscene.

Hallie had watched the swing from zombie to warrior woman, and wondered where the pendulum would come to rest.

"We used to be measured by our catch, like fishermen. Land a good one and you were somebody, too." Megan was off and running. It was often tiring lately. "I'm somebody on my own. I don't need to be completed."

Luckily, before she recited her entire creed, they reached a yellow Victorian house with every gingerbread curl highlighted in white. Chez Hansel and Gretel, Hallie thought.

The spirit of the house had been preserved inside as well, with gleaming woods, stained glass, and period furniture in jewel tones against patterned wallpaper. They were greeted by a woman who looked as if she'd escaped from a "Leave It to Beaver" episode, and were encouraged to join the others in her spacious living room.

Hallie had assumed that the attendees—aside from Megan and herself, of course—would be either jaded sophisticates or sleaze-bags, but the group was astoundingly average. They looked as likely to sample detergents or crab dip as the flavored massage lotions and edible jock straps on the coffee table, let alone the assortment of vibrators, books, video cassettes, apparatus that looked like hardware store droppings, and only God, or the Marquis de Sade, knew what else.

Hallie wondered what the original lady of this house, in her wide sweep of skirt and bustle, would make of these knickknacks.

"All right, if we're all here and comfy, let's start. I'll explain everything, and let you gals examine them." The speaker was young and curvaceous, with a soft Southern undertow in her words. "Welcome to our Pleasure Party. I'm Bobbie Sue and we are gonna have fun!"

Her tense audience did not return her smile, looked in fact as if they'd be damned rather than have fun. The hostess bustled in with five bottles of wine, which she strategically placed on end tables. Bobbie Sue looked relieved.

"Gonna pep up your love life tonight."

Every woman's face went blank, as if she had no idea of what either *pep* or *love life* meant.

Bobbie Sue seduced them like a pro, easing them in with relatively innocent objects. Toys. Feathers. Scented candles. Titillating books. It became easy, natural, to relax the muscles, lean forward, smile, demonstrate interest. The wine also helped.

Edible body paints. Edible pasties. Edible G-string. Edible, bittersweet chocolate, penis.

"Only problem with this," Bobbie Sue said, brandishing the phallus like a pointer, "is you take a bite and say 'yummy' and scare the man to death. Their universal nightmare, you know? And a frightened man isn't a perky man. So we might as well eat this here and now. Good practice, anyway."

She passed the penis around. One by one, women giggled and

nibbled, holding it by the large chocolate testicles. Hallie remembered similar parties years earlier when women had been thrilled by burping plastic containers.

More wine was poured. Bobbie Sue put on a cassette. Background music for brothels, Hallie decided.

"Whoever do you suppose gave men the idea the race is to the swift?" Bobbie Sue asked. "This music's a subliminal coach, slowing them down. Isn't that great, girls?"

The liberated attendees who undoubtedly elsewhere demanded to be called women, nodded and chomped the last of the bittersweet testicles.

The hostess put out cheese canapés shaped like cheese canapés. Hallie was disappointed.

"I like to start with a massage," Bobbie Sue said. "You want something smooth that won't stain sheets or sting delicate parts. This musk oil sinks into the skin and makes it incredibly soft. But for flavor, I just love putting coconut lotion on my boyfriend, then licking him like a gigantic piña colada. But maybe you'd like peanut butter, or raspberry. Try a drop on your hand." A half a dozen vials made the rounds, and two dozen tongues tasted palms with the domestic detachment of women testing batter or the consistency of gravy.

Well, yes, Hallie thought. Her boudoir could use perking.

More wine was poured, words and appliances blurring as Bobbie Sue cheerily described and women passed, speculating.

"Now, sometimes, for fun, we tie each other up with these velvet ropes? It can be a real turn-on for us liberated females to feel helpless and ravished."

Megan, Ms. Independence, smiled.

"Now, this thing here, you slip this over his penis like so."

"I keep imagining Annapolis," Megan whispered. "Mrs. Whatsis's virginal drag house, the one where a spotlight blasted you if you turned off the lamp. All of us in Peter Pan collars unpacking suitcases bulging with Bobbie Sue's apparatus.'

"These are ben-wa balls," Bobbie Sue said. "Put them up your vagina and they move with your body motion, turning you on. Supposedly, Japanese women put them in and sit and rock and have day-long orgasms."

"Maybe that's why they're so docile," Hallie murmured.

"They don't fall out, so be careful." This from a plump woman with brown hair in a no-nonsense crinkly cut. Hallie could envision her leading a hike or cleaning an oven, not involved in esoteric no-hands masturbation inside her polyester double-knits. "Don't forget and wear them to the airport like I did," the woman said solemnly. "They set off the metal detector."

Bobbie Sue waved a bottle of breath freshener. "I prefer spearmint, but any flavor's fine. One drop in the mouth before you go down on him. He'll love it so much it'll be easy to ask him to return the flavor. I mean favor."

The sexual revolution meets the Fuller brush man.

"Now you take this feather," Bobbie Sue said, "and you run it slowly up the underside of—"

Despite all her adamant liberation, it was unnerving to have everything so *there*, so matter-of-factly displayed, so blithely described. To know in which positions Bobbie Sue's boyfriend did what, and how he differed from her last lover. Now Bobbie Sue flicked switches and demonstrated vibrators—against her palm, to Hallie's relief. Large and small, electric and battery-run, noisy and silent. "Hugh Hefner has a wardrobe of vibrators above his bed," Bobbie Sue said. "Now you know how he gets those bunnies."

Hallie eyed the array. There was much to be said for those vibrators. They didn't have moods. Never mentioned that you were putting on weight, or said they were tired or made you feel you were so slow getting there, you might as well quit and save the vibrator from exhaustion and boredom.

Bobbie Sue beamed. "This design has an attachment for the guys, too!" Egalitarian vibrators. "This cap fits right on the tip of him, and I want to tell you, he'll adore you forever for it. And then we have this anal stimulator."

The women were no longer restrained or shy. They had turned into smart shoppers, taking the measure—sometimes literally—of the merchandise, asking prices, weighing items, listening to their hum and spin, considering.

Hallie tried to imagine her mother's generation at a similar party. Women in housedresses and Fifties propriety. "Our private parts," Sylvia still called them.

"Now, this here's my favorite." Bobbie Sue held up a gherkin-sized vibrator. "It's got remote control. Slip it inside your panties before you leave for work, and whenever you're stuck in traffic, flick the switch in your pocket and zippedy-do-dah. Talk about power dressing!"

That had books-on-tape beat to hell. Commuting could be fun if when you came home, you literally did.

"Now I'll pass everything around again, plus this order form," Bobbie Sue said. Good timing. Hallie would be back in her bedroom by midnight. Complete with new toys.

She spent ninety-four dollars for the considerate vibrator with the little cap for him, a pair of rabbit fur massage mitts, almond oil, and a deck of cards, each of which suggested a semi-outrageous activity. Worrying about potential rush-hour pileups, she almost, but didn't, buy the gherkin.

At 10:05 P.M., Hallie stood staring at an oil spot on Megan's driveway where there should have been a trunk in which she'd stash her sexy goods before retrieving her daughter and getting in the car attached to that trunk.

She and Megan raced into the house.

Kat looked disheveled. "Fell asleep watching TV." She put her hands to her chest. "Next I know, phone's ringing. Police. Didn't know how to reach you. You didn't leave a—"

Hallie tried not to scream. "Where are they?"

"What happened, Mom? What happened?"

"Didn't mean to doze off." Kat's wheezing was worse.

"Mother, what happened?"

Kat, eyes wide, sounded like a bagpipe.

Hallie fought tears and an irrational but intense conviction that if she went outside and started over, the car would be there, the children inside the house. "Where are the kids?" she begged.

"Hospital." Kat looked down, plastic oxygen snakes drooping from her nose.

"Are they all right? Are they—"

"Alive," Kat said. "Banged up, they said. Car's wrecked."

Megan was already heading for the door, and Hallie, short of breath, heart pounding, followed.

"They'll be fine," Kat said.

"Please," Hallie said, "call Ted. Tell him where we are."

"The number's on the wall by the phone!" Megan shouted as she opened the front door.

"Should I call anybody for you?" Kat asked.

Megan's hand gripped the knob. "No," she said. "No."

Sarah's right shoulder dislocated, elbow broken. A gash on and under her chin, half her face scraped raw. Possible damage to Michael's ocular nerve. A concussion. Broken bones. Tests.

Big trouble. Both drunk, and unlicensed Michael missing a curb, a turn, outracing the police, crashing.

Hallie was torn between wanting to hold and heal her child and being so infuriated, so terrified by the fact that nothing but luck had delivered Sarah whole that she could have wrung her cut neck.

She could have lost her daughter while she drank wine and fantasized about exotic sex. What kind of mother? The shiny pink bag was still in her pocketbook. She pulled it out and tossed it across the hall. Purge the non-mother bad woman, unmake her. Protect Sarah.

"The car," Sarah said.

"Who cares! What about *you*? Your life?" She was crying. Outside the emergency room, her voice a controlled scream while ten times as much sound stayed caught inside her. "How could you?"

"He said he knew how to—"

"He said! *He!* For a *boy*, Sarah! Risking your life to please a boy! Being that stupid for a boy! How could you—why would you—what if—what if—" Hallie gingerly embraced her around the bruises and the cast. She couldn't even say the what-if's, couldn't think them, couldn't bear them.

And then the doctor needed to test Sarah again and Hallie went to where a drained version of Megan sat.

Hallie joined her on the cracked leather sofa. Another forty-five minutes at least before Ted would arrive. Not exactly the reunion she'd imagined a few hours earlier. And why has the romance gone out of your marriage, madam?

"I'm sorry," Megan whispered after a long silence.

"You always are. Sorry or not, kids are stupid."

"About Michael." Her voice had no luster.

Hallie finally looked at her. "Isn't he okay? His eyes?"

Megan looked down at her clasped hands. "They think he'll keep his sight." Her voice was thin as an airwave. "He's lucky. But he isn't okay." A tear snaked down her left cheek. "Ben was right and I was wrong and it could have cost his life. And Sarah's." She shuddered. "He isn't okay."

Hallie reached over and held her friend's knotted hands to stop them from wringing.

"He'll be sixteen in two months, and he gets drunk a lot, and I'm as bad as my mother, insisting things are okay when they aren't. Ignoring problems or acting like they're Ben's, not Michael's and mine because . . . bad mothers have bad kids. Mothers who don't love their kids enough, but I do, Hallie. I do!"

"I know. And he knows it, too. Don't believe every stupid child-rearing theory somebody makes up."

"Remember that poem? 'They fuck you up, your mum and dad, They may not mean to, but they do—' "

"So you start over. There are groups to help."

Megan stood up. "I have to call Ben. It isn't right, not telling him, not letting him be a part."

She walked down the long hall, a small but resolute woman, shoulders not quite as militantly set as they'd been. Then, before she reached the telephones, she bent over and lifted a bright pink bag, pointing at Hallie and mouthing "Yours?"

Hallie started to shake her head, to do penance forever, renouncing hedonistic pleasures. But then it suddenly seemed important to believe, or pretend, that there'd again be times so normal and low-intensity that rabbit-skin massage gloves would be relevant. "Mine," she said, nodding.

———— 2 ————

Hallie nursed a cappuccino, writing postcards while she waited for Ted. She wondered how Italy, given the same mortar, stone, earth, grass, trees, and rivers as every other country, translated them into art, kissing every sense. Except the ears, which were, instead, assaulted.

She blocked out the cacophony of Rome—car horns and Vespa motors in terrible counterpoint. "—loved Florence. I've had a crush on this guy since I was younger than you." She turned the postcard over and looked at the David again, wondering if Sarah was too sophisticated to react as Hallie had once with her first comprehension of masculine beauty, her first inkling of the possibilities in gender.

They sold postcards of only his genitals. A desecration, Ted had said as Hallie almost bought one with its male fruit in florentined pubic hair. Not a desecration, she still thought.

"Kiss Grandma for me. Are you watching the convention? Won't it be exciting having a woman Vice President?" Two months after the accident, it was still hard not begging Sarah, in person or by postcard, to be careful, to protect herself, to swear off fast boys and faster cars forever. It was easy, however, to avoid writing other things, like "Having a good time."

Nothing you could name was wrong. They were having a luxurious, civilized time. But even when Ted was not in business meetings, when they were together, they occupied separate space.

She had thought it would be different in this exotic place. They'd always enjoyed themselves when they shed their ordinary lives. But now the burden of their everydays was too enormous to leave behind. They were polite, but excitement, enthusiasm, and unqualified approval were reserved for art, architecture, other people, and cuisine.

She felt fat and tried not to be too enthusiastic about the food, but she had carried her growing hunger all these miles just as Ted had smuggled his chilliness into this warm land, and one fed the other.

She didn't know what had turned him disapproving. Couldn't name her crime. They were like a snake swallowing its tail and complaining of indigestion. He gave her no cause to smile, then accused her of the crime of not smiling.

She had never known despair could be calm and chronic. "In headaches and in worry, vaguely life leaks away." Who said that? Maybe she had.

And there was always the possibility that this wasn't a problem but an everyday case of reality. Maybe gravity sagged middle-aged marriages as much as it did middle-aged boobs.

"Buon giorno!" He stood backlit by a Renaissance sky shot with gold, clouds piled one on the other over turquoise. It made you believe in heaven, or at least in Ted Bennett.

Twenty-seven minutes later, over dinner, they'd exhausted the conversational possibilities of his afternoon meeting, her wanderings, and the restaurant, and Ted was again reserved, private, vaguely disapproving, and impatient. Her dull terror returned and she could no longer ignore it. "Teddy," she said, to clear the air of demons, "something's been going wrong between us, maybe for a while. Can we talk about it?"

"We're in Italy," he said. *"I'm* having a great time—why must you create problems? You complain when I'm involved in my work, when I'm away, when I'm not paying attention. And now, when we're together, when I'm with you, you still complain. Why?"

Tongue-tied, she could say nothing.

"I can't please you, can't satisfy you, no matter what. It's hardly worth trying."

"That isn't so." But there she was, complaining. He was innocent, aggrieved. If she challenged him, if she said he was the one who seemed chronically unsatisfied, it would be added to her record as one more complaint. "Are you happy, then?"

"Reasonably so."

She took a deep breath. She had to ask it. Had to. "Do you . . . think we'll . . . Do you want to stay married to me?"

He actually gaped, then snapped his mouth shut. "Have I given you one reason—ever—to say that?" He shook his head. "Give me a break!"

She tried to be cheered by his answer, although it took enormous effort. She'd read that couples talked to each other most on their third date and the year before the divorce, so maybe his terseness meant they'd last.

Ted ordered zabaglione. All egg yolks and bad for his heart, but she kept quiet. She skipped dessert, claiming to be full although, of course, she wasn't. Couldn't be.

"Want a taste?" he asked, but she declined and they sat through more silence until suddenly she was crying. "What?" he said. "What's wrong now?"

So much. Way beyond words, but a few found their way. "I just remembered." She sounded so strange, she wasn't sure it was her own voice. "We were newlyweds and your parents visited and we were so afraid we'd grow up to be sad like them. And we went outside naked under raincoats and danced in the rain at midnight. Oh, damn." She was middle-aged and over-married and overweight and under-loved, crying in a restaurant in Rome. "I wish—I miss—" She stopped before she humiliated herself more by asking him to love her again, really love her.

The muscles of his face closed in on themselves. "We all do," he said. "We all wish and we all miss."

They walked back to their hotel. "What's that?" Hallie asked as they crossed a piazza and faced a wide staircase. "Where are we?" The steps were alive with young people. Boys' guitars echoing the Sixties. Long-haired girls in tight jeans.

"The Spanish Steps," Ted said as they maneuvered between hipbones, hair, and laughter.

Hallie looked at the young girls. We are as perishable as fruit, she thought. Such a terrible difference between the fresh and firm and the soggy, spotted, old. "I keep forgetting there are so many young people, as if everybody's past forty by now." She laughed nervously.

His glance was withering, as if she were not only dim-witted but offensive. "How can you say that? We have children their age!" He looked away.

When you love a woman—when you are in love with her, she thought, you want to agree, you want to laugh if she speaks lightly, if you know she hoped to amuse. Deep inside, the gnawing began again.

She puffed up the Spanish Steps, then paused for breath. Several steps above, the profile of a couple caught her even though she tried not to watch. The girl, hair streaming down her back, straddled her lover, lips and blue-jeaned hips locked together. And they kissed. They kissed while Hallie viewed them from below. They kissed as she climbed. They kissed as she brushed by, and when she had passed and turned back for a final glance, they were still kissing. She heard her own soft intake of air, like a sob.

To be kissed that way, in a dream of desire, melting slowly, from the lips down until, without moving, he was kissing all of you, all your skin, all your surfaces.

She would have never dared when she was that girl's age. Never suspected it could be that way. And now that she did understand and knew she needed it, she was too old and too little loved.

She would die of not being wanted that blatant, obsessive, total way. She would die of not having that kiss. She swallowed hard and cleared her throat and finally reached Teddy at the top of the stairs. His face was dark with anger.

"Never played," he said, as if talking to himself. "Such a god-damned good boy. Straight to college, work every summer, marry, have kids. Take care of things. Duties. Obligations."

She saw, as he must, the girls, dark-haired descendants of the Medicis and white-blond Nordics, loose-limbed and easy in the warm Italian night, and she was chilled, because she also saw the aching sense of loss in his eyes.

"Never," Ted said.

They made love that night, but it was nothing like the deep dances on the Spanish Steps. It was awkward and solemn, mutual consolation and apology for what they were not, what they did not have, what they could not offer. A requiem.

Hallie lay wide-awake, staring at the ceiling. Someone, Camus, had said, "Love can either burn or last." They were lasting on a very low flame. Maybe that was the same as being all right.

------------ 3 ------------

Ted crept up the freeway, wishing he had left home earlier, beaten the traffic. It was morning, between storms and the sun was a blurred polished circle on a tarnished sky.

Should have bought the new house in Palo Alto instead of Los Gatos. Better commute. Too late now. It had taken Hallie two hostile, reluctant years to find a place and he wasn't about to start again. Besides, the down payment had been made and they'd close in two months and—please, God—sell their house so that he wasn't carrying two mortgages.

". . . current screening techniques there is little risk—"

Herpes. AIDS. Harder to get any when he was young, but you lived after you finally did. *Get any*. From what mental junk pile had that come? Hallie and her Feminist Police would torture him.

Was Erica careful? Talk about change. Hallie's father would have killed his daughter's lover. Erica's father worried whether his daughter's lover would kill her.

She was living with a guy off-campus. Hallie knew, but he wasn't supposed to. He wished he didn't. Erica said she'd never marry. Most kids, according to her, agreed that they weren't falling into their parents' trap. He couldn't bear to ask what trap she meant.

Thanksgiving and Erica's twenty-first. The years since her birth folded into nothing, like an accordion. And Andy, too, bearded and wary, with an earring like a pirate. Two gone, and Sarah with a foot out the door. He'd thought there'd be more time. Now, kids leaving and he was nearly fifty and soft around the waist, an old man timidly peering over his steering wheel.

". . . the Ayatollah Khomeini today declared that—"

"The Ayatollah Fritter," Hallie called him, and lately, Ted didn't disagree. He wondered whether Khomeini's second in command also had a perpetual burn in his gut.

At least the interminable feud about taking the company public was over. Fritter had wanted to wait until the campus was complete, but he couldn't. He'd dumped so much into the ground, literally, borrowing against real assets more and more until now they needed additional capital to finish it. The modern-day Medici had become Nero, fiddling while he burned his own empire.

". . . Iranian offensive against Iraqi—"

"I hate being asked what I'm going to *be*," Andy had said a few weeks ago. "I'll be *me*, not a job title." And Ted lacked the guts to correct him, admit that the idiom was accurate. Your job sucked you in until you and it were one and the same organism.

I'll be me, not my job. He wished. Ever since Lucy left, Fritter behaved as if the company were last year's Christmas toy, alternately absorbing and annoying him. He instituted cutbacks, then spent wastefully, hired people, then changed his mind, always leaving Ted to clean up, explain, defend the about-faces, pay off enraged victims.

His head banged, his stomach burned. He crawled along, inhaling exhaust fumes. Then he squared his well-tailored shoulders. He had an interview on piracy problems. NBC evening news. He was Theodore Bennett, President and Chief Operating Officer of The Fun Factory. A definite somebody. It could be worse.

Nervously, he opened the envelope left sealed by his secretary because of the PERSONAL underlined three times below its address.

Dear Ted,

I've been meaning to write you *forever*, to tell you what a surprise and thrill it was for me to see your picture in *People* magazine!!! How does it feel to be inside the covers with Michael Jackson and Brooke Shields and Debra Winger??? I tell everybody I knew you when!!! (grin)

He couldn't remember if she'd always used a triple dose of punctuation. She spoke that way. Her wildness, excitement, contrasted with her sleek surfaces, her pose of blasé sophistication.

But now I finally actually *am* writing because I just found out I'm going to be in San Francisco (somebody told me to *never* call it Frisco!) in May!!! My husband has to read some *incredibly* dry paper about attachment theory (his specialty) at a medical convention (even though he's a Ph.D., not an M.D. Maybe they heard the word "doctor" and invited him???) (smile)

His secretary buzzed through. "Mr. Marks would like to see you as soon as possible."

His stomach jets spurted acid. "One minute."

Do you think you'd have time for a drink (for old time's sake) while I'm there? (Please?—It'll be *fun*!!!) The third of May. (Mark it on your calendar!!) If you don't hear from me, it'll be because I couldn't get through your *thousands* of assistants and secretaries!!! (joke)

Fondly,
Chris

Well, he thought. Exclamation point, exclamation point, exclamation point. (Grin.)

Maybe she'd catch him on the evening news tonight, too.

Then he heeded his master's call. Fritter was probably finally ready to talk time schedule for going public.

"Sit down," Fritter said when Ted entered his office. He, however, stood like an upright whale, looking out the window.

Ted waited, listening to the distant buzz and whine of heavy machinery eating ground for the campus.

"This isn't fun anymore."

Ted wondered what "this" meant today. Life? Meetings? Computer games? Television interviews? The window treatment?

"Seven years is longer than my short attention span."

The air currents stopped with the clear dead silence that people called earthquake weather. Ted barely breathed.

Fritter turned, hooked his thumbs into his belt, and looked toward the ceiling. "Don't like a thousand people depending on me. I want out."

Out? He wanted to quit his own company? Oh, Lucy, come back. Put Humpty Dumpty together again.

Fritter sank into his desk chair. "I'm selling out."

"The company?" Ted tested it, ready to be ridiculed.

Fritter nodded.

"Selling the company." Ted gave him a second chance, wondering if this was a practical joke, if hidden cameras were filming his astonishment for future laughs.

Fritter nodded again.

"This company. Sell. The Fun Factory. Now?"

"Yup."

"But aren't you going to— The plan was to take the company

public, to . . ." He had brain damage, aphasia. He couldn't make sense of the language anymore.

"That was the plan," Fritter said. "It isn't anymore."

"I have to advise you that . . . in light of commitments made—" Ted stopped himself. Don't panic. This was only a whim, and before word got around, certainly before they found buyers, Fritter would forget it. Ted tried to unclench his jaw, unlock the muscles in the small of his back.

Fritter leaned back in his chair. "Japanese group wants it. They came to me. I've agreed."

"You've already—"

Fritter straightened up. "It's a done deal."

"But—"

"It's my company, if I'm not mistaken."

"Listen, Fritter, you've gone through a difficult time. Why not wait before you make serious decisions that affect—"

Fritter exhaled with a soft, explosive pop. "Japs don't want our R&D people," he said, "but they'll take over the campus, finish it. They can use part of it, modify the rest, make it an upscale industrial park–office complex. We're in the hole, you know, so they're getting the company for peanuts, but I want out."

"Wait a minute. What happens to our R&D people?"

"They find something else."

"We just moved some of them across the country. We can't—"

"The Japs'll decide about the game team later, so we don't have to—"

"Wait—I'm still not clear about the R&D's." Fritter looked at Ted as if he'd never seen him before. "They all get fired? Guys who relocated families, bought houses? Fired, like that?"

"No written guarantees in this life. It's a volatile business."

"But their shares—everybody's stock when we go public. It was part of their contract, their deals. *My* deal."

Fritter shrugged. "Everybody's contracts include the words 'when' and 'if.' "

Seven years of that carrot. He'd busted his balls for that man, believed him. Built him a company. "But it could be done. Should be. We're ripe for it, and there'd be much more money for everybody," Ted said. "Then you could quit."

"Place is a drain on my mental health. Life's too short. I don't need the money."

Sure. He'd long since made back his investment and he had the zillions from his first company. Whatever the Japanese paid him, however low the asset sale evaluation, Fritter Marks definitely did not need food money. Not mortgage payments on a big new house. Not college tuitions for three kids. Fritter Marks had his fuck-you money.

Ted Bennett didn't have his. Seven years ago, Fritter had offered five percent of the new company, attractive compensation for the risk, but the vesting schedule had been extended and wouldn't become a hundred percent until they went public.

And now there would be no public offering and Ted owned less than two percent and the Japanese weren't paying much. He pushed figures, estimates into his numb, frozen brain.

"People counted on those shares," Ted said. "All those contracts." Bet he'd get around $200,000. The promise had been millions—five, six million—with the public offering.

A $200,000 check would have been nirvana to his father. But his father wasn't carrying an inflated California mortgage, and his father hadn't put a down payment on a new house. His father didn't have three college tuitions to pay. His father had savings.

And why the hell was he thinking about his father, anyway?

Because he couldn't think about anything clearly except that he was finished, with nothing ahead. He and his father had that in common.

"There are ways of cashing people out," Fritter said with a shrug. "No big thing."

Not even a warning, Ted thought. We're nothing to him.

"Think I'll produce a film. Harry Bevan wants to work with me, and the women involved are certainly prettier."

You think I give a shit what you do from now until you die? You jerk me around, and think I still wish you well?

"L.A. has a definite excitement," Fritter said.

"What's your timetable?" Fuck your future delights. "How's this going to work?" His stomach lining shriveled and ulcerated. To have to ask, like a servant. What's next, boss man? It was

Ted who knew engineering and management and marketing. Ted who'd made this company.

And Fritter who was breaking it. All that paternalistic crap about the Fun Factory family. An abusive family.

"It's a ninety-day thing, so we aren't futzing around," Fritter said. "By March, we'll speak Japanese. Get it over with. Not today, tomorrow being Thanksgiving and all, but Monday."

Ted loosened his tie. His throat was sealing and he had problems breathing. Ninety days and what about him? He had fiddled, like the grasshopper. Nothing put by for winter, and winter would last the rest of his life.

"I'm not an ogre," Fritter said. "Three months' notice, three months' severance pay. Six months' lead time to find something."

I am ruined, Ted thought. Dead. Destroyed.

"I'm not talking about you, Bennett. You and I, we'll sit down, work out the package. Basically, a year's pay. After the three months, of course. I think that's fair."

Ted focused on the wooden inlay work on the back of Fritter's desk. He wouldn't answer, wouldn't lick Fritter's boots. A year's salary was not a future, was not retirement, was only twelve mortgage payments, food for the table. And Fritter could have saved him. "Did you . . ." He was sure his throat was hemorrhaging. "Is there . . . did you talk about . . . an employment contract for me?" He choked over the words, the groveling. "With them?"

"They weren't much interested."

Translation: Less shit from you about my buildings, my budget, my dreams, and maybe I'd have lifted a finger to help you. It wouldn't have been hard.

Ted could not remember hating as purely, as cleanly, as he now hated Fritter.

"Better get ready for that piracy interview," Fritter said. "No better publicity than NBC News. The Japs were pleased about it. They're keeping the name, you know." He sounded merry.

Ted would tell the six o'clock news that he'd been had. Raped by reality, Hallie called it. He'd ask them to write in care of the Ted Bennett Defense Fund. Send money. Save me.

He was going to cry on-air, nationwide.

"Okay, Bennett? Go make those motherfuckers copying our game repent their sins." Fritter winked before he walked out.

Ted sat alone, taking deep breaths. He'd been on TV before. No sweat. Except those times, he'd gone on as president of The Fun Factory and he'd known what that meant. He'd gone on as Theodore Bennett, and way, way back, he'd known what that meant, too.

— 4 —

Hallie and Sarah sat close in the comfortable family room, an afghan over their knees against the damp chill of February and a bowl of popcorn balanced between them. Sarah watched a movie about a woman whose missing husband had reappeared after ten years.

After eight months, you could barely see the scar on Sarah's chin, and her arm reached easily, gracefully, for popcorn. So lucky, Hallie thought again. She compared her daughter's progress with Michael Farr's. Though physically intact, Michael was still struggling and rebelling.

Of course, she thought, on the positive side, Megan had Ben now. They'd been living together the last few months. On the other hand, since Thanksgiving, Hallie and Ted had merely coexisted.

Hallie returned to her book, *The Tristan Syndrome*, an examination, the ads said, of what you absolutely needed to know about love. The author's message was disheartening. It appeared that romance flowered only when love was in danger or doomed, and passion, with a life span of a few months to three years max, developed only when future satisfaction and happiness were doubtful. All of which made a marriage of nearly twenty-five years inevitably bloodless and limp.

Accept it, the author said. Grow up.

The hell with him. You could have a passionate marriage. You could have a passion for the real, for the really how it was. That was what being grown-up meant.

She looked at the other half of her great romance. Ted sat in a deeply cushioned chair, feet on an ottoman, drumming his fingers on the leather upholstery, impatient with the TV movie and mostly, consumingly, with his own existence. Back at Thanksgiving when his life had first been turned upside down, Hallie had tried to console him, but he was unsoothable. Nowadays, it was all she could do to console herself.

Fame, mild though the variety was, had kissed and ruined him. No matter that she was the bitch goddess, a known whore. He'd tasted her and everything that followed was peasant fare. A man didn't quit Camelot for the real world, at least Ted didn't.

What was the antidote for mentions in the *Wall Street Journal*, a *Newsweek* sidebar, a photo in *People*? Hallie's aging body, over-familiar caresses? Her humor, which fell flat on his ears? Her casual conversation, which he picked up in loose strands and questioned, as if she were threatening him? As if there were a subtext and secret meaning to every word.

She remembered with terrible pain that she'd once believed she could make him happy.

Ted stood up.

"Popcorn, Daddy?" Sarah wooed the wounded male, offering what she could. Hard to kill that instinct.

Ted shook his head. Sometimes he seemed feral—a desperate trapped animal—and she felt sorry for him, forgetting that such animals confuse helpers with attackers and counterattack.

Other times he seemed a fool, too sleek and superficial to comprehend that there was life after Fritter Marks.

Almost never did he seem Ted Bennett. There he stood, a furious silent mass. Her pulse rate elevated. He was as aerobically effective as jogging.

He was, in fact, an accidental diet, because when the tension had become unbearable, she started hiking the hillsides, metaphorically running away until one day she literally ran and found it to be release and escape. Plus, when she'd progressed from unhappiness to chronic depression, she lost her appetite. The misery diet. All you give up is the source of your happiness. Not painless, but effective.

"Have some popcorn, Daddy?"

"I don't want any! Would everybody stop nagging? Am I hurting anything? Am I bothering anybody?"

Sarah's limbs stiffened below the afghan. Enough was enough, and children were off limits. "There's no need to—" Hallie said.

"Lay off! I asked a question. I didn't upset Sarah. I didn't upset you, did I, Sarah? If I did, I'm sorry! Jesus Christ Almighty!" And he stormed out.

Right after Fritter's announcement, they'd pulled tighter as allies, as what she thought of as husband and wife, even the night he'd terrified her by being so lost and distraught she'd feared for his sanity, as if Fritter had sold Ted's ego along with the company. But even then, they were in it together, partners. Until Ted spun off on his own trajectory, becoming so erratic she thought he was on drugs. But his bloodstream was poisoned by fear, depression, and rage, not narcotics.

"I have a job," she'd said time and again. "You aren't Samson, holding the temple up alone. Nothing desperately horrible will happen to our family, no matter what. Erica's nearly finished. Andy can apply for student loans. We'll be okay until you find something. We'll sacrifice the deposit on the new house."

Only then did he react. "You never wanted to move, anyway. You're probably happy. We're losing a sizable chunk of money and you make next to nothing!"

"I'll pick up private work. We'll make ends meet. We've done it before, we can do it again."

"Living like—after everything, to live like—to be supported by my wife."

She mentioned the plans he'd always talked about. Reminded him that Skip was ready to be his partner. Told him to take the chance, put his severance pay into a new business. He looked as if he didn't understand.

They sacrificed the deposit on the new house, pulled theirs off market, reworked the budget, recomputed tuition bills, household maintenance. They worked out logistics and finances, but the most important issue, Ted Bennett's once and future identity, remained unresolved.

"Don't mind Dad," Hallie told Sarah. "He's—you know. Tense. Maybe I'd better go and . . ." What was the word? Wife. Verb, active. I have to wife.

She kissed Sarah's cheek. It had been nice, that almost normal interlude.

She felt a stab of pity at the sight of him brooding in the living room. He didn't look as large, as strong, as she always imagined.

He didn't even look healthy. "Don't shut us out," she said. "We love you."

He nodded ungraciously. If she had offered a high-profile job instead of love, he'd have turned on the charm.

"You have alternatives." She sat down across from him.

He turned his head away so that she was left studying his handsome profile.

Sarah tiptoed past the living room on her way upstairs. In a few minutes, the TV in Sarah's room blared.

"This is a good opportunity to rethink how we live, to simplify," Hallie said. Variation one thousand and one. "We could find a smaller house, lower our overhead."

"The American dream in reverse. Why are you so *defeatist?*"

Sometimes he broke her heart. Literally. She felt the crunch as it fractured. "I'm your biggest fan," she said, "and you know it. But we don't *need* all this."

"Life is more than making do, than subsistence, than what you *need*. And I don't want to talk. That won't make it better."

"Then what will?" She couldn't help screaming. She seldom could. That's why Sarah played her television so loudly.

He looked startled, then icily remote. "Probably nothing."

Then their marriage was dead. She was impotent and he was no more than the cold corpse of somebody half-recognized. This must be how it was to love an Alzheimer's victim, to have the body left, but not the person.

Oh, but. Twenty-five years next month. A history. The oldest established marriage in California, and you couldn't walk out on that. Shouldn't drive him away, either, even though that made him sound like a brainless sheep who wouldn't cling to a valuable position. One more try. "There's no reason to panic. You're getting the money from the sale of the corporation and the salary payoff. We'll coast for a while. Think of this as a well-earned vacation."

"A vacation is when there's something to come home to! I was the president. A company has exactly one of them, so you know how many opportunities there are for me? Zero. Except the New York offer, which, of course, I didn't accept."

She couldn't bear seeing herself distorted in the funhouse mirrors of his eyes. "That offer stunk and you know it. High risk, not worth quitting my job, finding a school for Sarah—"

"I didn't take it, did I?" But his face accused her of selfishness and cowardice, of having thwarted his one and only chance. He was irrational, and she was an inverted Lady Macbeth driving her husband to obscurity.

She didn't feel joined anymore. She felt captive. "You only considered it because they wanted to get into films, more glamor. It was an expensive, destructive way to save face!" Screaming again. "Buying time! It was underfinanced, doomed. We couldn't survive on the money—they thought you were a billionaire—I wouldn't have had a job—but you wouldn't have sounded *ordinary* again, like us mortals." She pounded the arm of the loveseat with her fist. "All that talk—years of it—about how you wanted to do something *real!*"

"Real was for after I got my money, remember, but suddenly you can't add numbers."

"I know the numbers on the New York thing were insane. You were going to be their front, their way into investment money—"

Like Santas, with grudges, not gifts, in their sacks.

"Some people would have taken the chance," he said, tight-lipped.

He twisted everything, unmade logic. Damn him for needing to blame and for picking her, the nearest, easiest target. "I don't know you anymore," she whispered.

"My own wife! The one person who should understand the humiliation! I was a patsy."

"I do under—"

"You're more interested in Girl Scout aphorisms than reality. You're right—you don't know me and you never did! So wrapped up in *your* career, *your* life, *your* ideas!

"Me? *Me?* I've spent every single day of the last three months— the last two miserable years—holding your hand, listening to you, being there for you—"

He became engrossed in a painting on the wall. She moved toward him, understanding how people sprung wires and suddenly murdered their nearest and formerly dearest. "*You* don't care! You don't even *ask* how I'm doing. I only exist to understand you! You're always in some big deal—good or bad—while I— you just—I'm so sick of—our life—" She sat down, winded, nauseous with failure. She had worked hard to keep her concerns partitioned off until this passed, had so wanted to be the good wife, to run the course of the disease and get the blue ribbon for spousal excellence.

The road to hell was paved with good intentions, but so was every other road, and dammit, the question remained, rose and burned her throat like vomit, choking her—*when was it her turn?*

She was sick of wifing, of being a supporting player. His worries mattered, his interests counted, his crises warranted attention. "Who am I? Your groupie?"

He aimed his face at her, or at least at the space she occupied, but he was blind and deaf. He didn't hear a word.

5

"I was afraid I wouldn't recognize you!" Chris swiveled on the bar stool where she'd been waiting.

"It's wonderful to see you again." Ted kissed her cheek. She looked slender and put-together in an unusual shade of gold-green silk. Not the same as she'd been, of course. The face was tighter. Half her good looks had been happy expectations, and now she had the air of someone too often disappointed. The red hair was brassier, coarser, and . . . tense, he'd have to call it. Well, none of them were getting younger. It seemed especially true here in this bar filled with the new generation. "Enjoying your trip?" he asked as they slipped into a booth.

"San Francisco's fun."

He didn't find it particularly so anymore on his visits with venture capitalists and headhunters, but he said nothing.

"I hope you didn't mind my writing you at your office."

"Not at all." He noticed how she held on to the stem of her wineglass, how the veins of her hands stood out now. He wondered if she worried over things like that, the way he did. "It intrigued my secretary, that 'Personal' you wrote twice and underlined. Made her think I was a man of mystery." He waved

over the waitress, ordered another spritzer for Chris, a Bloody
Mary for himself.

"I didn't want it filed away, or answered by somebody, like a
fan letter."

Fan mail? Hallie would laugh at that one. Of course, he
wouldn't tell her. He hadn't mentioned the gushy note months
ago. It was his. Separate.

"Were you impressed that I tracked down The Fun Factory?"
she asked, head cocked.

"It isn't exactly a state secret."

He hadn't told Hallie about Chris's phone call two days ago
either. About this date. Well, it was nothing to talk about. A
drink with an old . . . someone.

She must color her hair now. That's what it was. There was
something off about it.

"It's been fifteen years," she said, looking directly at, into, him.
"Fifteen and a half years. Since the reunion."

Ted felt relief when the waiter's arm cut the air between them.
"Well," he prompted, "bring me up to date."

"You know Grady and I went pfft." She put her hands up in
a gesture of defeat.

"No. I didn't." She looked annoyed.

"We should never have married. I made a lot of mistakes." She
traced loops on the table with her swizzle stick. "It took me a
long time to grow up. Too long."

She stumbled as if she was thinking it through, but the pauses
had the ring of a well-rehearsed speech, although he felt ashamed
of thinking so.

"But," she added, "it was a growth experience. It led me to
study psychology and I've been involved in the human-potential
movement ever since."

"Ah, yes. The bright new hope. Seminars, courses, and revela-
tions. How come we seem more screwed up than ever?"

She raised her eyebrows. "You've become a cynic."

"Sorry. Forget it. Any kids?"

She sipped her wine. "Two. My daughter's a school counselor
in Minnesota and my son's at Franklin and Marshall. And you?"

"Three. A daughter in high school, another who's a senior at

Penn, and a son at U.C. Santa Cruz." He was oddly uncomfortable talking about his children with her. "And what about you? What keeps you busy?" He hoped something did. Such an awkward question nowadays.

"I have a party business." Chris laughed. "Not likely to put me in *People*. Or on TV! I saw you a few months ago. I was in bed, watching the late news, and there you were, in my—" A tiny shrug. "Very intimate."

He smiled, over-aware of appearing in her bedroom. Over-aware that she'd made him over-aware. Subtlety was not her strong hand.

"You were very good, you know."

He didn't know to what bedroom performance she referred. "Thanks. So. You've remarried."

She nodded. "David's a psychologist. He's written a book about love, *The Tristan Syndrome*." Her voice lowered. "He's not nearly as romantic as that makes him sound. But I want to know about you. How are you?"

Lost. Terrified. Stupid. Washed up. Unemployed. Luckily, she didn't require an actual answer.

"Did you ever dream you'd run a glamorous company?" she asked. "Know famous people? Be famous?"

He saw himself through her eyes, clean. A star. Still a somebody. "It's not one hundred percent glamor," he said. *Hypocrite!* The censoring voice sounded suspiciously like a wife he knew. He hushed it.

"For most of us, life's one hundred percent unglamorous!" Her face softened when she was flushed and excited.

"In actual fact," he said, "it feels time for something else."

"You'd leave?" She looked so stunned, he could sense the rich forest of fantasies she had planted around his life. "Why on earth?"

Because the place was sold and I'm out on my ass? "I've wanted to do research for a long time now." He felt bilious, dangling above omissions and downright lies. "Tired of games." Fritter games. Video games. Mind games. Not this game, though. "And trust me, famous people aren't necessarily smarter or funnier than your friends at home." Sure. Drag in the famous people again.

He felt a twinge, saw Hallie at the side of the booth, hands on hips, eyebrows raised above white-water eyes, demanding to know what this act was about.

But Hallie wasn't there. And Chris, who had been a star to him when he was a poor scholarship boy, sat, mouth soft and admiring, positive that his life was pure enchantment. Chris yearned. Chris ached. Chris envied. Chris regretted. He hadn't felt this good in a long time. Who the hell cared what the facts were?

Her earrings were pearl clusters with a green stone in the center. Knowing her, an emerald. He liked that she cared about the details of how she presented herself, about quality. Hallie was big on "making do." He preferred people who didn't settle, who demanded the best.

"You don't sound exactly . . . Are you happy, Ted?"

Happy? His children were almost gone, his career was in ruins, and his wife had emotionally deserted him.

"I didn't realize it was a complicated question."

"Everything's complicated." He hadn't talked in this charged code, done this oblique dance, in eons.

"Sometimes," she said haltingly, "I think back." She leaned closer. "I remember. Do you, Teddy? Ever?"

Decades ago, her betrayal had boiled and fermented down to a dark residue. Then even that became irrelevant, seldom remembered. But these last few months, since her note, memories had flooded him. "I remember," he said. And when he did, his mind summoned something besides Chris. It summoned himself. He felt again how tightly his skin had fit his muscles, how easy everything seemed. How Chris glittered, rich and different, the key to the larger world of privilege.

He remembered how it felt to have the future spread clear and endless like a summer sky. To be on a quest at an age when fairy tales came true. Youth and hope were what he remembered with great pain. It wasn't so much Chris. Or perhaps it was.

She leaned over the table, put a hand on his wrist, her thumb on his pulse. Her eyes glittered in a damp glaze. "I was a fool." A single tear ran down her cheek and she made no move to check it.

He felt his heartbeat pulse into her fingers.

She twisted the hand on his so that she could see her watch. "I have to leave. I promised to be back." She took a deep breath, then lifted her pocketbook.

It had a pattern of designer's initials. He wished he hadn't noticed. It was the pretentious kind Hallie made fun of. Okay, the kind he made fun of, too. His monogram was a disease—TB—and maybe that had turned him off initials, his or anybody else's.

"Here's my card, if you're ever in Phildelphia." She bit her bottom lip. "Or I could travel some, too," she whispered. "On business. If you're anywhere . . . this is my private line."

"Chris, listen . . ."

"That wasn't easy to say." She kept her eyes averted. "But I had to. For old time's sake, that's all." She smiled and stood up, brushing her skirt smooth.

He stood too.

"It was wonderful seeing you again." She kissed him, a moment too long, with a pressure too subtle to be about friendship or old time's sake. She pulled away and smiled. "I remember so much," she said. And then she was gone in a green-gold flash.

Her kiss had been salty. A trace of that solitary tear, perhaps. But he remembered salt kisses after a night of dancing, skin hot with lust and sun, heart racing with expectation.

He licked his lip, tasting his youth again.

He knew he was plunking a ball-bearing into a Rube Goldberg contraption and it was rolling, pushing levers that pulled arms that moved gears that triggered wheels that . . . who knew? He watched as gravity and inertia, the very laws of nature, took over.

He put Chris's card in his pocket and went to pay the bill.

Clichés and Aberrations

1985

> To say that they clashed in many ways and in many ways
> disappointed each other is to say no more than that they were
> married, and for a long time.
> *Phyllis Rose*

----------- 1 -----------

WE HAVE to leave, Mom."

Hallie stared at a shot of Ted hoisting a laughing infant Andy into the sunshine, reliving that moment, the azalea bush in exuberant bloom, the wet grass between her toes, the love.

"Reorganizing snapshots is, like, compulsive. Anal retentive." Sarah had taken a psychology elective.

"Someday you'll understand."

"Look, Andy was actually cute once."

"All my babies were and still are."

Sarah grimaced, too young to value even sincere compliments. "Where was this?" she asked.

Hallie stood in tall dune grass, hair teased and tugged into semi-straightness, Sarah, in sunbonnet and diaper, balanced on one hip. Erica and Andy, both holding green buckets and shovels, stood at her side, squinting. "The Cape," she said. "Nineteen seventy, maybe?" How beautiful we were. Perfect. Did I know it, or was I thinking about what to make for lunch and whether my stomach looked fat and how the baby wouldn't stop fussing—absorbed always with what wasn't right?

"I hate that we had fun I can't remember." Sarah picked up another snapshot. "Dad was quite a hunk."

A picture of their first day in their first apartment. Ted, barely more than a child, leaned an elbow on a stack of cartons. She remembered her infatuation with his forearm, its blond hair like gold chasing. "Never on Sunday" serenaded them from the boxy record player while they unpacked, breaking for slapstick gyrations and kisses. Remembered the peppery shock of comprehending that she was this beautiful man's forever wife, and he her forever husband.

Photographs were like the scratch-and-sniff cards her children used to have, potent with memories waiting for release. "Daddy still is a hunk," she said.

"Well, of course. To you."

And Hallie comprehended a portion of Ted's panic.

She flipped snapshots, pieces of a puzzle called The Bennetts. Erica by the Minuteman statue in Lexington. Andy at the zoo. Sarah, cheeks puffed, blowing three candles on a birthday cake. Erica with no front teeth. Andy in a fifth-grade production of *Julius Caesar* in which he was prematurely stabbed by Brutus. He'd risen from the dead to demand his rights. "Hey!" he'd shouted, punching Brutus. "You forgot my line! 'Et tu, Brute!' " And then he'd dropped dead again. Hallie could still feel Ted squeezing her hand, the two of them shaking with silent laughter.

Ted carving a Thanksgiving turkey, family and friends lining the table. Sarah, up at bat in the championship game. All three children in Halloween getups. Erica in cap and gown. Ted, the children at his feet, singing and playing the banjo.

The measure of her days.

"We'll be late, Mom." Sarah was less eager for her grandmother's bridal shower than for the prospect of seeing Michael Farr for the first time since the accident a year ago.

Hallie put aside the photos. She wondered how much they were a proof of happiness and how much a proof of being photogenic.

Hallie had met her mother's intended a month ago, in Philadelphia, at Erica's college graduation. He was so unimpressive that she assumed he had money, because of a favorite Yiddish proverb of her mother's. "With money in your pocket, you are wise, you are handsome, and you sing well, too." Leo Braverman sang beautifully. But he was poor, plain, not noticeably wise, and a complete contrast to Hallie's prickly but interesting father.

Sylvia had met him four months earlier on a flight west, when both, they learned, were visiting their children. A whirlwind, bicoastal romance followed. "Of the geriatric variety," Sylvia said. "Not like in the songs. But at my age if my heart pounded and I gasped and lost my mind, they'd put me in intensive care."

With hair strands glued across a bald pate and a pencil-thin mustache, Leo looked out of a Thirties nightclub scene. He spoke with peculiar syntax, like one for whom English was a second language, although he had no accent. "Your most gracious mother has made me the happiest man on earth by consenting to be my bride," he said. "And now, we wish for your blessing."

If the agnostic afterlife included grave-spins, her father was whirling.

Before retirement, Leo had been stage manager of a small theater in Jersey. "In the arts," Sylvia said with awe, as starry-eyed as a woman with trifocals could be. He in turn was dazzled by Sylvia's domestic skills. His late wife, an actress, hadn't cooked. She had, in fact, removed the doors and used the kitchen shelves as display cases for theatrical memorabilia.

So today the future stepdaughters of Leo Braverman and assorted others sat in the July heat of Sonoma, feting the bride-to-be in a fragrant color-splashed garden.

In old wedding-shower tradition, Leo's daughter Connie wove the gift-box ribbons into a large bow, although Hallie thought that had something to do with how many babies the bride would have. Maybe Connie wove simply to avoid speaking to anyone, because she was less than ecstatic about the merger, insinuating that Sylvia was after Leo's minuscule pension and Social Security check.

No one knew Leo's other daughter's opinion. She had shaved her head and was selling flowers on Wilshire Boulevard in L.A.

Hallie looked at her sister rather than at her sour future stepsister. Vicky reminded her of W.P.A. photos from the Depression. Her body was weathered, muscles hard from work, not workouts. She looked older than her forty years, but in a well-used way. She still wore her hair in a long braid that reached the small of her back, and dressed for utility, not style.

It was easier to envision her in a cabin on the plains, dust seeping through planks and barefoot children clinging to her, than having a successful business and a fleet of delivery trucks. Next to her, thirteen-year-old Polly, toffee-skinned and black-eyed, giggled with Sarah.

Still a bit of a Mary Sunshine, Megan attempted conversation with dour Connie. "I hear the newest thing in wedding preparation is the plastic surgery timetable," she said. "You have to plan for it early, right after the proposal, because pouty lips, tummy tucks, liposuction, breast augmentation take time. Should we tell Sylvia?"

Connie glowered and tied another ribbon in her bouquet.

"Is it grounds for annulment if the bride looks nothing like the girl he asked to marry?" Hallie asked.

Kat, oxygen tank attached, wheezed a laugh.

"Thank you all." Sylvia lifted her wineglass. Open gift boxes leaked creamy silk lingerie, frou-frou for a woman who'd been practical for too long and who'd confided to her dumbfounded daughters that Leo was "a very sensual man." Connie's gift was a blender. "My daughters think that as a bride of seventy-one, I should have something wise to say, but I don't. Having a wedding shower at this age feels very odd." She looked around the table. "But then, it's all quite odd, isn't it? An adventure. And that, I think, is how much I know for sure."

Before dinner, Hallie stopped in at Megan's store.

"Does Sarah realize how middle class Michael's become?" Megan asked. "He'll bore her to tears."

"Never. She'll always see him as her wild past. She'll make up what she needs to see like we all do."

Megan raised an eyebrow. "Maybe. There was this woman on TV in love with a mass murderer. The man slit his family's throats because they got on his nerves, but she insisted he was sweet, and only she knew who he 'really' was. I got this creepy feeling I once sounded like that."

"Everybody does," Hallie said. "It keeps the species going."

Megan showed Hallie the back room, expanded for catalog orders. "I have a present for you. Guaranteed to boil the blood."

Not Hallie's. She'd lost all feeling and even the memory of it. In retreat from the domestic battlefield, she'd pulled her nerve ends after her so that she existed only deeply and secretly within herself. Can't see me, Ted, can't touch me, can't hurt me.

They had tacitly negotiated a nonaggression pact, avoiding squabbles by speaking only of logistical necessities. "What time will you be back?" she'd say. "Is the TV too loud?" he'd ask. Peaceful, noncombative, and platonic.

One morning, cleaning out a cabinet, she found the rabbit-fur mittens. The Pleasure Party and her expectations at the time seemed ancient history. She threw away the mittens.

They slept as far apart as a king-sized mattress allowed. For a while, they'd yawned extravagantly, insisted on unendurable exhaustion, salving each other's pride with nightly alibis. Then they stopped bothering. They crept onto opposing edges of the mattress and picked up books.

One of her first clients had been stunned that her marriage was over, but had matter of factly said that she and her husband hadn't been intimate for seven years without once mentioning it. At the time, Hallie hadn't believed such an arrangement was possible. Now she knew precisely how it happened.

Megan held up a black nightgown.

"It isn't me," Hallie said.

"Maybe that's because you aren't yourself lately." Megan spoke softly. "Did the shower make you sad? About your dad?"

She shook her head.

"Is it still Ted, then?"

"It's a rough phase. The terrible twos, multiplied. He'll grow out of it, I guess."

"Not every problem phases out."

"This will."

"I thought that about Daniel, and later about Michael, and I was dead wrong, nearly literally, both times. Trust me, there's no virtue in long suffering. Get help."

"It'll pass!" Customers in the front part of the store could hear. "It'll pass," she whispered. Miracles happened. Had to, because they were Hallie and Ted, the ideal couple. Ask anybody. There was all that love and history. There were all those photos.

After dinner at Vicky's, a sedate and dangerously adorable Michael drove off with Sarah and solemn promises, Leo took his bride-to-be for a drive, Polly had a baby-sitting job, and Ben and Megan went home.

"*Casablanca*'s on," Vicky said. "I need to cry. The kids'll be late no matter what they said, so relax. Michael is a very responsible driver. Nothing's as effective as learning the hard way. Sleep over. There's room. Nobody here but us chicks."

"Where's Dreadlocks?"

"Left months ago. Remember? Gave me herpes and stole my dope." Vicky pulled out a little tin. "I was ripe for celibacy anyway. The party is definitely over." She pulled a cigarette paper out of a miniaturized tissue box. "I tested HIV negative."

"God, Vick, that's so scary."

"Positive is scary. Negative is lucky. I miss the Sixties. Drugs and sex were fun, not matters of life and death, and what a high believing we could change the world."

Hallie watched her set the paper on the roller. "People seem more fucked than ever nowadays. I miss the Kennedys. Camelot and the perfect marriage. I wish they'd kept up the pretense."

Vicky rolled a joint as symmetrical as a Marlboro. "Excuse me for asking, but speaking of marriage, what is your husband doing in Pennsylvania this Saturday night in July?"

"His dad's sick."

"His dad's been sick for ten years. Besides, he saw him at Erica's graduation last month." Vicky lit the joint and inhaled.

Hallie had said the same to Ted and gotten back annoyed bluster. "He has an interview in New York Monday, so he's visiting Johnstown first."

"New York? You'd move?" The words were compressed in tiny inhalations.

"The company's headquartered in San Francisco."

"Then why cross the country for an inter—"

"Ask him. I don't understand anything he does anymore."

"Shit." Vicky passed over the joint. "Let's get high, stuff our faces, and feel sorry for ourselves."

"It's the best offer I've got." They sat on Vicky's bed surrounded by wine, trail mix, Fritos, Oreos, and a *TV Guide*. Across the room, Bogart and Bergman confronted love, duty, and pain. Tears immediately welled in her eyes. Lately, nothing could plug the easy weeping. Commercials made her cry as soon as people reached out and touched somebody. Cared. "Maybe we should switch to 'Saturday Night Live' and laugh a little," she said.

"Please?" Vicky pulled apart an Oreo. "All those people on the screen are dead. Have some consideration."

"Why aren't lovers ever married in love stories?" Hallie was dying of thirst and downed a glass of wine. "They *yearn*, and then they split or get a fatal disease or jump in front of a train. What about the rest of it? You think they'd make a movie about Bergman staying on with Bogart? Managing Rick's bar, keeping the books, and making eggs the way he likes?"

Vicky's forehead wrinkled. "Streisand and Redford are married in *The Way We Were*."

"*They get divorced!*" Her wail surprised her. "They never show us how people get on with it. For long. For keeps." Her mouth was still dry. She drank more wine.

"Who needs men, anyway?" Vicky said. "They're like trail mix. You think you're buying cashews and pineapple chunks, but you wind up with a handful of sunflower seeds."

"You are either smart or wasted."

Vicky opened another Oreo and slowly, precisely, licked off the white filling. "Except," she said rather dreamily, "there's something to be said for being special. Out of the billion people in the world, somebody says, 'Hey, you, you're different.' I mean there are so many people, otherwise."

Bogie and Bergman hazed the air with tragic yearning. Sam played it again. On this you can rely. What lovely words. There was a break for a word from our advertisers.

"Hey," Vicky said during the second commercial. "Know why women will always be inferior to men? Because they don't have penises to carry their brains in!" She lay flat on the bed laughing. "Isn't that the funniest?"

The movie resumed. Ingrid Bergman told Bogart that she'd always loved him, even though she'd left him.

"That's who I meant to be," Vicky said. "The one he loves forever because she broke his heart. They never love the ones who love them back. Not forever. Not even for long."

"I never broke anybody's heart." It was too sad to bear.

"You think love's something we made up, like the Easter Bunny?"

"I didn't make up the Easter Bunny," Hallie insisted.

"The problems of a couple of little people like you and me don't amount to a hill of beans," Bogie said.

"He's so smart." Hallie picked the candied pineapple pieces out of the trail mix, guiltily leaving the sunflower seeds. If Bogie lost his job, he wouldn't howl at the moon, or be glacial toward his wife, or change his personality. He'd hitch his shoulders and do something about the situation. Bogie understood that mention in *People* wasn't worth a hill of beans.

She wondered if Ted was also watching *Casablanca* and thinking about them. And then she wondered if she cared one way or the other. If her marriage had, perhaps, run its course, hit the wall, and died. She drained her wineglass and poured more.

"What I like about movies," Vicky said, "is that they're inevitable. You never have to worry, because they always turn out the same way."

"Ted wants to develop ones that aren't predictable," Hallie said. "They'd interact with you. What you did would affect what happened next. Like in real life." She shivered, even though the evening was warm. Her flesh was blue in the cold flickering light of the television.

---------- 2 ----------

Everybody did it. It wasn't a cosmic aberration, a fall from grace. Wasn't like he was the only man ever. More like he was the only man who never.

And why not?

A fling. One time only, two adults. Didn't hurt anybody.

Wasn't like he was a letch. Hadn't picked up a stranger at a meat market. Wasn't like he was taking advantage of anybody. All he'd had to do was whistle. Call her with the date and the room number.

He was entitled to a little pleasure. He'd been pushing that rock uphill his whole life and he was tired.

He wished he still smoked.

He imagined himself, the evening, from outside. A man and a woman leaving their separate worlds, meeting secretly. Brief Encounter meets Airport.

Sometimes you had to break the rules, 'or else you'd become Simon Bennett, breathing but dead, so vague and timid he waited for the TV weatherman to tell him how it was rather than stick his own head outside.

The motel was not the setting he'd have chosen with its double-paned glass and nubby green drapes muffling the airport's roars, its standard-issue paintings of Venetian canals, its generic carpet the color of shoe soles. Neutral ground for takeoff and landing and nobody's destination. But this was the safest place. He had to leave early. His breakfast meeting in New York was the official rationale for this trip and she, supposedly at a movie, had only three hours.

He had opened a bottle of red wine, a choice made after great deliberation. White wine needed chilling. Champagne seemed a cliché, and he wasn't sure they were actually celebrating something. His red, however, was unimpressive.

He'd spent too much of Saturday in a Johnstown State Store cursing the repressive government of Pennsylvania for making it impossible to find decent wine. To explain his long absence, he'd bought two bottles, one for dinner with his mother, during which he discovered how mediocre his choice had been. He hated appearing—still appearing—uninformed, naive.

Two standard-issue bathroom glasses sat beside the bottle. Bringing wineglasses would have been self-conscious. Besides, good ones were too fragile to pack and thick ones were less sophisticated than the motel water glasses, which had a rough panache. European. Continental.

It was crazy to agonize over such issues, but he was supposed to have learned things since he'd last seen her.

He rubbed his hands. Sweaty. Nervous, like a kid.

Probably the aftereffect of being with his parents, of worrying what to do about his father, who looked like death, lacking only the hooded cloak. How would Ted pay for his keep, or for a helper to spell his mother, if he didn't have a job or the prospect of one? He'd lied about consulting, invented offers so his mother wouldn't find out he wasn't the person she believed him to be.

His mother. More tight-lipped American Gothic every year. Boxed in her antiseptic house. Last night, watching *Casablanca*, for Christ's sake. Even a lizard would mist up when Bergman came to Bogie's room, crying, to say she could never leave him again. She loved him. She always had. The past was a mistake, a cruel twist of fate. Inescapable, but agonizingly wrong. She hadn't loved the other man. Only him. Forever.

Jesus. Even if the words didn't have a new, intensely personal meaning. But his mother leaped up and raced to the kitchen, hellbent on never letting a coffee cup sit unwashed. The scene was a killer. Really got him. Just as well she didn't see, or ask questions.

He turned on the radio by the bed, found a mellow station, then debated whether background music was too contrived. Still, it further muffled the jets outside, so he left it on, and damned if the next selection wasn't "As Time Goes By."

There was a knock on the door. He paused, took a deep breath. For old time's sake, that's all this was.

And then she was in the room, smelling of something expensive and of summer, looking as unsure and hopeful as he felt, older than he remembered. And then, spotting the desk and the red wine, she lifted another bottle. Red, too.

He took it from her and raised it in a salute. "Here's lookin' at you, kid," he said.

She smiled with the bright animation he remembered from years ago. "I saw that last night! Got home so early, we—"

"I saw it last night, too."

"Oh, Ted! That makes me feel all . . . and did it make you think about—when she came to his room, when she said how she'd left him once—" The radio played the last refrain of "As Time Goes By." "Is that a tape?"

"Radio." Fate. An omen. A sign. Her eyes widened.

Obvious portents and same old stories aside, he still felt awkward. She stood, shivering in the air conditioning.

He poured two tumblers of wine—hers—and passed one to her. They clicked glasses, drank, still standing. He wasn't sure how to proceed. There was one wing chair, one desk chair, and two double beds. Should they pretend they were here for conversation? Exchange views on politics or recent films? Dawdling and rushing seemed equally wrong. He finished his wine in a few gulps and poured more.

She pressed against him as she put her wineglass on the desk. "I've made some terrible mistakes about you," she said, "but this isn't one of them." She lifted the glass out of his hand and put it next to hers, then she leaned over and turned off the desk lamp. "Time does go by," she whispered. "There isn't enough to waste a minute."

Her kiss was a jolt of memory and expectation, loss and rediscovery. Unfamiliar taste and shape, a new spice, the tempo and sound of her breath exotic, the skin around the lips, at the neckline, beneath the buttons of her blouse, all with the familiarity of a dream remembered. In the years since they'd touched, their cells had sloughed and been replaced until they were not even physiologically the people they had been, but memory possessed him until the edge of the night fused with the long-ago last time, and all the years squeezed between dropped away as irrelevant side-trips and detours. Everything, finally, had coherency, made sense. This, then, was the design, overlaying, obliterating, righting the mistakes, misjudgments, insults, and undervaluations between the last time and this time.

"Yes. Oh, God, yes." He hadn't felt this urgent compulsion since he didn't know, couldn't remember, but maybe since, probably since the time with her. He unbuttoned, unzipped, unsnapped, slipped off.

She stretched below him like a cat, her body thrilling with its new-old contours. No soft-edged, overripe, overfamiliar lushness. She was achingly precise. To the hands, a girl. The girl. The same as always, and he pressed against her, remembering the imprint of her bones, realizing he'd lost nothing, only misplaced it.

He was in her and it was then again, all muscle and lust when summer was forever and a woman loved him, shared her secret richness, and he wasn't poor anymore and the universe was waiting for him.

Chris moaned, the sound echoing back to her room at the top of the stairs, secret tiptoes, so her parents wouldn't hear, in the dawns of Indian summer. Forbidden and sweet.

Oh, God, the lost time, the compromises and substitutes.

Until now.

He'd never been this hard before, this strong, this enduring. He knew he was crossing a line, courting the devil. He might go blind, his head might burst, his spine melt. And it would be worth it to hear her cries, the whistle of the wind, himself, finally, again.

When he came, it was from his scalp to his toes, from his fingerprints to his intestines. He came into her and into himself because she knew who he was. She remembered. She still saw it.

"I forgot how it could be," she said afterward, while they lay, entwined and dazed.

On the night table, his travel clock glowed and softly chunked their time away. They lay close, skin slicked with sweat, and he felt the first stirrings of excitement again. He wanted to laugh and cry, drunk in the brain in a way that had nothing to do with wine.

"This can't be the end of it, Ted," she whispered.

She was right. She was wrong. No. Yes. He'd made promises to himself, set ground rules, or he'd have never . . .

But they lived three thousand miles apart. Too far to become a real danger, so if now and then, what was the harm of it?

"Meet me somewhere. Anywhere your work takes you. You travel, don't you?"

His work. The glamor job. She didn't know.

She doesn't know you at all, he heard in a chilly tone. She knows your press releases. She knows the somebody.

"Anywhere," she said, pushing the voice out of his skull. "New York, D.C., the shore. Wherever you say."

How would he explain the flights, the expense? But why did he have to? He wasn't a child.

"Wasn't it always good between us?" she murmured.

He nodded, although the only time he could remember clearly was now, tonight.

"What a self-destructive fool I was. I was hoping it wouldn't be this good. I—" She pressed her face against his chest and he felt the wet of her tears. He put his arms around her and stroked her bare back, her neck. "I know," he whispered. He pulled her closer, felt himself grow, swell, start the climb again.

"Will you?" She shifted so that she straddled him, sitting on his lap, her gold-specked eyes on his as he gently touched her nipples, traced a line down the front of her. The world waited between them. "Will you let it happen?" She was close to tears. "Will you meet me again?"

His answer rolled up from between his thighs. "Yes," he said. "Of course."

3

All summer long he'd radiated tension, strung so tightly he could ricochet off walls. All summer long there'd been silence.

Now the season had changed, but all else was the same, except that Hallie could no longer stand living this way. She watched Ted silently empty his suitcase. He thought talking made problems worse. It had always been her role to force him into speech. Now their silence was so impacted, she had to push with both hands. Megan was right. Things didn't end just because you wanted them to. If she didn't do something, they would be this way through autumn and winter straight ahead into forever. "We have to talk," she said.

"About what?" He clutched dirty socks, as if for support, and looked like an animal trapped in headlights.

"About what's going on. What you're doing."

Color appeared high on his cheeks, then drained. "Meaning exactly what?"

"For months, you've been flying off to talk with people I don't know for purposes I don't understand. You never say how the interviews went, what happened. I don't know what's going on, except that Fritter told you the score ten months ago."

"If you recall, the company didn't change hands until March, and I stayed for the transition and a while after."

"Fine, but what about since then?"

He put socks and underwear in the hamper.

"I don't want to hassle you, but the way you're job hunting isn't systematic or sensible and it obviously isn't working or gratifying. You're so *unhappy*."

He sighed heavily, jaggedly. "You're right. I am unhappy. I've been unhappy for a long time."

"You—what?" Derailed. Off jobs and into unhappiness. That was all he'd heard. She tried and failed to catch his eye. He removed shirts, replaced them in his closet, and circled back without once acknowledging her presence. She pushed down panic, watching him smooth a tie and hang it up, transfer a roll of film to a different suit pocket, put soiled sports shirts in the hamper and unworn argyles back in the drawer.

Unhappy for a long time. Like that. Flatly. But she'd known it, so why was it terrifying to have him acknowledge it?

"What's that?" He'd pulled an ugly, putty-colored, and absolutely un-Ted warm-up suit out of his bag. It had the name of the expensive designer in enormous block letters across the chest.

"A warm-up suit."

"I can see, but whose? Certainly not yours. You hate advertising designers. You always . . ."

He hung it up carefully.

"Ted." He rezipped his bag. His features were folded shut, his eyes opaque. She didn't know him. He was the holder of mysteries. She was the supplicant, waiting.

His mouth curled, anticipating annoyance.

She took a deep breath, as if she were diving underwater. "What do you think you should do? About the unhappiness?"

"Don't," he said. "Please."

"Don't what?"

"I'm exhausted. I can't think straight. Let it go, okay?" He was visibly middle-aged. He had no job or prospects and he'd just flown cross-country.

"I didn't mean to start anything." That wasn't true. She'd meant to jump-start them. She'd fantasized the night, their overdue reunion. They'd find a plan and direction for Ted and it would feel so cathartic that afterward, they'd fall into each other's arms and become themselves again and forever.

She'd left work early to shower, shave, pluck, lotion, polish, and perfume herself. Under her blouse and slacks, she wore one of Megan's confections, a pale lemon film skimming her new contours. A teddy, it was called, and she loved the unintended pun. She couldn't wait to be unpeeled, revealed. It had been so long, months—and why? About what? She needed her husband, her friend, her mate, her lover back in her life.

She sipped the wine she'd brought into the bedroom, trying to cover her confused embarrassment. The man on the far side of the bed was visibly mortal and achingly lost and whatever shape it took, however battered it sometimes felt, she loved him. She had chosen to love him a million years ago and now it was irrevocable, too late to unlearn. "Ted?" Her voice was deep with invitation. She would not let them be like her sorry client, unjoined until the connectors decayed.

"Hallie," he said. "I'm tired. Please." As if she were a chore, like taking out the trash.

Still sweating from her morning run, Hallie drove to the supermarket. Its air conditioning chilled her and she hurried through her rounds.

A client had given her a fish he'd caught and smoked and she'd saved it for Ted, for a special brunch.

She picked up a loaf of his favorite sourdough bread. Supermarket love. Let me thrill your intestinal tract, your esophagus. The way to a man's heart.

She pushed her cart to the produce section, staring at the patchwork of greens, oranges, and purples. Cucumbers and tomatoes, she thought.

It would be okay again. They loved each other. She would feed him. Make nice. He would smile and say, for the first time in forever, "I love you, Hallie."

An onion. A perfect, pink-purple globe.

Then there was nothing left to buy and nowhere left to go but home.

Teddy, always an early riser, slept half the morning, and when he finally appeared in the kitchen, he still looked exhausted.

"Good morning," she said. "There's fresh-squeezed and coffee and I have some incredibly good smoked fish." Her voice was rushed and too high pitched, the nervousness audible.

"Where's Sarah?"

"Out. Why?"

"I thought she'd wait to say hello to her father." He was miffed, as if he'd been on a dangerous mission, in a war or in orbit, and his women should have put their lives on hold awaiting his return.

She said only, "I'll make you a platter."

"Thanks, but I'll make my own."

"You won't *owe* me if I make you a lousy sandwich!" Oh, God, snapping, but it was true. He'd been refusing small favors and simple acts of kindness, keeping the ledger debt-free. She had spent a great deal of the last decade resenting and renegotiating her traditional role as care-giver and nurturer. She had never thought about the pain of being forbidden to give anything at all.

"I'm trying to be fair," Ted said, "to pull my own weight. What you always carry on about."

So she stayed at the table and flipped the pages of the paper. Palestinian hijackers had killed a man on a cruise ship. Rock Hudson, her teenage image of romance, had died of AIDS. There were riots in London, landslides and floods in Puerto Rico.

The problems of little people like you and me don't amount to a hill of beans.

But they amounted to something. Not a hill, maybe, but a

bean. The one under the mattress. The one that broke the camel's back. You handled the challenges you were given.

She watched from a distance as Ted constructed his sandwich. He sliced an onion. A yellow one.

She went to the refrigerator. "I bought you a purple onion," she said. "It tastes better. Here."

He stopped, knife held midair, his face so agonized she thought he'd cut himself, but there was no blood, no visible wound. "I. Can't. Stand. It."

"Then—then don't. Use any onion you like. I'm sorry. I thought a purple—"

"You always think of me—you—" He dropped the knife, looked around wildly as if in search of an exit and began to shake.

"Teddy? What is it? What's wrong?" She moved near him, afraid to touch lest he shatter. She picked up the onion and examined it.

"You've never done a thing to hurt me," he said. "*Never!* I— Oh, God, what am I going to do?" He was crying. He who never cried seemed oblivious to the tears running down his cheeks. He who was so vain of his appearance stood in the kitchen, his face grotesquely contorted.

She clutched the onion. The purple onion that had made him cry. Because she hadn't ever hurt him.

God, dear God, dear God.

"You'll hate me." He whispered, but the words almost knocked her down.

It would be no small task to make her hate him. It would require a cataclysmic blow. An inversion of the natural order. A complete betrayal.

So, then. That was what this was about.

The landscape was sickeningly familiar. She'd seen this before. Soap opera, banal prefabricated dialogue and all. "There's somebody else," she said.

He stood paralyzed, stricken.

She noted the absence of denial or surprise. Noted also that his tears stopped, as if she'd lifted his secret burden. There was, then. Actually was. Unthinkable, but. There was. Another. Another person. Another woman. *Somebody else.*

"NO!" The word's sharp edges shredded her insides. The no swelled and filled her, pushing, exploding. *"NO!"*

She gagged. She would throw up. Faint. Die. Kill him.

The pungent bite of onion broke through to her. Her nails had dug into the purple sides and onion juice wet her hand. She let go, let it fall to the floor, but her eyes still smarted and teared.

There was another obligatory question. "Do you—" She couldn't say it. This could be apocalyptic, the code that shut the system. But there could be somebody else who had nothing to do with the heart of it. There could be hope. She had to ask. She grabbed the counter edge for support. "Are you in—" No. Being *in* meant some kind of commitment. Please, no. Back off. "Do you—" She dropped her eyes. She couldn't watch his face. *"Love her?"*

"I never wanted you to know." His voice cracked. "The last thing I wanted to do was hurt you."

Liar. The last thing you wanted to do was hurt yourself by not doing whatever you felt like. "But do you?"

"What?"

"Love her?" She gagged.

He shook his head. "I don't know."

"For how long?" she asked dully. For how long have I been the joke, the obligatory last to know? All those stupid lines, provided by and worn dull by how many women, how many times?

"Three months. Twelve, thirteen weeks."

Since back in the middle of summer. That whole unfathomable time.

"I think maybe I should go away and work this through."

Away? Moving out? Her husband was—her marriage was— Teddy was— She lurched to the nearest chair and held on. "Who is she?"

He shook his head. "It doesn't matter."

"Who?"

"Please don't."

She heard the two of them in a steamy bedroom, deciding, conniving, setting their parameters. "Don't tell, okay?" she'd said. And he'd agreed. "I don't understand!"

"It hasn't been good between you and me for a while," he said.

"A bad time. But I thought . . ." Who cared about her flimsy thoughts. It was too late for them now. He'd rejected her last night because he was faithful to . . . Her stomach heaved. To think of him. With. She could not bear it. Could not. She doubled over, kneeled, head on knees, breathless with the pain of it.

"Don't, Hal." His voice was strained and distant. "Things happen. You're strong. You'll be fine."

She shook her head, wordless. He was wrong. She wouldn't be fine. She wouldn't ever be fine again.

Fake Eggs, Real Feelings

1985

Higgamus piggamus, man is polygamous. Hoggamus poggamus,
woman's monogamous.
Medieval rhyme

————— 1 —————

AT 4:15 A.M. Hallie jolted awake, mind screaming, heart thudding, every molecule whirring.

In the dark, she dressed and left, jamming the key into the ignition, backing furiously down the driveway. She drove down the hill, shadow trees menacing in a predawn wind.

She wouldn't endure this, refused to.

Her mind was white and wide, blank except for harpy voices accusing her of every failure and crime. She drove recklessly, her foot too dead and heavy to raise. South on the open, unclocked freeway until she climbed the cleft in the Santa Cruz Mountains. Cautious, timid, good-girl Hallie, speeding to whatever wanted to happen, running away until two hours from home, on a spectacular, easily fatal cliff on Pacific Coast Highway, she realized she was condemned to see this out the hard way, in person.

She pulled off at a sandy observation point and watched the morning sky streak pink. Wherever you go, there you are.

The drive home was sluggish, the car dragging.

Ted was still asleep. She stood at the foot of their bed watching the rise and fall of the comforter.

She hated his hypocrisy, his tears while he turned the knife. Despised him for not being where he should have been when he should have been and who he should have been. The one person in the entire world she thought was in this with her all the way was a liar. A cheat. A betrayer. Adulterer—adulterator, fouling what had been unique and precious.

She grabbed a ceramic frame from beside his loose change on the dresser. Pennies fell silently to the carpet. The picture. So happy. All five of them on a picnic four years ago. Sunshine haloes around smiling faces. And it had been true. That's how it had been.

"YOU STINKING SON-OF-A-BITCH MOTHER-FUCKING BASTARD!" Neck veins popping as she screamed and hurled the heavy flower-sprigged frame, but at the last second not daring, shifting her wrist and aiming not at his skull but at the wall above the headboard.

The frame ricocheted and landed on the carpet, unbroken. She hurled it again, and again it survived.

She couldn't do anything right. Not keep her husband in love with her, not break one goddamned picture frame. She whirled around, bashing it on the wall again and again, splintering paint and doorframe, her hand aching until finally, she fractured the image of what they'd been.

A still-clutched sharp ceramic edge cut the pad of flesh below her thumb. She smeared her blood on the doorframe, tracking her hand across the wall, until she collapsed, sobbing, against it.

"Hallie." She spun around. Ted's expression mixed wariness and respect.

"Don't mess with me!" Her breath was as jagged as the bloody fragment of frame she waved. "I might kill you."

He had never been a stupid man. He nodded and stayed where he was.

*   *   *

They worked hard at stasis while Ted read his entrails. Mornings kept breaking, life going on and platitudes persisting despite Hallie's desire to curl into a fetal position and hide. To meet the challenge of the everyday, she had divided like a paramecium. In hyperspace, unmoored, one Hallie orbited her life, out of control until Command Central signaled direction. Back on earth pragmatic Hallie stumbled along. The orbiter, rigid with tension, ripped out her hair and, having no more constants or givens, scanned for signs and portents. Sometimes she stopped screaming, curled tight and wept, as if forever, into the void.

The earthbound Hallie observed traffic signals, remembered to buy milk, saw clients, and fed the dog.

She'd become a touristy split-screen feature. "The Hallie Experience." In Sensurround.

Crazy Hallie howled and tore at herself. Robot Hallie, earthbound and tied, imitating a functioning human being, made Sarah's lunch and fought to contain the madwoman.

Sometimes she couldn't. Yesterday she—they'd—burst into tears at the checkout stand because *Women's Something* had "How to Keep Him Faithful Before It's Too Late," when it was already too late.

But other than that and some nervous twitching and not sleeping more than an hour at a time and the sense that the earth had liquefied and every step was life-threatening—other than that, and the fear that people were saying things she needed to know in a code she couldn't unravel, she went on as normal, listening with neck taut, furtively and with terror skimming books and articles to find out whether she was addicted to love or codependent or a woman who loved too much or merely unlovable and about to be discarded.

Other than that, she was pretty much fine.

Oh, and she couldn't eat, but of course it was what she'd always wanted, bones moving out toward the skin. The dumped-wife recycling trick. Down to the minimum, the cultural ideal, narrow and ready for another Mr. Wrong.

He doesn't love me. The worst. Even hate was better, was something. The opposite of love was indifference.

"You look tired, tense," they said at work. But stress was a badge of merit, proof you were important enough to be over-worked. More stressed than thou, so she passed for normal and dealt with the deaths of other people's marriages. Except that if a client was the dumpee, Hallie became obsessed with finding the flaw that differentiated the loser from herself. And if the client was the dumper, she listened only for what had triggered the decision. Knowledge was power. Anything might save her if only she could understand, could find the secret word.

But otherwise, she was okay. Except two days ago, when a client lamented laws that permitted a one-sided divorce and Hallie had to leave and hang on to the washroom sink breathing deeply, as if in labor. Or later that day when she saw an ancient Chinese couple in front of the Legal Center, the woman with a tremor, the man, a limp. Arms joined, they leaned to the center like two sides of a bridge, buttressing each other. "I wanted that," she'd cried, surprising her secretary, and then she'd burst into tears, surprising her even more.

Should this marriage be saved? After all, marriage had become outmoded and hers had fulfilled its reproductive function. Every-body knew the thing was an illusion, as impossible an ideal as religion and art, but less worth the discipline and effort. Besides, you couldn't work this particular number on your own and she lacked a willing co-illusionist.

They had evenings of stumbling, convoluted talk, Hallie chas-ing nuances like a child with a firefly jar. She listened, catching flutters that might answer what could have happened in a few meetings, a few matings, to counterweigh twenty-five years.

Sarah entered in faux bag lady, thrift-shop hemlines, lace-edge slips, and skirts dragging over high-top sneakers, an ensemble that begged for parental protest, except Hallie's armies were busy on another front.

She sliced the sandwich. What would this do to Sarah's SAT's? To her life? He'd held Hallie's hand through labor, laughing when this girlchild slipped into life.

Seventeen years later, Hallie was embarrassed that eyes that could turn unloving had witnessed her most ultimate, earthbound, moment. "Ready for the exam?" She remembered her mother-lines.

"Nearly." Sarah popped earphones on and pulled out a paperback.

It took five tries to zip the sandwich bag.

The other woman must be exceptional. The new breed, not a retooled Fifties number like Hallie. Assured, accomplished, afraid of nothing. And, of course, blindingly beautiful. Who could blame Ted for upgrading? He'd been the last kid on the block with an antique wife.

"Morning."

The sight of him fresh-shaved and naked-faced always evoked a loving, pitiful pull. She fought to squelch it.

She didn't ask if he was off to a job interview. It was possible that she'd be no part of the new occupation, the new location, the new, improved Ted Bennett. A lot of topics had yellow caution strips around them. "Coffee's made," she said.

"What in the name of God kind of getup is that?" he demanded of his daughter.

Sarah, earplug deaf, sipped grapefruit juice, read *Lord of the Flies*, and tapped her foot.

"What are you listening to?" the paterfamilias demanded.

Sarah, blinking, took off the plugs. He repeated his question. " 'Like a Virgin.' " She replugged.

Ted looked disoriented, then vanquished. He'd forfeited some measure of righteous indignation. Which was crazier—the middle-aged man trashing his life or a teenager with faddish clothes and music?

An apple for Sarah's lunch bag. A loser wife should at least be a decent mother. What else? Carrot sticks? She brandished the vegetable peeler.

"I have these dreams," he'd said last night. He couldn't, didn't, define them.

She had these dreams, too, but you wouldn't play the love-death theme to them. They involved the familiar. Beloved married nonevents. Sharing popcorn through a rented videotape. Talking. Buying purple onions or peaches because he loved their taste. Hearing his surprised-sounding laugh. The way he knew how to mend things, make things grow. How he'd cried, secretly, when Erica left for college, and again when it was Andy.

She liked the way he went at life—or used to. His humor, his zest, his tenderness, his knowledge, his basic, underlying goodness. Those were her romantic dreams.

Sometimes, the down and dirty, the essential. The elemental grunts and sweat of childbirth, shared. The silent holding, the support and shoring up, after her father died or when the children were ill. And all their nights.

But nobody wrote love songs about constancy, about delights beyond the shuddering now of the untried. Only about the thrills of blight and doom, of uncertainty, loss, betrayal.

She believed in a different passion, one for the authentic, discovered person. She knew it was possible and true because she felt it. Passionately. And she wanted it, wanted it back. But to imagine that it could be was to risk a wrenching optimism. To be vulnerable and in pain. To be fearful and brave all at once.

He said he loved her. But not enough. Not *romantically* enough. He felt more the memory of their love, awareness of how much there'd been between them, a demon of guilt requiring exorcism before he could leave. Tears lubricated his path to freedom. The sensitive new man could cry his way out. Progress.

"Cereal?" she asked.

"I'm not hungry, but thanks." They behaved like good house guests.

Ted searched for evidence that they'd always been unhappy, pulling only files of bad times and sore points, insisting not only on his long-term misery, but on hers. Backing out, easing the way, giving his exit legitimacy.

"When I went to grad school, don't you remember how angry you were? And what about when I didn't come to the beach that summer? And when you couldn't go to Harvard? Or about Fritter, or moving, or those fights about my being an oppressive chauvinist pig?"

"What about the good times?" But the memories she served up sounded vague compared to the clash of remembered battles. The humor was lost, the tenderness, the private delight, the public pride, the ambience of joy. The precious moments that had cushioned their life didn't make great anecdotes.

"We were good together, Ted." She was a peddler with shop-worn wares. "You said we were the luckiest, the best." How did you cure someone of happiness amnesia? What if he said he'd been pretending all those years? Or worse, that he hadn't known what happiness was until now?

A car honked.

Ted patted Sarah on the shoulder. "Your ride," he said when she unplugged. She grabbed her lunch bag, blew them kisses, and headed for the door. "I'm sleeping at Deenie's!" she called. "There's a party. See you tomorrow."

Down to the two of them. The three. The Other Woman was always with them now. The heat-driven succubus sat on the kitchen table with her swinging long legs, briefcase, stunning bone structure, genius I.Q., and perfect body. Superwoman. The one Hallie had failed to become. The one who actually not only wanted, but had it all. Including Hallie's husband.

Her. New ears eager for Ted's old stories. New eyes for Ted's frayed self-image. Her, with legs always smooth, stomach never cramped, underwear never unraveled, and instantaneous orgasms that multiplied like an abacus.

The madwoman wept, tortured by the image of Ted lavishing on someone else the attention she had craved for so long.

"How do we handle tonight?" She carried her coffee to the table. "It's Friday. Do the rules of our situation allow entertainment? Or should we sit around and keen?"

He gave the question serious consideration. He had probably ejaculated his sense of humor into the bimbo. Vicky was right. Men carried their brains in their penis. "I'd like to see a movie," he answered gravely.

He no longer used the words *we* or *us*.

She rinsed her cup, put it in the dishwasher, and sponged the counter. "I won't be late. We can see an early show." Are you seeing her today? Do you tell me the truth? Can I trust anything about you anymore?

"Have a good day," he said.

Why don't you love me enough anymore? How long can I hold on? I'm going mad, I feel myself sliding even now. "You, too."

She went into the garage, pressed the button that raised the door, entered her car, put her briefcase on the seat, smoothed her dressed-for-success suit skirt, and turned on the ignition. She couldn't breathe, couldn't live for the pain of it. She opened her mouth and screamed at the top of her lungs. *"MAKE IT STOP! MAKE IT STOP! MAKE IT STOP!"*

Then she carefully backed out and went to work.

They laughed so loudly and frantically that the people in front of them moved to other seats. Like nervous kids on their first date, Hallie thought. Or nervous adults on their last.

"That was fun," Ted said on the way home.

She owed Woody Allen a big one. The laughter had been a bonus. All she'd required was time involved in somebody else's drama. She had rejected serious films. She didn't want meaningful statements about life. She had also ruled out love stories, lest the happy ending be between the wrong players. Wives were seldom film heroines and she didn't think she'd ever seen a movie where the throbbing finale was played for the old lady.

Weeks into their impasse, they had his and hers shrinks. Hers didn't want her on tranquilizers, but she didn't need a prescription for alcohol and every atom of her cellular system anxiously quivered, so once home, she opened wine and poured. Teddy had a different shrink with different principles and he popped pills when he shook.

The rest of the evening loomed. It was not easy finding topics when one had to avoid the present, the future, and all emotions. Even inanimate objects, potential community property, had to be carefully approached. "How are you doing, Ted?" she finally asked. They stood around the kitchen counter like commuters having a quick drink before catching a train.

"Pretty much one fucked-up mess." He smiled shyly, with visible embarrassment.

Don't be lovable as you leave. Please.

He looked into his glass. "I feel so guilty," he said. "About what I've done to you, how I've hurt you."

She almost felt cheered, but then her system rebelled, sick of trying so hard, of hanging in suspension, waiting for the crumbs and clues he dropped. She remembered the dim-witted squirrel, vacillating, paws up, wrongly, stupidly trying to outguess her. Road kill.

She stood straight. Paws down. "Guilt's cheap and easy." Her voice surprised her with its calm. "If you feel guilty, stop doing what makes you feel that way." She held her chin higher.

Was Ted his own squirrel, feeling doomed, fearing he'd done too much to turn back or make a difference? She offered him safety. "Listen, if this . . . thing of yours . . . ends, we can put it behind us, history, and get on with our lives." She hoped she could hold on to the rational sliver of her brain that had just spoken. Hoped she could proceed without recriminations, that the fury and pain would die down, or at least that she could maneuver around them. Because she knew she could choose either the rage or the future she wanted, but not both. She hoped what she knew would be what she did.

"Impressive sentiment," Ted said, "but impossible." He smiled sadly, insisting on doom.

"How *dare* you tell me what's possible, Theodore Bennett! I'll make whatever I damn well choose be possible!"

His surprised laugh, for so long unheard, sounded exotic, evocative. "You're so . . ." His body tilted toward her. "So—"

"Lonely." It popped out before she could censor it, before *fool*, *pride*, and *no shame* lassoed it.

Ted lifted a hand as if to touch her, then let it drop.

There were lots of ways to be brave. "Remember those experiments with baby monkeys?" she whispered. "If they weren't touched enough, they died. 'Failure to thrive,' they call it. Grown-ups can get it, too." Don't turn away, don't.

"I didn't think I had the right. I—"

"Hold me."

Which he did. Tentatively, letting her establish boundaries and limits. She pressed into his embrace, ran her hands over his back, over the cables of his sweater, to his waist, under the knit to the soft fabric of his shirt, her hands saying what her mouth couldn't. He stroked her hair and she heard his ragged breathing. She turned her head so that their faces nearly touched, and he kissed her forehead.

"Ted," she said. "Oh, God, Teddy—" And she tilted her face up, stood on tiptoes, and kissed him back, on the lips.

It was as shocking as a first kiss. She pulled away, ashamed. This man was in love with somebody else.

Then she realized she'd reverted. So he wouldn't respect her in the morning. This wasn't for him or about him. This was for her. She was dying from the outside in. She didn't need guarantees, she needed flesh. Life. "Come with me," she whispered.

He was frozen in place, caught in his own web of ethics. She took his hand and led him silently up the stairs, seducing him.

Just the way She probably—

And there She was, on the riser above them, wagging her perfect ass, taunting, enticing, comparing, flaunting—

Hallie pushed Her out of the way.

"Let me." She worked his sweater up and off, unbuttoned his shirt, unbuckled his belt. He stood like a baffled child.

"It's all right." She unzipped him and guided him back to the bed. "We're married." She slipped off his shoes, his socks, his slacks, smiling because the mustn'ts muddling his brain hadn't traveled to his groin.

He seemed hypnotized. She ran a finger under the elastic of his underwear, cupped the bulge with her hand, then she pulled away and began to undress.

Her blouse slid off her shoulders, down her arms, onto the comforter. She was always beautifully gift-wrapped now, secrets next to her skin as a personal pledge and validation.

She unclasped her belt, unbuttoned her slacks, and, hips swiveling slowly, lifted one leg out and then the other, watching him, eyes locked all the while, unmaking decades of quick sheddings, attention on whether a child cried, the trash was out, the gas range off.

If this was her kiss-off, it might as well be one hell of a kiss.

She stretched beside him in her teddy, tracing a fingernail path down his inner arm. "I need you." She was startled by the open husky urgency of her voice.

He pulled his arm away, but even so, she saw him register the details of her, and she realized he hadn't truly seen her in a long, long time. "That's a very . . . the pink silk . . . you look . . ." Her nipples stiffened and she watched him watch them while she stroked his arm. "But."

She moved her hand to his legs, the inside of his thigh. "I can't bear not to be with you. I need you, need to taste you and touch you and feel you inside me. And you need me. You don't remember right now, but you do."

"But Hal . . ."

She didn't let him finish. Right now she knew more about wanting than he did, more thoroughly, and not only about hers, but his, too. After all these years, she and Theodore Bennett had exchanged their DNA, and she could feel, under her own skin, the soft explosion of his nerve ends when she touched them. She knew him all the way through, just as he knew her, if only he would remember.

She leaned over him, kissing and stroking. "Let me," she whispered. "Let me love you." She was crying, or parts of her were. "We know how to love, Teddy. That's all this means. It isn't a contract. It isn't a promise."

Touching him sent such jolts through her fingertips and lips, directly and deeply into her center, that she thought she might die for the wanting of him.

The other woman floated through the plaster, crawling close to observe and compare, to push in, compete. Did she do this, too? Or this? Did he moan that way for her?

Out of my bed! Oh, God, crazy here, too. Except she wasn't going to let that be. She had power, was a force, an element. The center of life lay below her belly, and that was what she would think about, only of that, only of the two of them and only of now.

Ted forgot to be confused about what was permitted between them. It was belovedly familiar and brand new, more intense than ever as everything converged, confused yearning and love, wounds, desperation, time standing still and running out, pleasure and bereavement.

She had forgotten how it was to turn inside out and meet at the core, to lose all boundaries, have skin burn and dissolve to the naked organs, until she was he and he was she and they were something unnameable.

She had forgotten and she had never known, because they had never needed to be this way before.

"I've missed you," Ted said, his lips on her neck. "Missed you so much."

Later they found each other again with equal heat and urgency. Then in the morning, once clothed, he was as remote and unfathomable as before. Whatever had happened appeared to have nothing to do with their future. Hallie didn't think of it as making love. She had no idea what they were making or what to make of it.

"Once, that's all. He cheats on me, he's out." The heavyset woman folded her arms over her chest and the audience applauded. "It would be ruined. Women who take runarounds back have no *pride*."

More applause. Donahue moved to the next waving hand.

"It would never be the same," a quieter voice said. "I could never forgive him."

"But isn't it possible," Phil said, "temptation, you know. Our culture—"

"The stores are full of temptations," the quiet woman said. "Does that excuse shoplifting? You pay for what you get. Either way."

"Is this what you do every afternoon?" Spot jumped off the sofa, looking guilty.

"Mom! How long have you been standing there?"

"Why is it, when I come home early you're either watching soap operas, MTV, or this trash?"

"It's not trash. This guy wrote a book about adultery, and—"

"It's *easy*, how these women are. *Easy* to give up!"

"Mom?"

"Turn it off! Do your homework."

"In a min—"

"Good riddance to bad garbage," a lantern-jawed woman insisted. "Who wants a liar who can't keep a promise? Forsaking all others doesn't mean except now and then."

Wild applause from the all-female audience.

"Junk!" Hallie snapped off the set.

"Lighten up, Mom."

But Hallie couldn't lighten up or ease up or let up.

"And after the clinch, the happily ever-afters, right? Fade to black, the drama's over. It's been nonstop. Um, a lot. Sex, I mean. Every night and morning and sometimes in the middle of the night, too, and on the weekend, daytimes, whenever our daughter isn't . . ." She looked down at her hands. It still embarrassed her to talk about her sex life with somebody she barely knew. "And, um, intense.

"It might not be about sex at all," she said. "It might be because it's the only safe place." The past had been polluted, the future was murky. The now was all.

"This must be what an affair feels like. Of course, I can't ask. But desperate. Endangered. Obsessive. Very dramatic. Threatened. I can't stop touching, wanting. And he's the same."

Time had become undifferentiated, days and nights fused and glazed by their heat. She stammered through appointments, flushed with graphic memories of lovemaking, said it was a hot flash.

Sex was the only appetite she had, and it was constant. She was consumed by the memory of pleasure and the anticipation of more, aware of the sensuous potential of the world, of exquisite tastes and smells and textures and sounds, of the nonstop thrum between her legs.

Except she was also in despair, because the pleasure had no aftereffects, eased nothing, was only of the moment, the now. "He's still deciding whether to *leave me*, so how is it possible that we're so . . . He says this is the best sex of his life, which has to include his affair, doesn't it? He says, we joke, that he, we never dreamed it could be this way, just like in a bad script. So what is it? Pity? Regret? The Pillsbury Fuck-Off?"

"Do you ask? Do the two of you talk about it?"

Her hands looked alien, foreign on her lap. "I'm too afraid." Ted spoke only body language. Otherwise, Hallie pressed against him, ear to his chest, listening for a sign of life, a clue. He mentioned resurfacing the driveway. She rejoiced because that suggested a long-term stake in the place, and their marriage. Or wait—maybe it was about readying the place for resale. She crashed.

Every morning as she ran, she told herself that the loss of Theodore Bennett would not destroy her. I can survive, I can, I can, she said in rhythm with her feet.

Not really, the rest of her answered. Some things you just

knew. In the dark recesses behind her navel where shapeless tubes and pumps worked with no drama, no attention, maintaining the embarrassingly human and matter of fact—that was where she knew she and Ted had to be together. Facts had nothing to do with it.

Maybe she could have given him up twenty-five years ago when desire was based on intuition and hope. Now she knew what they could be, and worse, what she could lose.

How could she love him that desperately and still have the supernatural strength to pull free?

By doing it, she would answer herself. She could do anything she had to. She was strong, she was independent. She would survive. I can. I can. The Little Wifey Who—Kind of—Could.

And then she'd collapse, not only incapable of surviving her marriage, but helpless to endure the moment.

Sometimes, like the day before, he didn't seem worth the struggle. "I feel like Gulliver," he'd said. "Ropes pulling every appendage every which way." He was proud of his literary allusion and oblivious of the pain it caused her.

"Who am I, your *mother*?" she'd shouted. "Don't complain to *me* about counterdemands on your cock! Our life, our history, boils down to a pull on your prick? You egomaniacal asshole!"

He didn't understand passion the way she did, no matter what he thought. He didn't understand pain, either. He didn't understand her. She despised his stupid assumption that she'd be his true friend, the person with whom he could share anything, just as always.

He'd gone pale and sickly. "I didn't think. So used to telling you everything. Give me time."

"What are you deciding? An affair doesn't test anything. That's its point. Only life tests. Head colds, deaths, disappointments, humiliation." She sounded like the seven plagues or her own mother, and she remembered how wearisome such advice sounded to somebody blindly in love.

And perversely, again, fury, despair, a deadening, desperate love compressed and burned at her center. Make me feel better, not so alone. Make me forget. Here. Yes.

She tried to hold on to the thread of their marriage, pulling on skills acquired from young children who interrupted and diverted conversations. They'd taught her to sidetrack and double back, remembering the point she wanted to make. She told herself this was merely another interruption. She held tight to the point.

"I'm falling apart," she told the doctor. "Shaky afraid all the time, even while we're— I can't stand it much longer." She burst into tears, grabbed a handful of tissues, sniffled.

He nodded. "You know you can't control him, can't stop him from leaving. You can, however, decide what you want or have to do. You are in control there. You don't have to remain passive, do not have to wait for him to hand down a verdict. You can be in charge of your destiny."

The squirrel again. I can, I can.

He spoke gently. "How would it be, living alone?"

She pulled at her tissues. "It doesn't make sense. We're right for each other, better together. We add up to more than the sum of our parts." It hurt to say those words, to know they were true and that they made no difference.

The doctor waited. Hallie thought about cutting out the parts of her life that included Ted, and saw only a web left, a skeleton. "But," she said, stumbling over the words, "I'd find out how to live without him, how to make it work for me." It was her mind speaking, but she tested it against her heart, and at long last felt the two of them attempt a nodding acquaintance.

"It's like being terrified of earthquakes," he said. "You can dread them, try to make them not happen and be afraid all the time. Or you can realize there is nothing to be done except take the necessary precautions. Once you know you can't control something, it's easier to live with it."

She summoned her old fantasy of the uncluttered white room. Now she put herself into it and added her favorite paintings and pottery. Friends, good meals, books, work, children. A valid life.

"Think about it," he said. Their time was up. At least with the shrink she knew with certainty when that was the case.

There was nothing to be done. If Hallie stopped or slowed down, she'd cause an accident.

"Poor guy," Paula said. Their friendship had survived the collapse of the house purchase and, since both women had daughters in twelfth grade, they carpooled to parental events. They were returning from one when they saw the ducks at the end of the freeway approach.

A mallard male leaned into traffic, wings out to shield his mate, who lay crumpled behind him. Cars whizzing by ruffled his feathers, and he stood in their exhaust, warding them off. There was no safe way to stop the car, nothing to do even if they could. "What'll he do?" Hallie whispered. "They mate for life."

"Ah, that's what their PR says. But so does ours. Till death do us. Bet those feathery guys also change their minds and fly off in the night."

"Maybe not." Hallie gripped the wheel. "It's a decision, isn't it?" She tried to keep the strain and fear out of her voice. "Maybe they keep their word. Or maybe they're realists. They decide a duck's a duck, so what the hell, and they stay."

"Still a romantic, aren't you? Don't worry about him," Paula said. "He'll get over it. Now he's an eligible male. He'll be invited to dinner parties every night, so he can meet a nice duckling."

Hallie burst into tears.

"Oh," Paula said, the laughter gone from her voice. "Like that, is it?"

She lifted a glass of beer and winked. "This year we're exploring the second option in 'for better or for worse.' "

"Hallie?" Vicky and Megan asked in unison.

Since the day with Paula, she'd avoided people and unpredictable situations, but Megan had called, just back from a trip to Washington and the Vietnam Memorial. She sounded understandably melancholy and Hallie had no decent alternative but to go. She was lonely, anyway, with only a shrink as confidante. She needed to go public with the shame and terror of it, stop making it her dirty secret.

And now she had and had not died. Survival was possible. "He was peculiar for a long time," she said. "So many signs. Billboards. Skywriting. I didn't have the brains to add two and two."

"That's what trust means," Vicky said.

"Yes, but it's also what ignoring somebody means. He's been

in a tailspin since The Fun Factory was sold, but I couldn't stand it. I stopped listening and looking and caring. But this is so . . ."

"Predictable," Vicky said.

"Another middle-aged cliché," Hallie said.

"But not necessarily the end of the world," Megan said.

"Why not?" Hallie regretted having spoken. "Because it's me and nothing really bad ever happens to me so I'm complaining about nothing again? But it's *important* what happens between two people. What people do to one another means something. Or is it because everybody cheats nowadays? Because we give it fluffy names like playing around, fooling around, having a fling? It *feels* like the end of the world. Hurts like hell. Like virginity, once lost always lost, but faith's a much more valuable commodity. To have had it, to have believed, to have been that close . . . and there's the not being loved," she whispered. "The being lied to."

Megan spoke gently. "I didn't mean it's okay. I meant it's not like we're twenty. We're older, smarter about expectations of perfection. A marriage isn't celery that's either good or it's garbage. People make mistakes. People recover. A few scars make you more interesting."

There was discreet throat-clearing beside the table. Their waitress, an orange-blond in a kimono, put a tray of fish and rice in the center of the table. "Nonna my business," she said in a Brooklyn accent, "but I couldn't help overhear. No offense, but don't let the creep enjoy home comforts while he plays house somewhere else. I told mine to go to his slut. You think she ironed his shirts? He crawled back in no time flat and he's been housebroken ever since." And then she bowed in a most traditional manner and turned away.

Hallie stared after her. Anyone might have the answer.

"She's wrong," Megan said. "Don't make it more complicated or worse by giving him an ultimatum. He's going through a mid-life—"

"Not that!" She sounded much too sharp and unforgiving. "Whose life isn't one long crisis? Why should Ted's crisis give me one? Great timing, too. Just when marriage is back in style, when somebody noticed that being single doesn't automatically mean being happier, when commitment and monogamy are back in. They're calling togetherness cocooning, for Christ's sake. So just when it's safe to be married again, even fashionable, mine self-destructs. I'm never in synch, am I?"

Vicky lifted sashimi. "Everybody grows up in different ways, at different times. This is when you do."

Hallie closed her eyes. "Please. You don't approve of marriage, you don't approve of me, you've never been—"

"I approve of growing up, of deciding what you want and fighting for it. Everybody gets tested, and then retested, and you don't pick your exam. It can be terminal—death, sickness, or scary things with kids. It can be abuse. It can be money or drugs or sick parents or war or—there's no end to the bad variations. The test isn't about what happens, it's about how you handle it."

"It's so hard," Hallie whispered. "So scary."

"Nothing important's easy." Megan reached over and held her hand. "Ben likes to quote Thurber. 'Love is what you've been through with somebody.' Get through this. See where you wind up."

"I've known a lot of liars and cheats," Vicky said. "The slick ones have to be amputated. But Ted's so bad at cheating, it's almost endearing. Anybody who cries over a purple onion is worth the good fight."

And Hallie felt a wobbly smile pull the ends of her mouth. "Why is there always low comedy in the most solemn moments of my life? For a purple onion to trigger the worst . . ." And then the impulse to smile faded. "Everybody cries over onions," she said.

They were in the family room, the two of them watching the late news when Hallie realized that the madwoman in her brain had stopped sending semaphore signals. She was instead sitting in the lotus position, self-contained and serene. Enough, she said, leaning over so Hallie would be sure to hear. There is nothing more to do. Hallie's muscles unknotted. She turned off the TV. "Ted?" she said. "I'm letting go."

"Of what?"

"You."

"I don't understand."

"I thought if our marriage was hurt, we'd heal it, not shoot the beast. But things are the way they are, so this is a quit-claim.

You'll notice I'm no longer hanging off your trouser cuffs. I still want you, but I don't need you anymore." She might have been speaking Hindi for all his visible comprehension.

"But—but I don't want to leave."

The heart she had just declared finished with needing him did a small pirouette.

"Yet."

And flopped into a heap.

"Maybe. I think, not at all." And the heart, the madwoman, and Hallie herself, tired of the routine, untied the puppet strings. Her cells disengaged from his and remembered that they were separate organisms.

"There's this," she said. "If you stay, it has to be because you want *me* and a real marriage again. Not because you feel guilty, or because I'm the easier choice or a consolation prize, or because you're testing me out while Brand X hovers in the background. I'm pretested. Twenty-five years and seven months. If you stay, she has to be history so we can relearn trust. Stay if I'm worth loving exclusively. Otherwise, leave. For keeps."

"I asked you not to push me out."

"I won't until I have to, but I may have to soon." She was heavy with peaceful power.

"Is that an ultimatum?"

"Probably."

"This isn't easy, Hal."

"It kills me to know that."

"So, then," he said. "What exactly are you saying?"

"Just like the song says. Thanks for the memories. Honestly. It was, indeed, great while it lasted."

"Don't write me off with smart-ass lyrics."

She had been standing on the edge of a precipice for weeks, maneuvered there by Theodore Bennett, clinging to him, begging him not to finish her off, not to give the final push.

Now she'd relaxed her grip and felt a glorious release as she took the leap on her own. And to her amazement, didn't fall, but soared. She could fly. Solo.

She smiled and, for the first time in weeks, meant it.

*   *   *

The bathroom shower roared behind the bedroom wall. Hallie, prolonging the afterglow of that morning's lovemaking, yawned. Spot stood up on her doggie bed, bright-morning expectant.

Hallie looked out the window. Foggy. She noticed Ted's briefcase propped against the night table. What did he carry around anymore, except his empty calendar? His presumed empty calendar.

Three months, he'd said. Twelve or thirteen weeks before the day of the onion. The shower pounded. He no longer sang while he bathed.

Unethical, but then, what did ethics have to do with her marriage anymore?

Spot smiled and panted, tongue lolling. Hallie kissed the fuzzy top of the dog's head. "I forgive you the stain in the upstairs hallway, pal. At least you never pissed on me."

Spot thumped her tail.

Ignorance was not bliss. She opened the clasp and pulled out his calendar and personal address book, then clamped the briefcase shut again. Her breath came with difficulty. Thief.

The shower stopped. Shaving time. Only a few minutes left. She shoved the guilty evidence into the pocket of her terry robe and ran downstairs to the powder room, locking herself in. Spot clawed at it until she let her in, then relocked the door, her hands trembling. What a bad liar, a bad cheat she was.

Twelve or thirteen weeks, he'd said. She flipped backward. Cryptic entries, routine appointments, time notations, and, now and then, a flight number. Eleven—twelve, thirteen. Mid-July.

Johnstown? She remembered. His parents, then New York. That stupid trip. The weirdness of flying three thousand miles for an interview with a company based in San Francisco.

He'd be out of the bathroom soon, wondering, and she had to leave for work. She opened the address book, fingers fumbling over the gold-edged pages. She looked for unfamiliar names or numbers, nearly ripping the sheets of paper in her urgency.

Claudia Best. A mistressy kind of name. No address. A city phone number. But she couldn't memorize it. Couldn't think straight.

She unlocked the door and tiptoed out, sneaking through her

house, into the kitchen, where she snagged the memo pad and rooted around for a felt-tip pen that hadn't dried out. She heard Sarah's radio blare into morning upstairs before she relocked the powder room door.

Claudia Best. An unromatic-sounding Vera Melman in L.A. A Betsy Harkness in San Jose until she remembered Betsy, their neighbor's unemployed aunt. As a favor, Ted had asked around about a job for her. Scratch Betsy Harkness.

Which left only one entry without title or business or visible explanation. C. Allen, male or female, no address. A 215 code. Philadelphia. A business contact?

None of the unknowns were in New York or Johnstown, so maybe the date was wrong. Or maybe the succubus traveled with him.

Spot whimpered. Hallie unlocked the bathroom door and let the dog out, started coffee while two small leather books burned through the pockets of her robe.

She needed more. His secrets had to be buried somewhere.

"Where've you been?" Ted asked.

"Let out Spot, started coffee." He wore jeans, a cotton sweater. "What's on for today?" she asked.

"Meeting Skip for lunch," he said, almost grudgingly.

Skip. The technical wizard, potential partner in the interactive learning games. Did this mean he was actually doing something sane? Starting the business he'd talked about for years? But he seemed belligerent and secretive, so she kept silent.

The important thing was that there might be a window of opportunity, a clear coast. It took twenty minutes to get home from her office. "What time?"

"Huh?"

"Lunch. What time?" She panicked. What if he needed to find the answer in his calendar, which was in her pocket?

"Noon," he said. "Why?"

"No reason. Making conversation. Where?"

"Where what?"

"Lunch. Where are you eating?" What if it was right around here? Or if they were bringing in sandwiches? Or—

"Cupertino somewhere."

Good. An extra half hour. Very good.

He shook his head and went back into the bathroom. She unclasped the briefcase and dropped in the books, feeling faint.

At eleven-thirty she called home and got the answer machine. Ted had left. At eleven-fifty, she carefully approached her house, deciding to say she was ill if for some reason he was still there. It was a murky day, with dirty-looking fog as she sat, staking out her house like a detective in a tired old film.

Spot, overjoyed, followed Hallie into Ted's study. Such a nice room, so family oriented, with framed pictures of everyone, even Spot, and more to come. The snaps of Sarah's Sadie Hawkins Dance were still in their yellow and orange envelope on his desk. A nice person's study. Too bad. She went to the file cabinet and pulled open a drawer, feeling a twinge because it had no lock, innocently assuming no breaking and entering.

Tidy files. Tax information. Frequent-flyer plans. Utilities. Mortgage. Teddy had always been meticulous about records. Telephone. Miscellaneous. Receipts.

She pulled files and checked her watch, her pulse banging in the hollow of her throat. If his lunch went poorly, or had been canceled . . . Or if it hadn't been a lunch with Skip at all, but cover for a visit with his honey, the time and place a lie altogether . . . Her heart pounded. How did criminals avoid having strokes? How did cheats? How did Ted?

She began with the "Miscellaneous" file, thinking he might toss whatever didn't fit the nice-man image in there. But she found newspaper clippings, handmade cards from the children, a letter of congratulation from an MIT professor, a thank you from the Director of the Children's Cancer Clinic for time and the donation of Fun Factory games. An ancient Boy Scout award of merit. His sailing school certificate. The errata of his life. She replaced the depressingly wholesome collection.

She opened the thick "Receipts" file and slowly, meticulously, examined every slip of paper. American Express, VISA, travel chits, pharmacy tabs, bookstore expenses, department store charges. She stopped over September's American Express statement and stared at a two-hundred-and-fifty-dollar charge at a jewelry store in the city. The purchase had been made in early August.

She never bought jewelry. She hadn't received any gifts. She put the statement aside and pulled out July's, looking for clues in Johnstown or New York.

Instead, she saw a charge at a Philadelphia Airport motel on July fourteenth. Bastille Day, her mind idly registered.

SPEEDY CHECK-OUT was stamped on the receipt. Not speedy enough.

Philadelphia. The 215 area code. C. Allen. Did C. Allen travel with him?

She continued through the file. She found a second jewelry charge at another local store for yet another two hundred and fifty dollars' worth of trinkets. Generous man, that Ted. She took out her datebook, in which she'd noted all of Teddy's out-of-town trips and their theoretical destinations, and she checked his travel receipts against it.

He'd been in Virginia Beach when he was supposedly in D.C. She found a hotel charge in New York that was bloated for a single room, even for that city. And another Philadelphia, right before the onion, right before he'd come home to dismantle their marriage. No pretense here—this one stated that the room would be occupied by two parties. This was an open and sincere hotel, even listing all phone calls by number. Arm and forehead numb, she compared the numbers with those she'd copied from his address book.

Two calls home.

Five to C. Allen.

So C. didn't travel with him. He visited her. Hallie envisioned him rushing in, fresh from the airport late in the day, calling C. Later, C. herself, naked except for the jewelry he'd given her, checks in at home the same way Ted had checked in with his wife, laughing away Teddy, who was kissing her belly while she invented her whereabouts . . .

There were room-service charges. She added drinks beside the bed to her mental image. Dinners, never leaving the room.

Hallie sat with the damning evidence. If Ted were a client's husband, she would rejoice.

She kept the hotel receipt and closed the file cabinet, but felt too weak to move. The third party had become flesh and blood, a woman with a telephone, jewelry, and room service.

She used both hands to push herself out of Ted's chair, noticing again the photo envelope. Something gnawed at her.

That night. Unpacking. The putty warm-up suit. Of course. He gave her jewelry, she gave him status sweats. Damn them both!

But that wasn't it. Something else. She looked again at the yellow film packet. YOUR PICTURES ARE BACK! it said in bold black letters. Yes. He'd taken a roll of film out of his suitcase and put it into a suit pocket, but not even Teddy documented interviews. Photos of her.

She opened every drawer, stuck her arm behind the files, then she did the same at his desk. Nothing.

His negative file was neat and tidy, Ted's style. Examining twenty-five years of reversed and miniaturized candids was an appalling prospect, but she didn't have another appointment for an hour, so she began.

It turned out to be simple. There were countless yellow and orange narrow negative envelopes and a single green one, from a one-hour rush place in San Jose. Not even the one near home.

She pulled it out, trembling, and held the negatives to the light. Little figures. Sometimes one, female, sometimes two. A man and a woman. Clothed, thank God. Embracing. And even seeing them in reverse, not flesh, but white-eyed specters with dark faces—she cried in pain. How could old news hurt so much?

Hand shaking, she put the negatives in her pocket along with the hotel receipt and the phone numbers and left his study, sorry she had ever entered it, but determined to follow this through.

"We'll have these for you Thursday."

"But this is Tuesday!" There was no way she physically or emotionally could wait. She shook her head to make her point, then couldn't stop. "No, no, no."

"Ma'am?"

She had to see. Pictures. A dozen pictures worth twelve thousand words. "Not Thursday. No." The growl didn't sound like her own voice. She looked around to see if anybody she knew was in the store. No. Good. Because even if they were, she couldn't help herself. It had come to that.

"We're backed up. Maybe late Wednesday, I could ask the manager if—"

"*NO!*" Here it came. Breaking down in a fast-photo shop and no way to stop it.

"But ma'am, I—"

Words poured out, staccato, unstoppable. "Your–sign–says– one – hour – photo – so – you – better – have – these – ready – in – one – hour – or—"

"Lady!"

"I'll–sue–you–for–false–advertising–I'm–a–lawyer—"

"But lady!"

"*I'll – do – it – so – help – me – you – can't – screw – the – public – your – sign SAYS!*" Her hands shook from the shoulders down and made bumping noises on the glass counter.

The man backed away. "Right," he said. "Gotcha. We'll see what—"

"*NOT SEE! ONE HOUR! SIXTY MINUTES!*"

He raised his hands as if she were holding him up. "You got it," he said.

She met with her client, checking her watch every three minutes, then, pleading an emergency, she left the office again. She ran into a coffee shop, her pocket full of change. She had photocopied the receipts at the office, but she didn't want odd calls showing up there or at home. She stood at the pay phone near the rest rooms, her hands jerking almost uncontrollably.

"This is Christina Allen at Party Girls," a cold voice said.

Party girls? Call girls who said so on a message tape?

"We handle your affairs."

The whole thing was a joke. A wicked prank on his part because he knew she'd track it and get this message and laugh.

"Parties, anniversaries, weddings, showers, bar mitzvahs, you name it. Leave your name and number and one of us will—" Hallie hung up and clutched the ledge beneath the phone. C. Allen. Christina Allen. *Christina?*

"Excuse me." An unhappy woman dragging an even unhappier child waited for her to unblock the route to the bathroom. Hallie nodded, but it took two repetitions to make her body move.

Hallie had been mining the wrong cliché. Not the twenty-six-year-old bunny. The old girlfriend.

She stood still, overwhelmed with pity for the poor, sad trio of them. What fools, what pathetic old children.

But of all the women in the world . . .

Christina. She dragged her feet to the One-Hour Photo. The sky was still a despairing yellow gray. Christina. She had expected more imagination of Ted, more than unfinished business. The old flame reignites. Love's more wonderful the second time around. The road not taken can still be. Never too late to start over, change course, defeat death. No decisions, however right, are final.

Two Isoldes, remember? The one he couldn't have and adored and the other one, the dull wife, who doesn't matter.

She heard a screech of brakes, an angry "For Christ's sake!" and she stepped back on the curb without looking to see what had nearly killed her. How dizzying it must be to see twenty-five years, three children, and Hallie as a detour, an erasable error.

He could have had anybody. Why Christina, who'd treated him like raw sewage? And why had she reevaluated her discard? It must have killed her that Ted had acquired status and value, that she'd missed the best buy of her life. So she shoplifted it. Or what she thought was it. Hallie wondered how much reality Ted had admitted.

Christina Young. Christina Young Houston Allen, star-fucker. And Ted the former star, current fuckee, had fallen for it. They deserved each other.

She stormed into the photo shop and the clerk scuttled into the back and returned with an envelope.

She waited until she was in her car to open it. She took a deep breath, ready to be humbled by Christina's transformation from a cute teenager into a mature, irresistible beauty.

But there'd been no miracles. Her body was flimsy, moving toward stringy. Veins stood out on her shins. Her face was drawn, lined, marked with years of scowling. Even smiling at the camera, at her *lover*, God help us, even then, her narrow features were tense and drawn, angry lines etching parenthesis around her nose and grudging smile. As if she suspected she wasn't getting her fair share.

Incredible. The other woman in worse shape than the wife. Not as good-looking. Not as smart. Visibly unhappy.

There they were in matching red shirts and white shorts, like twins. Embarrassing, if it weren't agonizing.

Ted had set the timer and raced around to plant one on her. Or they had asked a passerby to immortalize their kiss. The sunlight glinted off their wedding bands. How lovely, the passerby must have thought. A married couple still in love.

Hallie felt finally, irrevocably ripped out of innocence. And cheated in a new way. She'd deserved a formidable foe. This desiccated creature without radiance, sheen, or light—who was she to author such pain?

An unfit enemy. An afterimage. An opportunistic infection.

It was now even clearer that it wasn't about her at all, only the idea of her and what she meant to Teddy's lost and aching heart. It wasn't about either one of them, only about what both of them had lost.

She had to laugh. It was so pathetic, it was funny. She really had to laugh.

So why was she sitting inside her car, in a shopping center, crying, sure her heart had finally, fatally, broken?

He drove by the lump and pulled into the garage. Horse manure, it looked like, but there were no horses on their suburban street. Concerned, filled with an unidentifiable dread, he went back to examine it. Something dead. Something killed at his garden gate.

The front door opened and Hallie, accompanied by Spot, walked down the short path. Spot jumped greetings, but Hallie said nothing, only watched from her side of the gate. Her face and pale eyes were impassive. She looked mythic, hair a soft wild halo, breasts swelling under her sweatshirt, hips curving her jeans. Exactly the way a contemporary no-nonsense goddess of justice might look.

The lump was as big as a mid-sized dog, but it had never been alive. It was made of trash and garbage, coffee grounds, paper, twine, rubber bands, eggs, spaghetti. He felt relieved, then anxious again. Who had done this, and why?

"I did it," Hallie said flatly. "I threw the garbage out."

He looked again. It wasn't twine or rubber bands. It was strips of fabric. Putty-colored. Soft. The warm-up suit, cut and cut and cut again.

And not plain paper. Photographs, ripped. He saw a flash of face. Red hair. He flushed, couldn't breathe.

She held her head at a stiff dare-you angle. Her face, usually so mobile, was contained and expressionless, except that her eyes glittered, threatened to be the leak in her rigid determination.

Garbage, she'd called it.

He burst out laughing.

She looked shocked and suddenly nervous, which intensified his laughter. "Sorry," he said, "I shouldn't—" But he had to. It was release, relief, hysteria, and pure admiration for the woman who'd julienned that warm-up suit.

Ah, Hallie. There you are. I've been looking for you. He caught his breath. "I admire your style." He looked at the mess at his feet. "I take it you don't admire mine."

"It's not flattering. It's not you." Her hand clenched the latch. "Hard to believe you considered it. Other men, maybe. But I thought you were different."

"A sorry choice." He watched her intently, afraid he had long since lost the password.

But her face softened, and for the first time in months, he wasn't sure that the earth was about to open and swallow him. "Tacky," he said. "Tawdry. Unsuitable."

"And much too expensive." The late-day sun edged her curls with fire.

"Hallie, it's over. It's been over. I've been giving myself time to be sure. I needed to know I would never look back or doubt. I'm sure I never will. I'm sure I'm sure." Say it right. Fix what you've broken before you lose everything. "I don't know what it was. It wasn't about her. It didn't even seem about me. Not this me. It was exciting for the wrong reasons, like being crazy might be exciting. But you need to know there's never been a time since the day I met you that I didn't love you."

She turned her head away, disbelievingly. "Sure. Even while you . . . ?"

"Even then. I tried not to love you, but it didn't work." He put his hand on top of hers, on top of the gate latch. "Tell me we can start over."

She shook her head. "Nobody can do that."

The tension returned, pulling tight his chest, pounding behind his eyes and along his jaw line. He'd gone too far. Ruined the one real thing. Broken something he couldn't fix. He stepped backward and his foot splatted into coffee grounds and tomato sauce. "Please. Believe me. I'm committed in a way I didn't know I had to be before. I thought I was committed twenty-five years ago, but I was a kid, didn't know enough, didn't realize—" He knew what he meant, had thought about little else for weeks, he understood now, but he didn't know how to say it.

"We've both had learning experiences," she said dryly.

"Please. Give me a chance. Give us a chance."

"Things have happened."

"Hallie—"

She shushed him. "You already tried the myth of starting over, didn't you? Dropping inconvenient facts of your life. It doesn't work. We can't do it."

"Please, I—"

"What we could do instead is keep going."

He looked at her. Her eyes widened, waiting. Keep going. It sounded grim, and they had never been that, not for more than moments, not plodding, dour-faced, duty-bound. But maybe that was the only option left. He had marks on his permanent record, so perhaps this was as good as it was going to be. Maybe all he deserved was garbage on his shoes, coffee grounds on his jeans, the dismal prospect of endurance.

Hallie waited, her arms crossed over her chest.

He looked at her, the woman who'd sliced his warm-up suit. He looked down at the runny mess he stood on, yellow egg smears oozing into his shoes.

But there were no egg shells. Of course not. Too much cholesterol. When they weren't trying to kill each other, they tried to keep each other alive.

"Imitation eggs!" he shouted. "Hallie, you threw fake eggs!" They were certifiably ridiculous. Mismatched from day one, only they hadn't noticed in time and now they were too far gone. They were going to keep throwing eggs—real or imitation—shouting, pulling, and pushing, for better or for worse, but for keeps.

Above them, a turkey vulture soared on a thermal current. "Stay away!" Ted shouted. "Nothing's dead here yet!" He saw a smile tickle the edges of his wife's mouth. A tentatively loving, nostalgic, very young Hallie smile, and he knew their future wouldn't be grim forever. Their marriage was bruised in the bone and might heal with a new shape, but the new form could be even better than the best had been, couldn't it? Which came pretty damn close—close enough—to happily ever after.

"Oh, what the hell." Hallie sighed and, with the trace of that smile, unlatched the gate. "Come on home," she said.

Strong in the Broken Places

1989

After all these years, I see that I was mistaken about Eve in the beginning; it is better to live outside the Garden with her than inside it without her.
Mark Twain

A TOAST to Erica and Jeff," Ted said.

They had announced their engagement after the pumpkin soup, before Ted carved the turkey. The kissing and hullabaloo was only now simmering down.

"To Erica and Jeff," Hallie echoed. Her daughter was getting married. Incredible.

There was something miraculous about the joy an engagement triggered, despite all prior knowledge of what it could mean. Megan and Ben, former casualties, applauded. Sylvia Saxe Braverman wept and avoided cynical warnings. With only the disappointments of her own marriage and widowhood as referents, Miriam Bennett, like a wobble-headed doll, nonetheless nodded approval. Even Chloe lifted her glass in an exquisitely theatrical manner and proposed another toast to the happy couple. "Here, here!" said Vicky.

Perhaps it was the bravery of it, the audacity.

Hallie's brain had become swampy, hackneyed sayings, like Burma-Shave signs, sticking out haphazardly. Happy the bride. For better or for worse. Through thick and thin. Happily ever after.

Oh, but the ever afters were a bitch.

She was supposed to pass wisdom on, make the road easier for her child. But what should she say?

"So much to be thankful for today," Sylvia said. Even before Erica's announcement, they'd been toasting Ted's business, which after four rocky years was finally on its feet and out of the red.

"I'll drink to thankfulness, too." Hallie was drinking to everything. Disorderly conduct unbefitting a mother of the bride.

What to tell Erica? Hallie's mother had warned her of depression and war and illness and tragic loss, all of which she'd been spared. But Hallie could speak of the hazards of change and flux, of trying to find your balance on uncertain ground.

"I'd like to toast Mom and Dad." Erica held Jeff's hand. "You made marriage seem like a good idea."

Hallie raised her glass to Ted, far at the other end of the table. He looked the same as he had the day they'd informed her parents they were marrying. Another reason to grow old together. Their eyes were going at the same rate as their looks.

They'd made their daughter a believer. Although why not? They were true believers themselves. She reflexively checked off another good day on a mental calendar that had begun at ground zero, her front gate, four years ago.

There might not be happy endings, but there were definitely happy beginning-agains despite scars and inoperable bullets lodged near their hearts. Many things besides diamonds were forever. But their injuries weren't mortal or crippling, even if they ached in bad weather, as old wounds do.

The two of them were survivors of a near disaster—relieved and joyful to be intact, happier than they could have been before they had to define and fight for what they wanted. They knew how close they'd come to destruction and how easy it was to get that close, and so they protected each other now.

She'd always thought she'd been born too soon or too late for the interesting revolutions from the Russian to the sexual. Then one morning as she kissed Ted good-bye and went to win their daily bread, she realized that in their own lurching, balky fashion, they'd reinvented the Bennetts. She'd been so blinded by its day-to-day battles, she hadn't noticed her own revolution. She'd simply called it marriage.

Ted blew a kiss from across the room. "To my bride," he said. He began carving. "To the turkey," Andy said.

Not quite storybook perfect. But still, quite a story. She would find a way to extract its meaning and explain it to Erica.

"Erica! I hope you won't live in San Francisco!" Hard-of-hearing Miriam Bennett shouted across the table.

Erica and Jeff had already been living there for two years. Miriam didn't approve, so she didn't acknowledge it. "Our jobs are there, Grandma," Erica explained.

"It isn't safe! I saw on TV. The fire, the buildings, the bridge."

Six weeks earlier, nature had rattled their teeth, brains, homes, and whatever illusions of safety and permanence they harbored while, at the same time, underlining the need to live, gratefully and fully, in the moment.

Miriam, viewing events from back in Johnstown and being Miriam, had missed the meaning altogether. *"There could be another quake!"*

"But we love the city," Erica said, conceding and discounting its hazards. "And no place is really safe."

"What?"

Erica spoke slowly, enunciating each word. "We know that sooner or later we'll be jolted. But our building's on bedrock. Good foundations, and bolted down. And we've made provisions. Stored water and food."

Clever child, Hallie thought. Understands about risks. Living on a fault line was probably terrific training for marriage.

"The trick is surviving. Then you rebuild," Erica said. "Look at Mom and Dad."

Hallie was startled. She and Ted had tried to keep their catastrophe private. And then she realized Erica hadn't spoken metaphorically. They had also literally rebuilt. The chimney was standing again, the carpets clean after the upended pool had sent a tsunami over them, and the remaining fissures, scars, warps, and fragments would eventually be mended.

As long as there was something there to begin with, you could repair, reinforce, become strong in the broken places.

"But what if you aren't in the safe place, aren't home?" Miriam either could not hear or did not care about the rest of the table. Andy passed the stuffing. There were compliments for the chef. Vicky's Polly and Sarah talked about college and S.A.T. scores. Chloe Wister and Michael Farr discussed the theater, his new love and ambition. Miriam ignored all of it. *"What if you're some-place dangerous? I saw on the TV those people on the bridge!"*

"Terrible," Jeff said solemnly. "Nothing to do but hope we're lucky, that we're in a good place when it hits, and that it doesn't hit with everything it's got."

Hallie wished parents still had to give permission to their daughters' suitors, because she wanted to formally endorse this young man. He understood.

"Luck's part of it," Erica said. "So is danger. That's how it is. But being so afraid that you avoid it, or run away, seems too high a price to pay."

They both understood.

The mother of the bride-to-be relaxed. Her daughter was ripe and ready for marriage and there was nothing Hallie needed to tell her, except that it was worth it, and to please pass the turkey.